JOHANNA AT DAYBREAK

Johanna at Daybreak

R. C. HUTCHINSON

LONDON

MICHAEL JOSEPH

First published in Great Britain by
MICHAEL JOSEPH LTD
44 Bedford Square
London WC1
APRIL 1969
SECOND IMPRESSION JANUARY 1980

ISBN 0 7181 0443 9

Printed in Great Britain by
Hollen Street Press Ltd at Slough, Berkshire
and bound by Redwood Burn Ltd, Esher, Surrey

FOR

ERNEST

AND

DIANA
RAYMOND

ACKNOWLEDGEMENTS

I have to thank Dr William Berijder of Alkmaar for his patient answers to my many questions about the article in *Leiden's Medisch Maanblad* which first acquainted me with the history of 'Johanna von Leezen'.

I am deeply indebted to Frau Arnold Rewental, whose gracious hospitality at Schloss Griesenberg in the autumn of 1959 enabled me to hold the conversations with her cousin which crystallised in this book.

RCH

1

It was perhaps an hour later, or perhaps in the following
night, that I was once more wakened by the stammer of a
tugboat's engine, and now I seemed to hear beneath it a
troubled, human cry. This time it was futile to hold the bedclothes against my ears; I could not escape a sense of responsibility.

From the sound of Tilka's breathing I judged that she was
fast asleep. That could have been pretence: she might be
listening to every movement of mine, ready to make a full
report in the morning. But the urge to see what was happening had become so strong that I was ready to forsake my
usual precautions—to assume, at worst, that a creature in
Tilka's physical state could do me little harm. Without stopping to put on a coat I crept to the window and opened one
leaf of the shutters an inch or two, so cautiously that no
sound escaped from the hinge.

Empty, lit by an almost full and naked moon, the scene
recalled a silver-point drawing by van der Neer which I must
have known in childhood: while the recent furniture of
kiosks and electric wires was hardly visible, the ancient roof-
line on the farther side of the square—a row of high, stepped
gables, the frosted cupola which crowned a massive water
gate—was as sharply edged as if, newly built, it stood in the
high sunlight of an August day. As though this picture had
been smudged at the bottom corner, the canal bank was invisible: the mist which had hung all week about the square

had settled now to form a fluffy quilt across the water, and the iron bridge which in daytime carried an unbroken chain of traffic gave the appearance of a solitary object floating on that coverlet of cloud, a toy which a child had left forgotten on his bed. I had come to know it so well, this view from the window, that in daylight I found it drably commonplace. Now, brought to stillness, a pattern of shadow and silver light that seemed as insubstantial as the backcloth of a stage, it was at once beautiful and stored with menace; so that as I stood barefoot on the floorboards I was shivering not so much from cold as from a sense of helpless solitude.

What use, if they came for me, to shout towards those lightless houses! Even the echo of my cries would be submerged in the enormous silence as they led me through frozen and deserted streets.

Either a breeze was loosening the mist or my eyes, getting accustomed to the quality of light, had increased in penetration. The throb of the tug's engine had died, but now, within and above the haze, its suite of barges was faintly visible; they emerged in close succession from the cave of darkness below the iron bridge and passed like somnolent sea monsters, perfectly soundless, to where the next bridge absorbed them. For some time this endless train held me in hypnotic fascination: the constant, noiseless progress of dark shapes through a phosphorescent veil had the grave beauty of cloudscape—as if in one of Capelle's tremendous skies the drifting stratus had been set in actual motion—and since the power which drew them was neither seen nor heard I almost took them for living creatures, advancing with a purpose of their own. The sight increased my feeling of isolation: soon, imagining that all existence was comprised in the passage of this convoy from a vanished country to an unknown terminus, I became convinced that my last hope of living with others of my kind was drawing away; and under this compulsion I descended without further reflection to the square.

I had suspected that the boats bore no ordinary cargoes, and as I went nearer to those still passing I saw that the decks were alive with passengers; at first I took them to be convicts, they stood so still and impassively, but none was manacled and I saw no warders. As the faces grew clearer a few seemed familiar: this—a nun's face with a fluff of white on the high cheekbones—was surely one I had worked from in my portrait-painting days, this man resembled a labourer who had been in the camp with me, and here, grown up, was a girl I had played with in my childhood. With mounting curiosity I called out:

'Where are you going—where are they taking you?'

And a sharply bearded man who recalled to me a picture of my father answered, 'We can't tell you unless you come as well.'

I might easily have sprung aboard—the gunwale of the boat which carried him was passing no more than a yard from where I stood—but I was not convinced that those travellers were indeed friends of mine or people I could trust. In the frame of darkness they bore some likeness to pilgrims of an earlier age, with their honest clothes and the resolution in their eyes; they were the sort to whose companionship I had once looked for inspiration as well as comfort. But what would happen if I joined their voyage and found myself en-closed in a circle of silent, hostile faces! I wanted no adventures, I longed only to be secure and private. Daylight would discover this flotilla in country I neither knew nor could imagine; some bare and shadowless tract, it might be, where nobody could hide.

That boat had passed, another and another came. I was still searching for the source of the cry which had so disturbed me, and now I caught sight of one more figure which I thought I knew. It belonged to a child who stood apart from the rest, a dark-haired boy whose serious features wore a dignity remarkable in one so small. I waved, and he responded with a smile which, though it did not part his lips, lit his face for an instant with a melting radiance; it touched me so poignantly that I began to walk and then to run along the bank, keeping level, calling:

'Look—if you want me I can easily come.

He must have heard, since he turned his head and for a few moments his eyes were almost meeting mine, but he did not smile again. My legs were weak and I could not keep the barge's pace for long; one cordial word from the boy would still have impelled me to join him, but when no one made even a gesture of recognition my courage failed and I began to fall behind. Soon, exhausted, I stopped altogether and stood watching as the stern lights disappeared one by one at the bend below the railway bridge.

I think that when I turned away the barges with their cataleptic loads were still passing, but by then my eyes were almost out of use. Not that I was weeping: the grief which came from the finality of that experience was not like a fire, which tears can mitigate, it was rather such an arctic wind as invades the whole being, benumbing all one's senses, freezing the heart. As soon as I had recovered some self-command I returned to Tilka's side and listened again to her breathing. It was just as when I had left her, there was nothing to suggest that my movements had broken her sleep.

I was still not wholly reassured. In the morning I brought her breakfast as usual—small chores like that helped to fill the long, bare days—and when I had made her comfortable, with a suitcase propping up the pillow, I asked in a casual voice how she had slept.

'Marvellously!' she said. 'Last night I didn't even dream.'

'Does the noise of the tug-boats never wake you?'

'The tug-boats? I've never heard one.'

That, I thought, could not be true: I knew that deafness was not among her disabilities, for however quietly I spoke she never missed a word. But I did not press the point directly. I said:

'You seemed rather restless—I thought your back might be hurting.'

To which she answered, 'Johanna, dear, you worry too

much about me! I've got so used to my stupid back I hardly notice it at all.'

How could I pursue with questions a creature who spoke so bravely! Day after day she lay helpless, often in pain, but whenever she caught me looking in her direction her face took on a smile, serene and even gay. Now she was actually laughing, as she said:

'Oh, how serious you are! Darling Johanna, you mustn't take things so solemnly, you're much too beautiful to go about with a face like a judge. And truly, you shouldn't ever worry over a fag-end like me!'

In a sense different from hers I longed to take her at her word—to forget the dangers of confidence and accept at face value the affectionate young woman she appeared to be. Had we come together in other circumstances we might well have been devoted friends, in spite of our disparity in age. Her voice would alone have endeared her to me—she was fluent in German, which she spoke with the softest foreign intonation—and her physical grace had only been etherealised by the illness resulting (I was told) from a long period of near-starvation. Her flesh, so wasted that it seemed almost transparent, showed too emphatically the virile structure of her face, the high cheek-bones, the salient forehead; but her shell-white skin had still the purity of Chinese porcelain, the wide-arched eyes and the lean mouth were exquisitely fashioned, the marvellous aureole of fine gold hair made womanly what might else have been the face of a handsome boy. An adorable being: but was she to be trusted? The widow of a cavalry officer, she came—by her own account—of a land-owning family settled from the time of Stephen Bathory in the province of Bialystok. That might be the truth; but even in those days of mental exhaustion I remembered that Bialystok was not far from Vilna, with its large Jewish population, and it would have been rash to assume that Tilka's sympathies had totally escaped that influence. I gave her willingly what her invalid state demanded—some care for her physical needs, a cordial interest in her personal history. But

I steered away from every topic which might lead to questions about my own.

Indeed, I had long felt it would be safer not to share quarters with a person of such lively mind, and one whose personal charm might put me off my guard. And I think it was on the morning after my experience by the canal that I went to the Superintendent's office to request a change. Speaking slowly —for he sometimes pretended that my Dutch was difficult to understand—I said:

'Mijnheer Dekker, I don't in the least want to be a trouble, but I shall be glad if I can be moved to another room.'

His reply was, 'Oh, dear me, dear me! Another customer not satisfied!'

I noticed then that the lame girl Agatha Lange was standing in the recess beside the bookcase, her cheeks tearstained and her mouth fastened in the shape of childish obstinacy. There was nothing unusual in this—Agatha spent half her life protesting against imagined injuries to her comfort or self-esteem. She said now:

'I refuse to share a room with that crew of monkeys any longer. Not one more night! That's final!'

'Then would you two like to share?' the Superintendent asked of us both.

'God forbid!' I said under my breath. And simultaneously Agatha answered, 'That I refuse absolutely! I'm not going to sleep with *old* women.'

The door had opened again, and while Agatha was speaking some object flew across the room, narrowly missing my head. From the corridor a voice—belonging to Anna Wiedlich or someone like that—shouted, 'If Agatha's going she can take her things!' A pair of court shoes and a tin cash-box landed in the middle of the room, then came a Bible, a suspender-belt, a jar of face-cream. The Superintendent looked appealingly at me.

'Would you, dear Mevrouw, be so very kind as to shut that

door,' he said.

I did so, and then made my customary protest. 'I'd be glad, Superintendent, if you'd stop addressing me as "Mevrouw". It's a joke that doesn't amuse me any more. My name is Johanna von Leezen and I am not a married woman.'

This brought the standard apology: 'I'm sorry, Fräulein von Leezen—I'd forgotten. But really, you know, I was only speaking with our ordinary politeness—and in the papers which came with you from Ysseldoorn you were described as being married.'

'Very likely!' I answered. 'At Ysseldoorn the authorities were very good at attaching titles and histories to everyone, to suit their own ideas.'

For some moments then the Superintendent sat in silence, turning his large, watery eyes first to Agatha and then to me. The twitching of his lips suggested that something was amusing him, but that was habitual—he had reached the age of sixty or so without really growing up. To me he constantly resembled a frog: he was pitifully undersized but very wide in build, almost bald, with an over-large and restless Adam's apple, a sagging jowl and frog-like mouth. The black suit which he wore through every season had acquired a greenish tinge, and his hands, like his face, were flabby and damp.

'Look,' he said at last, peering at Agatha as if from a hiding-place behind a clump of reeds, 'I think it might be a good plan for you to have a talk with Mejuffrouw Potgieter. She's bound to have some suggestions for making you more comfortable.' And then he addressed himself to me: 'Tell me, gnädiges Fräulein, what don't you like about your room? We thought—Mejuffrouw Potgieter and I—that as one of our senior residents you would prefer a room with only one companion.'

Naturally I could say nothing to reveal my suspicions of Tilka. Instead, I answered, 'It's impossible to sleep properly on this side of the house. The noise of the tug-boats is always waking me.'

He registered surprise. 'Tug-boats? Where?'

15

'Why, on the canal there!' I pointed through the window. 'Don't you realise, they're passing at something less than 200 metres from my bed, at all hours of the night, splitting the air with their klaxons.'

'But my dear Fräulein,' he said, almost as if he were addressing a child, 'that section of the canal has been closed for more than a year, while they're re-building the Boden-straat bridge. All the traffic goes by the old channel, right the other side of the town.'

'Then how was it that I myself arrived at the quay over there?' I demanded.

'Arrived—when?'

'When I was brought here from that other place.'

'Oh, but I think you're forgetting: from Ysseldoorn you went by train to Hilversum and then you came on here by road.'

In his eagerness to contradict me he had ceased to notice Agatha, who was behind me now, laboriously recovering her property—letting go her crutch, dropping the Bible, starting all over again. But she would not tolerate his inattention for long.

'Those bitches,' she said fiercely, 'they despise me because I'm not interested in all their gossip. And because I take a little trouble with my clothes they think I'm showing off. The fact is they're no better than gypsies themselves.'

The Superintendent gazed at her with the look of courteous incomprehension which was part of his stock-in-trade.

'But I myself adore the gypsy folk,' he said apologetically. And now he fell into his paternal manner: 'Listen, please, Agatha—and you—gnädiges Fräulein. I know this isn't an ideal place to stay in—we're overcrowded, there are many discomforts. But then it's not meant to be your permanent home. As you know, what we're aiming at—the Association I represent—is to move you on as soon as possible to where you can start fresh lives in complete independence—some of you, I hope, in your own countries. This is only what you might

16

call a staging post, one where you can be cared for better than in a large camp—especially as regards medical care.'

I was about to ask him what sort of medical care he thought I was in need of, but a certain uneasiness stopped me; although I had heard all that rigmarole before it came to my ears now with a freshly sinister note. And as if he partly read my thoughts he continued, addressing me alone in a voice of deceptive sympathy:

'I imagine you'd really rather be here than back at Ysseldoorn?'

'At Ysseldoorn?'

He nodded. 'You don't want to live in that overcrowded camp again?'

I could not answer, for the practice of trying to explore the past was one I avoided—it would bring me nothing but hideous confusion.

'And you, Agatha,' he went on, 'surely you'd rather put up with us than go back to Eschlingen. There you were in a hut with forty others, and you've told me that none of them were easy to get on with.'

He spoke softly, but the thrust was shrewd: in a numerous company of angels Agatha would not have found one as *sympatisch* as she required. I no longer remember whether she prolonged her resistance; I am only certain that she was never put in any room except No. 5 (the former library), where at least two of the other girls continued to respond to her conceits and vagaries with immutable patience.

For myself, I was obliged to yield to what I interpreted as the threat of removal to a sterner, perhaps more dangerous place of confinement. This house depressed me: all its smells reported the obsession of the Dutch with cleanliness, one felt that the comfort of civilised upholstery was largely banned for fear it would harbour specks of dust. But here there had been no formal inquisition, and I had begun to hope that if I stayed long enough in so obscure a backwater Authority might forget I was still alive. To be private, that was my single objective. For I had come to see that my one chance of safety lay in surrounding myself with a fosse so wide that gaolers and fellow-prisoners alike would cease to think of me as a creature of any significance.

I forget how the conversation ended. All I remember is that he spoke with a certain earnestness of Tilka's virtues, and casually asked if I would make a portrait of her face, if he got me materials; to which I answered that I was quite incapable of portraying anyone, having no talent of that kind.

A few days later (or it may have been in the following winter) the Superintendent and I had another disturbing conversation. My regular business in the office was to type his correspondence, on an ancient American machine: I generally welcomed this employment as a change from kitchen tasks, and there was always a chance that some letter passing through my hands might give me useful warning of impending danger. On this occasion I had finished the typing and was entering-up the postage book when Mijnheer Dekker came in.

He seemed to be in his sunniest humour, and for some moments he stood watching me with a gently patronising smile, as if I were a child displaying unexpected intelligence. Then he said:

'Fräulein von Leezen, we have two new guests arriving today. They belong to your part of the world.'

Instinct told me that this apparently innocent remark was meant to draw me. So I nodded briefly and went on with my work.

'Actually they're coming from Ysseldoorn,' he continued, 'but their time in the camp may not have overlapped with yours. Their name is Stahl—an elderly couple. Did you ever meet them?'

'Not,' I said, 'as far as I know. There were some thousands of people at Ysseldoorn. A dozen families may have had the name of Stahl.'

18

'Walther Stahl?'

'I never met anyone called that.'

That was true in reference to Ysseldoorn.

It was also true that when he uttered that name (common enough, though faintly exotic on the lips of a Dutchman) it lit a spark in my mind, as if I had once seen it on some sign-post or in a newspaper headline, but there was no reason to mention this mental flash to him, or to pursue it on my own account. I had learnt the folly of such researches. Here I was surrounded by women who gorged themselves with retro-spection—one found them weeping in corners over the imagined happiness which attached itself to their dim memory of earlier years—and I was disinclined to join them in that sort of amusement. The past, for me, was such a region as precocious children invent to scare each other, a cavernous darkness peopled with menacing shadows, and I did not need to distress and alarm myself by turning in that direction: the present was enough for me to cope with.

'They involve us in some problems,' he continued con-versationally, as he wriggled out of his appalling overcoat and hung it on the nearest picture hook. 'We're not really equipped for looking after old people.' And then, sitting down, he gave me a sidelong, schoolboy glance. 'I don't know if you'd be kind enough to help me a little?'

'You mean, you'd like me to prepare a room for these people?'

'Well, Mejouffrouw Potgieter is attending to that—I think Rosa Kossuth is helping her. No, I was going to ask if you'd care to meet them at the bus station—it would make a lot of difference to them to be welcomed by someone who speaks their language as they speak it themselves.'

'But who would go with me?' I asked.

'I rather thought,' he said, 'that you might go alone.'

'That is allowed, on this occasion?'

'Allowed?' He was sitting at his desk now, mechanically polishing his spectacles, he put them on and immediately took them off again to stare at me over the rampart of papers with a curious look of counterfeit innocence. 'But do you still not realise,' he said, 'that in this place you can go about by yourself as and when you like?'

We had been through this *opéra bouffe* before, and I saw no sense in repeating the whole performance. I said, 'All the same, I'd like a note of your permission in writing, in case anyone questions me.'

And to this he agreed: 'Very well, dear Fräulein! If you will please make out the certificate you want I'll put my name on it.' Then he sighed, as if I had committed him to a task of Heracles. 'But tell me, do you think there's a man with a rifle up there on the water-gate, waiting to take pot-shots at anyone he sees crossing the square alone!'

He was smiling again, but I could not join him in his gaiety. Only a few days earlier I had seen not just one but four or five men on top of that building, with ropes and ladders. Ostensibly they were cleaning the dome; but I had noticed that one or other of the party was nearly always idle, simply gazing down into the square.

No, I did not share what occasionally seemed to be Mijnheer Dekker's view—that the very ugliness of life, its terrors and humiliations, could be turned to a source of amusement. And yet it was hard at times to resist the friendliness which he constantly affected. He had risen again, to come and stand behind me with a hand resting on my shoulder. He said, as if caught between laughter and tears:

'Dear Fräulein—may I say, dear Johanna—you find us the most dreadful folk to live with! But all the same we love having you here. It fills me with gratitude, all the jobs you do for me every day!'

It was the kind of talk which discovers feminine weakness. How easily could I have responded with a cordiality like his! And how soon would he have led me into self-indictment, some disclosure dredged from a memory which the years of weariness had left in utter devastation.

* * *

My outing to the bus station in Roemerstraat must have been in an interval of sunlight—that light which the still, intense cold of a Dutch winter seems to bring to peculiar brilliance. I have retained some visual impressions as sharp-edged as pen drawings—a white bobble dancing on a girl's scarlet cap, the anxious eagerness on the face of a waiting soldier, the old-style lettering of 'Wilpenschoen' on the headboard of the bus as it swung majestically into its allotted bay.

It was a day of curious experience. Fearful of being hemmed in by hostile strangers, I stood some distance away until the crowd of alighting passengers had dwindled. Then, as I went nearer to the group, I saw at its edge an old man— thin, stooping, shabbily dressed—whose face seemed familiar, so that I automatically murmured a *guten Tag* as I passed him: he did not answer, but in the puzzled glance he gave me there was, I fancied, a hint of recognition. I remember vaguely supposing he was someone I had seen at Ysseldoorn —perhaps one of the camp scavengers, certainly no one of consequence—and a moment later I had ceased to think of him, for a second surprise was awaiting me. Close to the door of the bus a woman too flamboyantly dressed for her years was standing alone, faintly smiling at—I supposed—her own thoughts. As I approached she brought her eyes to focus on my face and said rather imperiously:

'At last someone I know! My husband's finding the luggage, then we shall want some sort of conveyance.'

Taken aback, I said in confusion, 'I'm afraid I've no time— I'm looking for some people called Stahl.'

To which she answered, 'Stahl—yes yes, that's my husband's name. You've come of course to fetch us.' And then she called, 'Walther—come here! Here's a lady who's come to look after us—I think it's someone we know.'

She was not a person to be contradicted. She must have been shorter than I, but I think of her as a tall woman— chiefly, I suppose, because of her bearing and composure. To say she had a commanding presence would be inexact: rather she good-naturedly awaited the service of other

21

humans in the way that lazy but attractive mothers rely on the devotion of their sons. The aura of the *grande dame* was enough to offset the crudities of her appearance. Her clothes, at this encounter, were of the shabbiest, and the violet scarf which topped her aged moleskin coat was in outrageous discord both with the copper dye of her hair and with the crimson parakeet surmounting her conical hat; the barbarous jewellery loading her ears and fingers might have come from an oriental bazaar, while of her real face only the Jewish contours were discernible beneath the coat of gums and pigments with which it was plastered. But these extravagances did not mislead me. I should have recognised her as a woman of some status even if she had been a total stranger; and as to that, I could not be sure that this was our first meeting: a faint reverberation from the past made me doubt whether her name was Stahl, whether she and the old man I had noticed, who was now limping towards us with a battered valise in his arms, were in fact husband and wife.

'Ah, you've found our things—how clever you are!' The old lady's eyes shone, the mat of rouge which stood for her mouth was split in a wide smile. She turned to me again. 'You've met Walther?—I can't remember. He's splendid, you know, the way he looks after me. Now all we need is a taxicab. You say you've come from our hotel?'

I saw no urgent reason to answer; it was desirable to find out more about Frau Stahl—if that was indeed her name— before I satisfied any curiosity she had about me. So with only a gesture of complaisance I left them, and returned three or four minutes later with a taxi under command.

By then she had ceased to worry about who I was: to women of her age names are generally elusive, and not of first importance. It was the old man Walther who had become inquisitive. As we drove along by the canal he was nervously fussing about his wife's comfort—pulling her coat together over her knees, removing a drip from her nose with his own handkerchief—but he contrived to keep me under sidelong observation, rather as if I might suddenly attack them. He exhibited the professional reserve one associates with old-fashioned servants; and I could see that he had overcome a high rampart of diffidence when at last he spoke to me directly:

'It is—surely—Frau Josef?'

The question startled and strangely moved me. And such was the gentleness of the old man's manner, so touching his humility, that I might easily have answered, 'Yes, I am charmed that you should call me by a name so dignified and so euphonious! Let us agree on that, and use it as a basis of friendship.' But to do so would have opened that voyage into memory which I most needed to avoid. I replied in a voice as temperate as his:

'No, Herr Stahl, I've never had such a name—I am not a married woman.'

He looked incredulous. 'But she was so like you, Herr Josef's wife! Though a younger lady, of course.'

I said with a certain firmness, 'Then it must have been someone with similar features. I'm sorry!'

This brought a murmured apology; and to excuse himself he turned to his wife: 'You remember how she looked, the young lady Herr Josef married!'

But Frau Stahl was not to be drawn from her own pre-occupations. 'What a nice town!' she observed, spreading her indulgent smile over the market stalls, the pollard limes, a bomb-wrecked cinema. 'This is still Holland, I suppose? I like this country very much.' And now she leant forward and took my arm, to announce with a confidential air which would have turned the Gorgons to loving allegiance, 'The Dutch, you know, are generally most agreeable. Often stupid, but extremely good at heart.'

Clearly she was enjoying the ride, and I found my own feelings responding to her radiance; though her unmistakably Jewish appearance kept me on my guard I already felt an eagerness to serve her as far as my own safety allowed. Presently she asked me:

'This hotel we're going to, I hope it's not too expensive.

23

Nowadays we haven't a great deal of money—Walther will tell you.'

Nonplussed, I could only answer, 'I don't think there are any charges. It's a very simple establishment, we get no luxuries.'

'Well, really that doesn't matter,' she said affably. 'The place we've come from was all timber huts—I forget the name—we were there for a long time and really there was no comfort at all. Besides, we shan't be here for long, only while our own house is being got ready.'

A troubled glance from Walther came too late to warn me. I asked, 'Your own house—?'

She nodded. 'Our house at Eisenach—you must remember it, dear! Of course we shan't find it just as it used to be. There was the War, you know, there seems to have been some damage, and the grounds must be in a sad state after so much neglect. Still, my dear Walther here will soon have everything to rights.'

She gave him a look of infinite trustfulness, and now it was fascinating to see his handling of the wandery old woman; to watch how he retrieved a cigarette from the depths of his coat pocket, smoothed and tidied it, put it between her lips and held a lighted match with a waiter's professional carefulness, so that this tiny service expanded into a ritual of chivalrous devotion. At the same time I experienced a certain discomfort. Perhaps it was all to the good that one in Frau Stahl's predicament should fancy herself a free woman making a dignified tour of Europe while her estates were set in order. This, at any rate, could be no affair of mine. But the name Eisenach had waked for an instant a pattern of sensations—a wind which bore the scent of water weeds and the faint notes of a Mendelssohn overture, sunlight flashing on the many windows of a long stone façade—which made me feel as if I were fleetingly involved in her hallucinations. It was another warning. Intuition had told me that the coming of this pair was a new threat to my security; now I faintly saw that what I had to fear from them was not a hostile observation but a show of friendliness which could seep through my defences and gradually undermine them.

It was something of a relief to come in sight of Coenraad's Lodge (as my house of bondage was still called), for there the interest my charges still took in me was automatically dispersed.

Whatever the purpose of their coming, they were granted an impressive reception. Mijnheer Dekker, who must have been keeping watch from his window, was at the front door to greet them, beside him Mejuffrouw Potgieter with her apron off was bowing with the dignity of a chatelaine, parading her formal smile, and before the taxi stopped the Moravian imbecile Vaclav had waddled out to the kerb, had flung the door wide open and seized the aged valise from Walther's hands to bear it ceremoniously indoors. Nor was Frau Stahl unresponsive to this welcome. I thought I saw a look of despondency in her face as, with one sweep of the eyes, she took in the dingy front of the 'hotel', but in the next moment she advanced on Mijnheer Dekker with a brilliant condescension, extending her hand for him to salute, exclaiming:

'A charming place, Herr Gastwirt! Our room is ready? I'm sure we shall be most comfortable here.'

I was surprised yet again when she turned back to speak to me:

'Perhaps you would pay the chauffeur, Johanna dear. And Walther will settle with you when we get inside.'

When a score of unrelated people are living in a house of sparse amenities, every newcomer is welcomed for his or her novelty if for that alone; and although it so gravely threatened my tenuous peace of mind, I could not be altogether sorry for the coming of these Stahls. Their speech was neighbour to mine, there was about them a distillation of familiar experience which, even against my will, played on my spirit like the sun of early spring.

Looking back, I find it remarkable that Debora Stahl took her place so readily in the Coenraad establishment. Far older than anyone there except her husband, she demanded no special privilege. At her first meal she sat herself comfortably at one of the long tables, perhaps imagining that a waiter would presently bring her the menu; but before anyone had explained the routine she noticed that others were taking their plates into the stone-floored passage that led to the kitchen and without hesitation she did the same. Thereafter everyone in turn offered to save her this fatigue—even the selfish Agatha Lange volunteered. But she would have none of it—Walther himself was not allowed to take her place. And one of my liveliest memories is of her red head seeming to float above the queue like a personal standard as she moved towards Mejuffrouw Potgieter and the great saucepan with the air of a landgravine at an imperial reception, spreading over the squalid parade a smile of settled indulgence.

In other departments she needed help, but never claimed it as a right. At about the same time each morning I would find her stationed on the second landing, wearing the look of a benevolent tourist who has slightly lost her way; her eyes would light when she saw me and she would embark on a formula which scarcely varied from day to day:

'Johanna, dear, I wonder if you could spare just half a minute to put me right. I seem to have been rather stupid over my dear man's bed.'

So, in the tiny dormer-windowed room which the Stahls had been allotted, I came each day upon a hardly credible confusion: a cocoon of sheets and blankets sprawling over the wash-basin, the floor littered with underwear and the beds with shoes, the mattresses and bolsters so tumbled that sometimes I could only just squeeze in at the door. She would hover, serenely helpless, murmuring, 'Oh, my dear, how practical you are! What a magician!' while I wrestled with this chaos; and when the job was done she would even kiss my cheek.

'Thank you, *thank you*, dear Johanna, with all my heart. What a relief—I can't tell you! I simply had to have it straight before Walther comes—he's such a tidy man himself, he doesn't realise how things get in a muddle of their own accord.'

Always her gratitude seemed genuine, and she even tried to repay my trifling services in kind. Once, when she saw me carrying Tilka's dinner tray, she said, 'Oh, is that for the Polish girl?' (She seldom remembered anyone's name.) 'Let me take it for you, please!' and giving me no chance to refuse she seized the tray from my hands, to turn and stumble up the stairs, swaying and quivering, so that it rattled like a milk-float. Caught unawares, I could only submit to this foolhardy philanthropy. Later on I went to see if she had reached Tilka's bedside without disaster, and found her settled there in spirited conversation: with the innocence that charmed us all she was telling of the parties she would give on her return to Eisenach, while, taking a forkload at the end of every sentence, she absently devoured the meal she had arrived with.

I still see clearly how it was that I allowed her in those days to treat me as a grown-up daughter. When your past with its consolations has been removed as if by surgery, when you are quite alone, it is easy to accept whatever new comforts may reflect the old ones. Debora Stahl must have been in the middle eighties then, and at that age people seem to be harmless. With Walther, who appeared to be playing a part for which nature had not designed him, I always felt some threat to my security. But everything in his wife—her independence, her chaotic modes of thought, as well as her cheerful kindness—served to weaken my mistrust.

Occasionally Walther would still address me as 'Frau Josef', sometimes inattentively, sometimes with a penetrating glance. In a way which sounded wholly ingenuous he would speak of people known to him in earlier years:

27

'Frau Josef, I think you must remember the name of Herr Oskar Rubensohn. He came to Eisenach very often, he had an important position with one of the newspapers.'

'No, Herr Stahl, I don't remember that name. And I've told you, Eisenach is a place I've never been to.'

At which the old man's face would grow sorrowful as well as puzzled. 'But you yourself, gnädige Frau, you must remember my meeting you at the station when you came with Herr Josef first of all, and later on with the children.'

'No, Herr Stahl, it wasn't me—it's someone else you're thinking of.'

I was sometimes vexed by these gentle inquisitions. Once I had a bad night, first kept awake by Tilka's painful moaning, then alarmed by sounds which seemed to come from the canal; and on the morning that followed, when Walther and I were washing dishes together, he chose to chide me for my feeble memory:

'You will pardon me, gnädige Frau—I do believe you don't *try* to remember things. You were at Ysseldoorn for a long time—so Herr Dekker tells me—and yet you say you can't remember what section of the camp you lived in. Or even how you came here. If you really thought hard—'

I found suddenly that I was in tears; and I burst out, 'Why must I think hard, to satisfy your stupid curiosity! You're only a servant, after all, whatever you pretend to be.'

'So you do remember I was a servant!'

He spoke without rancour, so quietly that he hardly interrupted my vehemence; and in a surge of resentment I went on:

'I know you're here to spy on me, you and your Jewish connections! You can't expect me to help you! I've a right to my own thoughts, haven't I—I don't have to be told by you what I ought to think about!'

That brought him to contrition. 'But, gnädige Frau, I didn't mean to offend you. It was only that I myself think so much about the old days....'

His sorrow sounded so genuine that my temper began to subside.

'I'm not offended,' I said, struggling to get my voice under control. 'But I can't have people telling me what I ought to remember. You, you can make it a sort of holiday, going back into old days. I suppose there's nothing whatever for you to be afraid of. Well, you're wrong if you think everyone's the same—some of us can't afford those luxuries. If once I started to look back I'd see everything, *everything*—don't you realise that!'

Of course he did not: essentially he was too simple a creature—perhaps too virtuous—to conceive the terror which could press on lives less homogeneous than his, to imagine an existence where a mere shift of the eyes may carry you over the volcano's edge.

And here I should record that his bewilderment never turned (as far as I could see) to animosity. From the time of that sharp exchange he became more cautious. Now and then, forgetting the tacit agreement between us, he would begin to talk as if he and I had shared a large area of experience, referring socially to children he supposed I knew, to the gaieties and splendour of life in a great country house. But then he would check himself, and fall back on a sad benignity, as if he were dealing with someone who had wantonly preferred the delights of vagabondage to a rich inheritance. In the end it was owing to him that the thin integument on which I depended for safety was punctured. But before that time this humble and devoted man had gone some way towards winning my parsimonious affection.

I was not alone in responding to the Stahls' conspicuous good nature. They were often laughed at by the younger inmates: Rosa Kossuth, in her rustic simplicity, could never look at them without giggling into her grubby handkerchief, while the sight of Debora Stahl's face in the morning, copiously smudged with fresh cosmetics, would put the idiot Vaclav into vociferous laughter. But before long even so shrewish a creature as Anna Wiedlich was ready to speak of the old couple with a certain fondness.

We were in need of variegation. Outside the office we never saw much of Mijnheer Dekker—as a pastor he had other duties, I suppose, elsewhere—and Mejuffrouw Potgieter had been, as it were, the queen of our society: at meals, when she had finished serving in the kitchen, she generally took her place at the head of one of the two long tables, and between those wan gatherings one was never far from her ambience— the organising voice, the faintly antiseptic smell, the bleak efficiency. Internally, Coenraad's Lodge was mainly her creation: in a way not easy to define, the personality of this virtuous, flat-chested woman seemed to be impressed on the physical frame of our daily lives, on the sickly paintwork and the odorous draughts, the chill of soaped and flooded passages, the savourless food; and I mean no ill when I say that if you scanned the rows of pallid, empty faces confronting each other across the oilcloth-covered tables you saw in each of them some reflex of our overseer's forthright countenance— not the hardihood, but a cast of mind which accepted as immutable the barren state we lived in. There was in our company a one-armed man from Maramures who, if you carelessly wished him good morning, would burst into tears; there were bloodless girls content to fill the day by labouring to beautify their sallow skins, and a widow rigid with arthritis, the product of a camp at Verkhoyansk, who tirelessly employed herself in copying the Scriptures on to the backs of envelopes: these various beings had one element in common—they had ceased to consider the possibility of any change in their condition, to believe in or even hope for any future at all.

No wonder, then, that the climate was affected by Debora's expansive presence. To her the ascetic temper of our governess was as a mountain wind to a seasoned climber, and apparently she never remarked the difference between Mejouffrouw Potgieter's status and ours. Her own pre-eminence among us did not depend on her reputed wealth, since there was nothing to support that reputation, or on the dignity which accrued to her from her husband's devotion. It came, I think, simply from her boundless self-confidence. The preposterous toilette was symptomatic: at times, to say the least, her hand-glass must have told her that she looked a freak, but to one so comfortably established in her own eyes it did not matter if her cosmetic exuberance was an entertainment to her fellows. She counted on their loving admiration: that was enough. Slowly and sometimes painfully—for she suffered from varicose veins—she moved from room to room as a steamship in too small a harbour, flying the effulgent smile which would be dipped impartially to honour Mejouffrouw Potgieter, or the dribbling Vaclav, or me. Often she would be searching for Walther, since she could not keep in mind for as long as five minutes that he had gone to buy her cigarettes or was cleaning her shoes in the yard. She laughed a great deal; the oddity of the 'hotel' and its complement never ceased to divert her; but chiefly her laughter was directed at her own fumblings and confusions, perhaps at the incongruity between the old woman whose reflection she saw in our faces and the one whom she herself would have recognised.

Struggling to recover the feelings which possessed me at that time, I believe that if she had been a total stranger I should have held her in total affection—I should even have rid myself of the latent terror which her transparent Jewishness provoked in me. But the mind will not be totally immured. Behind Debora's exotic features and egregious behaviour there appeared the spectral image of a younger and more collected woman, bearing some other name, a picture to which I could not invariably stay blind. Sometimes she addressed me with a special, familiar tenderness—'Dear Johanna, how lucky I am to find you here, you of all people!' —and then her voice would touch a fibre in my brain, starting a current of ephemeral happiness like the scent of forgotten flowers. Those were the moments of my greatest peril, when I felt a violent impulse to yield to the siege of memory, though I knew instinctively that any sweetness the past could bring me would be instantly submerged by anguish and fear. Once, when her special kindness had fluttered my emotions, I went to stand before a wall-glass overhung by an unshaded light. The face which anxiously stared back at me was of a woman advanced in middle age, with grey hair cut short like a boy's. The features had been good, the long nose and the brow firm in structure, the mouth finely shaped; but now the flesh was so impoverished, the cheeks were so devoid of colour and the eyes of lustre, that I could barely connect these lineaments with any notion of formal beauty, still less of loveliness. And here, strangely, was a kind of reassurance. No one could easily identify this woman with one who had lived in any other state than subjection and solitude; and in the set of these lips, the coldness of the eyes, was a guarantee that she would not readily be inveigled back to the haunted tracts of mind which she had long abandoned.

But in the fitfully lighted ante-room through which one passes into sleep there were always insidiously smiling faces which made me feel defenceless; and among them I caught, that night, a glimpse of Walther in livery, holding open the door of a luxurious car, repeating, 'Frau Josef, you are to come with me. Listen, Frau Josef, you have to come now, you know you can't escape.'

I think I knew intuitively, on a day in early spring when I was bidden to the Superintendent's office, that the trap had started closing. But this may be due to the falsities of retrospection. There was nothing unusual about the summons, which was probably issued in the standard form, 'Mijnheer Dekker would be very grateful if Fräulein von Leezen could spare a few minutes to kindly assist him with some clerical work,' though as Anna Wiedlich chanced to be the bearer it reached me in her characteristic wording: 'The boss wants you for his office jobs.'

32

Certainly I realised as soon as I entered the room that I was there for an object more serious than clerking. With the Superintendent himself, who was standing near the window, were Walther, occupying the little basket chair, and Dr Hofdijk, the Lodge's regular physician, with his enormous bulk astonishingly perched on the edge of a filing box; the silence of those three showed something different from mere politeness, and in a single glance I saw on all their faces the near-paralysis which commonly invests the male when he has some delicate business to transact with a woman. I went to my usual place and began entering the previous day's out-letters in the register, while the men resumed their conversation, or pretended to—their talk sounded entirely artificial. This performance continued for two or three minutes before Mijnheer Dekker gathered courage and, in a tone which was meant to sound casual, addressed himself to me:

'Fräulein von Leezen, you remember Mijnheer Tollens in the Search Department at Ysseldoorn?'

I said, 'Tollens? Yes, I believe there was someone of that name.'

'Oh, but I think you knew him quite well,' he said didactically. 'Surely you were in his office for a time, doing the sort of work you so kindly do here for me.'

To this I replied, 'Very likely, Mijnheer Dekker. But I really don't remember. I never dwell on things which are past and done with—there seems no point in it, in these days.'

That loose utterance was not far from the truth. In the circumscribed existence of Coenraad's Lodge I found that the years at Ysseldoorn had already receded far enough for most of the details to be lost; it was no longer easy to connect the names and faces of people in the camp I had lived or worked with; and I welcomed this clouding, for I supposed that if these years were finally blotted out the more distant past was bound to remain invisible.

But my answer seemed to increase whatever trouble was weighing on Mijnheer Dekker's mind. He said with laborious

33

patience, as if to someone of sub-normal intelligence, 'But you know, dear lady, the faculty of remembering is one given to us humans for our use. If we cease to exercise it we cease to be—in the fullest sense—ourselves.'

'For some of us,' I said shortly, 'that may be an advantage.'

Clearly this was an attitude that a man of Mijnheer Dekker's limitations could not penetrate. To cover his perplexity, he turned to Dr Hofdijk.

'Tollens is very remarkable,' he said, 'the way he traces people. Of course he has all the best contacts—he works chiefly through the S.I.P. bureau at Bern.' And then, more nervously than ever, he spoke to me again: 'I expect you know, Herr Stahl has been anxious to get some news of Frau Stahl's relations.'

I shook my head. 'No, I know nothing of Herr Stahl's private affairs.'

It was Walther's turn to speak for himself. 'Frau Josef—' he began, but a look from Mijnheer Dekker stopped him and he changed his opening. 'You realise, gnädiges Fräulein, I'm eighty-seven, I might go at any time. And then I can't think what would happen to my wife, I don't know who would be responsible for her. I mean to say—everyone here is kind, but if I was gone it wouldn't be the same as if she had her own flesh and blood to take responsibility.'

There was nothing factitious in the old man's concern—his mouth was trembling and I thought he would presently burst into tears. It was greatly to my relief, then, that Mijnheer Dekker quickly took charge again.

'But now we have good news from Tollens,' he said to me, '—excellent news. He has found that Frau Stahl's grandson is living at Astelbrucke, with a young wife. It seems that this young couple are ready to provide a home for their grandmother—and of course for Herr Stahl as well.'

I said to Walther, 'Then it looks as if your problem is solved!' but his face did not reflect my optimism. He answered pathetically:

'I don't know what to do! My wife is always talking of her

house at Eisenach, she thinks I'll take her back before long—she has no idea what things are like. And then, Astelbrucke is a place she's never been to, she might not settle down there. She's not even clear who I mean when I talk about Felix.'

I said, 'Felix—that's your grandson?'

'My wife's,' he answered, in quick correction. And then, with his old look of perplexity, he said, 'Little Felix—surely you can't have forgotten *him*!'

He was staring as if I had come to him in some absurd disguise, and the eyes of the other two were fastened on me as well.

In fact I had known a number of Felixes. The picture his words brought at once to my mind was of a man abnormally small in stature, with conspicuously Jewish features, seated at the head of a long table. That fleeting vision was enough to warn me of a likely ambush—however guileless Walther might be, the others were obviously angling for some reminiscence they could use against me. And because I was on my guard defence was easy. As one flicks over the leaf of an album I extinguished in my mind the portrait labelled 'Felix', and I said gently, with an assurance barely short of conviction, 'Herr Stahl, I think you always confuse me with someone else.' Then, while he stayed silent and bewildered, I continued, 'Surely you'll do whatever Mijnheer Dekker recommends. I'm certain you couldn't have better advice.'

It looked as if the Dutchmen had been waiting for some opening like this. I saw a swift exchange of glances between them, and then Mijnheer Dekker addressed me in a way which suggested rehearsal:

'It would all be easier if we could meet the young people—there's so much one wants to know. Unhappily the young man seems to be something of an invalid, and he has work which makes it difficult for him to leave home at present.'

'That's a pity,' I said.

'But his wife Luise is visiting Utrecht early next month—she has relations living there. We were wondering—Herr

35

Stahl and I—if you would possibly consent to go and meet her. You would learn something of what sort of home she has to offer. And Herr Stahl would greatly value your judgement, I know.'

Taken aback by this strange proposal, I said to Walther, 'But you, Herr Stahl, why shouldn't you meet her yourself?' 'It would mean a whole day away,' he answered simply. 'I couldn't leave my wife as long as that.' And he added with a touching earnestness, 'It would be a great kindness, Frau Josef, if you would do this for me.'

Here was crisis. In this old man one saw an essential goodness which would have made me eager to serve him; but the question was not one of obliging a casual friend. Ever since our meeting at the bus station I had shut my eyes to what I obscurely recognised in the faces and gestures of the Stahls, had made myself deaf to names in their conversation which sprang at me like things alive. But I had failed to exorcise the dull suspicion that they belonged to the region in my life which I had consigned to oblivion, and now I vaguely feared that every step I took in following Walther's wishes might bring me nearer to a viewpoint where the whole of that abandoned countryside would rise to confront me again. For some moments, then, I was silent, dumb with irresolution. At last, with Dr Hofdijk watching me obliquely, the Superintendent betraying an open and eager curiosity, I said crisply:

'I'm afraid I don't feel up to such a journey.'

Again the two Dutchmen exchanged glances. It was the doctor who asked, with apparent sympathy,

'You mean—the complications of getting tickets, finding the right train, that sort of thing? I know you have some trouble over remembering things.'

'Exactly!' I answered, with gratitude. 'I'm not used to business of that kind.'

He nodded gravely—on the surface he was a man of extensive tolerance. But now it was necessary for Mijnheer Dekker to launch a fresh attack:

'But I should have thought,' he said, 'from the work you do

for me, that business of any sort would be no worry to you.'

'In any case,' I countered, searching for some other escape, 'I don't know what my legal position would be if I were found so far from here.'

To this, with his eyes turned up in mock despair, he answered, 'Oh, not that again!'

Of those two men I had always looked on Dr Hofdijk as the more mature, and now I was grateful to him for taking no part in the other's facetiousness. He addressed me as if he regarded my intelligence as equal to his own:

'Of course, Fräulein von Leezen, it's for you to say whether you can manage the journey. But I have one suggestion which might help a little. You know I've been trying to get a bed for Mevrouw Zamoyska in the Coligny Hospital at Utrecht? Well, that's more or less fixed now. And I thought if you were to go along with her in the ambulance it would be a simple matter for you to meet Frau Stahl's grandson's wife at the same time.'

Any fool would have seen that this was a stratagem which the Dutchmen had shrewdly worked out between them, using Walther and Tilka Zamoyska simply as their instruments; under the orders of a superior authority (probably of Jewish complexion) they were leading me into some position where I should be ready to make a confession—or so I supposed, though at the time my mind refused to tell me what I was meant to confess. But what could I do! If I declined to follow the path they had mapped for me they would soon bring other pressures to bear—they could make my life at the Lodge intolerable until I submitted to their will. How was I to fight them, when I had no weapon and no one on my side!

Yet I think it was a certain feeling for Tilka which finally persuaded me. She, perhaps, was on their side as well; but she and I had been living close together, no one could have been insensitive to her beauty or her courage, and now that I was to lose her I saw that the loss would not be insignificant. I owed her at least a gesture of goodwill; and it seemed likely that the hardships of her journey and arrival among strangers would be eased a little by the presence of someone she knew.

A whole minute must have passed in painful silence. Then I said to Mijnheer Dekker, 'I shall need a document to certify that I'm travelling with your authority and at your instigation. If you're prepared to take full responsibility, I shall be happy to do this errand for Herr Stahl.'

Dr Hofdijk, at least, seemed to realise that my decision had not been costless. Later, he took some trouble to explain in detail the arrangements made for my journey, with such an air of sympathy that in spite of my suspicions I found myself warming towards this gargantuan, deliberate man. Even when he spoke about my weakness in memory, and suggested that I should make a habit of writing down whatever I recovered from the lost years, he did it with a show of understanding which—if I had not been on the alert—would have convinced me that he meant only to be kind.

The day of my excursion to Utrecht was one of heartbreak, but it admitted moments of astonishing delight.

Even now I hate thinking of how Tilka must have suffered. The ambulance was roughly driven, and where the road surface was uneven the jolting must have brought her agony; yet she did not once cry out, she only put her knuckles to her teeth and waited, very white, till the pain had subsided enough to let her smile again. We did not talk much on the journey; she had hardly the physical strength, and with me the sense of impending loss almost prohibited speech. Kneeling beside the bunk for most of the way—since the attendant's seat was of awkward height—I did what I could for her comfort, turning and bunching the pillows, giving her sips of water, letting her frail hand rest in mine; while she, when her eyes were open, winked and made droll grimaces, as if we were a pair of girls escaped from school.

At the hospital they made me wait in an ante-room furnished with charts and surgical trolleys while she was put to bed. Then I was allowed to spend ten minutes more with her, and I remember how small and ghostlike she appeared, how cruelly robbed of identity, when, in what looked like the covered deck of a liner, I saw her as one of perhaps a hundred breathing puppets filed in a perfect uniformity of beds with scarlet blankets and with metal cabinets to wedge them apart. But her spirit was untouched by this assimilation, the little lights in her eyes were burning brilliantly again.

'I've been catechised already,' she said, 'about my religion and relations. I fancy that tidy funerals are what these people take a pride in.'

In that farewell conversation she was affectionate but also mocking. Not for the first time she asked me how old I was, and when I told her once more that as far as I knew I was in the middle forties she said:

'And I'm only twenty-nine, yet I always itch to be a mother to you.'

'A mother? How?'

'I want to lecture you, to tell you you mustn't take life so seriously.'

I said, 'Is that what mothers do?'

'After all,' she pursued, 'the War's been over some years now. You're still alive, and so am I, theoretically. And at present we're not starving. Is there anything else to worry about?'

I had to take refuge in evasion: 'I don't like leaving you here, all among strangers.'

'Me?' She made an airy gesture with the finger of one hand. 'Oh, I shan't be here long, and it ought to be quite amusing.' A spasm of pain brought her to silence, but presently she said, 'Johanna, dear, what is it you're frightened of? Sometimes you look as if you were wearing someone else's jewellery and you thought everyone round you was a policeman in disguise.'

I longed to laugh with her, but laughter would not come. I said, 'Perhaps that's what I feel like.'

'But darling, why? You're not the sort of person who could

ever have done frightful things. Like me, for instance—*I* nearly killed a man once, a poor idiot who tried to rape me in a labour camp. *You'd* have been very polite and correct, you'd just have said, "Excuse me, but I must decline to take part in a Non-permitted Recreation".'

That was spoken with the gaiety I loved in her. Yet it so hurt and alarmed me that I found myself suddenly weeping. I said in a gust of impatience:

'Tilka, I've told you—often—I don't want to think what I'm really like, what I did in the time I've forgotten. I did frightful things, I know that—and that's *all* I know. I'm not going to hunt them out again—ever—to please anyone. Not to satisfy your curiosity, or mine.'

My outburst brought her, in turn, almost to tears; and in those few moments the ordinary, human grief of leave-taking was changed to a sour misery by my suspiciousness and her incomprehension. Through the malice of circumstance it was just then that a senior nurse bore down upon us, her face set in the frozen sweetness of her craft, to say in a voice that could only be obeyed, 'I think Mevrouw Zamoyska ought to rest now, after her tiring journey.' I stooped and—for the first time—pressed my mouth against Tilka's cheek. Unable to speak, I turned from her and went the whole interminable length of that sepulchral ward without once daring to look back.

So wretched a parting left me, for the time, not so much in sorrow or remorse as stupefied. With the mentality of long-term prisoners I continued to carry out orders: mechanically following Mijnheer Dekker's precise directions I found my way to the Nieuwe Gracht Hotel, where the wife of Frau Stahl's grandson was to meet me, and there established myself in an inconspicuous corner of the vestibule, beside a child who was ingenuously devouring bread and paste from a newspaper spread on her thighs. At least my nervousness had gone, since the underlying fears had lost importance: the motives of those who had engineered my mission, the way I was to conduct my business with the young woman, the

40

suspicion that I was being followed and spied on—those anxieties seemed trivial when my spirit was empty and deflated. I watched the hotel traffic, the swarming of rotund and voluble matrons, the darting passage of harassed business men, as one sits through a dull and unconvincing film.

I was faintly surprised when the child I shared a settee with, having finished her picnic, took a half-smoked cigarette from the top of her stocking and lit it with the air of a veteran. I had vaguely put her at thirteen or so; now, covertly observing her large hand-bag and high-heeled shoes, I added a couple of years to my estimate. My glance drew her attention, and presently she asked me, speaking schoolgirl Dutch in a grave and grown-up way, if I would be kind enough to tell her the time. This I could not do—I had sold my watch with most of my other possessions some years before.

Even so small an exchange was enough to make her a different creature. In the too short, home-made dress and with meagrely developed breasts her body was still a child's, but now there was something unchildish about the pale, corneous face in its proscenium of straight black hair—in the slightly oriental eyes an adult anxiety and hunger, in the shaping of the mouth a capacity for anger or endurance. Simultaneously I thought, 'I must contrive to paint this girl,' and, 'Here is a creature too young for her experience, one whom it would be happiness to adopt and care for.' She, of a generation not easily embarrassed, showed no disquiet at my patent curiosity; and soon, as if from a well-established friendship, she addressed me again:

'I suppose you haven't seen an old lady wandering about? It's someone I'm supposed to be meeting, and the bother is, they say her memory's gone all to bits, so she may have teetered off to the wrong hotel.'

Till then I had still been largely occupied with thoughts of Tilka, but those words brought me to the surface. I asked, in German:

'It wouldn't be me—Fräulein von Leezen?'

'But how silly of me!' she cried. 'Why ever did I think

41

you'd be old! I'm Luise.'

This was flattering. But conceit was only a small ingredient in the sensation of that first encounter with Luise; my delight came chiefly from the artless way in which she seized my hand in both of hers, and from her smile which, as a baby's does, accepted me without reserve. I see now how my own mood contributed to the shock of pleasure her welcome gave me: the loss of Tilka had so increased my sense of isolation that the warmth of this young stranger was more than comfort, it was like a readmission to the human race. But at any time I should have found her irresistible, for her radiance came from a deeper source than the charm which any girl keeps handy for social use. She was tired and undernourished—the amateurish cut of her hair would alone have signalled the straits in which she was living—but I was conscious less of her poverty than of her means to sustain it. She was a quick, active person who expected no easy marches; needing to fight for a sufferable existence, she made a pleasure rather than a virtue of fighting. Formally her features were not remarkable, but the fortitude that burnt in her dark and burdened eyes, the vein of humour that a special twist of her pliant mouth exhibited, made a face which, even if that had been our only meeting, I should have remembered with fondness and gratitude.

'Yes, we've got a house,' she presently told me, '—or rather, a bit of a house. Not ours, of course—we sub-rent from a Baltic couple upstairs, they're slightly adulterous but rather nice. Our bit's nice, really. Or we think so. A bit tatty, but it does for us all right. It's the first place of our own we've had since we were married—that was nearly two years ago—the first proper place.'

We had moved to a café on the other side of the canal where, with the travel money Mijnheer Dekker had doled out to me, I was able to give her coffee and *pils*, and she seemed as much delighted by this slender entertainment as a girl at her first grown-up party. With a show of ease and dignity she sat with her skirt pulled as far as it would go

42

towards her knees, and flirted a paper napkin, and constantly eyed the handsome waiter with admiration thinly veiled by a ladyish hauteur. Yet already I discerned in this play-acting juvenile a person of resolute intelligence.

'There'll be a money problem,' she said composedly, 'but then there always is. I mean, if the Stahls come we'll have to take over one or two rooms upstairs—the Pavaakas have more than they really need. Well, I can work that out. Franz thinks they ought to come—he has rather a strong sense of family, he was thrilled when he heard his grandmother had been traced. The only question—'

I interrupted: 'Franz—is that your husband's name? I was told—'

'He changed it,' she said, 'while he was living with his Uncle Albrecht—his uncle thought it would be safer.'

'Safer?'

'Yes—from Himmler's boys. They took Albrecht's surname, Franz and his sister. So they've always been Franz and Agnes Weckerlin to me.'

It amused but also touched me, the mystic look which visited her face when she uttered her Franz's name: beneath the shell of a mature woman one saw so vividly the tender innocence, the agonising vulnerability, of bridal love. I remember that I felt a sudden envy, the envy one must always feel of brides; and that this was followed by the thought, 'With all her devotion centred on a husband, what has this child to spare for an aged couple she has never seen?' But now the remote expression gave place once more to the practical, and as if she had traced the working of my mind she said:

'Tell me, please—Frau Stahl, is she bedridden?'

I replied that both the Stahls were reasonably active, though Frau Stahl lacked concentration and—as far as I could judge—had never been used to domestic work of any kind.

'Well, if she's up and about that makes things easier,' Luise said. 'You see, we're both out at work all day, Franz and me, and Agnes isn't awfully reliable because of her eyes, so a complete invalid would be a bit awkward to cope with.'

It was not hard to see the vein of anxiety which her eagerness was meant to disguise; and I said spontaneously:

'I'm sure the Stahls would appreciate your kindness, but I think it might be best if they stayed where they are. At Wilpenschoen there are lots of people with nothing to do, we can all help in looking after them.'

'But what sort of place is this Coenraad's Lodge?' she asked. 'Is it some kind of hostel? What do *you* do there?'

The last was an unhappy question: it recalled the strange and invidious position I occupied.

'It's supposed to be a sort of staging-post,' I answered lamely. 'That's really all I can tell you. I'm there myself—as far as I know—because there are people who want to keep tabs on me.'

She nodded, with a look nearer to sympathy than to surprise, and I guessed that the authorities at Wilpenschoen (or those above them) had given her at least a hint that I was a suspected person. She was looking at her wedding ring, avoiding my eyes, when she said:

'Whatever I tell him, Franz won't be satisfied till they come. It's partly having lost his father so young—that makes him feel responsible for his relations.' With this she smiled again, and let her eyes meet mine, as if we were two mature women discussing a boy's caprices. 'Oh yes,' she concluded, 'you *must* persuade them to come!'

A faint discomfort persisted: it was painful to think that she too, this gay and gallant creature, had been informed against me. But so imperative, that day, was my need for affection that I could accept a humiliating status as long as it was screened by the warm, spontaneous friendliness she showed me. When she said impulsively, 'Look, why don't you come as well? We could fit you in, and you could help me manage things,' I could easily have answered—had I been a free woman—'Yes, of course I'll come!'

Truly, I was ready to live in almost any place that was not

an institution, any society where the only ties were mutual fondness and understanding. Yet I could not forget that the Stahls were the link between Luise and me, that surrendering to Luise's friendship would mean involving myself still further with them and their connection. And that, as intuition told me, was to turn back upon my flight, to abandon every chance of safety.

Again she may have read my mind, as children do—less with intelligence than with instinctive sensitivity. For a little later she said cautiously:

'If you did come to us you wouldn't be worried at all. We'd see to that, honestly.'

I said, ' "Worried"?'

'Herr Dekker told us in his letter,' she said, 'that you didn't want to talk about the War and so on—things that are over. Like lots of people. Franz is the same, really, he never talks about what he's been through, except to me when we're quite alone. And he's marvellous at keeping off the subjects people don't like. Whatever anyone says, I think being Jewish makes you more tactful than other people.'

I said, 'Your husband's a Jew, then?'

It was a foolish thing to ask about any of Frau Stahl's kin, and I was not surprised to find Luise eyeing me with a peculiar embarrassment. She answered patiently:

'On one side, yes. And of course I am too.'

So! I had noticed what I took as evidence of a Balkan strain in the shape of her eyes and her rather dark skin, but I still saw no sign of diplomacy in the cast of her features or in her smile. And now, in the way of young wives, she wanted to expatiate on her man's abilities and virtues, but that was a path I was not ready to follow. At the first opening I said as warmly as I could:

'Luise, it's sweet of you to even think of having me in your home, but it just isn't possible. I wouldn't be allowed to leave the Lodge, certainly not to stay anywhere outside Holland.'

She appeared to be genuinely disappointed, and murmured something about Franz wanting to meet me as well. But she

45

was too sensible to press me further, and we did not refer to that subject again.

When the time came to start my return journey she insisted on coming with me to the station; and though I suspected that this was a duty laid on her by my controllers I was freshly moved by her charm in performing it—our ages might have been reversed, so great was her solicitude in looking after me, getting my ticket, finding me a window seat. As Dr Hofdijk had hinted, I needed such help. For years I had been so little used to independence, or to the pressures of a great city, that I felt like a country child, bemused by the kaleidoscope of mature and confident faces; and in the last moments before the train started I nearly gave way to alarm and distress. Already, that day, I had parted from an old friend, and now I found it almost unbearable that I should lose for ever, after a single meeting, one who had brought me something like a daughterly affection.

Mijnheer Dekker was not about when I returned to the Lodge, so it was Walther himself to whom I first reported on my mission. He laid wait for me after supper, led me conspiratorially into one of the pantries and there brought me a cup of coffee which he had begged from Mejuffrouw Potgieter. He was touchingly grateful, as if I had given him some costly service, but also nervous and excited.

'You found her?' he asked earnestly. 'It went all right, the meeting with the young lady?'

'It went very well,' I answered. 'I liked the child immensely.'

Then, steering my way between his impetuous questions, I gave him an account of the situation at Astelbrucke as I understood it. The young couple, I said, appeared to be people of signal goodness, genuinely concerned about the welfare of the young man's grandparents. The offer of a home for them was entirely serious. But I judged that they were short of money, their household was largely unorganised and the space available extremely small. In short, I was certain that he and Frau Stahl would do better to stay where they were. I must have expressed all this with too little appreciation of the old man's anxieties, for his face, when I had done, showed a piteous disappointment. He said:

'I was hoping they had a proper establishment, to give my wife the sort of things she's used to.'

The only response I could make was a sympathetic silence. And now he spoke with an intimacy that surprised and disconcerted me:

'Forgive me, gnädiges Fräulein, but I don't think you know even now what rests on me. It was just a few days before my old master died, he sent for me to talk like one man to another. He said it was easier for him to die because I was there to see no harm came to his wife, whatever happened. He said, "I trust you, Walther, like I've always trusted you." Well, that was right—I could take the responsibility. But when *I* die, what happens to her then, unless she's with her own relations? That's what rubs against my mind, all the time.'

More than once in our earlier exchanges he had spoken of 'my old master' with the sentimentality one finds in servants of long standing. Hitherto I had not encouraged such reminiscences, which he had evidently meant as an entrance to the subject of my own history; but that evening he was so woebegone, like a boy when a long-promised treat is cancelled, that I could not hold him at a distance. Without reflection I asked:

'Frau Stahl had an earlier husband, then? You were in his employ?'

He looked at me with an expression, now familiar, of patient wonderment at my childlike ignorance; and then, as if I had accused him of some misconduct, he exclaimed, 'What was I to do! She had to leave the house—there was no safety for her there, with those police and people coming all the time. The only place to keep her hidden was my own little house. And then it wasn't my idea to make her my wife, it was hers.

47

It was safer for her—that I had to agree.'

The humility of that utterance brought me almost to tears. Even from so bare an outline of the facts I could see that this simple man's conception of loyalty had led him to a course demanding abnegation and probably courage of no ordinary kind; yet, far from parading his virtue, he was offering excuses for behaviour which seemed to him presumptuous in a servant. My picture of him at that interview has stayed sharp and alive: the square grey head against a row of yellow china mugs, the deeply wrinkled flesh, the sombre, dutiful eyes; and with that image I recall the sense it brought of my own moral poverty. Just then I would have done almost anything to prove myself his friend. But friendship cannot be founded simply on a current of emotion. His next words, innocently spoken, were enough to put me on my guard again.

'You won't mistake me,' he said laboriously, 'I'm glad I can call such a lady my wife—one I have a long respect for, and more beside. But for me she will always be Frau Schechter—I can't ever feel it's right to call her anything but that.'

That name had been on his lips once before, and now, as then, it startled and alarmed me; for I had come to recognise it as a warning of the dangers to which any new road might lead. In a recurring dream a footman would ask my name as I stood dumbly facing a circle of old friends, and when I told him I had forgotten it he would cry, with a spiteful grin, '*Frau Schechter!*' at which the faces would become so cold and scornful that I would take to screaming flight. Searching despairingly for somewhere to hide, I would come on a house I thought was mine, with its door wide open, but as I was about to go inside the same derisive voice would whisper, 'Welcome, Frau Schechter, welcome, traitress!' and I would wake, shouting, 'I don't know who you mean!' Sometimes the exhalation of that nightmare, like the flavour of a nauseous meal, returned in my waking hours; and now, simply because 'Frau Schechter' had come so easily into his talk, I was almost ready to identify the homely, self-effacing man before me with the insolent lacquey of my dreams. He

48

must have sensed my sudden coldness. Shortly afterwards he said that his wife would be looking for him, and when he had thanked me once more for going to Utrecht on his behalf our conversation ended.

But how idle to suppose that I should have any influence on the Stahls' affairs, or the plenary right to conduct my own!

I made my report to the Superintendent next morning, and in the afternoon, after a long talk with Walther, he sent for me again. Not surprisingly—for his temperament embraced a broad streak of sentimentality—he had been more impressed by Walther's views than by mine; he thought now, he said, that the future of the Stahls would be better secured if they were established with their own kin, even if the physical conditions left something to be desired. To this I could only shrug my shoulders. I was about to leave the office when he called me back.

'If you could spare a minute more, Fräulein ... I've been thinking: you know how much Frau Stahl values your help—more than once she's told me you're the one person she leans on here. I was wondering if you would be willing to go along with the old couple and see them settled in. You'd only have to be there a few days—unless you found you were happy and wanted to stay longer.'

His smile, as he uttered this startling proposal, had the innocence of a child's—I saw him for a moment as a small boy asking a much older sister to play with him. Once more the charm of his misshapen, quizzical, appealing face so touched my warmer sensibilities that I was almost ready to yield not only to his wishes but to his seeming cordiality. A sharp appreciation of danger supervened: the man was calmly inviting me into a nest of Jews. And I said with some asperity:

'Have I any option?'

'Oh my dear, dear lady,' he answered, as if in humorous exasperation, 'do you really think I'm such a tyrant! If you

49

have any fondness for the Stahls I imagine you'll want to go. But of course it rests entirely with you.'

Perhaps it did! I could either place myself in the bosom of a Jewish family, where every careless remark of mine would be recorded, or I could decline to go—and that refusal might in itself be taken as evidence of guilt. For want of a determinant, I said I should like to think over his suggestion, and he agreed that I should give him my answer next day.

I was not allowed, however, to make up my mind alone. An hour later I was summoned to the room which Dr Hofdijk used as surgery—ostensibly he wanted me to help as nurse and chaperone with some treatment he was giving to Agatha Lange—and as soon as Agatha was disposed of he asked in a general way if I had enjoyed my trip to Utrecht. I answered that I had not found much pleasure in seeing Frau Zamoyska suffer the pain of travelling, or in parting from her at the end of the journey.

'Well, of course not!' he said warmly. 'I myself, I share all your feeling for Mme Zamoyska, that infinitely charming and courageous woman. No, I was thinking of your errand for Walther Stahl.'

'That was pleasant enough,' I told him. 'The child was delightful.'

'The child? Oh, you mean the grandson's wife.'

'To me she's a child,' I said. 'She's so young I can't think of her as a married woman.'

'No?'

'But in any case I'd rather not gossip about Frau Stahl's relatives,' I said.

'Well, I'd hardly call that gossip!'

He was narrowly observing my face, as if I had come to him complaining of some trouble with my eyes. This was slightly disturbing, for as a rule his manner when we were alone together was cheerful and masculine, suggesting that he and I shared an adult outlook. He said:

'I wonder if it can't be carried too far, the admirable notion of never intruding on the privacy of one's neighbours.

I mean, if we strictly avoid knowing anything at all about our friends' affairs it must limit our power to help them.'

'I expect you're right,' I answered briefly. 'But the person I'm engaged to help just now is Mejuffrouw Potgieter. So if you'll excuse me—'

Still he would not let me go. 'There's something I've been wanting to ask you,' he said sociably. 'The period just before you arrived at Ysseldoorn—what was happening to you then?'

I answered, 'I'm sorry to disappoint you. It's gone from my memory completely.' And under the stress of his inquisitorial eyes I added, 'Yes, and I'm glad of that because it was like being in hell.'

'So you do at least remember the feel of it?'

'I remember nothing!' I retorted. *'Nothing at all!'*

I found myself in tears then. It was not a weakness I gave way to often, and I was ashamed of yielding on this occasion, since it must have looked like the crudest feminine stratagem. But Hofdijk behaved well—no doubt he was used to blubbering women. He offered no comforts of the obvious kind; he only said, when I had calmed enough to hear him:

'Really I wanted to be helpful. You seem to live such a shut-in life—I feel we should all be on better terms if you could tell us something of your history. But there it is! If your memory simply won't function it's no business of mine to plague you.'

With this his boyish smile returned, and whether or no there was anything genuine in his profession of sympathy it moved me to further submission. I was wretchedly in need of counsel. And as if he were a life-long friend instead of a hostile agent I said impulsively:

'If only you'd leave my memory alone and just advise me!'

At once his humour turned to an almost paternal gentleness.

'What about?'

'They want me to go to Astelbrucke,' I said. 'The Stahls have made up their minds to live with the grandson. Mijnheer Dekker thinks I ought to travel with them and settle them in.'

'Well, why not?'

The simple question was not to be simply answered. I said precipitately:

'There wouldn't be room for me. Luise would be nice about it, she'd pretend to give me a welcome. But I shouldn't fit in with a gathering like that.'

'Not even for a few days?'

'No. They'd all be longing for me to go.'

'What a curious notion!'

He produced his pipe, the sort like a miniature kitchen stove which I had seen old farmers smoking in my childhood, and started the filling process with all the devotion of a lady's maid packing a ball dress. After a while he said:

'No, I'm not the person to advise you—what am I, after all, but a workaday leech! One thing, though: if you do go, I'd recommend you not to turn it into a home-made martyrdom. If you're imagining all the time that your hosts can't stand the sight of you—well, you'll be making things unbearable for them as well as you.'

'In other words, I'd do better not to go?'

'On the contrary, I think the change of scene might do you a world of good.'

The pipe was filled to his satisfaction, but before he could speak again he had to perform the slow, hieratic task of lighting it.

'It's a question of courage,' he resumed, as if arguing the matter with the spent match which he held between his fingers. 'At Astelbrucke you're going to be surrounded with people of your own nationality, the sort of people you've known in the past. And that will scare you, because the past is what you're always running away from. Well, either you hide yourself in a cloud of worries and suspicions—in which case you might as well not be there—or else you accept the

52

friendship they offer and stop fretting over what it might lead to.'

His lecture had at least the sound of honesty. It led me to respond with equal bluntness:

'Yes, I see what you mean—and I'd go through with it if I had the sort of courage you talk of. But I haven't, and that's the end of the matter.'

'Is it?' He stopped playing with the match and looked into my face again. 'Listen!' he said. 'You're of North German stock—I could tell that from your voice alone. Well, I'm not sure that I greatly love your countrymen, but I wouldn't call them cowards. And you, fundamentally you're a brave person, but sometimes you fail to use your intelligence— because it's foolish to be afraid of oneself, and really that's what you're afraid of.'

That was spoken from a copious ignorance of my nature and situation, but not unkindly—I never suspected this rather simple-hearted man of any personal animus. And later I often recalled his judicious words as a general guide to behaviour. But words have small effect on those deep, impetuous currents which shape the twisting channel of experience. People who have no fear of heights cannot conceive the horror of living on a narrow ledge from which, through drifting smoke, one catches sight of roofs and pinnacles far below; they will not understand how those in such a case are blind from choice, since the only defence against that terror is total blindness.

No, nothing said by the genial Hofdijk or the insinuating Dekker could much have impressed me; and I think when I review those anxious hours that I was brought to a decision simply by resurgent loneliness. Tilka had gone; the Stahls, mysteriously trailing the fragrance of a bygone happiness, were going too, and at Coenraad's Lodge I should be left with no one but foreigners or people who meant nothing to me. In a restless night, full of confusion, I found myself arguing that for a short while the fear of exposure by those who at least shared my language could hardly be worse than living under

53

alien observation. In the morning I told Mijnheer Dekker that I was ready to make the journey to Astelbrucke, and to stay there for a few days, as he appeared to wish.

As the time of the expedition came nearer I regretted my complaisance. In the night before we were due to start I hardly slept, and the day that broke, through a low roof of cloud, found me sick with depression and forebodings. Nor was there anything to cheer me in the circumstances of our departure.

On the ground that he had lost his wife through tuberculosis (and his money through addiction to Geneva gin) a sour and hairy man called Asselijn, owner of an antique motor-sedan, was employed by the Superintendent as often as occasion could be found. This ne'er-do-well had been told to come at half-past nine to drive the Stahls and me to the station. That was the pith of Mijnheer Dekker's responsibility for the manifold disorder which marred the start of our journey and to which Debora Stahl herself, in her simplicity, made the largest contribution.

Some time before nine o'clock she established herself on the pavement, flanked by a big cardboard box which held her summer hat. Everyone begged her to return indoors and wait sitting down, but she would not listen: her legs were perfectly sound, she said, and she was following a dictum of her father's that it showed only a lack of culture to keep servants waiting. I myself was in so nervous a state that I could not reason with her—I soon retired to watch events from the office window—and her obstinate behaviour was too much even for Walther's loyalty: at the end of an argument where the two sides scarcely joined he went back to their room—perhaps with some latent thankfulness—to finish his packing undisturbed.

She did not wait alone. Two or three of the younger women, always ready for acts of virtue which would cost them nothing, went out to form a bodyguard. These were soon joined by Vaclav, who sometimes chose to regard himself as Debora's footboy (I think his sickly mind comprised a streak of romanticism which responded to hers), while a few townswomen of the infinitely leisured sort lingered to watch from the promenade in the centre of the square. These were hardly to be blamed: the appearance of the Coenraad girls with their gaudy makeshift clothes and their imbecile smiles would nowhere have lacked attention, but it was commonplace beside that of their centre-piece. Today Debora was bareheaded. One of our Czechs had re-dyed her hair, heightening its colour to that of a copper beech in spring, and dressed it to fall in sparse, uneven coils about her neck, while in pursuit of what she understood to be the post-war fashion she had caused another girl to shorten her skirts so ruthlessly that her gnarled and spindly knees were preposterously displayed. I suppose these oddities of toilet were disturbing to the citizens of Wilpenschoen, with their innate respectability. I myself was troubled by this visual travesty of the woman I knew, as if I witnessed in the theatre a piece of shameful miscasting. For within the gross embellishments one still perceived a certain aristocracy: she faintly realised, I think, that there was some irregularity in her position, and yet supposed that her own compound of dignity, good nature and hopefulness would restore to her her natural environment of sunlight and calm.

By a quarter to ten the spasmodic rain which had been falling since daybreak had turned to continuous drizzle. There was still no sign of the driver Asselijn.

Mejuffrouw Potgieter and I were sent in turn to implore the old woman to come indoors. She was obdurate. Thrown a trifle off balance by the pressures of the occasion, she declared that Walther Stahl, her driver, was never late; if the clocks said it was past the time he was ordered for, then it was the clocks which needed correction. By then my own nervous impatience had brought me almost to tears. When I remarked to Mijnheer Dekker that Asselijn was utterly irresponsible he answered in effect that there was no need for feminine fuss—a later train would serve us equally well and he would send a telegram to give our hosts the new time of arrival. But thereafter he tried repeatedly to reach the man by telephone, and at last, when those calls were unanswered, he agreed to summon a taxi from a less irresponsible firm.

This one came in under ten minutes; but, to crown my exasperation, Asselijn's disreputable car had arrived, rattling and belching smoke, a few seconds before. Leaving it some distance from the kerb, Asselijn had strolled into the Lodge, had made his way upstairs and was leaning against the jamb of the office door, filling the room with the stale smell of Bols, while he addressed the Superintendent with lush familiarity: on an earlier run, he said, he had found his engine short of oil, and because of that mischance he was perhaps a trifle late.

Left to himself, Mijnheer Dekker would probably have accepted this ridiculous excuse. But Mejuffrouw Potgieter was standing nearby, and she was no friend to bibulous tradesmen; before her employer had a chance to say one word she had launched her own attack on Asselijn with a passion which brought even him to sobriety and to some alarm. While this was going on I slipped away and went down to the street.

The almost simultaneous arrival of two cars had shaken Debora's satellites into such bewilderment that I found myself assuming authority. The luggage was to go in the respectable car, I said; the other would be dismissed. Both Walther and Vaclav were ready to accept my direction, but the scurry of mindless girls got in their way; the hat-box and my own valise were still on the pavement when Asselijn reappeared, with the Superintendent and Mejuffrouw Potgieter beside him. He had reached the stage of truculence. In a voice that must have carried to the corners of the square he protested that his vehicle had been engaged and whether used or not must be paid for, adding that Mijnheer Dekker was a common thief dressed up as a man of God, that he—Asselijn—would go to the police and also send for lawyers from Den Haag. Like all such mountebanks he appeared to be winning some sympathy from the lookers-on; but again Mejuffrouw Potgieter showed a spirit equal to his insolence, and under her fresh assault he could only withdraw to his driving seat.

It had begun to rain more heavily; and now I saw with anger and acute distress that the confusion this wretch had engendered was not yet exhausted. Debora had remained aloof from the complexities of our situation—a native decorum forbade her to interfere with the minor details of living. Moving a little apart, she must have scrutinised the sedan, and to her, I suppose, it had seemed the shape of car to which she was most accustomed; now, at all events, she was established in the back seat, waiting placidly for the journey to begin. The mistake was realised too late. Asselijn had already started his noisy engine when a warning cry from Mijnheer Dekker reached him; he was in no mood for further parley and like a phaeton with scared horses the car leapt forward, throwing its passenger with shocking force against the back of the seat. Another woman of her age would at least have uttered a cry of fear: Debora was above such weakness. When a blue cloud had dispersed I saw with painful admiration that she had regained her balance, and showing no more than a faint surprise was inclining her head to right and left, like royalty in a ceremonial parade. Now it was evident that the works of the car were in shameful disrepair: in a crippled way it came almost to a halt, then bounded on with a noise like rockets bursting, and this sickening performance was several times repeated, with the victim lurching forward and back, forward and back, like a puppet on a spring. Divining that something was wrong, the onlookers had started to run after it, a wild regatta of spread umbrellas and splashing feet, frustrating the other car which Mijnheer Dekker had ordered to give chase; everyone was shouting at Asselijn to stop, and this provoked the ruffian to a fresh salvo of laughter. Through sheeting rain I caught sight of Walther's face as he struggled in the tail of the pursuit; it

57

was tearful and white with alarm. But the face of Debora herself never lost its august complaisance. Doubtless the shock had numbed her mind: she may even have taken the tumult as some sort of congratulation. I know that throughout this violent promenade she continued to bow and smile, waving when possible a gracious hand, and that when the congestion of traffic at the canal bridge brought the ordeal to a close she uttered no word of censure. To Walther, when he rejoined her, she remarked that the motor seemed to need some attention, but added that the village folk had been so welcoming, so kind.

The train we caught after all that hindrance started not much before midday; through the long afternoon it trudged laboriously across the flat, unchanging meadowland, stopping (or so it seemed) at every bridge and windmill for an old man with a pair of cockerels to alight or a group of country girls, shaped like bartizans, to climb aboard with huge baskets of broccoli. The clouds never lifted, and before we reached Broekenvoord, where we had to change, there were lights showing in cottage windows. The train to take us on was not leaving till late in the evening. In a corner of the waiting-room we ate the basket meal that Mejuffrouw Potgieter had provided; and in the remaining hours Debora, with her head on Walther's shoulder, was mostly asleep. Till then she had been asking at intervals of an hour or so:

'Is this Eisenach? What time do we get there?'

And with unflagging patience Walther had answered, 'Not Eisenach, no, dear wife. We're going to Astelbrucke, *Astelbrucke*, to stay with your grandson for a while. The house at Eisenach won't be ready for some time yet. You do understand?'

'Of course I understand, Walther dear—the little Dutch pastor explained it all to me. We call on my grandson—for the moment I forget his name—and presently he takes us on to Eisenach in his motor-car.'

On the second stage of the journey our fellow-passengers again seemed nearly all to be Dutch—provincials whose wooden features matched their lugubrious conversation. But the presence of a man who sat in the corner opposite mine, ostensibly engrossed in a trade paper, would alone have made me uneasy. He had entered the carriage almost on our heels. He was of humble and kindly appearance—his clothes and accoutrements suggested an old-fashioned commercial traveller—but more than once I saw him glance in my direction, and we had not travelled far before he was writing with studious concentration in a notebook, which left me in little doubt that his business was to watch and report on every movement of mine. To be under surveillance was no new experience, but the closeness of this quiet observer was a reminder that I had been led to make a perilous decision; that with every repetition of the rataplan of wheels below me I was nearer to regions where I might be known, where others would remember what I had forgotten and the substance of any charges brought against me, however far back in time, would no longer be distant in space.

That fresh invasion of fear took a physical shape: although the carriage was hot and stuffy my blood felt cold; and when nearly everyone else seemed to be sleeping, and my own eyelids were heavy, I felt it impossible that I should sleep.

By chance a woman sitting near the informer, with features of greater refinement than her neighbours', somewhat resembled my mother (though shorter and less dark in colouring); and in my somnolent state, to which the poor light and the rhythmic motion of the train contributed, I came to imagine that my mother was actually travelling with me, that she and I were still engaged in an argument which had started more than twenty-five years before. I was insisting that in our time it was normal for a woman turned twenty to lead an independent life, and I heard her say, in a voice almost as clear and individual as when I had first known it:

'Johanna, listen! If you want to be an artist you can do that sort of thing quite as well at home. Here everything's provided, and there are servants, after all, to keep you comfortable. Your father would never have approved of your living alone. And surely no one of culture works for news-paper people!'

To which I answered, 'But Mother, the people who want to employ me are perfectly respectable—they themselves belong to an established family. And I shall be living quite near my cousins—they can keep an eye on me, if you think I need protection.'

These words were spoken with a confidence I could no longer feel: I had come to know that the demands of a newspaper office were often too severe for a girl accustomed to no working discipline but her own. And now, with the train's even pulse annulling my sense of time, I found myself once more in tears because I was late with an illustration needed for the weekly edition. Herr Nietzold, to whom I confessed this dereliction, was grave and unsparing: I must see the Editor, he said. And when he had led me through a chain of connecting rooms I stood before a desk where a young man sat with his hands hiding his face. He neither moved nor spoke; so at last, because I could not bear the silence, I said humbly:

'I am Fräulein von Leezen—I was told to report here.'

Still the young man made no movement—it might have been a dead body I had addressed. But after a long time I heard him speak in a voice of dreadful grief:

'I'm sorry, Johanna—I should have known you were not to be trusted. There's nothing more to be said.'

From the depths of sadness in which those words left me I was glad to be drawn to the surface by fresh and loudening voices, by a light that burst on my fallen eyelids. The train was standing still, the carriage had been invaded by men in uniform and one of them was pointing a torch at my face.

'Your papers, please.'

'I am Fräulein von Leezen,' I told him, in wretched con-

fusion. 'I have always been considered a trustworthy person—
I've held positions of some responsibility.'

'Yes yes! Your papers, please.'

I was almost certain that I had come to the hour of reckoning: it was possible that I should be faced with no charges after all, no questions—they would simply take me to some yard not far away, perhaps to the side of a field, and there finish the business. I said:

'I'm ready—I'll come with you.'

'Your papers!' he repeated.

I found in my bag the certificate which Mijnheer Dekker had provided. The official gave it only a cursory inspection and returned it to my keeping.

'Thank you,' he said.

'That's all?'

'That is all.'

As the train moved on I noticed that the man who had sat in the corner making notes was gone, and I concluded that his tour of duty had ended at the frontier. Who, then, was to watch me now?

I would not let my eyes fall shut again, but the voice of the dream pursued me in wakefulness; repeatedly I caught the echo of that withering sentence, *'I should have known you were not to be trusted,'* till I almost wished the men in uniform had dealt with me as I had feared. To be spared the torment of interrogation, to attain the final safety of unconsciousness—what greater mercy could I ask! Yet I could not see myself accepting with simple resignation so passive a way of escape. If there was any substance in the charges to be brought against me I desired to speak in my own defence: though the facts were out of reach, I knew that in the dark tract where my mind's beam would not penetrate I had been alone and frightened; I wanted at least to say, *'Make your judgement on the woman who stands before you, recognising whatever loyalties, whatever strengths of heart or will she has to show now; not on a creature so different, left so far behind, that this one can no longer re-create her thoughts and feel-*

61

ings, let alone remember how she acted or what she said.'

From that small spring of protest there flowed not courage but a fresh current of resignation. I had begun this journey of my own will, and if I was advancing towards destruction this folly might be better than waiting in such desolate outposts as Ysseldoorn for disaster to creep up and engulf me. I was still locked in drowsiness; but while my fellow-travellers continued to sleep noisily, slumped against each other like bodies in a bombed street, a trickle of curious excitement was now enough to keep me awake.

At a feebly lighted station where we stopped for half an hour I saw notices in German, with the rusted remains of a once familiar advertisement, while just below the carriage window a group of workmen talked in voices not far different from those of my birthplace in the Lüneburger Heide. This abrupt revival of old sensations was enough to quicken the embers of a fire which had appeared to be extinct. I had come to look on exile as a natural state—beside my long estrangement from every fellow-creature the loss of father-land had seemed of small significance. But now an unexpected sense of homecoming served even to blunt my dread of hostile witnesses. The countryside that emerged as a grey film from the loosening darkness was wholly different from that on which night had fallen: the undulating corn-land, heroic beeches massing towards the carriage windows, the silhouettes of gigantic barns and crouching churches, these by contrast made the country which had sheltered me—its featureless and sodden plains, the toyshop prettiness of its little towns and hamlets—seem as insubstantial as pictures thrown on a screen. It came as a forgotten music, this gravitation of the heart towards the land of my child-hood. Like other loves, it was seamed with distress; but in an hour when drowsiness had turned to a cloak of contentment, subduing even the ache of cramped muscles, I felt something akin to the warmth and exaltation of one restored to a husband's arms. With the rest of the carriage still asleep I enjoyed a peculiar solitude; and as the new day came to birth, as the ground mist floating by the window parted now and again to show red cattle grazing, a cobbled lane with a parapet of lupins, a high-wheeled dray with its driver dozing over the reins, I felt as if, long dead, I had returned as a ghost to the country where my life had transiently held shape and meaning.

2

Astelbrucke: I thought I had been there before, perhaps on the business of my employers, perhaps to make a portrait of some rich man's wife. Or else I had visited a neighbouring town of the same complexion. In the place we came to there was less to be recognised than in the face of a friend some hours after his death.

The first thing to catch my eye in the hazed early light was an old tramcar lying on its side, then came a mound of rubble as long and high as an ocean liner. Where the track curved steeply, following the course of a stream, what first appeared to be a tall villa revealed itself as a wall with nothing behind, and a road which rose to cross the river finished in space—of an ancient bridge only the piers had survived. A block of flats standing high above the mist lacked nothing but glass in the windows and the factory beyond them seemed to be undamaged, but those buildings alike revealed no sign of habitation. Where the train began to slow for the station a wizened cat, heraldically poised on the crest of a refuse-heap, was the only living thing in sight.

The station itself lacked its roof, and at that early hour the central platform, an endless vista freckled with casks and boxes, was almost empty of people: descending from the train, stiff and heavy-eyed, I felt as though we had landed on the wharf of an island which its population had long abandoned. In those moments the sense of returning to a cherished land deserted me; I was assailed by the misery and fear which a child suffers in an empty house, and but for the presence of the Stahls I might have surrendered to childish tears.

That wave of desolation was soon past. An object in the far distance defined itself, approaching, as a ramshackle perambulator which a girl was pushing at a lame trot. This was Luise. She was wearing a man's raincoat buttoned askew and her hair was in rats' tails; I thought she must be starved and ill, her thin face was so white, but as she came towards us the cold, lifeless look gave place dramatically to the smile which had first set my heart alight in the hotel at Utrecht. Leaving the pram, she made a little rush to catch hold of me and kiss my cheek, murmuring, 'Dear Fräulein Johanna—so sweet of you to come as well!' Next, quickly turning, crying, 'Welcome, dear Grandmama!' with a half-curtsey that a ballerina could hardly have bettered, she kissed Debora's hand. And then, facing Walther, she curtseyed again:

'And you, sir, Franz and I have so longed for you to come!'

If the old man was slightly flustered by the deference in her greeting, his wife responded copiously to Luise's warmth. In a moment the fatigue of the journey seemed to slip like a stole from Debora's shoulders and the blood returned to her cheeks. Laughing, and with tears welling from her grateful eyes, she folded her grandson's wife in a motherly embrace.

'Dear child! How like your beautiful father!' (She was seldom accurate about relationships.) 'You must come and stay with us at Eisenach, for weeks, for months, as soon as we're settled again.'

It was, then, a party lit with the phosphorescence of instant friendship, though ragged in formation and still half-asleep, which moved slowly towards the station exit, Debora distributing her unsteady weight between Luise's arm and mine so that the three of us described a zigzag course, while Walther with the luggage in the pram trudged manfully in our wake.

'And you have your motor somewhere near?' Debora asked of Luise, as we halted for a rest.

'No, Grandmama, at present we haven't a car at all. But it's not terribly far to go.'

'We could hire a droshky, perhaps?'

'Well, I don't think we'd find one, not as early as this. There aren't many about, even at ordinary times. And their charges are fabulous.'

'It's about how far?' I asked.

'Oh, fifteen minutes,' Luise said. 'Perhaps a bit more when there's luggage as well.'

When—still in the station precincts—we stopped for the third time for Debora to recover breath I saw that the walk would be far beyond her powers. With hardly anyone about it seemed that questions of dignity might well be waived, and as the pram was a big double one, sturdily built though now advanced in dilapidation, I suggested that Luise and I should manhandle the luggage and let the old lady ride in its place. To Walther, with his persistent respectability, the proposal was clearly ungrateful, but not to Debora herself, who from girlhood (I imagine) had cherished a taste for dashing novelties: to ride in a perambulator at the age of eighty-five must have seemed to her a welcome escape from the dullness which had come upon her world, and almost before we had the cases out she was trying to put herself aboard. This, with Luise's help and mine, she presently accomplished, leaving Walther merely to frown and fret, to cover her salient knees with his coat and then to load himself with the hat box. From that point Luise and I did the pushing together, with the rest of the luggage in our spare hands; and in the new order—very slowly and precariously, often pausing to rest ourselves or to equip our passenger with a fresh cigarette—we crossed the station square, trundled past the ruined Rathaus and over the river by a makeshift timber bridge.

On the farther side it looked as if one town had ended and another lay ahead, for in a space of several hectares nothing stood more than a few feet above the ground: vaguely the scene resembled a view of Herculaneum, except that in place of plinths and arches there were wheels and shafts of steel protruding from the crumbled masonry, fragments of machines so broken and contorted that they might have been

66

implements of torture from a Bosch's imagination. Yet to me there was nothing satanic in this wilderness. The violence which had forged it was far behind. No creature but ourselves was moving, and the flat, silken light of early morning, finding flecks of green in the dun waste, heightening the colours of thistle and ragwort, of poppies that blazed from cracks in concrete floors, turned the quietness to a strange serenity. In part, perhaps, the magic lay in a sense of escape from real existence. At Wilpenschoen I had never for a moment lost the consciousness of being in subjection. Now, though one night's journeying could not have altered my status, I could not picture any member of the trio I walked with putting me directly in my place. I knew this freedom was illusory. Yet the total change of scene, the day's calm and freshness, the apparent sympathy of my companions, were enough to persuade my spirit—so long as intelligence lay dormant—that I had returned from a fearful and humiliating voyage to the safety of a family's care and understanding.

It seemed that Debora as well responded to the morning's gentleness. The jolts and creaking of the pram disturbed her not at all, she blew large cumuli of smoke into the calm air, smiling at Luise and me with an impartial and fond indulgence. Even when an erratic wheel plunged into a deep fissure, almost tipping her out of the pram, she maintained her genial temper.

'This place needs a lot of renovation,' she remarked judicially. 'I think, Walther, you ought to speak to the men about it.' Then, perhaps remembering that her responsibilities had lately narrowed, she said with a worldly tolerance, 'Well, it looks as if this part had been used for military business. I expect the officers will see to it in time.'

Her attitude must have been a comfort to Luise, in whose face I saw a growing anxiety about her charges: her concern was natural; for Walther, encumbered with the hat box, bravely picking his way between loose masonry and potholes, could not entirely hide his distress, and the quarter we came to now, with streets too narrow for the early sun to enter, was not an easy one to commend to strangers.

"This part is all going to be rebuilt,' she said in shy apology. 'They've not got round to it yet, because it's rather low on the priority list.'

And Debora nodded in grave acceptance. 'So interesting!' she said, surveying the altered scenery with patient eyes.

At first approach these streets appeared to have been comparatively fortunate, escaping the fury which had flattened everything between them and the river. But the houses had still a lifeless look, and you realised soon that most of them were uninhabited: some were roofless, some had glassless windows; here a row of old, half-timbered buildings had been shored with steel girders, here a tall one had fallen forward to make a Gothic archway with its opposite neighbour. Such were the more patent wounds in what must once have been a frame of modest but tolerable lives. And beside those major blemishes were a hundred signs that no one any longer thought this place worth caring for: all the woodwork needed painting, walls were stained with the effluent from broken conduits, where a drain was blocked there were tins and paper bags afloat in a slimy pool which had spread across the road.

'The next bit's rather uphill,' Luise said diffidently; adding, 'but it's not far now.'

That was a useful reassurance, since the narrow street into which we turned twisted upwards at so steep a pitch that the footpaths had perforce been laid in steps; for me, pushing one-handed, with only a slip of a girl to share the pram's weight, this meant an onerous progress, and for Walther a fresh alarm. When Luise stumbled, and the pram slipped back some way before I could block the wheel with my foot, he cried out tearfully:

'This is hopeless! We must get a proper conveyance!'

I think he would have dropped his load and gone in search of a taxi, had not Debora asserted herself, as she was wont to do in any crisis.

'Dear man, we mustn't fuss,' she said with the decision of a kindly nursemaid. 'These girls are doing splendidly. I get a better view from this palankeen than I ever do from a stuffy motor-car.'

My own doubt was whether Luise was fit to go further: having fallen, she remained on her knees, panting heavily and giggling in a girlish way which I thought was dangerously near hysteria. I looked about to see if any help was available, but—how typical of Astelbrucke!—the one old woman staring from a doorway was plainly too feeble to be of use and in a group of children gathering to feast on our predicament not one looked wholly sane. (Even Debora was faintly disturbed by their curiosity. 'These little things, what are they staring at?' she demanded. 'Do they think I'm going to lay an egg?') I asked Luise if she was hurt, and she answered, sobering, that she only wanted a few seconds' rest. That we willingly allowed her; and though her breathing continued to sound painful she used the time, still kneeling, to give us fresh encouragement:

'I do hope you won't think the house too awful. It was terrible when we found it, but Franz is doing things as fast as he can—he's done quite a lot already.'

'Franz?'

'I mean your grandson—he's called Franz now. I'm his wife, you know.'

'And he's a housebuilder?'

'No—he's really a musician, but he has another job at present. And he does things to the house in his spare time.'

'Well, that's excellent—one's husband ought always to have some spare-time occupation, it keeps them young. My own husband did—of course he's been dead for some time now—he used to buy statues when he wasn't working at his newspapers. Yes, my dear, I look forward very much to seeing this house you speak of, I'm sure it's in every way delightful.'

Her spirits—so differently organised from mine—were responding as they always did to the stimulus of a new audience: I noticed she was sitting up more stiffly, and again there was a tincture of royalty in the smile, the slight inclination of the head, which she awarded to the gaping woman on the doorstep. 'A lovely day!' she called, though from this high-walled alley a day of any sort was hardly visible; and now the rays of her benignity were spread to include the swelling corps of urchins: 'Be careful, dears—this little cart might run back and crush you all. Perhaps you ought to go to your mothers now—I expect your suppers are waiting for you.'

At the next laborious advance she did her best to assume entire responsibility. 'Not too fast, Johanna dear!' she commanded at almost every forward thrust. 'This is an old machine, it won't stand up to much.' And then, 'Walther, dear, I think you might put down that box—someone can go back for it. If you'll just put a hand on these dear girls' behinds it will help to steady them.... Home now, children —*home*, you dear disgusting grubby things!' In a peculiar way I think her buoyant autocracy refreshed the courage of us all: hating the operation as I did—the attrition of our self-respect by the children's witless curiosity, the sheer agony from straining legs and lungs—I could yet feel something of the inspiration which soldiers are said to draw from a trumpet call. We gained no more than two or three metres in each effort; but with only the shortest pauses we attacked the work again and again, till in ten or twenty minutes, trembling, soaked in perspiration, we arrived at level ground.

The street we had come to offered no conspicuous reward for our exertions: it was one that commerce had laid hands on half a century before, planting small factories and office blocks, a stark warehouse and a nest of oil tanks, where trees and cottages once stood. Here again I felt that the whole assemblage of haggard and decrepit buildings had suffered some mortal infection, like a forest which termites have invaded. But now I was too tired to care. We went on for perhaps half a kilometre, steering deviously to avoid the worst of the ragged paving, and then turned into a covered passage barely of carriage width.

It led to a courtyard ruled on the street side by a house of four storeys. This had been a more pretentious building than its neighbours, with copious ornamental tiling and elaborate architraves; but at the first encounter my main impression was of broken or fenced windows, a canopy of underclothes slung on lofty airing lines, a nightgowned woman leaning from a high, wrought-iron balcony which looked about to crumple under her weight. Here, it seemed, was the consummation of our long journey. I reflected with some complacence that it was not I who had planned it.

'It's really nicer than it looks,' Luise said bravely, 'I do hope you'll like it after a time.'

I had witnessed Debora's arrival at Coenraad's Lodge: her first sight of 'the Warren' (as some of its residents had named it) seemed to me a sterner test of her adaptability. She survived it with fresh credit. While we were disembarking her—an arduous business, incompatible with much decorum —she was noticeably silent, and in a moment when her face was close to mine I had a glimpse of tears in the old and weary eyes. By the time she was on her feet, however, every trace of sadness or chagrin had gone.

'But how romantic!' she exclaimed, sweeping the barbarous edifice with a glance which admitted no more than a blurred impression. 'I remember another house like this, my mother's family had it for a hundred years or so—I think it was at Posen.'

And now she did not wait for Luise to lead the way. At the top of a short flight of steps what had once been the servant's door stood open. Neither diffident nor offensively presumptuous, with something of the calm that courageous men may show on their way to execution, she went inside. Luise solicitously followed. With his ineradicable meekness Walther would have made me go next, but that was not as I wished. I held back, and was left in the yard alone.

For I had not forgotten my position. Throughout the journey I had been treated in the friendliest way—as if, indeed, I belonged to the family of my companions. But I knew that in reality I had no rights to this place: I had been brought here with a judicial object, nothing had changed but the scene of my detention.

The woman in the nightdress had disappeared. I found a fleeting pleasure in being entirely by myself, and as the sun surmounted the jumble of low roofs behind me, lighting in turn a trough of marigolds on a window ledge, the faded green of an eaved board, the drapery of traveller's-joy which dangled from a gutter over the doorway, I was heartened by its placid warmth on my neck and shoulders. It was yet very early, nothing pricked the stillness but the song of a linnet whose cage hung by an attic window, and in those moments of unearthly peacefulness I saw afresh that for me perfect solitude was the only bearable existence. To my tired eyes the house itself appeared now as a painted scene, at most a hollow artefact, enshrining no genius of its own; but I knew that presently it would come awake, that I should be called inside and very likely flattered with a further show of geniality, as if I came both with the rights of an intimate friend and with a stranger's innocence. I needed this respite, if only to steel myself anew against yielding to an insidious parade of affection.

It was not Luise who came in search of me, but a spectacled female in an overall—a girl of perhaps eighteen whom at the first glance I took for a much older woman, since her hair was almost as grey as mine. She stood at the top of the steps, a squat, round-shouldered figure with elephantine legs, peering as if into heavy fog, with her lips parted in a faint, foolish smile. Assuming that this look of random benevolence was meant for me I went towards her, and in response to a vague gesture made with her head I preceded her into the house.

In a wide passage we came on Luise carrying a loaded tray. She had the appearance of one required to do half a dozen things at the same time.

'I've got you a room at the top of the house,' she told me rather breathlessly. 'Agnes will show you—I've got to get off to work now.' Then, divining that the spectacled girl and I had so far exchanged no word, she said, 'Agnes is my sister-in-law, you know,' and to the girl herself (after a moment of curious hesitation), 'I expect Fräulein von Leezen will want to sleep for a bit—she must be worn out. It's so sweet of her to have looked after Herr Stahl and Grandmama on their long journey.'

To this introduction the dumpy girl (whom I had previously supposed to be a servant of some kind) made no reply, but her vagrant smile appeared to hover for a moment about my head. Then she picked up my small valise, and bidding me with a movement of her chin to follow her she stumped upstairs.

The stairs were carpetless, the flaking and discoloured walls chequered with dark patches where pictures had once hung; at this early hour the ruling odours were of dampness and disuse. I remember thinking, as I wearily ascended behind my silent guide to one bare landing after another, 'This is a house inhabited by birds of passage—those, like billeted soldiers, with nothing to replace the essence that departed with its owners.' The jetsam that caught my eye from the gloom of successive corridors, a child's tricycle without a saddle, a pair of slippers parted by a heap of soiled linen, only heightened the air of dereliction. We had reached the top floor, and the end of a passage, when Agnes turned to open a door.

'This,' she said.

The room was scarcely more than a cupboard under the roof—you could only stand upright on the door side. At the other, a narrow bed had been placed under the round chest-high window (which I saw was barred); beside it was an old piano stool and next to that a bamboo table bearing a chipped jug and basin. That was nearly all the furniture. But in this Spartan cell someone, unaccountably, had girdled the ceiling lamp with a gay pink shade, and a shock of cornflowers stuffed in a pickle jar adorned the window sill.

The girl Agnes, standing awkwardly by the door, continued to avoid my eyes. Peering towards the basin, then at her own feet, she said, 'Will do?'

'Why, perfectly!' I answered, and took my case from her hands.

It was hard to tell whether her immediate role was that of gaoler or chambermaid. I thanked her for conducting me, and then, as she lingered, I said, 'I think I'll rest for a while, as Luise suggested.' Still she did not move. So, giving her a friendly smile, I took off my shoes and skirt and lay on the bed.

There was silence now, and with my eyes closed I thought she must have slipped away. But after a while a floorboard creaked, then a hand carefully lifted my head while another bunched the pillow about my neck.

Because it came as a surprise, this action greatly touched me. Again I thought of my mother, but now in an aspect which I had almost forgotten: she, no sentimentalist and never at ease with children, had yet consoled me in my illnesses with just such tenderness as this. Indeed, for an instant I imagined that the quiet hands must be hers, and so vivid was this illusion that I thought, as I opened my eyes, 'Why, yes, this is my mother's embarrassed and evasive smile.' In truth the thick-lipped mouth was in no respect like hers, and nothing could have been farther from my mother's spare, northern physiognomy than the heavy nasal bridge and lumpish brows framing the eyes which deviously scanned my face. But the faint echo from my childhood had its effect. I could almost have cried out to the new acquaintance dawdling at my bedside. 'Stay with me, please—I can't stand being alone, high up in an unknown house!'

In actuality one does not say such things—one does not flourish shapeless fears before strangers. I shut my eyes again, and when the girl asked in her straggling mode of speech, 'Bring something? ... Milk?' I only murmured, 'Thank you—no.' Soon the door was quietly shut, and the clomp of her heel-less slippers along the passage dwindled to silence.

The fatigues and responsibilities of the journey were over, I had earned the right to rest. But now I could not sleep. I lay torpid, not much connected with the material world but never quite unconscious of the things close to me, blobs of light and shade which the sunlight made through my eyelids, a ridge in the bedding under my waist. In this lethargic but sleepless state I found my thoughts returning to the callow, goodnatured creature who had brought me upstairs, embroidering the fantasy that in this strange form my mother had come to life again; wearily I once more traversed the history of our quarrels, her chronic resentment of my independence, the rancorous pride which had kept me away in her last weeks of lonely suffering, and I found myself whispering, 'But now I shall make it up to you, now that I am middle-aged and you are young I'll give you the devotion you should have had from me in years gone by.' From this conceit there flowed a current of warmth and sweetness. That the young woman who had suddenly entered my life lacked every physical grace was only an advantage—so much the more did she need my care. For it seemed to me now that the cataleptic state in which I had so long existed was nothing but a symptom of futility, of a hunger for some being whose impotence would call for my service and all my tenderness. I had forgotten where I was. For a span of time, measurable perhaps in fractions of a second, I imagined I had entered a life of freedom, to be surrendered only to the claims of a consuming affection.

Soon I was reminded that what surrounded me was not an empty shell. There started at some distance a lawless orchestra of children's cries—the raging misery of one lately born, the war whoops of little boys and the petulant screams of their sisters. A closet was flushed, a rasping female voice broke out in a spasm of scolding, and now, from the other side of a plywood partition, came the gross noises that a man will produce on waking: the long, plaintive yawn, the boisterous ventilation of nostrils, a convulsive pectoral cough.

Simultaneously I was aware of a new aroma permeating the stale air of the room, a compound smell, oily and sweet, which I presently identified as that of Jewish cooking. But the fresh alarm which these sensations started was not enough to rouse me and was quickly past. I had known that I was entering a Jewish stronghold, and when you have lived for years in the company of fear you become insensitive to its abrasion, as Arctic travellers to that of freezing winds. Dimly I felt that I had learned long before to merge myself in a household of the sort these odours projected, attuning my sensibilities to its exotic flavours, suppressing what was discordant in my own temperament and outlook. So, I might reach that state again. With this thought came quiescence. As the sunlight in the room strengthened, as, in the unknown house surrounding me, the bustle increased, I sank into a rare illusion of innocence and thence at last into sleep.

In one of those dreams where space is confined by no laws I heard, as if from far away, the clink of china, and then my own voice saying collectedly, 'Thank you, Agnes.' But when my eyes came open the face hanging over me in the fading light was that of a man with a black beard.

I asked—my speech at least was calm—'You've come for me?'

He did not answer, and while he continued to gaze at me in silence I saw him rather as an insect under examination might see the entomologist—his sombre Jewish eyes concentrated in an earnest inquiry, his finely modelled mouth set in such gravity as a judge's might wear when it has just pronounced a sentence of death. He said at last:

'You've had a long sleep!'

To me this sounded like an accusation, and I made what might have been a schoolgirl's answer: 'I thought I could—I wasn't told to do anything else.'

'But of course!' he said, with a little bow.

He stood back and stretched to turn on the light. Then,

with a fleeting formality, he announced himself: 'Franz Weckerlin! I'm Frau Stahl's grandson, you know.'

Still not fully awake, I found myself responding with the dull politeness of a town councillor's wife: 'So? I have a great respect for Frau Stahl and her husband.'

He bowed once more. 'I've brought some soup,' he said. 'My wife thought you must be hungry by now.'

I said, 'That is extremely kind.'

'No no—a pleasure!' he replied.

Again he was closely watching me, as if I were an animal of rare interest, and now that the light was on I found myself observing him in equal fascination. His lean body, with the large head and heavy shoulders, was of a sort one automatically pictures stripped for fighting, and I am not sure if at that first meeting I noticed its mutilations: I may have realised from the stiffness of his right trouser-leg that the limb inside was artificial, but since he habitually kept his left hand out of sight I doubt if I saw just then that the three middle fingers were lacking. It was his face which held my gaze, the splendid forehead, the burning intelligence of eyes far recessed under rankly sprouting eyebrows, above all the sadness in a mouth as straightly ruled, as delicately thin, as an elderly priest's. This virile and compelling face was in no neat order—it was smeared with dust and sweat, the overlong hair needed at least some combing, the beard looked as if it had been trimmed with garden shears—and I remember thinking, 'How shocked I should have been in earlier years to find at my bedside a creature so barbarously unkempt and in a labourer's dress!' He may have read my thoughts, for after staring for some moments at his enormous, mud-caked boots he said pensively, as if he had slowly arrived at an unwelcome truth:

'No, I suppose I'm not quite properly turned out as a chambermaid.'

Now he smiled, and instantly I felt that a new person had taken the first one's place—here was such a man as I could travel with.

'It's a misunderstanding,' he continued pensively. 'At the regional labour office they asked if I was ready to work in dirty conditions, and I said yes. So now they have men hunting the whole district for oozy mud, and when they find a specially filthy patch they say, "This'll do for Franz—he'll love this. Send at once for Franz Weckerlin."'

I asked in some confusion, 'Then you're a geologist?'

That made him laugh. 'Yes, that's it exactly! This bull-dozer thing my kindly employers entrust to me, I use it for delving into all the most fascinating strata.'

He had begun to look about the room, and this survey seemed to recall him to sobriety.

'Not only a sluttish chambermaid,' he said judicially, 'but a wretched chamber! Really I'm terribly sorry—for the moment it's the only one we could get you. The Pavaakas, you see—they're the main tenants—they will keep letting off more rooms to old people they come across. (Do have your soup, won't you—it's starting to freeze.) Still, we *will* grab you a better room the moment there's one going.'

I told him that as I understood the arrangement I had only been sent from Wilpenschoen as courier for the Stahls, and to settle them in at their destination. 'I expect to be recalled,' I said, 'in a day or two.'

'Recalled?' He looked at me with puckered brows.

I nodded. 'By the authorities in Holland.'

This simple statement seemed to trouble him—just then I had the impression that he did not greatly care for his role as an agent of discipline. Simultaneously I realised that he was a pitifully tired man. His eyelids had fallen, and for some moments he was silent; then he spoke very slowly, as if he were repeating a piece he had tried to learn by heart:

'Dear Fräulein Johanna, we want you—Luise and Agnes and I—to stay with us as long as possible—as long as you're happy here. And my grandparents too, I know already how much you mean to them.' There he paused: he seemed to have forgotten his lines. Then, 'There's not much in the way of comfort here. But we beg you, please—whatever you think about us—to try and feel you belong to our small circle.'

That was spoken with a note of sadness, and so humbly that it nearly overwhelmed me. To save myself from tears I had to be stiff to the verge of rudeness in my reply:

'I'm afraid it's not for me to decide how long I shall stay. I can only say I'll do my best to be useful. I mean, in return for the shelter you're giving me. I'm anxious not to abuse your hospitality.'

To this he made no answer; and soon, either in embarrassment or from charity, he bowed himself away.

Once more alone, I went through some moments of wishing I were back at Coenraad's Lodge. It had been a kind of liberty to live among those—the stolid Dutchmen, the polyglot crew of vacuous women—who made such small demand on one's mind or feelings. Here such detachment was impossible. The people responsible for me now were my compatriots. It was easy, since they were conspicuously Jewish, to be mentally on guard against the traps they might set for me; the hard thing would be to rule my feelings, to stanch the springs of emotion which people of my own tongue and with such kindly manners were likely to evoke from my inmost being. This Franz had been at my side for less than five minutes: it was enough to show that instincts had survived in me which I had thought were finally extinguished —the longing to honour another creature and myself to be honoured, to sink so deeply in a lake of affection that the shame and terror of the real world would be for ever forgotten. Recalling vividly those earliest hours at Astelbrucke I see it was not the menace of the Weckerlins so much as their gentleness that—if the means had been available—would have made me take again to flight.

But I have to beware of illusory 'memories'—of imagining that from the moment of arrival I knew what the Warren had in store for me. I suppose, for example, that I was there for some days or even weeks before I heard any reference to Albrecht Weckerlin, yet now I find it hard not to believe that some mention of 'Uncle Albrecht' came into my earliest talk with Franz and that, from the very first, I intuitively recognised this name as signalling the principal threat to my security.

'Uncle Albrecht had the room you're in when he stayed with us last winter. He found it horribly cold.'

I do remember that when Franz said those words he was in the kitchen, alternately bending to tie his bootlaces and swallowing a spoonful of the stew I had made for his breakfast. It was some time later—one evening when I was helping him to repair the paving in the yard—that I asked:

'This Uncle Albrecht you talk of, is he an old man?'

'Oh, heavens, no!' he said. 'About your age, I should think. I think he was younger than his wife—she was my father's sister. She's dead now. He married her not long before the War.'

I see him, as he spoke those words, handling a mortar trowel with an artist's concentration; his casual utterance gave the impression that neither the dead aunt nor the living uncle meant anything much to him. But a little later, when he was resting, he said spontaneously:

'I owe him everything—Uncle Albrecht. He took us in when we were just about *kaput*, Agnes and me—we'd been on the run for months, and she was no more than a kid. He could have been shot for that. And later on when Luise and I got married he said we could go on living with him as long as we liked.'

That speech is joined in my memory with another, belonging to a different occasion and not addressed to me. Luise had just come in from her work one evening and I was arriving in the kitchen to give her her supper when I heard Franz say:

'Of course, yes—Albrecht must come and stay whenever he wants to.'

To which Luise answered—she had her back to me—'But

it's not only the room problem. You know how he feels about things—his frightening sense of what is right and wrong.'

A remark so commonplace—so typical of what young people say about the middle-aged—might have passed without my attention had not Franz, catching sight of me, directed at his wife a vehement look of warning; this brought a moment of embarrassment, and in the hope of clearing the situation I said impulsively:

'You do know—if you want the room I'm in at any time, I'm perfectly willing to go back to where I was before.'

'Oh, but dear Fräulein Johanna,' Luise said quickly, 'we couldn't manage without you for a single day.'

The topic was discussed no further. But in Franz's eyes I had seen a spasm of anxiety too deep to have come from a small domestic concern. From that time I found myself always with an ear open for some mention of 'Uncle Albrecht', whom I somehow pictured as a burly, square-built man with an officious mouth and patronising eyes; one whose care for Franz and Agnes would lead to a jealous and destructive hatred of any stranger found in their house.

I had in fact written to Mijnheer Dekker within a few days of my arrival, requesting his instructions about my return to Wilpenschoen. I had to wait a week or more for his answer, which—as I judged from its literal oddities—he had typed with his own hands on the office machine:

My very dear Fräulein von Leezen!

I am delighted to have your letter, which—though it tells me nothing about your journey—is at least evidence of your safe arrival and that of our dear friends the Stahls.

As to your returning here, this (as I thought I had explained to you) is entirely a matter for your own decision. You know, of course, that as long as this somewhat rugged institution is in being you will always be welcome here, and I greatly miss all your kindly services. For one thing, nature has made me incapable of placing any letter or other document where I can ever find it again—according to my own broad observation this disability comes, I know not how, as a by-product of theological study. But in other departments I have dear Mejuffrouw Potgieter, that queen of domestic efficiency, as my assistant (or, should I say, as the General to whom I myself am a modest Chief of Staff), also the ladies Rosa, Anna, Agatha *et al*, who give me the benefit of their several gifts (as varied, though not always as valuable, as the ones St Paul enumerated to the citizens of Corinth), while where you are living at present there is, as I understand the situation, no Mejuffrouw Potgieter, and there are, on the other hand, dear Frau Stahl and her devoted husband, people too old for care for themselves, who have come to look to you for daughterly ministrations that no one else, I think, could give them. Again, I understand that your young hosts both have outside occupation, and I should be surprised to learn that they do not equally value having in their household a guest of such helpfulness as yours. If you will assiduously re-examine the problem in the light of what I have said, I think it most likely that you will decide to extend your stay at Astelbrucke, perhaps indefinitely.

Meanwhile I send you, dear and honoured Fräulein Johanna, the most affectionate greetings from us all.

Your devoted friend,
Nicolaas J. Dekker.

The arch manner in this letter offended me less when I summoned up an image of the writer: small in stature and of simple intelligence, he had always seemed to me an undeveloped creature whose whimsicalities one accepted as one accepts the innocent foolery of a child. There was still much for me to disapprove of: his answer to my question was evasive, and the artless flattery which he used to cover the evasion would have deceived no one. None the less, his argument that there was more to occupy my time where I was than at Coenraad's Lodge carried some weight with me. It was true that in some ways I could be useful to the Stahls, who at first were hardly more at home in the new ménage than in the old; it was also true that the young people had neither time nor resources to care for them as their age demanded, and if Luise was pregnant, as I already suspected, that situation would not improve. When you have no real life of your own, and no security, you tend to fill the vacuum with bustle and with a passive absorption in the lives nearest to hand. Like a locomotive shunted on to a fresh track I had, when Mijnheer Dekker's letter came, already fallen dully into a new routine, and it would have needed a will much livelier than mine to return to the old one.

But that, perhaps, is not the whole truth. When I try to recapture the peculiar feel of my apprenticeship in that household it is always Franz who stands in the foreground, though in fact I saw less of him than of the others. I used to give him his breakfast as early as half-past five, he was at work all day and when he came home in the evening he was too tired as a rule for conversation: he would eat his supper in silence, following (I supposed) some train of thought which had started in his working hours, and afterwards it was clear that he wished for no one's company but his wife's. Sometimes, however, he and I would find ourselves together, washing the supper things or doing some repair in the Stahls' room, and on those occasions he might emerge from his mental camera to look at me with curiosity and something resembling an amused affection, as if I were a dog of unusual breed (or none) which he had acquired through absence of mind. He would address me then with an air of shyness which I found peculiarly engaging.

'Really I don't know why you slave for us!'—that was a typical opening. 'Of course you ought to be getting a proper salary. At any rate you're to have half the next allowance we get from American Relief. Luise insists on that. And I do too.'

I told him repeatedly that my needs were small. This was true: a prisoner without relations wants little in the way of material things; authority gives her shelter and food, and personal vanities are largely in abeyance. But then he would continue, sombrely teasing out his thoughts.

'They say I ought to get a clerk's job, but I'm better paid as a navvy. And to get anywhere at clerking you need a solid education. I haven't got that. Mine went all to hell even before the War came—all I've got is what I've picked up from Albrecht Weckerlin.'

When he talked like this, ingenuous, self-mocking, confidential, I almost ceased to think of him as my gaoler; and the Jewish cast of his features no longer much disturbed me, for a physical beauty such as his—the head cut with the savage power of a Meunier, the hooded eyes smouldering with a prophet's fire—served to blur such demarcation. His curious way of smiling, which would start as a veil for sadness and turn—like a lamp when the wick is raised—to a core of radiance, was what first set him apart from all the others whose existence bordered mine. Recurrently it brought a sense of familiarity; I felt that I had known at an earlier state in my life the strange coalescence of grief and hopefulness which it revealed; and this perplexed me until I remembered a distant dream (so vivid I could still confuse it with reality) where a train of barges had been slowly passing and among the crowding passengers a child had seemed to recognise and signal to me with that same engrossed, endearing smile. In Franz it belonged to the most benign and boyish of his moods. On other days his face was old, that of a man desiccated by the slow furnace of experience, and there were moments when a lode of bitterness in him was exposed in caustic observations or fits of ugly laughter. Early in our acquaintance I learnt to expect those revulsions, and to keep my distance when they were imminent. Even then he did not seem a stranger.

His sarcasms were never directed at me, and only once was I a target for his anger. It was when, late at night, I heard unaccountable noises from a shed in the courtyard and went to investigate. From female nervousness I opened the door with a jerk, and in the light of a bicycle lamp saw Franz standing with his back to me, his awkward legs far astride; he was playing a violin—or rather, trying to play it—with the instrument in his right hand, the bow in his left. When the draught warned him of my entrance he swung round, trying at the same time to hide what he was at; and in a burst of weeping like a tired child's he shouted at me:

'*What do you want?* I let you live your private life—why do you stick your nose into mine!'

I could only shut the door and creep away, myself not far from tears.

Like any woman of middle age I had an appreciation of male mentality sharp enough to tell me that in a creature of such gentleness as his the intervals of rage or despair were nothing to wonder at. I accepted him as a whole person, and with the kind of loyalty an animal will give to the man who keeps it. If I had to spend my final weeks as a prisoner—and I could no longer see myself in any other state—I wanted no one but him to be in command.

Yes, the value of any settled life, any semblance of tranquillity, is magnified when you feel that it cannot be permanent, that a threat from outside is always drawing a little closer. In that situation you are grateful for every familiarity; you draw drops of contentment from the known looks and gestures of people about you, from the way your small possessions come readily to hand.

Of course it is never easy to live as if in total trustfulness with those who are concealing their real thoughts and feelings. Often I could talk to Luise as to a favourite daughter, but there would come a moment when I caught her observing me with the patronage of one who wisely indulges a child's caprice—at those times her expression made me think of Walther's when he was trying to involve me in his reminiscences. On some days I seemed to see that look reflected on every face: even Agnes, regarding me through the narrow aperture which connected her with the world outside herself, would show within her clouded eyes a fearful curiosity, a deliberate restraint. That air of adult forbearance became oppressive if two or three of my companions wore it at the same time. When, for instance, Franz and Luise were together I was constantly aware of their collusive glances; I could feel that the moment I left the room they would start discussing me as schoolteachers discuss a wayward pupil. And yet it was the solidarity of these young people with each other and with the Stahls which, as much as any other cause, made me want to stay with them. Here I caught sight of something I had long forgotten, how kinship alone can hold together individuals far apart in age and outlook. I could not be neutral in the face of that enlightenment. For one like me, debarred from every genuine friendship, it was impossible to enter such a circle; but I wanted to be near, to serve and cherish it, even to win for myself a little of its warmth.

The domestic comforts were small. Few of the doors or windows fitted their frames exactly; the second lavatory, of primitive design, was on the far side of the courtyard; a single bathroom with nineteenth-century equipment was expected to serve the whole house.

To share an antique kitchen with several other women would be relatively simple where a common speech and a common gift for planning enabled every user to be familiar with the others' programmes. Those conditions did not obtain. There was no means of knowing whom, or whose utensils crowding the sink and stove, one would find in the kitchen at any hour of the day or night. Maria, the mistress of Pavaaka, was no trouble—she was touchingly anxious not to let her operations clash with mine. But another Baltic woman known to me as Hanna, a yellow-haired creature with breasts like half-filled flour sacks, seemed always to arrive when I was busiest and would stand waiting for me to free the oil cooker, her enormous mouth sagging despondently, her pinched eyes smoking with impatience. Congenitally stupid, she never learnt to manage the archaic oven, and frustration put her into infantile rages.

'This damn-devil stove!' she would shout. 'These German idiots, why cannot they make a thing so simple, a stove to cook with!'

More than once, when sheer incompetence had reduced some concoction of hers to reeking ashes, she threw the casserole on the floor; and on such occasions her fury would reach its climax in a physical assault on the cooker itself, which she would hammer with her fists or kick with her square-toed clogs, crying:

'Bastard—bitch! Cookstove? *Foosch!* Hell-damn-furnace! Made by German fools for German whores!'

The complaint was groundless, and it needed no special insight to tell me that I myself was the real object of her resentment. But though such outbursts were a constant irritation when I was trying to cater for the widely varied needs of my own party, this shiftless woman troubled me less than Frau Reuben (I knew her by no other name), a pale bedraggled creature from Memel who would not have raised her voice to escape death by torture. When I was working under the greatest pressure—with Agnes, perhaps, laboriously ironing Luise's smalls on one half of the kitchen table and Walther cleaning shoes between the mangle and the larder door—a gust of eucalyptus would tell me that Frau Reuben was in our company again, doubtless garnished with her three children, for she would hardly move a dozen paces without them. Like herself they were pallid and thin, these latest products of many centuries' migration, and too young to have learnt the use of handkerchiefs, but even the smallest of them had eyes above the table level and fingers which darted like frogs' tongues upon every attractive morsel. Their mother seemed seldom to notice their depredations. With me, as with them, she was infinitely patient, never complaining of my being in her way, never even asking when the cooker would be free. But she would stand close behind me, and in the hoarse whisper which was all the voice left her by some tracheal infection she would inform me about her current anxieties:

'Yes, she's like her father, Esther is—she just won't eat, not except just what she was brought up on. Children are funny, aren't they!'

I answered that being childless I could not say.

'I don't really know what to do,' she said supinely, '—I suppose she's like my little Simeon and my little Miriam, I don't expect she'll live very long.'

This seemed to me foolish talk, with the child Esther almost under our feet, observing the mother with unmistakable intelligence and languidly chewing a slice of beetroot from a salad I had prepared for Franz. But it is useless to be vexed by exhibitions of mindless parenthood, and I tried at least to show a civil interest in her concerns.

'Little Jakob,' I would say, 'looks better today. And I don't think he's coughing quite so much.'

This was a waste of breath: to women of her sort optimism is always an affront, and she met it with stock replies:

'Ah, but have you heard him at night, Fräulein von Leezen? And it's three days now since he kept anything down.'

'I'm sorry to hear that. Has he a weak digestion?'

'Digestion? Fräulein von Leezen, you ought to see his motions! It's something you wouldn't believe. I'll show you sometime.'

I said that this was needless. But she persisted:

'Things, Fräulein von Leezen—things I wouldn't like to talk about. Right in the middle—crawly things. If you'd like to come to my room sometime I could show you one of his little motions.'

To one with no special interest in paediatrics that branch

88

of kitchen talk can soon grow burdensome; it added to the strain of cooking with wretched tools and scant supplies. But when you are working for lenient employers, and with an illusion of safety, you bear with such irritations. If you have spent months in flight, if you have twilight memories of sleeping with a dozen other kitchen servants in the basement of a cheap hotel, of scrubbing floors in the billets of foreign soldiers, escaping from that slavery only to be stored in a depository for outcasts, you will not be much deranged by the vagaries of a few callow females.

At worst they did not frighten me, since the close and familiar is seldom alarming. I was more in fear of the people I saw only in glimpses. In a house so large and populous you could not always tell whether those you met on the stairs were residents or visitors—tradesmen, rent collectors, political spies. But it was not those passers-by who haunted the dark places in my mind, it was the figures which appeared to be almost a part of the fabric. On the first floor my path was crossed again and again by an old man with a civet's face who, wearing a soldier's coat over ragged pyjamas, and bent almost double, pushed himself along—rather as ferrymen propel their boats—with two short sticks. Often, as I stood to let him go by, his eyes were pointed directly at my waist, but he never showed a sign of realising that anyone was near him. Then there was the youth with a keloid covering almost half his face—at dusk, as I turned at the summit of the stairs to go to my room, I would come upon him gazing through a bull's-eye window, as motionless as a wax model. Those, and others I encountered always in the same places, were apparently harmless beings, but to me there was something sinister in their attendance. They belonged to the past rather than the present. Obscurely I felt they were there to witness that one cannot finally obliterate a previous life by shutting the doors of memory and turning the key.

Such acquaintance as I had with other residents in the

Warren I owed first to Debora. Hers was not a spirit which confines itself to small compartments. She had come, I think, to realise that the state she dreamed of—her old position as mistress of the great house at Eisenach—would not be restored to her in a matter of days or even weeks, and now she resolved on social adventures to leaven the weight of time that lay on her shoulders.

'Johanna, dear, Luise tells me that these Pavaakas—they are her lodgers, I imagine—she tells me they are most agreeable.' (She had failed to grasp the irregular relationship of this couple, which Luise had more than once explained to her.) 'I think I must make a call on Frau Pavaaka—it's a courtesy I feel she would expect of me.'

For me those neighbourly excursions meant some clerical activity: before they could be undertaken there were notes to be written, replies to be studied and in turn acknowledged. It would sometimes take a week or more to arrive at a date and hour for the meeting. But for Debora those tourneys of politeness were part of the pleasure: from the time when Agnes was sent upstairs with the inceptive letter the old lady would live in feverish but joyous impatience for the arrival of a return messenger, and she would give to the laboured missive which came as earnest a scrutiny as if it were a ducal commendation.

'You must read it to me, dear—the light in this house is the wrong focus for my spectacles. . . . On Friday, yes, I think we can manage that. Five o'clock? That seems a curious time! Ah, but perhaps that's the calling hour in Lapland, or wherever these interesting people come from. Will you come to me, dear, a few minutes before that. I shall want a little help in getting ready.'

On the first of these occasions I went to her room an hour before the time of the appointment. It was not too soon. From the litter of drapery in a cabin trunk which had followed her from Ysseldoorn she had extracted what she termed 'my calling stays', and she thought it essential to be encased in this formidable garment. 'You see, dear, the jersey-silk has a feeling of its own, it longs to cling to solid things—do you know what I mean?' I did not, but I never matched my lame perceptions with the acuity of hers. To gain more space, or for decorum, Walther was made to leave the room during the operation, and as he himself was already half changed it meant that he had to stand in the passage in under-vest and trousers. I thought this unfeeling on Debora's part, but she, absorbed in the business of her own robing, had little mind to spare for his comfort then: to her the tugging and the padding-out, the shortening of straps, the first-aid needlework performed close to her skin, were all a ritual suffering married with delight. Only the lack of choice in dresses grieved her:

'The cerise taffeta would have done so well. I can't think what has happened—Martha seems to have packed none of my best dresses. I think she rather lost her head when the War came.'

She was fond, however, of the blue jersey-silk, and when she had tapped a long-empty scent bottle against her wrists and throat, had mounted and adjusted the flamboyant hat in which I had first met her, she was ready to squeeze the last drop of pleasure from her outing.

'Walther! You may come in now.'

He came, to complete his dressing with a Bismarck collar and a black jacket, the only one he had without stains or patches. This coping of extreme respectability gave him the manifest appearance of a servant, and I fancied from a shadow which passed across Debora's face that she was aware of this effect. But the zest of the occasion overcame all other feelings; she said, kissing the side of his head:

'Why, you look splendid, my old friend—like royalty! And you, Johanna, charming! It suits you so much better, to have your hair growing again.... But *of course* you're to come too—what should I do if you weren't there to tell me when I forget things!'

With that encouragement we were launched on our arduous progress upstairs, two steps and then a pause, a longer rest at the half-landings. I doubt if Debora in her elated mood had any idea that Walther was bearing a fair proportion of her weight while the rest of it fell on me; so that when we reached the second floor, with him and me breathless, she, only a little damp and rosy-faced, was ready to advance at once upon the objective.

'Are you all right, Walther? Ring the bell, Johanna dear.... No bell? Then knock on the door—a firm rap is the best.'

I knocked. And when we had waited for half a minute or more, hearing from within the sounds of hasty tidying, the door was opened with evident misgiving to disclose the meagre person of Maria Pavaaka, for once shorn of her apron, her ragged hair tied back, her face wiped and drawn into a timid smile.

'Good day!' Maria said, as limply as if she hoped we might yet think better of our plan and retire downstairs.

It was not a fulsome welcome, but in its reflection on the face of Debora it seemed to grow large and warm. As though caught by a gust of wind, Debora left her escort and went forward with her hands at shoulder height.

'Frau Pavaaka, this is so very kind! Your letter touched me deeply—I can hardly tell you how I've looked forward to this afternoon.'

There was, I believe, nothing consciously histrionic in that approach. To Debora any encounter with a fellow being worked as a stimulant, it brought a gladness which the other party was bound to share and which sharing would intensify; or, if the new friend seemed too feebly made to accept the galvanic charge, her own incandescence would suffice to irradiate and warm them both. For a moment, now, she faltered: a name—it was her constant trouble—a name would not come. But she made a strong recovery:

'I want to present my old friend, my dear Walther—Herr Walther Stahl—who has been with me for *many* years— really I don't know what I should do without him. And my daughter Johanna, whom I think you have met already.'

(This was how she had taken to describing me. It would have been pointless now to raise an objection.)

So bidden, Maria fell back a little to hold the door wide open, much as a housemaid would. She cast an abortive smile towards Walther and me, and with Debora as the point of a spearhead we three moved a little raggedly into the room. The reception had begun.

For myself, although these outings made a break in the routine of housework and the terrors of lonely rumination, I could see little pleasure or sense in them. Our hosts—later to become our guests—lacked most of the apparatus needed for entertaining; we were also short of common topics and, in practice, of a common speech, since the German these people used, adequate for such business as marketing, would hardly stretch to the requirements of continuous conversation. But perhaps it was only I who suffered at once a lively embarrassment and monstrous tedium. It was true that Walther, sitting bolt upright and holding his thighs as if he were guarding high explosive, seldom uttered a whole sentence, but I think he took an unfailing pride in his wife's social gifts and found his own contentment in hers; while Debora herself seemed no more conscious of any dullness in her audience than a gifted pianist at the summit of his performance.

In my memory of that first visitation there are fragments as sharply defined as a blackboard drawing. There is Debora seated with a studied grace in the one armchair, shedding her smile as a lighthouse circulates its beams, consciously the prima donna in this scene but never indulging in patronage. At a distance of two or three metres the frail Maria is primly perched on the higher end of a sofa which has two legs appreciably shorter than their fellows, and at the lower end Larin Pavaaka, her cadaverous protector, is crouching over his rampant knees with the grim patience of a peasant sheltering from a storm. Behind him a child, a few weeks old, lies asleep in apparent comfort with nothing but a linsey shawl between him and the floorboards, while a sister of perhaps eighteen months, clad only in a short chemise, comes plodding sturdily towards the sofa; arriving, she pushes up her mother's skirt to plant a wet kiss on the flesh above her stocking; goes on to where the baby lies, bends double to kiss him on the stomach, laughs, and with her lips pursed to utter a wavering, insect hum waddles off to the next room. In a few moments she makes another entrance and the simple drama is faithfully performed again.

This ceaseless perambulation was in effect the only active part of the entertainment. Debora was not slow in turning it to conversational use:

'Your little one is going to be musical, I think.'

A nervous laugh from our hostess was the only response.

'And you,' Debora pursued, 'are you fond of music?'

'Music?' Another girlish laugh. 'Well, I don't really know.'

In no wise discouraged, Debora went forward with her theme like a swan making its quiet passage through still water: 'Myself, I'm very fond of music, it runs in my family. In my own home we have little concerts from time to time—in summer I sometimes stage them out of doors, we all sit beside the lake and the artists perform on a little island close to the bank. Last year we had Kukuchin to play for us—or no, I think it was longer ago than that. Walther, when was it Kukuchin came?'

'I think it was 1936, ma'am.'

'Yes yes, I expect you're right. A wonderful man, a marvellous interpreter of Mozart—and himself so modest, so charming. You know him?'

It seemed the Pavaakas did not know Kukuchin.

'But you've heard him play, I expect. Perhaps Herr Pavaaka plays some instrument himself?'

Herr Pavaaka failed to understand this question. His mistress, suddenly provoked by his feebleness, said sharply, 'Larin! Attention!' and continued in a vernacular I could not follow. On Larin's primitive face I read in succession the conspicuous signs of shock, resentment, helplessness, and these emotions finally brought him to speak.

'Cousin,' he said gruffly. 'I have a cousin.'

Debora received this confidence with kindly interest. 'A cousin? But how nice for you! I myself have had some most engaging cousins.'

'He used to play music,' Larin said. 'But they shot him.'

'What—for playing, Herr Pavaaka?'

'For playing? No. It was the Russians. They were out to get him.'

I saw Debora's face change, as if at the pressure of a switch, to unaffected sympathy.

'Oh, how very sad!'

Larin slightly shrugged his shoulders, as one who felt himself unequal to making moral judgements.

'Harmonica,' he said, '—that was what he played. He got it off a sailor.'

'A sailor—how romantic! The harmonica, yes, I believe that's an instrument which calls for a great deal of artistry. Kukuchin's special instrument—I expect you know—is the viola.'

'No,' Larin said firmly, 'My cousin never had a viola.' He turned suddenly upon the child who was humming contentedly behind him. 'You stop that row, Zebilla, or I'll slit your gullet.'

'I expect those things cost money,' Maria said apologetically. 'I expect Larin's cousin couldn't afford a viola.'

As the ponderous exchanges went on and on I wondered if they were to be relieved by any kind of meal: when an hour or more had passed there was still no sign from the Pavaakas that they had considered this aspect of hospitality. At last some intuition seemed to tell Maria that the afternoon would pass more fluently if her guests were given refreshment; she bent towards Larin; for some time the pair was absorbed in whispered colloquy, then Larin left the room. A few minutes later he returned with three vessels on the lid of a biscuit tin: to Debora he handed a large tumbler, to Walther a smaller glass, a coffee cup to me. In each of these was a spoonful of (I think) diluted vodka. Under Debora's leadership we accepted and drank this offering with ceremonious gratitude.

'...And I wish you may live to see your children's children enjoying great prosperity!'

Those, I remember, were the last words of Debora's long, circuitous benediction. She had risen to declaim it, and I dared to hope that she might be planning to bring our visit to an end. But her pleasure in the Pavaakas' society was not exhausted. After returning the tumbler to her host, and quietly ferreting in Walther's pocket for a cigarette, she resumed her seat. I realised with dismay that the same sort of colloquy, exasperating in its lack of coherence, was to start all over again.

The baby had waked but miraculously had once more fallen asleep. Maria re-settled herself on the sofa, with what feelings I could not tell. She asked, perhaps with some anxiety:

'You wish—something to eat?'

'Dear Frau Pavaaka, how sweet of you!' Debora answered. 'But no! A thousand thanks, but to eat anything now would spoil the taste of your delicious wine.' She turned again to her host. 'If you are fond of music, you should visit Wiegenstadt. The concerts they have there are world-famous. But perhaps you have been there already?'

The question was too difficult for Larin. He said, after some reflection, 'I have a cousin who went to visit Hamburg.'

Debora nodded agreeably. 'Hamburg, yes—that's a rather different sort of town. But not, I expect, without its own attractions. Wiegenstadt is a place I myself know well, because my husband used to work there—he owned some newspapers.'

'Please?'

'Frau Stahl is telling you,' Maria explained to Larin, 'that Herr Stahl has a newspaper shop in Wiegenstadt.'

This brought from Debora a soft correction: 'Not Herr Stahl—my other husband. And what does your husband do, Frau Pavaaka?'

'My husband was the stationmaster at Varjuli.'

'At Varjuli? How very nice! I believe I should enjoy that kind of work myself, waving a flag to send the trains in all directions.'

'But then the Russians put him in prison.'

'Ah, those Russians—you never know what they'll be up to! Still, he looks very well now.'

'Well? I don't think so. He remained in prison. I speak of Witold. Like you, I have here this other husband.'

'So? But he looks well too.'

That was spoken with diminished confidence, and I could see from Debora's face that for once she was conscious of having lost her bearings. Sensibly she again turned her attention to Zebilla, who was still engaged in her monotonous promenade.

'Perhaps your little boy is hoping to grow into a stationmaster too?' she said to Larin.

It was Maria who answered, again with a note of apology: 'Well, Zebilla is more a little girl, really.'

Debora leant forward to regard Zebilla's person more attentively, and then she nodded.

'So! Then her little brother, I expect, will follow his father and manage the trains.'

'Perhaps...' Maria said doubtfully. 'Only Simeon isn't Witold's child—he's Larin's.'

I might have tried to resolve these misunderstandings, but I lacked the needful energy of mind. Was there anything to gain? I judged that Debora herself was still in good spirits, while the Pavaakas, as far as I could see, were but faintly troubled by social misgivings: to people living so modestly as they it was perhaps a source of pride to be visited by a woman of sumptuous presence, or perhaps both parties were imbued with that pervasive sympathy which—as I believed—drew together people of Jewish strain far apart in language or status. I did not intervene. And soon the child Simeon, doing at once everything of which babies are capable, effected a desirable break in the conversation.

With the measure of intelligence that time brings, I have come to see it was a failing in myself which made that kind of party so sore a trial to me. There is no enjoyment in gatherings to which you make no contribution. I furnished nothing, because I was remote from the people we encountered, and in constant fear of their trying to overcome the estrangement.

In contrast, Franz and Luise respected my privacy; they seemed in some way to realise that for me the past was an immensity of darkness which had to be kept from any wayward beam of the mind's light; and I had the impression that Agnes, for all her dullness, was their partner in that understanding. But how could I expect such delicate consideration from our neighbours! These, in fact, hardly tried to conceal their curiosity about the gaunt gentile whom Frau Stahl presented as her daughter and who was manifestly nothing of the kind. Always I could feel them watching me with inquisitive eyes, and sometimes they would probe me with ostensibly amiable inquiries about where I had spent my childhood, what I had done in the war years. Those questions I answered with stock evasions, murmuring that I had lately recovered from a long illness; but they were always frightening, for they could easily have led me into dangerous speculation. And since my arrival in this house my defences had come to feel so precarious, so thin.

Nor could I take refuge in a total indifference to these acquaintances, whom I often saw as vessels lying alongside me in a breakers' dock. For only the blind and deaf can live entirely in their separate worlds.

'But you and I, Fräulein von Leezen, we've met before—surely I once sat for you, at Munich, a long time ago!'

In those terms, during one of Debora's visitations, I was addressed by a middle-aged Jewess whose sallow flesh overflowed the collar of her blouse like a sunk soufflé, and who surveyed my face with a penetrating intelligence. I answered that she was mistaken—that I had never been to Munich—and she said with a shrug:

'So? Well, I was painted a good deal in those days.'

But a name so vigorously shaped as hers—she was, in fact, Klara Kielreuter—could hardly fail to make some impression on a wakeful mind, even one conditioned as mine was never to dwell on names with a familiar ring. As soon as she had ceased to scrutinize my face I started scanning hers, and within those ruinous features—the puffed eyes, the chapped and drooping underlip, the small chin couched in a great scroll of flesh—I saw for an instant a face shaped by exquisite sensibility and brave with purpose. As if a pencil of light had pricked into the past, that vision waked a chorus of sensations: the smell of pigments diluted by a draught of air from an open window, air warmed by the Bavarian sun, enriched by sylvan odours from the Englischer Garten; and so vivid was that return of lost experience that I wanted to cry out:

'Why, yes, you chattered so much about your work that you ruined mine! And we laughed like schoolgirls about your beaux, who were always steaming with impatience down in the hall, and you were so gay that your happiness flowed into me. . . .'

In fact, I naturally kept my counsel. She did not challenge me again, and it was most unlikely that a second person whose path had once crossed mine should have drifted to this house. But that encounter emphasised the risk in all these meetings—the chance that anyone of my own generation might wake the faculties I had put to sleep and set my thoughts to run in the vast tract which I had forbidden them.

Yes, if you have once given yourself to making pictures your eyes will never lose the painter's habits in observation. To me a new face was always a technical problem, instinctively I looked for the strongest visual aspect, balanced the claims of charcoal and pastel, lay in wait for the moment when some subtle change, involving a million cells and fibres, would light the individuality which is latent in the dullest cast of features. There was a woman of about my own age called Hilde Oestmann—she must have been one of Franz's protégées, since there was obviously no connection between her and the Pavaakas. She had mouse-coloured hair and a shiny skin, she wore rimless spectacles and, as a rule, clothes which appeared to have been bought by post; practically she was unpaintable, and at first her only interest for me was that an agent sent to keep me under observation might well have assumed that colourless appearance. Her room was on the same floor as mine, we met in the passage often, and having been introduced at one of Debora's small parties we added each other's names when saying good-day. These might have remained our terms of acquaintance indefinitely—for a long time I saw her merely as a thing that happened, like showers of rain or the sound of trams passing, and her view of me may well have been the same. But this picture was abruptly changed. At first light one morning I woke to find her standing by my bed. As when the immigration officer had roused me on the train journey, this was a moment of great alarm; and in something like the words I had used with him I mumbled:

'What—have they come for me now?'

For a moment she regarded me in silence and apparently with some astonishment. Then she said uncertainly:

'I came to ask—I wonder if you could very kindly lend me some money. Two marks would do. I'm right out till Tuesday.'

At this point I thought the woman must be sleep-walking, or perhaps out of her mind. But I automatically got up, drew round my shoulders the man's coat which served me as dressing-gown and pulled out my valise from under the bed. I had, in fact, nearly ten marks—Luise gave me every week what was called housekeeping money and she would never take back the change. I said sleepily:

'I could give you five.'

'No, two would do,' she said. 'It's to get some medicine—my father's had a bad turn.'

This slightly increased my confusion—till then I had not known even that she had a father. I cannot recall how I answered, or any detail of the small transaction which followed. What has remained in my memory, distinct as a Dürer engraving, is the wholly altered appearance of Hilde Oestmann herself as she stood, now calm and patient, between the door and my bed. She was, of course, abnormally dressed: she had put on trousers and a skimpy woollen jacket over her nightdress, the spectacles were missing and the hair which as a rule was drawn from her forehead to an uncompromising chignon now hung in two thick pigtails which gave a curious, archaic dignity to the stolid structure of her face. But those obvious changes were not the important ones. It seemed that a climax of anxiety had lighted in this nondescript person both the tenderness and the courage of a real woman: her lips were tremulous but her eyes brilliant with resolution, the effusion of blood beneath the dingy skin gave to her whole face a vitality I could not have imagined. Here was an individual I should have gone far to please, both from respect and because she had touched a chord, long idle, in my sympathies. I knew that I should never again see her as a mere appendage to my surroundings.

I must have given her some money, and I naturally asked if she needed any other assistance. To this she answered, modestly but with confidence, that she would like me to sit with her father while she was out of the house.

'If he's left to himself,' she said in her even, cultured voice, 'he might get up and move about. That could easily be the end.'

And with no more delay she led me to their room.

As I picture it now, the room was not much wider than the span of my arms, perhaps three times as long, and in that small area space had been found for a paraffin cooker, a wash-hand-stand, a high iron bedstead. There was also a mattress on the floor, where evidently Fräulein Oestmann herself had been sleeping. The bed was empty and open; in a chair beside the stove a small figure wrapped in a blanket was curled up with one wrist on the chair's arm, a cheek lying on the back of the rested hand. The head was entirely hairless, and yet as I saw it then it might have belonged to a young man, for the wrinkles of age were almost absent—indeed, the white skin was nearly as flawless as a healthy girl's. The eyes were shut. The breathing was soundless, and except for an occasional twitch the body was perfectly still.

'Father, Fräulein von Leezen is kindly going to sit with you till I get back,' Hilde said.

She cleared a stool for me, smiled quickly, and was gone.

It was still in a part of my mind that my new friend—so different from the cipher she had seemed before—had deliberately planned this meeting: she, or her superiors, might well have thought that by rousing me in the small hours to put me in a strange and awkward situation she could surprise me into lowering my defences. The fear was strengthened when I saw that the man in the chair had opened his eyes. Those eyes, which were watery but far from vacant, he gradually brought to bear on my face, but without moving his head; and this was particularly disconcerting—to be so silently, so freakishly observed by a naked-headed stranger who might be of almost any age, any mentality. It was nerves, then, rather than duty or compassion, which after a long silence led me to ask:

'I wonder if I could make you more comfortable, Herr Oestmann?'

'Comfortable?' He took a few seconds to consider the question, and then he said, 'Well, thank you, but I have to stay in this position—almost like a foetus—because I get a kind of stitch if I try moving, and that's so disagreeable. If Hilde can get the digitalis that will solve my problem almost at once.'

His speech, not easy to pick up, would alone have betrayed a cardiac weakness, but he still contrived to use a pleasant, urban voice with delicate modulations. And as far as I could tell, the grotesque indignity of his posture embarrassed him not at all.

'Though why it should do so,' he continued, 'remains largely mysterious to me. I've tried to inform myself—there's a very able man called Heffter, I once attempted to read his great work on experimental pharmacology, but with only the late evenings for that sort of reading I found I had insufficient concentration. And you, gnädiges Fräulein, are you in the last agonies of discomfort?'

'Why no!' I replied.

'But how good of you to say so, sitting on that abominable perch! All the so-called furniture in this room was built by tradesmen of such primal innocence that they simply knew nothing about the human form. Only please don't repeat that to my daughter, or she'll think I'm grumbling.'

I assured him I should not repeat it.

'And truly,' he said, 'I don't complain about the inadequacies of our present accommodation—at seventy-four one can't expect a very full life, so the framework of living no longer greatly matters. And you know, the restriction of one's movements can lead to a kind of mental liberation. When I had a large legal practice I was always running in every direction, meeting everyone, hearing what everyone had to say, packing my life tight with transitory experience. It was like travelling in an aeroplane, you see everything and you discover nothing. But when I was in a prison camp for some years—when the living-space allotted to me was not much larger than my own body—then I began to overhaul my previous knowledge of the world, to ask what it all amounted to. And here, as you see, I have an equally restricted view—the newspapers Hilde gets hold of, the radio we sometimes borrow from the people below, those are my only peepholes. Of course it often makes me restive—poor Hilde, she'd be better off in charge of the reptile house at the Frankfurt zoo. But then, all old men are a trial. And I do believe that as one's field of vision narrows one sees to a greater depth.'

As he spoke—and I am satisfied that I have remembered with fair fidelity his way of talking as well as the substance of what he said—he was faintly smiling. He must have been in considerable pain, but perhaps to one so practised in the pleasures of the mind the body's ills are never dominant. I know that as I watched that bloodless, ageless face, lying on its side like a thing discarded but alive with boyish eagerness, the light and shadow in his voice so far engaged me that I ceased to think of my responsibilities or the incongruity of our situation.

'To be still,' he said, 'to be always observing from the same viewpoint—that brings great advantages. And in a queer way it makes you rather more flexible in your attitudes. For instance, I am more intensely conscious of my Jewishness than I ever was before—and that has a dual consequence. It fills me with pride and gratitude for what my forbears have given me—the power of survival, the mental independence you always find in minorities, the gift of discriminating between what's merely attractive and what is permanently beautiful. But just because I've completely realised my nature as a Jew I feel I can penetrate some distance into non-Jewish ways of looking at things. I've come to understand profoundly some of the gentile resentments—the uneasiness they feel about people who can never be fully assimilated. I think of Pharaoh's subjects, the gnawing fear they must have suffered when they found the control of their economy had been idly surrendered to foreigners—prolific tribesmen with a metaphysical deity who appeared to sanction all their acquisitions. Yes, I honestly think I can put myself inside the minds of those Egyptians. And to look at history with intelligence one needs to start with that sort of perception. You see what I mean?'

The question seemed purely rhetorical: I suspected that my face was no more than a blur to him, and that in the excitement of riding a hobby-horse he had forgotten whom he was addressing. That was desirable, for I was a little disturbed by the turn his thoughts had taken. But now a new shift in his talk showed that he was by no means lost in the smoke of his own eloquence.

'I'm not sure,' he said, 'whether young Herr Weckerlin follows me in that view—I was airing it not long ago with him and his uncle, Albrecht, that able and courageous person. Franz Weckerlin is a young man of enviable gifts, I think. But you must know him much better than I do.'

I answered that I knew him very little.

'But it was Franz who brought you here?' he said. 'I thought there must be some connection.'

That remark gave me a shock I could not wholly account for. Although it was uttered so simply I saw it as one more attempt to violate my privacy: I remember thinking, 'These Jews, with their inflated sense of family, they expect everyone to be wrapped up in a parcel of relations—they simply can't believe there are people whose only wish is to be free of all entanglements.' Dimly I must have known it was irrational to be so much put out by the old man's artless observation, but here reason had no authority: his words had revived the sense of insecurity in which our conversation had started, and now I was fully on my guard again.

I think I pretended not to have understood him; and a little later I suggested that he was using his voice more than a sick man should. He agreed quickly and humbly, as if accepting the authority of a professional nurse; but almost at once he began to discourse again—on his strict but happy childhood in Liegnitz, the joyful feasts of Simchath Torah and of Canucah, when one candle was lit each day from the Servant Light until the nine-branched candlestick was all ablaze. And though he told me nothing which was not familiar I found myself listening once more to his rhythmic voice and being lulled to a new quiescence. All the same, I was glad when Hilde returned to relieve me of my charge.

The incident was a fresh reminder that all these people were continually watching me; they were pretending to identify me with my keepers, doubtless in the hope that a false confidence would lead me to self-betrayal. For some days afterwards I was determined to campaign for a transfer to my former place of confinement.

But in those weeks when the talk about 'Uncle Albrecht' had not yet become a threatening cloud it was far from easy to think of surrendering the superficial calm in which Astelbrucke was enclosing me.

Was it in reality so fine a summer? My picture is of mornings freshened by early showers, of one cloudless day following another, the air so warm it dissolved the frontier between indoors and out; days that aged into velvet evenings with men still in shirt-sleeves and girls in cotton frocks lolling on wooden benches in the courtyard, smoking and flirting in murmurous groups all along the street. Such gentleness of climate becomes a drug for the senses: with the body set at ease the eyes approve, the heart accepts what in a harder season would look plain or ugly. That part of the town must have been thrown up almost in my lifetime, with nothing but utility in the builders' mind, and now with its broken roofs and pitted streets, its silent workshops, one could hardly see what use it served except as a petrified encampment. Yet there was in its incongruities something which exercised a kind of spell upon one's vision. Above the glassless front of a shop where two old men with massive seats and lank moustaches spent their day repairing bicycles the title ROSA-MUNDE—*Moden* still showed in a florid silver script; the crumpled building which had housed municipal departments served as a store for salvage now, so you saw the town's officials working at the back of a drapery or issuing permits from a table outside the Café Nordhoff, and in an old insurance office where the sisters Essenschneider sold me swedes and cabbages the gaps between folding screens gave copious views of the strings on which they hung their clothes, the Napoleonic bed in which they slept. From such blurring of boundaries came a peculiar sense of freedom; and I could not repress a certain fondness for those grim streets because

of their visual surprises. In a region lost to any thought of
elegance the scarlet of Ida Essenschneider's blouse, the gold
of an old counterpane shielding a trader's barrow, were like
the first notes of a reveille; through the porch of a roofless
church you were confronted by a foam of philadelphus and
laburnum, and where one house had been plucked from a
terrace in Welckerstrasse you saw beyond the smoking railway yards, always with a new shock of pleasure, a scarf of
beeches hung on the foremost shoulder of a chain of gentle,
blue-grey hills. Those casual enchantments did not make the
place a fairyland: rather it resembled a body left on the
battlefield, too far maimed to be worth collecting, avoided for
fear of contagion; and in daytime the people you saw
about—the old and arthritic, children with lupus and with
grown-up eyes—reflected the dilapidation of the streets surrounding them. For them existence could mean no more
than the bare avoidance, day after day, of destitution, and I
myself had lived too much in poverty's companionship to
view it as romantic. Yet I saw in these burdened people
something which challenged my own hopelessness. Perhaps
they still wondered at being alive and on their feet. At least
their look was of endurance, not despair. They had what I
recognised as a pre-eminently German quality: they sought
no comforts, no reliefs, only the honour of starting to rebuild
a shattered edifice, recovering the heritage of brave and
seemly living which a wanton generation had thrown away.

At the time I found it anomalous that my one link with
this resurgence was of Jewish complexion; I mean that the
Weckerlins, to whom I was now in established service, were
assuredly no less involved in it than any of their neighbours.

That came home to me on a day when Franz forgot to collect
his picnic lunch and I had to take it to the place where he
was working.

From a contractor's office in Kriegsstrasse I was directed to
what had once been a Junker's estate on the northern edge of

the town, and there, as I approached the former stables, I came on a scene of prodigious activity: at the site of a demolished mansion a score of almost naked men were loading rubble into a file of lorries, others nearby were sawing through the enormous bole of a felled cedar while an engine managed by a girl in shirt and knickers rocked and shuddered in its efforts to drag the roots from the ground; farther on, where veterans with picks and shovels were dismantling a terrace wall, a chain of women and boys were wheeling away the debris in barrows, and a mobile crane with another young woman in control was shifting the major pieces—wrought-iron gates, a cast of Aphrodite, a pile of paving-stones—as a spoilt child snatches and abandons a succession of toys. In this engrossed and sweating concourse no one seemed to be in command; but a little toothless fellow I accosted beckoned one of his mates, who was able to guide me.

'Weckerlin? You mean the one who works the Kuppe-Schneider? Look—over there, where those two trees are coming down—if you go that way you'll see his machine.'

Following that indication I reached a place where, with the ground falling away, I could recognise below me the remains of formal gardens in the Spanish style, with an ornamental lake beyond. Plainly this area had long been left untended, and now, from corner to corner, a trench wide and almost deep enough to hold a row of cottages had cut it in two; other trenches branched towards the lake, and on the hither side were pits and furrows such as an animal of fabulous size might have dug in a search for food. In fact, the sculptor of this savage landscape was visible: a huge red machine, like a military car with steel claws instead of guns, was crawling over the hills and canyons, rolling like a ship in heavy seas; as I watched, it swung to assault a cliff of yellow rock with a violence which made it tremble from front to rear; drawing back, it attacked again, and then in a series of manoeuvres, marvellously deft for a thing of such unwieldy shape and size, it set itself to collect and lay aside the spoil, much as a housemaid clears her sweepings with a dustpan. From a point a short distance down the slope I could see for myself that Franz was the driver. I was afraid to go nearer, but soon he caught sight of me and waved enthusiastically; after attacking the cliff once more he silenced his engine, clambered down and came towards me, limping over the cratered ground as fast as he could.

'Dear Fräulein Johanna, what are you doing so far from home?'

Those words swam in a surf of laughter, and the sight of him as he approached—cheeks red from the labour of breasting the hill, mingled sweat and oil running from brows to beard, eyes alight with welcome—remains a luminous memory. Then, as he came quite close, the jovial face was suddenly shadowed with apprehension.

'There's nothing wrong?' he asked. 'Luise—?'

I reassured him: 'No no—only you forgot your lunch.'

'What—and you've come all this way with it? On foot? Oh but my dear Fräulein Johanna, that's ridiculous! A man who forgets his lunch ought simply to starve.'

In truth he could hardly have shown more gratitude if I had come to him through fire and flood.

'At least you must share it now,' he said. And when I objected that it was far too early for a midday meal he only laughed again, and started to unwrap the package. 'Sit down, sit down!' he commanded, kneeling to wipe a patch of grass with his oilstained handkerchief. 'There isn't a clock in sight to control us. A meal does you far more good if you have it in the best company.'

There was a full morning's work waiting for me, but his genial authority was not to be resisted. I sat as he bade me and obediently ate a token portion of what I had prepared for him alone.

We had no protection from the sun, which on that cloudless morning cast a harsh glare on the baked and lacerated countryside. And I think it was partly the massive investment of light (which Franz seemed not to notice), partly the fortuitous nature of this meeting, which set it on a different plane of feeling from every other happening in that memorable summer. The heat and the hardness of the ground denied all comfort to my body, and my eyes were not much rested by the cataclysmic scene confronting them; but the nearest workers were a hundred metres off, their voices no more than a pale smear on the field of stillness which seemed to divide us not only from the active world but from the coercion of time, and with that isolation came a narcotic sense of freedom. No darkness from the past could withstand the flooding sunshine, and the underlying relationship between me and this young man, as prisoner and indulgent warder, grew insignificant: enough, that we were both of the human kind, and in this fragment snatched from an ordinary day I recovered a fact I had almost forgotten—the peacefulness one may find in having a single person as companion.

He lay on his side, his body oblique to the slope, his head supported on his good hand. He munched contentedly, accepting the sun's heat as a kitchen cat accepts the warmth of the stove, smiling at me as if we had plotted to share a delicious truancy. When the silence began to make me nervous I said:

'That machine must be difficult to handle.'

And at this his smile widened. 'Difficult? No—but I make everyone think so. I talk to Prütz the foreman as if it was like playing a church organ. Actually a child could work the thing after half an hour's instruction.'

'All the same, you do it very effectively,' I said. And I added, without thought, 'It's a pity these gardens had to be destroyed.'

'You think so?' He smiled again, with a faint patronage. 'No, I can't say I shed tears over anything so artificial. All those hedges they chopped into fancy shapes—battlements and colonnades—it's the sort of thing Frenchmen do with their miserable dogs.'

'But what's it going to be now?'

'This burrow? A sewage plant. The town's sewage system got badly knocked about in the bombing—they've patched it up, but it won't last. This thing is the right solution—it ought to cope with the town's needs for at least a hundred years.'

He spoke with a certain warmth, as if I had accused him of dilettantism. And now, with the masculine zest for technicalities, he sat up to instruct me in the future splendours of the undertaking:

'What I'm digging out at present is the place for the secondary sedimentation tanks. The aeration tanks will come on the farther side of that shrubbery. You can see where the new channel comes in—over to the left of the farmhouse. There'll be a pumping station at that point, bringing the sewage up to the level of the screens and the grit chambers. Later on I'll be working somewhere about the middle of that wood—that's where they're siting the sludge digestion tanks. On its own scale this outfit's going to be about as advanced as anything in Europe.'

I asked, 'But where have you studied all this?'

'Oh, the plans are in Prütz's office—anyone can see them.' And now he returned to his attitude of self-defence. 'Yes, I suppose this was a handsome property—it must have been a pride and joy to the family who owned it. But when you think what this plant's going to do for the health and comfort of thousands!'

I agreed: 'Yes, I see that.'

'Though why I should worry about their comfort I really couldn't say!'

The access of bitterness in those words took me by surprise, and the shock was such that I did not immediately speculate on what lay behind them. I said nothing; and in a few moments he seemed to recover his calm.

'The interesting thing,' he said, 'is that this box of tricks has all been planned by a Jewish engineer—from the first survey right through to the blueprints we work from. Then there are two Jews in the drawing office, and eight or nine on the site here—three of them operating machine tools. And me—I've no education, I'm not an engineer, just a common labourer, but when they have a machine that really scares them they hand it over to me.'

Again his expression showed a cryptic amusement, which blunted the arrogance in his speech; but it seemed to me that the joviality was no more than a cover spread thinly over suppurating wounds. With my attention fixed on his face rather than on what he said, I found myself wondering that features so young bore so great a burden of experience, that a boyish smile could betray such inveterate sadness. Here was a grief which dissolved the common boundaries of sympathy: for the time, the difference between his situation and mine had become no more than incidental, and I felt as if a dark vision of my own were reflected in these profoundly suffering eyes.

'Yes,' he said, addressing a blade of grass which he held between thumb and finger of his defective hand, 'they seem to need us nowadays, this tribe of cockadoodle Caesars.'

Because I had still not stirred my mind to grasp his meaning, I put the question, 'You do enjoy the job? I should think it's rather satisfying, to have a share in the work of reconstruction.'

'Reconstructing what?' he asked politely.

'Well—our country.'

'I don't call it mine!'

He had stopped eating. Fishing in a trouser pocket he found a half-smoked cigarette which he put between his lips, but he did not light it. With his eyes turned away from me he said:

'These people I work with, they're friendly enough, we get on all right. We even have our jokes—they're rather simple-minded. But I don't belong to them—I don't feel the way they do. Why should I! They think of this as Fatherland— they say so aloud, they're incurably sentimental. Well, this Fatherland of theirs, it cost me these three fingers to start with—just a bit of carelessness in the Collecting Centre for Juveniles! You can't quite expect me to feel a burning ardour or a Fatherland of that sort.'

He snatched the cigarette end from his mouth and stuffed
t back in his pocket. I said timidly:

'You've never told me about the fingers. You say it was an
ccident?'

But now he was too much engrossed in his theme to hear
ny question.

'All I want,' he said, '—apart from the money—is to prove
o these bastards they can't get on without us. As soon as
hey've got their country all smashed up they're in need of
ewish brains to rebuild it—that's what they have to be
ught all over again. Next time—who knows—they may
emember the lesson!'

I could no longer stay blind to the motif of his eloquence,
nd the passion in his voice might have alarmed me—it came
s a trenchant reminder that this man, smouldering with
nger against the kind of people I belonged to, had me
ntirely at his mercy. But in fact his invective had a different
ffect: I found myself longing to reassure and to shield him,
o offer my own friendship as pledge for that of everyone he
hought of as hostile. And this was no breeze of sentiment,
irred by a heart's cry from one who was young and engag-
ng: the revelation of a destined cruelty—of gentleness
arped by mindless animosities, a life irreparably broken by
he colliding chances of birth and historic circumstance—was
ke the breaching of the walls which enclosed my own
istress to discover tragedy in its true dimension. I did not
eep—not at the time. But with the sun scorching my skin I
ddenly found myself as cold as snow, my whole body
ivering.

Franz was watching me. He cannot have failed to see the
ate I was in, but his face showed no concern, and I
emember thinking, 'Yes, he knew the effect his diatribe
ould have on me—to him this is a sort of triumph.' A
inute or more must have passed in silence while I was
ulling myself together. Then, as I stood up, I heard a voice I
ardly knew as my own, saying:

113

'Yes, I suppose you ve simply no use for the rest of us—for people like me.'

Now tears were threatening, and to escape that mortification I turned and began to climb the hill. In a moment Franz was in front, facing me, with his hands laid on my arms.

'Look—' he said breathlessly, 'you mustn't pay any attention when I talk nonsense. Sometimes I can't help it, it just comes over me. Dear Johanna, please listen: think of what you've done for Grandmama—how you sweat for all of us even when you're not really well. You can't truly think it' *you* I'm angry with.'

Any gentle answer would have done, but I was voiceless and this seemed to increase his humiliation. Still holding my arms, he spoke with an earnestness which, as I think of it now, strikes me as German rather than Jewish in nature:

'You and I—Johanna—in the end we'll come to understand each other, then you won't mind the stupid things I say.' He hesitated, frowning and nervously smiling, hunting for the words he needed. 'You do realise—you do understand you've not been awfully well? Not for a long time. That's what makes it hard for us—we never know what could be harmful, we have to keep feeling our way.'

Such obscure and tangled phrases came to me almost devoid of meaning; and as vague references to illness are always disquieting I made no effort to understand him. I had grown aware that from some distance off a man was shouting, and this offered a way back to a comprehensible world. said:

'I think someone's calling you.'

Franz must have heard the shouts as well, but he pretended astonishment. 'Me?' The smile which came now was without affectation. 'That's Prütz,' he said, '—he thinks I'm scrimshanking.' And he tilted his chin to bellow, 'Stop fussing, General—I'll make up the time!'

He let go my arms, and when he said rather solemnly 'Thank you again for bringing my lunch—it was fabulous!

kind,' I thought our erratic interview was at an end. He had, however, one more surprise for me. About to turn away, he hesitated, again—as it appeared—searching the air for words; then, impulsively, he came close, and with the sort of desperate boldness that a timid lover occasionally shows he caught my neck in the crook of his arm to put a kiss—naïve and lavish like a child's—between my eyes. That done, he stood back and nodded with a friendly, childish gravity, as if some small matter had been finally agreed between us, and next moment he was away, descending with his long, limping stride to where he had left his machine.

I have since wondered whether the foreman witnessed that coltish embrace, and if so what he thought of such an incongruous exhibition; but when it happened I forgot that he was there and that a dozen others might also be watching. For my mind was in great confusion, so that some time later, when I was crossing the old clothmarket, I realised I had walked two or three kilometres without receiving a single impression from the streets I was passing through. That puerile gesture—that mime of honest affection—was it simply an apology for an aggressive speech? Or a token of the transient sympathy an executioner may feel for his victim? It had not offended me: in a way I could not understand I had felt it to be natural and kindly, the artless caress bestowed by a young man on a woman twice his age, a thing done with such simplicity. Chief among the complex feelings it left in me was one of gratitude; and this emotion did not die with the hour which evoked it, it remained as a small fire to which, on days of weakness and dejection, my spirit would often turn for revival.

Yes, we seem to be always in need of that refreshment of the spirit which only men can give us. But it is to women, I think, that we look for a more constant understanding.

That thought occurred to me freshly a day or two after my picnic with Franz, when a letter reached me with the

Wilpenschoen postmark and proved, to my great surprise, to come from Tilka Zamoyska.

'. . . Well, here I am, back at the Lodge, and Lore Schutze is most sweetly writing this at my dictation.

I left the hospital a fortnight ago. I had been moved several weeks earlier into St Martha's Ward, which, as one quickly reads from the surrounding mists of gracious reticence, is supposed to be "terminal"—in that salubrious anchorage any considerate patient departs this life within a day or two of admission. Alas, I failed in this simple test of good breeding, and as the days turned into weeks, and I still neglected to expire, the situation grew more and more embarrassing. "These Poles," everyone was saying (though not quite within my hearing), "they're entirely uncivilised, they just don't realise what's expected of dilapidated bodies in a genteel Dutch lazaretto." But in all their actual dealings with me they were so infinitely courteous—so long-suffering, so genial—that I grew more and more ashamed of my unco-operative behaviour—my tedious longevity—and in the end I besought them to return what was left of me to Wilpenschoen to be stored in a dark place and forgotten.

Not that that has happened! Here I am treated as if I had returned in triumph from some honourable enterprise—from being, shall we say, the first Polish widow to sing the entire part of Manon in a bathysphere submerged off Rotterdam. I am back in our old room, and everyone spoils me all the time.

But I miss you terribly. Not only for the meals you used to bring up to me, for all your kindnesses, but for yourself, Johanna dear. I need to be with someone older than myself, and far more sensible, who will yet be patient with my foolishness. Can't you come back? Won't you at least pay us a visit—even if it's only for a few days? (I ought to mention that my gossiping is rationed—Dr Hofdijk won't let me natter for more than half an hour in every twenty-four.) I ask, of course, out of pure selfishness. But you know, a change would be good for you as well. I'm sure you're working much too hard for the dear Stahls, and worrying too much about imaginary mistakes, and what people are thinking, and fearful misdeeds in the murky past which everyone including yourself has long ago forgotten. What *you* need is something feminine and feather-witted, to listen to your sadness and cry for a while, to tell you you are shamefully misunderstood and then go off into schoolgirl giggles....'

So? If that was a sound prescription, no one but Tilka herself could dispense it; her fine and supple mouth, the range of melody in her voice and laughter, the warmth which her frivolities could never insulate—these were not to be found elsewhere, and least of all in the Warren, where all but one of the women surrounding me were absorbed in their family affairs.

I had imagined that with Luise I might come to something warmer than a workaday friendship, but that expectation was largely disappointed. Of course we were far apart in age; and in practice we had not much chance to get to know each other better. She was employed as counter waitress at a canteen on the far side of the town, and there seemed to be no limit to her working hours; as often as not she came home very late, and pitifully tired, so our talk was confined to domestic matters: did the Stahls seem reasonably comfortable, would the shopping money stretch till Friday night? Naturally she kept for Franz such animation as she could wring from a worn body and brain; and I came to wonder if she was the ideal companion even for him; for though she had great intelligence—what Jewess is without it!—one saw in her the results of a fragmentary education, and she plainly lacked the flexibility to respond to a temperament as delicately tuned as her young husband's. When Franz was in his mood of eloquence, his talk larded with droll conceits and allusive ironies, she would sit with her dark Semitic eyes fixed on his face in wifely admiration, but to me it was apparent that the thoughts he uttered found little room among those which were crowding her mind. Of course she was not to be blamed for this; but I needed often to remind myself that in some degree her insensibility must be due to her condition. As the weeks went by she seemed to be drawing apart—in a way I recognised—from all of us: the chatter and movement in the kitchen, the tale of the day's random happenings, may have seemed to her of no importance, and almost meaningless, beside the advancing miracle in her own body.

Tilka's letter, then, only underlined a familiar truth, salient in this house where all the other lives were tightly woven in patterns of kinship—the bareness and futility of living without an intimate friend. And for me such friendship was manifestly impossible: what confidences had I to offer, when I could never allow myself to peer into the darkness of my own history! I could hope for no more than a sustained companionship; and there was but one person—Agnes—on whom I depended for that solace.

'Poor Agnes, she's terribly slow. But she does try to be helpful.'

In something like those words I hear the weary voice of Luise. And Franz, in one of his earliest talks with me, had spoken with the same forbearance:

'You have to remember, my sister went through a lot when she was quite small—there was only me to help her, and I wasn't a fearful lot older. That's why she seems a bit stupid—those hard times rather hindered her growing up, if you see what I mean.'

Chiefly they conveyed affection, those indulgent apologies. They told me almost nothing of what I was to discover in the lumpish young woman who served as maid-of-all-work in that unwieldy household.

Yes, her movements were ponderous, and she was maddeningly slow to grasp any change in routine. I would ask her to do the Stahls' room while they were taking a walk, she would nod with genial complaisance, and five minutes later I would find her serenely scrubbing the entrance hall—her normal occupation for that day and hour. But such vagaries could be ascribed first to my own failures in instruction: in time I learnt to be lavish with gesture, to get out the tools appropriate to any special task and often to lead her to it myself. From the start I found her at least a willing subject (as Luise had foretold). The hardships which had robbed her body of almost every grace had given it the vigour of a collier's, she would embark on the roughest task with patent cheerfulness, and never leave it from boredom or fatigue.

So much for her value as an under-servant. To me she was never a creature so impersonal as that. Because she had not much skill in forming sentences she and I could go no distance on the path of ordinary conversation; but she had, besides the shy and rather foolish smile, a hundred ways of expressing her feelings, and I naturally fell into a simple pattern of response. Without meeting my eyes she would half-turn to touch my fingers, and I would answer that signal by putting a hand for a moment on her shoulder; when, impulsively, she held me by the waist and rested her forehead between my breasts I would stay quite still, stroking her hair and the nape of her neck, till that small wave of sentimentality was spent. Palpably she enjoyed being near me, hearing my voice (especially when it praised her work), and in our earlier days together I had, I suppose, a feeling for her of the kind which lonely women attach to domestic pets. But as our acquaintance matured, her range of looks and gestures so extended that to think of her in those terms would have been repugnant and absurd. Even her speech developed to a degree which astonished me. She learnt such phrases as 'Grandmama—garden,' and then, 'Grandmama—garden with Grandpapa.' Later we reached a stage where, when I said, 'I'm going to the shops—would you like to come?' she would answer, 'With you? Shops with you, with Johanna? Agnes come? Yes, come-come-come!' And she would laugh exultantly, and link her arm with mine, and almost dance me out to the street.

I remember a trivial occasion which seemed to typify our ripened understanding. That prosaic but generous woman Hilde Oestmann had evidently noticed that I possessed practically no wardrobe, and one afternoon she asked me (with a touching diffidence) if I would relieve her of a dress and one or two other things for which—ostensibly—she had no housing space. Gratefully accepting these, I took them to the cubbyhole where Agnes slept and where I found her sitting on the bed, laboriously sewing a button on her better dress. I said:

'Agnes, look what Fräulein Oestmann has given us! I believe this jacket's going to fit you perfectly.'

And when she just gazed at me with a particularly obtuse expression I boldly put it about her shoulders. It was a pretty thing in crimson corduroy, bought—I surmised—in the Kurfürstendamm before the War and so well cut that it had kept its elegance. The softness, I think, appealed to her first, and I watched with interest how she warmed to it, stroking the silky stuff, with a remote smile forming on her parted lips. After a while she put her arms into the sleeves and went slowly, as in a trance, out to the landing, where a cupboard stood with a looking-glass in its door. I followed her, admiring; and when she had gazed at her reflection for some time first with a magisterial severity and then with that enraptured self-deception which gay clothes provoke in the plainest women, she turned to ask:

'For me? For Agnes? For me, always?'

I told her, 'Of course!'

We went back to her room. So obvious, so unbounded was her pleasure in this portion of Hilde's gift that I began at once to think whether another, a charming summer frock with a pattern of birds in rose and green, could be altered to fit her as well. I held it up against her. But now her mood abruptly changed, she pushed it away, crying:

'No! Not Agnes, no!'

Supposing that the colour did not appeal to her I nodded

and started to re-fold the dress. This brought a further display of impatience: excited, with a wilfulness I had hardly seen in her before, she snatched it from my hands and tried to throw it over my head, ejaculating, 'You! You!' with such vehemence that she might have alarmed me had she not, next moment, broken into laughter. To meet her whim I changed into the dress there and then, and went out to the glass to settle it on my waist and to straighten my hair. Now it was her turn to play the part of admirer, and this she did with an exuberance of smiling and gesticulation which no one could have taken for pretence.

It was a foolish scene—a woman who had lost all her looks preening herself in a far too youthful dress, beside her another, young but of dropsical appearance, giggling and applauding like a delirious child. And since we stood in the house's main artery it was too much to expect that this folly would escape all notice. A pair of legs, bare and blotched with red, showed in a top corner of the glass too late to let me escape; turning, I encountered the crumpled and peevish face of the Estonian, Hanna, arriving from her quarters on the floor above.

In words which matched the idiocy of the situation I said, 'Good afternoon, Hanna. Agnes and I are just trying on some clothes.'

Her answer was to stare as if she had come upon me naked in the street. But the scandalised expression which deepened my discomfort had no effect on Agnes; she, still radiant, pointing at me with her hand spread, was exclaiming, 'Dress! Look—new dress!' And to my amazement the churlish Hanna was caught by her fervour as a narrow valley is lit by the midday sun. She came nearer, exhibiting a smile which seemed as little appropriate to her rugged features as the frock was to my person, and with a sudden explosion of goodwill she addressed me in the most ambitious German at her command:

'The gown? The new gown! Ha-ho—so cosy, so sublime! You Prussian beauties, you spend the time only to lovely-up your bosoms, to make yourself like queens!'

Nor was she content to deliver this private encomium. Before I could find an answer she had moved to the head of the downward stairs, and from there she shouted at the top of her voice:

'Quick! At once! Come and see this Leezen in her famous gown!'

The cry must have alarmed Walther Stahl, who hurried out from his room, collarless and blinking, with Debora not far behind. At the foot of the stairs they stood side by side and peered upwards as if trying to observe a solar eclipse through layers of cloud.

'Johanna, dear,' Debora called, 'are you all right?'

I was not allowed to reply for myself. It was Hanna, laughing and triumphant, who called back:

'See, this gaudy Leezen in her latest gown! Superb—*hein?* A daughter of love—a fairy queen!'

In so populous a backwater the lightest whiff of drama will collect an audience. Before the Stahls had taken up their station I had realised that Frau Reuben's children, monsters of curiosity, were leaning over a handrail far above to imbibe their share of the entertainment, and now doors were opening on every floor. I caught sight of Larin Pavaaka surveying the exhibition from a higher landing with a face of decorous incomprehension, he was joined by an aged cripple in a military coat and almost simultaneously another observer appeared below, arriving from the street; this man of grey respectability, perhaps from the Bürgermeister's office, went to stand beside the Stahls, following their gaze with the specious reverence which passers-by show to a funeral cortège, while Debora, still confused and faintly anxious, was calling up to me:

'But why, my love, do you have to try on your clothes in the middle of the stairs?'

At which Hanna, now a little drunk with her own showmanship, shouted back, 'Because she wish to make herself a treat for all the men!'

I had never before been the centre of so ridiculous a scene.

There was an obvious way to end all this indignity—I had simply to retreat to the room I had come from. And had there been no one but Hanna in my way, that is what I should have done without a second's delay. But while Hanna was trumpeting my supposed glories it was Agnes who remained my true supporter. She must have felt—rightly— that she was responsible for my sudden promotion to the limelight; now she stood close to me, holding my arm, half shy, half proud and jubilant, like every photograph of a self-effacing bridegroom, and it came to me that such unsought, such groundless loyalty must not be betrayed by a sullen or cowardly response. That instant of perception was decisive. I forced a smile. Pointing to the jacket which Agnes was wearing, then to the flowered dress, I proclaimed for every-one to hear, 'All from Fräulein Oestmann—aren't they nice!' and in case she too might be watching I blew a kiss towards Hilde's room. Now, with an arm round Agnes's shoulders, I bowed to right and left, at once self-mocking and self-admiring, and flaunted my skirt as an actress would. Absurd as it was, this extravaganza kindled a creeping fire of genial smiles and applause. Somewhere a child cried, 'Na, she looks a proper tart!' in wondering approval, I could see that tears were welling in Debora's eyes as they often did when she was struck by gusts of happiness, and beside her the solemn stranger was murmuring, 'Bravo! Bravo!' and clap-ping with his finger-tips. The naïve extempore performance— Agnes's and mine—was clearly a success.

But what makes that interlude stand out in memory is the sense of enfranchisement it brought me. So spontaneous a display of friendship invaded my seclusion as a great wave sweeps over a sea wall: I ceased to think of myself as an intruder, alien to these people in every instinct and allegi-ance, I forgot that I was a person awaiting conviction, with no warrant—except the procrastination of my accusers—for living there at all. In those spellbound moments I felt myself a rightful member of a close, endearing circle, bound to it by the sort of ties which unite a family. That view, of course, I quickly recognised as illusion; but a desert traveller may be grateful for having dreamt—however fleetingly—that she is drinking from a mountain stream.

The trivial affair of the dress display was in fact the first in a chain of small events which signalled the end of an epoch— that season in which a prosaic routine, with the mildness of the people about me, had begun to make my terrors seem chimerical. In those long, tranquil days, when my enemies showed no sign of pressing for an arraignment, I had almost come to believe that what I had banished from my memory they too had forgotten. Then the warnings started again.

Among those gifts from Hilde Oestmann was an outsize petticoat which seemed to have no attraction for Agnes and would not have fitted me. I thought that Luise with her swelling girth might be glad of this, and later in the afternoon I went to put it in her room.

It was one I seldom visited, since she insisted on keeping it in order herself. On this occasion I found—though the bed was made—the venial untidiness one may expect where both occupants have had a scramble to get to work; instinctively, as any housewife would, I put together a pair of slippers which Franz had abandoned in different parts of the room, replaced a garment of Luise's which had slipped off a chair, closed a half-opened drawer. I was turning to leave when, amid the feminine litter on the dressing-table, I noticed a small, mildewed photograph in a home-made frame: it showed—as my eyes passed across it—a young man of Jewish features in severely respectable clothes, and my immediate thought was 'Franz, of course, without the beard.' Interested, I picked it up, meaning to examine it properly, and at that moment a footstep sounded in the passage outside: Luise, home a little earlier than usual, stood in the doorway, tired, showing some surprise at my intrusion.

I in turn was slightly confused, and it must have sounded as if I was covering up some guilty action when I said:

'Oh—Luise—I just came to bring that petticoat. It's a present from Hilde Oestmann.'

'A present?'

'Yes, she was turning out some things.'

'Oh,' Luise said. 'Oh, how kind! And you've been tidying?'

That was something like an accusation—no one cares to find that another woman has been spying on her negligence. In a little cloud of shame which seemed to envelop us both I said quickly:

'No no—I only picked up something which had fallen on the floor.'

With that I should have framed a smile and slipped away, but I was still holding the photograph and so betraying the kind of curiosity that servants are commonly charged with. I had to replace it, and though I did so as unobtrusively as possible I saw that Luise was following the movement of my hand with fascinated eyes. In fresh embarrassment I murmured:

'That's Franz, isn't it?'

'No, not Franz,' she said.

Now she was watching my face with (I thought) an expression of sad concern—rather as a mother will regard her child whom she has caught in some foolhardy escapade. Pensively she passed in front of me to take the photograph in her own hands, and it looked as if she was going to put it out of sight in one of the drawers. Then, apparently changing her mind, she said enigmatically:

'It's someone Franz knew when he was small. Do you want to see it?'

In the way she spoke I seemed to hear a note of warning, but that was only one source of the alarm which seized me then. Momentarily, as she turned the front of the picture towards herself, I had an oblique view of it, and with that fresh glimpse came an impression of familiarity: at some time in the darkened years I had known a face which, if not the same, had impressed me exactly as this one did. I asked obtusely:

'What did you say?'

And she answered, still holding the portrait so that the face was invisible to me, 'You can see it if you wish.'

Now I was speechless. While a tidal wave of curiosity made me long to get hold of the picture, the fear of what it might reveal was like an electric fence to keep me away. I know that another woman would have overcome such foolish panic. But when I look back at the quiet scene—the small shabby bedroom, Luise's strangely anxious face, the square of pasteboard in her hand—I find the sensations of that hour recurring so vividly that they still seem to excuse my feebleness. Suppose you are a shy guest among people you greatly want to please, that you have been given a bouquet, and now someone whispers in your ear, 'Those flowers are hiding a timed device, at any moment it will burst and disfigure you for life': that figment may give an impression of my feelings then. To Luise I must have seemed grossly ill-mannered as well as stupid—I remember saying, after a long pause, 'No, I'm not interested in your husband's friends,' or something equally ungracious. But she made no retort to this rudeness; her eyes were still not hostile, only troubled, as I hurried out of the room.

The encounter left me with a stabbing headache and in the lowest spirits: only the force of habit kept me to my normal routine.

In that household the time-table was fluid: I took the Stahls' supper to their room at a fairly regular hour, but Agnes had hers when she felt inclined, while Franz and Luise generally arrived in the kitchen, ready to eat, as soon as they came home. That evening Franz appeared when Luise was half way through her meal and took his place beside her at the end of the table; they chattered in low voices while I was re-heating the stew. This was a recurrent situation, and like any sensible woman I understood that a young couple were entitled to their secrecies, but in my prevailing mood of suspicion and distress I found it almost intolerable not to hear what they were saying. Inevitably Frau Reuben arrived, 'just to put my casserole in the oven', and stood at my elbow to narrate the sufferings of her child Simeon in his last hours: it was among her favourite recitals, and while her voice trickled on like oil squeezed through a pin-hole, and the living infant Jakob continuously mewled with his forehead pressed against his mother's seat, I was desperately trying to pick up at least a word or two from the conversation in the background. Luise would undoubtedly be giving an account, amused or resentful, of my absurd behaviour when she had caught me poking about in her room. Was Franz finding this an entertainment, or a cause for indignation? Already I was almost convinced that an unlucky chance, inflated by my own stupidity, had cost me the confidence of my young employers; and with this conjecture came the revelation that the friendship of these Weckerlins was no longer a mere emollient of my existence—it had worked towards its centre, becoming a purpose for living.

I think that Franz, with his quick and sometimes almost feminine perception, may have nearly read those thoughts; for when I put his supper before him he caught me by the wrist, smiling, and bade me sit down.

'You must rest a bit,' he said. 'You treat yourself like a galley-slave!'

I could only yield to his courtesy, and now Luise in turn seemed bent on being agreeable. She said, 'I've been telling Franz about Hilde's presents, and how you've very sweetly passed the slip on to me.'

The affair of the photograph might never have happened; superficially it appeared that the simple relationship between us three had not been disturbed. But I still felt as if something I valued had been impaired, that the danger which had seemed to be receding was drawing closer again.

Surveying that evening in perspective, I see that the turn the conversation took was coincidental; but I half-believed at the time that the name I dreaded was deliberately introduced

—it looked as if my folly over the picture had led the young people to give me a new warning about the insecurity of my situation. We had talked for a while about Hilde Oestmann's generosity, her devotion to the invalid father, and then Franz had dilated on the problem of one Herr Szamuely, who being strictly orthodox was troubled by the Sabbath infringements of the Pavaaka children, when Luise said casually:

'Darling, you did see Uncle Albrecht's letter?'

And Franz replied, 'Yes, I've got it here. He's coming this way towards the end of the month.'

As he said those words he looked warily at me, or so I imagined. I asked, in a voice which surprised me by its calm:

'You mean, your uncle is coming to stay here?'

'He'll probably look in for a night or two,' Franz answered. 'He does as a rule.'

He went on to tell me that Albrecht Weckerlin had for some time been a commercial traveller—he covered a large area, selling pharmaceutical products for a Brunswick firm 'He's always very busy, but he makes time to come here whenever he can.' He spoke rather haltingly, as if other thoughts were pressing on his mind, and I could see, glancing at Luise, that they were both in some embarrassment. It was she who said reflectively:

'He's very practical, Uncle Albrecht.'

This brought from Franz a studied contradiction: 'Practical? I wouldn't say so. When he gets an idea in his head—some notion of his own about truth or justice—he ceases to be realistic. He goes where it takes him, and to hell with the results.'

He stopped abruptly, as if he had been led into an indiscretion, and I think he would have dropped the subject; but I, increasingly nervous, was not ready to leave it. I asked, in a tone of indifference:

'You mean—political ideas?'

'You could call them that,' he said. He spoke hesitantly, as if afraid of abusing some confidence. 'Albrecht lost his wif in the War—that was political all right. And with him everything starts from there. People like Luise and me—oh, everyone we know, practically—we think there are things there's no point in remembering. Or finding out—we don't feel like spending our lives unearthing who exactly is to blame for every single thing in the past. Albrecht's different. He's a type who always wants to get to the bottom of things.'

Not much was new to me in this account of his uncle—it only firmed the outlines in a portrait I had mentally sketched long before from snatches of his and Luise's casual talk. Nor had he said a word to suggest that I myself would be an object of this uncle's curiosity. Why, then, did his speech so profoundly disturb me? It was, I think, that the incident in Luise's room had revealed more sharply than any previous happening how thin was the party-wall between the peacefulness I lived in and the realities from which I had taken flight. Previously I had tried to believe that the sense of moral infirmity which nagged me like the half-heard sound of radio would gradually fade; now, one sight of a yellowed photograph had told me that the sickness came from a lesion which was real and irreparable. A sore so deep and gangrenous could not be thought of as having only a private significance; and I could hardly doubt that this Albrecht, zealous invader of secrecies, would be merciless in exhuming mine. My fears remained shapeless, but they were vivid enough to affect me physically—they brought the cold contraction in bladder and lungs which you feel when a figure suddenly confronts you on a lonely path at night. I had some trouble to control my voice when I asked of Luise:

'You'll want my room, of course, when Uncle Albrecht comes?'

The question cannot have surprised her—this matter had been mentioned between us much earlier in my stay. But it seemed to renew her discomposure.

'I haven't really thought things out,' she said.

Here I was at some advantage: I had not been so long in dread of Albrecht's coming without mapping an escape. I spoke rapidly, and no doubt with a revealing agitation:

'I was wondering if I might go back to Wilpenschoen, to
stay for a time. I mean—if it's possible to get permission. I
could go straight away, if it's allowed. I'd manage the
journey—they say you can get lifts on English army lorries.'

Luise was trying to interrupt, 'Johanna, please listen—' but
I hurried on:

'The other women in the house could cope with my work—
I'm certain they'd be willing. For two or three weeks—I'd
write them out a programme, I've planned it in my head.'

'Oh dear!' Franz said mildly. 'Are you in such a fearful
hurry to leave us?'

I threw out an excuse: 'I have a friend at Wilpenschoen, a
Polish woman—she's bedridden, she may not last very long.
And you see, you'd have my room for your uncle, and also I
expect he'd rather have you three to himself, with strangers
out of the way.'

At that Luise smiled. 'In this house? It isn't awfully
likely!'

Franz was regarding me with the grave, masculine expression which with him was often a cloak for amusement. He
said:

'Johanna, dear friend, you can't mean to run away before
my birthday! Who's going to organise the party, if you do
that?'

'But your uncle may be here before the 26th,' I said.

He answered, 'I don't think so. As I read his letter, the 29th
is the earliest possible.'

Just then I noticed on Luise's face the faintly puzzled
childish look which odd remarks of mine seemed often to
provoke in her.

'Oh, you know,' she said, 'that Franz's birthday is the
26th?'

The question took me unawares. I replied that she or
someone else must have told me; though in truth I did not
know how the date came to be in my head.

We left the matter unsettled on that occasion; but the pair

seemed sympathetic with my wish to see Tilka Zamoyska, and in a later discussion Franz agreed, at my request, to communicate with the authorities concerned and arrange if possible for my accommodation for a fortnight in Coenraad's Lodge. He thought that what I needed for the expenses of the journey could be found. I was to remain at the Warren for the birthday party (as at heart I wished) and, if the plan matured, depart for Wilpenschoen on the following day.

Until the very hour of the birthday supper I doubted if it would take place at all. Everyone in the house had to be invited, and since any room which might have held so large a party was serving as a maisonette the courtyard was the only possible venue. There, in the morning, by putting together several borrowed tables I contrived to make one long enough to seat the whole expected company; and thereafter I was wondering all day if it would be feasible to eat in the open air.

The sky had been clear on the evening before, it had seemed as if summer would go on for ever; but after a poor night I had waked to find the window misted, the air in my bedroom chill, and though the sun grew warm again before midday there were clouds passing from the north which, travelling lower and more densely, increased in menace as the day went on. There was work enough to occupy my mind. And yet I remember noticing the altered, restless flight of birds which had long been content to bicker over crumbs and flap to the nearest gutters; and how a nosing wind with a tang of salt in it made tiny whirlpools from the silt of leaves and dust in corners of the yard. While everything about me was familiar all the feel of it had changed, as if a ship I was cruising in had sailed overnight from sheltered waters to the open sea.

No doubt it was partly from within, this feeling that the world was surrendering to winter; for by now I was convinced that my time at Astelbrucke was closing for ever. In theory I was to be away for less than three weeks—the exact date of my return was fixed already. But I reasoned that whoever was assembling the dossier for my indictment must surely be nearing the end of his task, and if so it seemed unlikely that authority would restore me to the care of such free-and-easy gaolers as my present ones. As I see it now, my own wishes were partly aligned to that assumption. For all their amiability, I had never come to terms of simple trust with these Weckerlins: in their intercourse with me, their looks, their way of speaking, I was always conscious of a certain reserve which barred me from their more intimate thoughts—often they reminded me of people at pains to withhold bad news from a sick friend. That would not have mattered had they been people I did not care about—else-where I had grown used to being treated rather as if I were a child. But these were young, brave and endearing, and though they held me unworthy of their confidence they seemed to put some value on my affection. Such duality cannot be borne for ever: best, perhaps, that this phase in my life should be recognised as one more failure, abruptly written off, added to the list of those to be absorbed in forgetfulness.

There are persons of morose intelligence whose pleasure is to plan their own funerals down to the carving of the finials on the hearse. In retrospect I see myself as not far removed from those. If today was to be the last act in my affiliation to that household I desperately wanted Franz's party to be a success. But there were other handicaps besides the precarious weather to stand in the way of this ambition.

I had helpers enough, among whom the sententious Hanna was not the least diligent.

'*Foosch!* These almighty Germans who mean to conquer all the wars, these impotents who cannot even manage a dog-size feast!'

Scraps like this from her sustained soliloquy, uttered in barbarous German with a voice scarcely softer than a riding master's, reminded me at every hour that Hanna was in her nood of exultant xenophobia. Yet she gave me better service han most. She fetched and carried, she scrubbed the pavetones where the table was to be set. I had only to murmur ome requirement and she was off to procure it, using the kind of tact one associates with Sicilian buccaneers.

'That Leezen,' I heard her shouting at someone on the econd floor, 'that crazy woman, she must have two more chairs.... Oh yes you can! ... Very well, I take this stupid couch—soon I clean up the dirty thing.'

And a minute later she was plodding into the yard, bent double under a sofa like a tortoise beneath its shell.

Her industry should have been an example to those on whom I had more right to depend. Luise had the day off from her canteen, but physically and mentally she was too much encumbered by her pregnancy to be of any use: she kept sinking (to Hanna's fury) on any piece of furniture which was handy, and when I passed near her she would whisper, 'Oh, Johanna, you're so wonderful—what shall we do when you're away!' while her vaporous smile told me that all her thoughts were in the cloud-cuckoo-town where infant cherubim, for ever soft and warm, eternally luxuriate in their mothers' devotion. Neither was Agnes in a serviceable state. She responded to any precise request, but when that job was done stood idle, observing the altered scene as children gaze at a firework show; or if I were for a moment still she would put her arms about me and indulge in fitful tears. On that day when I most desired to be friendly and gentle with everyone I constantly found myself ready to scream with exasperation.

I could not be always at the centre of activity. Anxious to avoid all possible offence to the pious, I went to seek final advice on questions of *kosher* from an orthodox couple named Szamuely who lived in the stable block; and as they spoke very little German (while I had no more than a bare acquaintance, gleaned in student days, with Hungarian) their earnest, kindly explanations robbed me of nearly half an hour. Shopping took some time—small shopkeepers who

knew the Weckerlins were eager to make special contri-
butions to the birthday feast, for which I naturally paid in
protracted conversation. Likewise, as I went about the house
to borrow utensils everyone had little offerings to make—a
hoarded bottle of Schluck, a box of sweetmeats from an
American parcel—and the reception of these meant listening
to many little speeches telling me of the love the donors had
for Franz and Luise, of how secret the gifts were to be kept
except that Franz himself—and Luise perhaps, and possibly
the other members of Franz's family—should be told of the
abundant affection they represented. Whenever I returned to
the yard from one of these missions I seemed to find my
helpers in some fresh altercation.

'Ha—you Leezen—time you come!' Hanna would scream
at me, with the pleasure the simple take in things going
wrong. 'The fat bitch is after the ladder again.'

The woman she referred to was Klara Kielreuter, who had
amiably put herself in charge of decorations and who swayed
towards me with a martyr's dignity in her face, her shoulders
draped with a string of bunting.

'Dear Fräulein von Leezen,' she said with her languid
smile, 'I wonder if you could have a word with Herr Pavaaka.
I simply cannot make him understand that if he'll give me
the ladder for ten minutes he can have it all to himself for
the rest of the day.'

It was Maria Pavaaka who had suggested that her protector should hang a light above the table—'Larin is magical
with electricity,' she said. Now I saw with helpless anger how
imprudent I had been to acquiesce. Conceiving that the yard
should be festooned with lights like a beerhouse garden, that
remote and difficult man had been about the town to borrow
quantities of cable which, recklessly looped about the furniture and impeding every movement of my other helpers, was
driving everyone to frenzy. He himself, standing with folded
hands, had the look of an artist defeated by the obtuseness of
vulgarians.

'You tell me to light up this paddock,' he said forlornly. 'I
134

ask you: how, please, with no ladder to rise on? Please, I am not a skylark or a flying machine. Above all, I am not a heavenly angel.'

I must have found some way to content him for the moment. But the problem of the ladder admitted no final solution, and I remember how whenever things were at their worst that day I seemed to hear the dreaded voice of Larin repeating once again his bleak and senseless observation: 'Gnädiges Fräulein, I wish to inform you I am not the angel Michael. Nor even an aeroplane.'

Walther, too, with all his virtue, became a burden on that occasion. Following his bent, he had set himself to polish the gimcrack 'silver' and cutlery I had collected, and it hurt him that others failed to see his task as comparable in importance with theirs.

'I only want this end of the table to work on,' he complained to me, 'but every time I clear it someone puts their own things there instead.' And a little later: 'Fräulein Johanna, I don't want to be any trouble. But really it's impossible to work at all with Herr Pavaaka deliberately twisting me up in his electric wires.'

Frequently he went to see that all was well with Debora, always returning to me with some fresh problem:

'I'm very sorry to trouble you, gnädiges Fräulein, but my wife is still worried over what she's to wear this evening. With the change in the weather she's afraid of catching cold and—if you'll forgive me for mentioning such things—she's not sure if there's room for a woollen garment under her calling stays.'

I had, of course, to go and offer the old lady such counsel as I was able—not once but two or three times. Despite her small misgivings she was in high excitement, having persuaded herself that the gaiety and splendour of the world she had lost was to be restored to her for at least one evening, and by contrast with her mirage I found the scene in the courtyard more depressing each time I went back. There was never much to raise one's spirits in that shapeless area between lumps of pretentious building, a reservoir of kitchen smells, a sounding board for the screams of children; and now I felt that the sadness of its normal scenery—the straggling rubbish bins, a crude latrine, the botched enclosure where Frau Reuben kept a trio of despondent hens—was only magnified by the garnish of white tablecloths and crumpled flags. Again I tried to smother those desolate thoughts with bustle: turning my back on the quarrelsome confusion which raged about the centre of the yard, I applied myself to fitting up a service table near the kitchen entrance; but presently Hanna was there to help me, continuing the while her wearisome report of everything I wanted to ignore:

'You hear the smash? That is Agnes—four more glasses she has tumbled on the ground. . . . Ha! Now the great bitch Kielreuter has fallen from the ladder, I think she hurts herself a good deal. . . . Now Pavaaka has set himself on fire. . . .'

I tried to remember that I had no real concern with this celebration—substantially nothing was expected of me but to be an attentive servant. By tomorrow night I should be far away, and the past summer, already shorn of reality, would be receding into the darkness which covered so large a tract of earlier experience. But I could not hope to go through the evening without a sense of being involved, or without the grief which would shadow that feeling.

'Night is the one unfailingly successful artist. You can struggle for hours with a landscape which refuses to compose, then dusk comes, and tells you at once what is important and what you may profitably suppress.'

This remark of an idiosyncratic painter who once taught me at the Munich Academy came to my mind that evening, when the prodigal embroidery of electric bulbs which Pavaaka had strung between the balconies served rather to disguise than to illuminate the garish detail of the buildings surrounding us, and the moonlike paraffin lamps which Klara had placed along the table gave to its sorry trappings, to the double row of pale faces surmounting undistinguished clothes, a surface lustre, even an air of opulence. It was Herr Oestmann, turning his head to right and left as far as his arthritic joints allowed, who said:

'You've done marvels, dear lady—it's as if Josef Israëls had made a sketch to guide you. And to me you've restored a lost delight—I thought my banqueting days were long since over.'

I had set my own place next to his, pretending that an invalid guest—and one of his standing—was entitled to special attention; in truth I chose him as companion because I thought his sinewed intelligence might guard me against any invasion of sentimentality. It was a sensible choice. For much of the time I was busy serving, but whenever I returned to my seat this aged, physically shrunken, lucid man would welcome me with the manners of a world which had vanished before the War, and as I recall that meal I hear his gracefully modulated voice reaching into every part of it like the veins of a leaf.

Somehow he had learnt far more than I about our neighbours.

'Our friend over there,'—he was discreetly pointing at Frau Reuben—'I find her features of absorbing interest. Do they remind you of someone even better known?'

I looked attentively. Frau Reuben sat as if alone and waiting to be photographed, her waxlike face set in a smile which might have stood for dim contentment or a mild disdain. She had not touched her soup; but while I watched I noticed she was quietly slipping bread into envelopes which then disappeared inside her blouse.

'No,' I said.

'Why, Catherine de' Medici!'

I glanced again and saw what he meant.

'And that is strange,' he continued, 'because I can't imagine she has any Florentine connections. At least, I'm told her family has been in Lithuania for some generations.'

'They wouldn't have much to talk about,' I said idly,

'Queen Catherine and Frau Reuben.'

'Perhaps not,' he answered. 'In fact, I should describe Frau Reuben's conversational powers as still awaiting development.' He paused, to move his body painfully into a new position. 'But then, a certain simplicity of intellect is often a practical advantage. For example, a well-educated woman, if her husband sets fire to their house and then shoots himself in front of her, is quite likely to go out of her mind. That's what Frau Reuben's husband did, when the political situation became too difficult for people of his sort. Frau Reuben's response, on the other hand, was simply to collect her two infants from the top floor room where they were sleeping— the third was still *in utero*—and carry them down the blazing stairs and drag them fourteen kilometres over the snow on a fuel sled. . . . Excuse me, I think Frau Stahl is trying to attract your attention.'

I went to her at once.

'Johanna, my dear, everything is wonderful!' Debora said 'I can't remember when I was last at a dinner so beautifully arranged. I'm very sorry my husband is so late, but I'm sure it's not his fault.'

Thoughtlessly, I said, 'Oh, but he's there—look!' (For I had placed the old couple at either end of the table, as their seniority prescribed.) But she would not even turn her eyes the way I pointed.

'You understand, dear,' she said, 'the management of newspapers is a great responsibility. Most likely something important cropped up—a political change, perhaps—something he has to deal with personally. He would think it un pardonably ill-mannered to be late for your party if he could possibly help it.'

I could only assure her that I should never suspect her husband of the smallest discourtesy.

It was time to serve the second course, a wistful version of Gulasch contrived largely from vegetables, and some minutes must have passed before I sat down again, but Herr Oestmann went on speaking in my ear as if there had been no interruption:

'And then there's the man who came to her rescue, our good neighbour Pavaaka—in him you have one more example of the indulgence fortune shows to the feeble-witted. A town councillor with a small grocery business left him by his father—you find such manikin dignitaries in every little place from Viborg to Cadiz. Almost nothing in his head except an atavistic hatred of all Russians. This man is suddenly asked to care for a pregnant woman—she's in flight with her two babies, already she's travelled some hundreds of kilometres in carts and lorries. Well, he himself has no sort of vehicle except a small motor-boat he uses for off-shore fishing. So he puts the little family into that, with another woman he's caring for—perhaps too ardently—while her husband's in prison, and enough food and water for a few hours. He has just fifteen litres of fuel. With that he steers this package out of the harbour—in broad daylight, under the muzzles of the Soviet machine-guns on the mole—and sails away towards the middle of the Baltic. The act of a finished imbecile. And at two o'clock next morning, when they're helplessly drifting, a Swedish freighter sights the little party and picks them up and takes them to Malmö.'

The dulcet voice was making scarcely more than an aural impression; for Walther, urgently signalling distress, had caught my attention, and at the first pause I went to his end of the table. He said rather pitifully:

'Forgive me, please, but I'm extremely worried about my wife. It has got so much colder—at her age I don't think she should be sitting in the open at all.'

I did my best to reassure him: Frau Stahl was protected by many layers of clothing—I had seen to this myself—and her hands, when I had felt them a few minutes before, had seemed perfectly warm. But now he turned to a fresh anxiety:

'What really troubles me is that she's not quite herself this evening. Before this meal—which you have so kindly and so excellently prepared for us, dear honoured Fräulein Johanna

—she was telling me that she must have the car at eleven. You see, she's thinking I'm still her chauffeur. Well, that wouldn't matter, not in the very least, but it means that she's looking out for her proper husband—the first one, you understand—and it's going to be a dreadful disappointment for her when he doesn't arrive.'

'I'll get Franz to talk to her later on,' was all I could say. 'She always listens to him, and he'll know exactly how to put her right.'

He seemed to draw some comfort from this simple proposal; in his modest way he took my hand to press it gratefully, and for a while I stayed beside him, our fingers still joined. For my part, I was glad to feel I was linked to this company by at least one member of it who, too guileless to realise my true position, accepted me simply as a friend.

It was a slender bond. I had shared in the ordering of this party, but so little did its appearance match with any I had pictured that I saw it as a tableau prepared by someone else for my inspection. By now the massed clouds, screening the stars, had completed the ascendancy of darkness, and the contour of roofs and gables which I knew so well was no longer even faintly visible; all I saw beyond the dancing jewellery of Pavaaka's illuminations was a few lighted windows like peepholes cut haphazardly in the grey flats of a many-angled stage. Within these squares of light faces showed as if puppets had been hung there. The aged Herr Szamuely, after blessing the meal with a moving dignity, had felt he could not innocently share it, so at the window of the tiny room they lived in he and his wife sat like twin statues of the Buddha, gazing with a settled kindness at the scene below them; elsewhere you saw small foreheads flattened against the panes (for the children's party I had promoted earlier in the evening, with Luise as hostess, had failed as a device for getting them early to bed), while in rooms less brightly lit I could discern the heads of some who had ignored the invitation, the pale mask of a boy with a giant keloid, an almost hairless woman whose eyes appeared as craters in a shrivelled skull—neighbours familiar to me by sight but hard to think of as belonging to any world I knew. Seeming themselves unreal, these quiet presences suspended in an amphitheatre of shadows lent a curious unreality to the area they commanded. I found my sadness deepening: what, of this evening, would remain as something to look back on, as a fire whose glow might follow me through a desolate journey? Back in my place, looking up and down the table at faces newly sculptured by the lamplight—at the faint, modish amusement on Klara Kielreuter's sickly profile, at Hanna's vulpine eyes and fungous cheeks bent down towards her plate, Luise's air of distant exaltation as she sat with one hand in Franz's lap, the other mechanically raising food to his mouth—I thought that for all their salient independence there was in this variegated company something beside the Jewish lineaments which gave them a mysterious fellowship, underlining my own estrangement. Again Herr Oestmann was leaning towards me, attentive and urbane.

'It distresses me,' he whispered, 'that you've eaten almost nothing. Of course it's the way with all good women—self-immolation is their calling. But I think you should sit still for a while and let my daughter sacrifice herself in your place.'

I could not share his frivolity. Trammelled by my own thoughts, I asked spontaneously, 'Do you think these people are enjoying themselves?'

'You mean,' he said, 'are they enjoying the excellent fare you've provided, the sense of occasion, the charming décor—all the fruits of a generous hospitality? Why, of course they are!'

That was evasive. I said, 'No, what I mean is—are they happy?'

'Happy?' He seemed to turn the word this way and that as a geologist will turn a specimen he cannot identify. 'Happiness,' he said, 'is something we've forgotten, something we don't look for any more.'

I was obliged to leave him once again: we had been short of oil for the table lamps, two of them had begun to smoke and I had to put them out. But he hardly seemed to notice that hiatus in our conversation.

'You see,' he said as I sat down again, 'happiness—as I understand the word—depends on an attitude of mind, one has to start by supposing it's a possible state for oneself. And that's what none of us believes any longer, because we carry wounds of the spirit which can't be healed. To give you an instance—one which naturally comes to my own mind. When I was arrested—that was before the War—my wife Naomi was very ill. I asked the man who came for me—he came to my office, he was young, and very good-looking, with a cultured voice—I asked him if he would take me to see my wife for just five minutes, to say farewell. He refused absolutely, he said my private worries were no affair of his. And to me that was like a final statement in philosophy, it seemed to tell me that in a world where the highest form of life—speaking biologically—could be so casual towards another creature's suffering the idea of happiness was just a romantic illusion. We here, I think we're all like that. We can't convince ourselves any more of people's goodness—when we look into a stranger's face we're asking all the time, What are this person's real intentions, what power has he to do me harm? It means that for us nothing is permanent, nothing certain. Today we're alive, we're not being molested, we're free to associate with those we're fond of. But we count on none of this, we don't even expect that everything will be the same tomorrow. That's something which you—I speak with great respect, dear lady—cannot imagine or understand, the idea of spending one's whole life with a sense of desperate insecurity. Instinctively listening all the time for the loud knock and the rasping voice, waiting for a new torture of separation.'

(Yes, he said those words to me! *To me*: 'You cannot imagine or understand ...')

He had not raised his scholarly voice, but a new intensity of feeling had made it more incisive, and guests on the other side of the table were pricking their ears. I was glad, then, to see Hilde sending him signals of daughterly admonition. Hiding my deep embarrassment, I said lightly:

'Then you count yourself among Schopenhauer's disciples?'

'Schopenhauer,' he answered with a certain weariness, 'was one of those ill-starred creatures who fabricate synthetic philosophies to serve as a frame for their own abnormal mentality. Listen: if you will grant me a little more of your patience I should like to explain to you how I differ from that noxious pedagogue.'

But a hush which travelled like a wave along the table put even him to silence. Looking up, I saw that Debora was on her feet.

The spectacle brought me a new disquiet. Against all my entreaties the old lady had insisted on adding to her evening toilette a favourite hat, and she made a disturbing figure, far short of her intrinsic dignity, as she stood with a hand on Pavaaka's shoulder, swaying back and forth as if to keep her balance on a pitching deck. No one else, however, appeared to notice the unconventionality of her appearance, and a seasoned lawyer could not have shown a greater confidence than hers when she began to speak:

'My dear, dear friends—I am sure I can call all of you that! And especially my dear Walther, whose kind face I see over there.' Her smile expanded into radiance. 'Walther Stahl has been with me for a long, long time. Longer than I can remember. I can only tell you that he has served me faithfully every day *for more than fifty years*. Yes, I am an old woman now. And little did I think, in years gone by, that one day I should have the happiness and privilege of proposing the health of my dear grandson on his wedding day.'

'The old mare speaks very well,' Herr Oestmann remarked in my ear. But he seemed to think that her oratory deserved no more of his own attention, for soon, in a whispered undertone, he was continuing his private lecture:

'No, honoured lady, you'd be wrong if you wrote me off as a pessimist—in truth I'm exactly the opposite. Experience may tell us that human beings are mostly cruel to the point of madness. But God who created them is not a madman. The very fact that we speak of cruelty as "unnatural", though we see it everywhere in nature (in ourselves as well), is enough to show that there's an entity outside us—greater than we are, less transient, calling for our obedience—one to whom cruelty is intolerable. How else can the mere idea of mercy have come to us, enclosed as we are in a system where mercilessness appears to be the principle of survival?'

I was newly afraid that his eloquence, muted though it was, must be disturbing our neighbours; but a glance at the nearest faces told me that Debora still held her audience. I heard her say:

'...to Herr und Frau Pavaaka for their kindness in letting us use this beautiful yard. Next year I shall be inviting you all to my own home, when the redecoration will be finished. By then I hope this young couple will be surrounded with lots of lovely girls and boys—that is really what marriages are meant for, and it's all quite easy and delightful once you have learnt the way.'

In Franz's face, resolutely fixed on his grandmother, I saw a reflection of my own discomfort; but the guests still wore a look of placid sufferance, and from time to time, when a sentence seemed to have petered out, there were murmurs of amiable applause. The last of the lamps was failing. I stretched to turn it out, and now the table and the company were only lit, a little eerily, by the electric ribands which high above us, swung and quivered in the erratic wind. Cadaverously pale in this fitful illumination, Debora continued staunchly with her address:

'...and I don't want you to feel under any restraint because you have a person like me amongst you. I think you may feel more at ease if you remember that when we've all been dead for some time we shall all look very much the same....'

I wanted her to stop, I wanted the evening to be over. 'But then,' I thought, 'I shall be going right away. From Franz

From Agnes. I shall be utterly alone.'

'Perhaps I may cite my own people,' Herr Oestmann resumed, 'as an illustration of what I've said. In our earlier history you find us guilty of appalling wickedness—greed, monstrous cruelties, constant religious infidelity. And for that we've been punished, again and again, by subjugation to tyrants, disasters of every kind. But that long record of depravity never extinguished our inborn knowledge of what is good and holy—there have always been voices from among ourselves to protest that we've betrayed our calling. In my belief that's why we've been allowed to survive—as a people, I mean—even when we're scattered round the globe. It's because we've produced in every age something greater than ourselves—a message, an oracle, insisting that righteousness is an entity independent of human kind, infinite in power, exerting a unique authority. Our tortuous history—the suffering which has followed all our deviations and our blasphemies—it has served to offer the world that awe-inspiring lesson at a terrible cost to ourselves. And if that's our tragedy, paradoxically it's our glory as well—the belief, the knowledge, that God so uses us to show mankind his power and his moral perfection. Forgive me: that is something—may I say—far greater than the "happiness" which others regard as the prize of living.'.

What he said meant little to me then—my mind had other occupation. His words made their impress chiefly, I think, because of the lapidary's precision with which his thin mouth shaped them. He spoke without gesture—one saw that the smallest of his movements incurred some physical distress— and it was memorably strange that from a body like his, motionless, bleached and shrunken, there came that steady flow of speech, those sedately chosen phrases uttered with an incandescent passion. I was not the only one who heard him. Franz was near enough to pick up at least a part of the discourse, and though his eyes were always fixed on Debora I could see that a part of his mind was grasping at my companion's words with the excitement such talk induces in people of racial sensitivity. This party, given in Franz's honour, was it affording him any pleasure? I tried to catch his eye, but it almost seemed that he was set upon avoiding mine.

Of his own speech in answer to Debora's I recall only a few sentences:

'... has advised us to equip ourselves with a swarm of sons and daughters. Luise tells me she has already asked for quotations for this equipment from the Stork Trading Company. But she and I think the *first* really important thing for everyone to have is a wise and adorable grandmother....'

And it was plain to me that these felicities came only from the shallows of his mind. I had moved to Debora's side, thinking she might need some help after her sustained exertion; from there I could watch her grandson frontally, and I saw more surely than before that the formidable structure of this face, freshly defined by the parsimonious light, must derive from indelible suffering: here was a configuration which new experience could no more soften than spring and summer can change the contour of Mont Blanc. No doubt my observation was affected by inward stress. Myself on the threshold of a new exile, I easily discerned in those recessed, afflicted eyes a loneliness akin to mine. 'Like me,' I thought, 'he must have travelled through country which one's mind cannot shelve and dare not recollect; those journeys have brought us both to a solitude which no friend or lover could penetrate.'

When he sat down there was garrulous applause. 'Well done, Sir! That was heart-stirring!' 'Like Esaias!' 'Why, yes, as good as the radio!' I should have joined in the congratulation, but shyness held me back: what had I to say in company to this man who had once embraced me! Now Debora was asking for comfort, as I had thought she would:

'Tell me, dear, did I speak foolishly? Sometimes I get a little bit muddled—with the light so bad it's hard to remember things.'

146

And soon there was a new focus of attention: Klara Kiel-reuter had begun to sing.

It was Hilde who had persuaded her to perform for us; myself, I should not have dreamed of asking an artist whose public career had closed long before to exhibit her voice again, in conditions so little suited for singing. The accompaniment was distant and uncertain: before the party the men had tried to get an old piano out through a first-floor window; it had jammed (as I had warned them it would) with the greater part hanging over space, so that Hilde, precariously mounted on a ladder, could only play it with one hand, and the weak notes she made had to traverse a barrage of minor sounds—the rustle of wind, an undercurrent of stertorous breathing and whispered conversation—to reach the artist they were meant to support. But Klara seemed hardly to notice these impediments. There were weaknesses in her performance which even I could recognise—it was as though one heard an instrument which had long been without professional tuning. But in this neglected, veteran voice some of the magic had remained. She had wisely chosen a song known to all the world:

> *Auf Flügeln des Gesanges,*
> *Herzliebchen, trag' ich dich fort,*
> *Fort nach den Fluren des Ganges,*
> *Dort weiss ich den schönsten Ort.*

and we who had turned to Debora's speech the face of patient courtesy listened to this late echo of a resplendent art in simple rapture. Some of those who had been staring from high windows came down to stand at the edge of the yard; as creeping things emerge from their hiding places late at night the children supposed to be in bed were all about us now in their vests or night-suits, gazing at the singer as if she had escaped from a fairy tale, and in the spell which lay upon us no one tried to send them back. Again my eyes turned towards Franz's face, and I saw with pleasure as well as jealousy how the singing soothed him: the taut muscles gradually slacked; with an arm fastening Luise's breast to his side, his cheek resting against her hair, he seemed to be letting his responsibilities and griefs detach themselves and float away on the sunlit stream of sound.

> *Dort wollen wir niedersinken*
> *Unter dem Palmenbaum*
> *Und Liebe und Ruhe trinken*
> *Und träumen seligen Traum*

The ovation which came at the end of the song was like the burst of sound when the doors of a schoolhouse are flung open, it was taken up and swollen by a group of men and girls who had filtered in from the street; and I who had heard this woman sing to delirious audiences in the Max Zenger Konzertsaal could only marvel at her shy response to this homely triumph. With tears on her cheeks Agnes was clutching my sleeve, as she often did when her feelings were disturbed; Franz, coming to stand behind us, put his arms about her shoulders and mine.

'Duckling, there's nothing to cry for,' he told her gently. 'It doesn't hurt her, singing!' And to me he said, 'So—that old witch still works her sorcery!'

I said, 'It's a marvellous voice, don't you agree!'

'What—now? I'd hardly call it a voice at all.' He was faintly smiling, but I could not tell how far he spoke in mischief. 'It's a matter of technique,' he continued dryly. 'She goes through a boxful of ancient tricks to serve up the contents of a rusty wind-pipe as the voice of Lilli Lehmann.'

'Lilli Lehmann?' Debora said, roused by the name as a dog is roused by a familiar scent. 'Why, yes, she used to sing at my parties, I regard her as my greatest friend.'

Franz nodded gravely. 'And Johann Sebastian Bach— didn't you and he, dear Granny, play duets on the clavichord?'

'Sebastian Bach? Oh dear no! At least, not after your grandfather and I became engaged.'

Klara was on her feet again. With mounting confidence

148

and power she sang the Schubert setting of *Gebet während der Schlacht,* and it seemed to me that the miracle of sound flowing from this creature in physical decline gave to the shapeless throng about me such unity as Titian imposes on his subjects. A loose connection was causing the electric bulbs to flicker, and the pulsing light brought a new appearance, at once jaunty and macabre, to the litter of refuse and utensils covering the table, the pale heads of infants clustered now like tubers about their complacent mothers, the anxious face of the pianist dangled (as it seemed) above the onlookers' heads. But for me the faint delirium brought by this spectacle was overborne by a splendour which, entering at the ears, took possession of all my senses.

> *Herr, ich erkenne deine Gebote;* Klara sang.
> *Herr, wie du willst, so führe mich!*
> *Gott, ich erkenne dich!*

and the sovereignty in that prodigious voice seemed to level all the barriers of custom and mood which lay between us. Among the interlopers pressing towards the table—the raffish youths, the thick-lipped girls with bosoms dragging on flimsy blouses—I remember seeing an old man with a scholar's brow surmounting the gaunt cheeks of hunger, and a boy with the eyes of Heine, and another whose undirected gaze and sagging underlip suggested the imbecile; but the vast divergence in looks and fibre no longer counted; and as we forgot our incongruities so, I think, we ceased to feel the evening's coldness or the poverty of our spare and futureless existence.

> *So im herbstlichen Rauschen der Blätter,*
> *Als im Schlachtendonnerwetter,*
> *Urquell der Gnade, erkenn' ich dich.*

The words recall the voice and with it, distantly, the dream-like courage of that hour. The nearness of those who had grown to be a part of my life, the trustful Agnes, Franz with his impulsive kindnesses, had given me an illusion of safety which the power of music brought to exultation: a flood of brave imaginings—the tireless fortitude of marching men, the stir and smell of foreign harbours in the half-light of dank mornings, the invention that subdues a fever-swamp to fabricate a city—took such possession of my spirit that I forgot I was an outcast, I saw myself and those about me as belonging to one legion, sharing equally the human inheritance, accepting the hardness of our state with equal resignation. In all that various company I was aware of only one who did not yield to the enchantment; in Debora's eyes the lustre had faded, and now her facial skin had the look of perished rubber. I heard her say in a limping voice I hardly recognised:

'I don't know what to do—they've taken my home and I don't know when I shall get it back. These people, I want to give them all a lovely time. How can I do that without a house to entertain them in!'

I must have whispered whatever comfort I could think of, but of course she didn't hear me. I remember how, when I took her hand, it lay in mine like that of a dead body, and how when she spoke again it sounded as if the voice came from another woman, remotely hidden inside her.

'What can you do,' she said, 'when you're old and silly and all the people you love are gone!'

Twice, before the party wore out, Franz said to me in an abstracted way, 'So—you'll be leaving us tomorrow.' And the second time he added, 'You do know—whatever happens there'll always be a place for you here.'

That vague remark, uttered almost as soliloquy, yet made me feel as if he and I had reached some sort of understanding which set us apart from all the rest; and an image of his face, slightly aloof, the social smile hardly veiling its recurrent irony, is one clear recollection from an evening which grew increasingly shapeless and confused. Submitting to a new mood in her audience, Klara had gone on to give them songs with rowdy choruses; and when Agnes and I had washed the supper things to an accompaniment of raucous chanting I returned to the yard to find the whole concourse of authentic guests and self-invited visitors, led by a make-shift orchestra of concertina, nursery drum and mouth harmonicas, involved in an amorphous dance. Some time later the electricity failed altogether, bringing shouts of 'Herr Pavaaka! Forward the engineers!' in a torrent of squeals and laughter. But the players hardly paused in their exertions, and in a sprinkle of light from electric torches the livid parody of a *Rathausball* came frantically to life again, a score of couples eddying about the table, a chain of men and girls advancing and retiring in a boisterous wave which broke and splashed against the containing walls. I had a glimpse of Hilde, gravely amused, as she danced with a cigarette be-tween her lips, a string of children linked to one arm and a portly tradesman to the other; Hanna pushed past me in a gale of raucous merriment, rearing her massive knees on either side of the bashful youth she was clasping against her stomach, and I noticed that even Agnes, standing bemused amid the swirling dancers, was moving heels and shoulders to the beat of the drum. But my own part in this festivity was finished: I saw the tangle of shuffling bodies as perhaps the dying see the movement about their beds, at once near and remote, a spectacle with which I had lost connection, while a pain which had smouldered all day behind my temples became a raging fire. A woman fully in her senses would have taken herself to bed. But where could I escape the plague of noise! And in truth it was better to endure a fever of sound and shadows, a besieging unreality, than to be cloistered with my own desolate thoughts.

I fancy the revels flickered on into the small hours. For me, however, the evening was brought to an end at some time earlier than that.

It was when the electric lights, having failed a third time, were once again restored by Pavaaka's industry that I caught fresh sight of Walther, who I thought had retired long before. He was talking to someone I didn't know, a small, fair, neatly tailored man, and my first impression was that this person might be imposing on him. With the vague purpose of rescue I made my way towards them.

In retrospect I seem to have known intuitively, even before I was face to face with the small man, that he was dangerous to me. That, I suspect, is hindsight. But I do remember vividly a look of deep embarrassment on Walther's face when he saw me approaching, and how he presented me to the stranger in a manner quite incongruous with his usual courtesy, merely saying in a flustered way, 'Oh, this—this lady—she is Fräulein von Leezen.'

The man himself, a gentile of about my own age, might well have been disconcerted by so crude an introduction, but he nodded placidly, as if it were only what he had expected. Then he took his time, surveying me with something like a cattle-buyer's discrimination, before he announced himself, 'Weckerlin—Albrecht Weckerlin,' and added with a fleeting smile, 'Yes, Fräulein von Leezen, I've been hearing about you for some time.'

In the rush of thoughts which came to my head the practical concern of a housekeeper took first place. I said hurriedly, 'We weren't expecting you quite so soon, Herr Weckerlin. But I'll have your room ready in a few minutes.'

'Herr Weckerlin has taken a hotel room already,' Walther interposed; while Albrecht, answering me, said, 'Yes, my plans got changed. My head office is full of idle nincompoops —"Let's send a wire to Weckerlin," they say whenever they're feeling bored, "to stop him going wherever he's started to go and send him in the opposite direction."'

This was spoken with gestures of languid tolerance, while a twitch of the muscles about his mouth suggested that for him life was a chain of comedies, monotonous in pattern but contingently entertaining. There was, indeed, a persistent aura of gaiety—a Hamburger's irreverence—about this compact and vigorous creature. But even then I did not mistake him for a frivolous person. Though the way he talked to me was cheerful and friendly his eyes were oddly disquieting: they continually scanned my face, as if searching for some deformity of which our friends had told him.

I found myself addressing him in a hurried and nervous voice, like a servant caught in some neglect of duty: 'At any rate your usual room will be ready tomorrow. I've been using it myself—just for a time. But tomorrow I'm going away.'

'Alas, I too,' he said. 'My despotic employers are only allowing me one night in this port of call. And where—if I may ask—does your journey lead you?'

'To Holland,' I told him. 'To Wilpenschoen.'

'Ah, then I can take you at least a good part of the distance in my car—I'm going that way.'

This was the last thing I wanted. I said quickly, 'You're very kind, but I think your nephew has got my rail ticket already.'

'But surely that can be cancelled!' he said. 'Let us find Franz and see what can be done.'

I saw that my only hope was to get my word in first. With a mumbled reply, 'I'll speak to him,' I set off towards the kitchen entrance, where I had last caught sight of Franz; dodging through the crowd so swiftly that Albrecht had no chance to follow on my heels.

I realised now that the dancing had stopped; the orchestra was being refreshed with mugs of beer, and to fill the gap a curly-headed boy with a violin had climbed on the table. He was devoid of artistry—at most his skill was that of a street fiddler—but he lacked nothing in fervour; he was playing, I think, some crude version of a Brahms rhapsody, and I can still see his lithe body in its heroic stance, the muscles tense from neck to knees, the eyes febrile from excitement, the bowing arm strained in ecstatic violence. That picture stands beside another: of Franz as I found him then, leaning back against a wall, his face deformed by such a blank, discarded

153

look as I had seen in fellow-campers at Ysseldoorn. I should
have been warned by that expression; but I was wrapped in
my own purpose, and I went to him with a child's naïveté.

'Franz,' I said impetuously, 'your uncle has arrived early
He wants to take me in his car—to Holland, or part of the
way. I don't want that. I just don't want to go with that
man.'

Apparently my voice failed to penetrate his understanding
His gaze was fixed on the boy violinist, and without a glance
at me he said:

'That bumpkin—even he can fake up some sort of music
Me—in a hundred years I couldn't be even as good as *that*!

Impulsively he held up his left hand, to stare with sardonic
eyes at where the middle fingers should have been. That left
me helpless: what words of consolation make any sense to a
man robbed of the faculty he would have prized above all
others! I said feebly, stupidly:

'I know.... Yes, all of us have suffered.'

And at that he turned upon me in a fury of contempt
which even as I recall it now chills me physically. With a
voice which passion made almost soundless he said:

'What sort of suffering? You, you took care not to suffer!

The sounds about us—the crowd's hubbub, the busy whine
of the violin—cannot have stopped, but in memory it seems
that those final words of his left us in a cavern of stillness
Presently his body appeared to crumple, as if burnt out by
his intemperance, and he limped away into the house. For
myself, I was ready now to travel with Albrecht: it no longer
mattered whom I went with, nothing that happened to me
now could matter.

3

I did not see the Stahls before I left. I had written out in some detail what had to be done for their comfort. For Franz I prepared breakfast and a picnic lunch as usual, but I avoided meeting him. Luise, before she went off to work, came to say goodbye and spoke warmly about my early return; but since I had decided not to return at all I could make no convincing response to her cordiality.

Albrecht Weckerlin had said he would come for me at nine o'clock. I think it was exactly that time when he arrived in the kitchen. I was already in my raincoat, and the case containing my possessions was on the table beside me; without being asked, Albrecht picked this up to take it to his car. By then the business of abandoning one course of life—which had come to be the only course with any meaning—was really over.

It must have rained heavily in the night, for everything about the yard was dripping, and now a screen of cloud dulled the light as if a sheet of canvas had been slung between the housetops, so changing the appearance and the smell of the place that I no longer saw it as one I had lived in. Parts of the composite table were still there, with a few utensils which had escaped collection; there were reels of cable everywhere, a chair lying on its back, broken glasses. Curiously, this debris alone seemed substantial; all that surrounded it looked like an artist's pallid reconstruction of a scene dimly remembered. The thought which came to me as I walked somnambulistically through the puddles with Albrecht at my side was, 'So, another dream, one touched with the colours of affection, has come to its end.'

The car was immense and old-fashioned, the plump up-holstery now leaking kapok with a whiff of stale cosmetics might almost have belonged in earlier days to the Aben restaurant. Installed in the seat beside the driver's, I seemed already to have left Astelbrucke behind, though the tissue of sensations which enwrapped me now—the flavour of tar-nished opulence, a compound solidity and softness—spoke less of new adventure than of experience long submerged. In that comatose state of mind I hardly realised that Agnes had followed me to the car, and when Albrecht gave her a part-ing embrace I watched them as one idly watches strangers at a railway station. It was perhaps a recrudescence of shyness, or merely slowness of wits, which prevented her from step-ping forward to say goodbye to me: she simply stood on the wet footpath with that look of sad bewilderment which a dog shows when it is being left out of a family excursion. For my part, I gave her only a casual wave of the hand, a conven-tional smile. Obscurely I may have been afraid of starting a more poignant emotion in that simple creature's breast, or in my own.

We left the town through a quarter I had not visited before, a sprawl of mean houses with here and there a row missing. I remember the spectacle of a queue, perhaps half a kilometre in length, of carts and lorries waiting their turn to use a pontoon bridge which a military convoy was monopolising: the driver's lethargic faces, a lagoon of yellow mud, the finespun rain. As we stood there with the engine running it felt as if we had never emerged from wartime.

Not that we stood still for long. Precisely organised in mind as in person, Albrecht knew of another crossing; he patiently manoeuvred out of the line, we bumped along a narrow secondary road and came to a damaged bridge which a large display of threats and warnings, reinforced by a row of tar barrels, forbade us to use. For Albrecht the removal of two barrels to afford us passage was the work of seconds; we had reached the other side of the canal when a policeman appeared and stopped us.

Had Albrecht not seen the notices? 'Then you will go back,' he barked, 'and read them properly, and close the bridge again, and return to the main road.'

Albrecht had lowered his window and was leaning out with his hands folded on the frame.

'Listen!' he said. 'I did two years in the army—Fifth Panzers. Head and chest wounds at Zhlobin.'

The policeman received that news without emotion. He said, 'Trooper?'

'Yes.'

'And I was a colour-sergeant.'

'Just so!' Albrecht said. 'But you are not a sergeant any longer and I am not a trooper *now*.'

With that he raised his fist, but the whip in his voice would have been enough. The policeman shrugged his shoulders and turned away.

'Bavarian!' Albrecht commented, as he drove on. 'His speech betrays him. Now he'll sit down and write pages of sub-legal jargon to commend his own brave but thoughtful handling of a critical situation.' The corner of his mouth went up in a tightly rationed smile. 'Those pinchbeck kaisers —their day, I hope, is done.'

He fell into silence then, but the topic must have expanded in his mind: some way further on he said reflectively:

'Yes, wars are nature's provision for men of that kind— those with just enough grey matter to see that in normal times they count for nothing. Well, it stands to reason, any refinement of the intellect is simply a hindrance in the business of killing, so in war the bossing jobs go to men of low-grade intelligence. And how they revel in getting their own back on the sort which has always despised them!' He paused, and then he said, 'But perhaps I oughtn't to express such views to a member of a military family!'

That was spoken with a sidelong glance, half confidential,

slily amused, which seemed to demand a reply. I said quickly:

'My name's quite a common one. There must be branches of my family I know nothing about.'

He nodded, as if accepting what I said. But then he continued: 'In the first war there was a General Marcus von Leezen—he served under Falkenhayn. The Rumanians took him prisoner at Dobrudja.'

I answered, 'Yes, I believe there was an officer of that name.'

Again we travelled in silence, for perhaps half an hour. Lounging in his seat, Albrecht appeared to be caressing the steering wheel as a lover will continue to fondle a woman's arm in moments when his thoughts are far away. Evidently his mind, like that of many amateur soldiers, would not leave the subject of warfare alone, for when he next spoke it was to talk once more of his army days:

'In the early part of my service we were blessed with a sergeant called Zuchau. He had only one idea in his head, that was to catch us out in some offence and get us savagely punished—he had the whole disciplinary code off by heart and he knew just what sort of job any one of us was likely to fall down on. All our lives became a misery because of that man, and he knew it—it was meat and drink to him. Sometimes I wonder if he never thought of what was bound to happen in the end.'

Involuntarily I asked, 'What did happen?'

'To Zuchau?' He frowned, apparently searching his memory, and then let the subject slide. 'Of course,' he said with resurgent cheerfulness, 'you find people of the same species in other walks of life. My present boss—the chief sales executive at Braunschweig—he's the sort that never offers you a chair when you go to report. He's about twenty years my junior. He sits with his back to the light, I stand facing him like an idle schoolboy summoned to his professor's desk. Still, my job gives me a measure of independence. At this very moment that papier-maché Jupiter is very likely ringing my hotel at Astelbrucke and squealing with rage because I'm not there to receive his latest whims. He'd love to give me the sack, only he's frightened of my customers—and he knows that no one any longer frightens me.'

Now he was laughing: there seemed to be a strain of the buffoon in him, one who relished his own virtuosity even when he had to perform to an unresponsive audience. In ceaseless rain we were traversing a belt of closely planted larch woods, the windows were opaque with mist and the screen-wiper on my side was out of order: the sharing of a cell so isolated from the world should at least have led us towards some mutual understanding. But I never mistook my captor's politeness for friendship or his gusts of joviality for a desire to please, and since I made only terse and bloodless replies to his effusions no real communication was possible between us.

Was he deficient in human sensibilities? I do not think so now. But in the early stages of that journey I saw him as part of its unreality. Before the birthday supper I had given too much time to picturing my return to Wilpenschoen—the nervous gloom of sitting friendless in the train, then the tired walk through dimly familiar streets, the wave of vacant chatter and hygienic smells which would engulf my arrival at the Lodge. Conversely, the peremptory change of plans had left me too short an interval to prepare myself for an entirely different journey. The decrepit luxury encasing me, the rustling flight through an endless tunnel roofed with foliage and rain, gave to this passage the quality of lurid dreams; and the figure planted at my side, appearing to wind-in the road with its indolent eyes, only increased the sense of hallucination. Here—my brain repeated—was the Albrecht Weckerlin whose name had haunted me all through the summer; and here, instead of the large physique and commanding presence I had imagined, was a small, neat, smiling man, spasmodically attentive to my comfort, ready to share with me his little hoard of gossip and pleasantry. In other circumstances I might even have found him an attractive person, with his speech that sometimes reminded me of dry

Moselle, his gentle divagations. But I did not forget for moment that he had forced his company upon me, an nothing he said or did could have weakened my distrust.

The complacent voice meandered on like a sunlit stream '...Franz, yes, the dear fellow is still young enough to thin that life can be governed simply by intelligence—especiall an intelligence like his own. Last night I heard him explair ing to Luise—in the kindest way—how to prepare herself fo the responsibilities of motherhood. How shocked he will b when he finds her paying more attention to nature's tuitio than his! But then I never forget how wonderfully he care fo⟩ Agnes. When they broke out of the *Kinderlager* she wa nothing but a terrified animal—so he's told me, and it isn hard to imagine. And yet by the time they'd found their wa to me there was nothing inhuman about her—except a tot⟨ lack of vanity, and that's a trait I personally find endearing

My mind refused to be involved in those ramblings—h might have been speaking of people I had never heard of. F⟨ now it was dull with apprehension. At an early stage of th journey I had suspected (or perhaps only feared) that I w⟨ being driven not towards but away from Holland. This fe⟨ had persisted, and by now had turned to conviction. Whe we stopped for a café meal in the outskirts of a small town summoned courage to ask him where we had got to.

'This place? This is Eiselberg,' he answered casually.

I repeated, 'Eiselberg?' I had not forgotten my geograph so far as to think that Eiselberg was between Astelbrucke an the Dutch frontier. 'But then we're going in quite the wron direction!'

'Oh, I should have told you,' he said with the sam indifference, 'I had to come here first—I have some custome⟩ to see. You won't mind waiting while I make a few calls?'

What was I to answer—what power had I to support a⟩ objection to this treatment! I could only say weakly, 'T⟨ people I'm going to may be wondering what's happened ⟨ me.'

Either he did not hear that or he pretended not to; inste⟨

of replying, he spoke from where, apparently, his erratic thoughts had led him:

'You were asking what happened to the sergeant—to Zuchau. Well, they waited—my soldier friends—till there was a lot of metal flying about and then they shot him from behind. You could call it a traditional operation—so beautifully easy, and with no fear of a Court of Inquiry. I myself saw it happen. And to tell the truth I was neither shocked nor sad.'

Those words forced me to glance at his face. He had turned his head, trying to get attention from a distant waitress, and for some seconds I was able to stare without offence. His voice had sounded as lively as ever, but the gaiety which so often showed in a corner of his mouth and in his eyes was absent now. It seemed that my earliest impression had been right: this was not a frivolous person.

At that meal I could eat almost nothing, and the hour I spent sitting alone in the car while Albrecht made his calls was one of miserable foreboding. I was almost glad when he returned, since the close and visible is not so frightening as the dangers that lie hidden. But when we set off again I felt certain we were travelling in the same direction as before. And I dared not question him.

By then, I think, the rain had stopped, but the clouds stayed low; not once in that day's drive did we emerge from the twilight which had fallen on the countryside. Fastened in a column of heavy vehicles we went at foot-pace through a long industrial valley, from which we rose into a forest of giant beeches; late in the afternoon we were threading a village made with patterned slates, and this wore a glancing familiarity, like the replica of a toy that formerly belonged to one's own nursery. That scenery was always insubstantial. Yielding to drowsiness, I ceased to realise that I was moving from one place to another; rather, I seemed to be installed in a stationary cabin while the faded simulacrum of a country I had known was joggled past its windows. For a time I even forgot the presence of the silent man beside me.

We were waiting against some barrier—it must have been at a level crossing—when he startled me with an incon sequent question: 'Have you any memories of Tübingen?'

I stared at him as a witless child would: that famous name, tossed at me so abruptly, would not at once connect with anything in my mind. I said, 'Tübingen?'

'I mean,' he said patiently, 'the university.'

I answered then, 'No, I don't think so.' And when I saw that this crippled statement failed to convince him I added, in growing confusion, 'I attended several universities—that was a long time ago. I've had other things to think of since then.'

He nodded acquiescently. 'I only asked,' he said, 'because my wife was there—some time before I knew her—and she used to talk about a fellow-student called Fräulein von Leezen.'

To which I replied, 'Well, I've told you my name is quite a common one.'

We were moving forward again, and for some moments he was occupied with the controls of the car. Then he said:

'Yes, but this was a rather uncommon girl. For instance she was the first woman student to win the Oberbayern prize—she got it for a dissertation on Reuchin's humanism.

'So?'

'And she was one of the founders of a student periodical called *Der Freisinnige Vorkämpfer*. You may have heard of that?'

'What? I don't think so.'

'It was regarded as something new and very remarkable in the way of student journalism.'

'Yes?'

'And I gather she wrote a great part of it herself. But later on she went over to exploiting her other gift, which was portrait painting.'

'So?'

'But you say you've never heard about that girl?'

'I don't think so.'

'And you yourself were never at Tübingen?'

His voice was still light and sociable, but clearly I was under cross-examination.

I said, 'I don't remember.' And realising that such an answer satisfied no one I went on hurriedly: 'There's no point that I can see in going over early years, trying to think what one was doing before the War. That was a different world entirely—it's finished, it's dead.'

Of course this was a foolish way of speaking: it came from a growing fear not so much of my inquisition as of damage to my internal defences. You cannot live what approximates to a normal life, you cannot behave as people expect, keeping some remnant of dignity, if you allow all the doors of your mind to stand wide open. I was still faintly hoping that a person so civilised as he appeared to be would now acknowledge and respect my reticence. But that was too optimistic. He said, again politely but with a growing warmth:

'I'm afraid I don't agree. No one's life can be divided into past and present with a thick line ruled between the two. Isn't it obvious that we're made out of our own history, every one of us—our past experience and the way we've dealt with it!'

I saw no purpose in commenting on that pronouncement, and for some time thereafter he had to give his attention to negotiating a narrow street crowded with country people and market stalls. But as soon as we were clear he returned to his theme, repeating forcefully:

'No, I can't agree with you! Pretending to ignore the past, thinking one can shut it out, disown it—that is facile. It's a way of suppressing disagreeable emotions, we use it to exculpate ourselves—or rather, we hope to. It's cowardly, and in the end it doesn't work.'

Again there was nothing useful for me to say. Men listen to women rarely, and least of all when in their didactic moods. I remained silent, then, and by degrees his excite-

163

ment seemed to evaporate. Presently he spoke in a steadier voice:

'For a long while after my wife's death I tried not to think about her. I went so far as to hide all the photographs, I shut my friends up if they even spoke her name. It seemed to me then that the cure for my misery was to pretend that our marriage—lasting such a short time—had been irrelevant to the course of my life, something which could be as-it-were discarded. In the end I saw the folly and cowardice of that evasion. And now I've turned right round, I do everything I can to keep them alive, those three short years which she and I had together. I try to recover her earlier years as well, to make them my own—in a small way I can do that from what she used to tell me and what her friends have told me since she died. You may not understand this, as you say you're not married, but to me every part of my wife's life is something to be preserved and treasured for always.'

This was the kind of talk I most dreaded, but there was no way to stop it. How, if you are terrified of heights, do you deal with a stubborn man whose greatest pleasure is mountaineering and who insists that you are to be with him on his next perilous climb!

'So you see,' he continued slowly, 'I feel a personal interest in all my wife's friends. The Fräulein von Leezen I've told you about was one she admired beyond measure—so much so, she invited her to spend part of the summer vacation at her own home. And that had an interesting result.'

At this point I found courage to protest: 'Herr Weckerlin, I'm very tired—I didn't expect this journey to be so long—and I can't really follow what you're saying. I'd be grateful if you would just let me go to sleep.'

'An interesting result,' he repeated, as if my interruption demanded no more notice than the noise of a passing aeroplane. 'Sara's father was so impressed with her friend's talents that he gave the girl a job on one of his newspapers. And that led to her meeting his son, who very soon fell in love with her. They were married about a year later.'

I left this chatter to expire, suffocated by my silence.

Thereafter he gave me the respite I had asked for—a few minutes of freedom from the voice which had seemed to feel its way like a surgeon's probe towards the dark places in my mind. But I did not sleep. When the last faint colour of trees and cottages and finally their shape had been absorbed in the strengthening darkness I still saw his face in profile against the window: in the sparse light of a blue interior lamp it resembled a marble effigy, the lips and brow cut with a Donatello's refinement; but the eyes remained alive, and these, compelling mine as a solitary lamp would in a dark arena, continued to warn me of a resolution so austere that I should be powerless against it. With the passing of un-measured time they grew more frightening, these eyes which never turned for an instant towards my face; and when he suddenly spoke again, as if in answer to an unseen questioner, his pale voice was like an arctic winter descending on my body and mind.

'I could have got out of military service,' he said slowly. 'There was a history of tuberculosis, I had the option of reporting or suppressing it. But I thought it would be best for Sara if I served—in those days I was a simple fellow, I imagined a soldier's wife would always be protected, what-ever her antecedents. Yes, and I went on believing that, even when I was getting no letters. Of course, mail was always very uncertain where I was, in the Kharkov sector. I thought when I went on sick leave that I should find her waiting at the station at Unsleben. Well, that didn't happen.'

The dry voice stopped, as if someone had lifted the needle of a gramophone. Presently it began again:

'I found an official note—a printed affair with the name filled in. It said she had been moved to an "accommodation area" for "security". No particulars, no address or anything. That was all the information I had to live with till another form came, to say she had died under hospital treatment. And some of her clothes came at the same time, done up with a flimsy piece of paper and string.'

I remember how, despite the impersonality of his speech, I thought he must be asking me for pity; indeed I was tempted to offer him at least a word of gentleness. But the sense of danger restrained me. Obscurely I knew even then that I could afford no sort of friendship with this person whose very name had long been a threat to me; that I must not involve myself in his affairs or emotions.

'Yes,' he continued, 'I tried to forget all that. But now I don't want to forget it. In a way I was responsible myself for what happened, because we all were—we stood and watched them making a world where things like that could happen. And we can't say, "Well, it's time to put all that behind us"—that would be just a cowardly evasion.' His voice had remained cool and colourless, but now, as a dry bay leaf under a magnifying glass will suddenly burst into flame, it yielded to the passion he had been suppressing: with a fury that pierced my ears and brain like a heated wire he said: 'Those things are not to be forgotten! *I tell you, I will not let anyone forget them.*'

When the car stopped again I woke from an oppressive dream where I had tried to talk to Franz and he would not even turn his eyes in my direction. Perhaps I had slept for a few seconds only, perhaps for an hour. In the moment of waking I did not remember who it was beside me, stretching to ease contracted limbs and then rather painfully getting out of the car; only when he turned back to speak through the window did his voice restore to me the formidable companion of that day's journey.

'I think they'll put us up here,' he said. 'Just wait where you are and I'll find out.'

Not yet in full possession of my faculties, I said hazily, 'But this isn't Wilpenschoen.'

'I wanted to come here first,' was all he replied.

He went a few paces down the road and I heard him knocking on a door with his knuckles. Then there was total silence. The only light there was came from the wing lamps of the car, it showed we were halted beside a high brick wall. Here the air which reached me through the lowered window was dry and warm, almost motionless, as if summer had returned: the stillness was soothing, and this time I found it a relief to be for a while alone. The days were long past when I had needed to think of my virtue or reputation, and in truth I felt no fear of any kind. Often an occasion for terror seems to provide its own remedy—a sense of detachment or disbelief. Here a man of wayward mentality, volunteering to facilitate my journey, had driven me all day in the wrong direction; but I merely thought in a sleepy way that such behaviour was too eccentric to be taken seriously.

High above me a rectangle of light appeared in the wall, then another at a lower level. A door opened, letting a long panel of light fall across the road, and now Albrecht's voice was joined by another man's. Presently he came back to me, to say:

'Yes, they can take us here.'

I still knew that I could only do as I was told. Without answering, I alighted from the car and walked to the open door. There I thought of my case, and turned to see if Albrecht was bringing it after me.

Now once more I was frightened, and this was fear of a new, convulsive kind. A faint breeze came up the road, it bore the scent of phlox strengthened by the warmth following rain, and simultaneously I heard, perhaps from a kilometre off, the industrious grunting of an old steam locomotive and the clangour of bogies on an iron bridge. This complex of sensations brought no image to my mind's eye, no name, nothing to be located in time or space; yet it seized me as brutal hands might have seized my body—as if a ghostly voice had whispered, 'Yes, here is the destination of all your journeys, this is the point on the circle of experience to which you must always return.'

An old man wearing a raincoat over his underclothes was holding the door open, his face was one of sad servility;

behind him I saw a passage floored with shiny oilcloth, a
door marked *Speisezimmer*, hats and walking sticks on a row
of pegs. Furniture so commonplace derides a sense of danger.
For a second or two no muscle in my body would respond to
any demand of the brain; then, as if the house might offer
refuge from the formless horror which had gathered about
me, I went inside.

Although he counted for nothing in my life, the features of
that man—the owner, I suppose, of the *Fremdenheim*—have
left a pellucid picture in my mind: the chaplet of grey curls
encircling a bare and shallow cranium, the hairy dewlap, the
timid, mournful eyes. He had, I think, no great intelligence,
and as he slowly led the way upstairs, with me following and
Albrecht carrying our baggage behind us, his whole body
seemed to express a certain wonder, tinged with regret, that
anyone should take advantage of the service he was there to
provide. Such people will always upset the minor mechanisms
of living, and no doubt Albrecht himself, for all his specious
confidence, was physically tired; but Albrecht had given me
no cause for compassion, and what I chiefly remember about
my entrance into that lodging is a weary anger at the
senseless muddle which two males could make of a simple
operation.

We arrived in a bedroom so crammed with chests of
drawers and garish ornaments as to resemble a second-hand
store. There Albrecht put down my case.

'And the other room?' he said.

The proprietor sleepily picked up my case and went on
down the passage, with Albrecht at his heels. Having no
instructions, I simply followed them.

'This one,' the proprietor said, opening a door at the far
end.

Albrecht went in and put his own case on the floor. The
proprietor put mine on the bed. Standing before a looking-
glass, yawning and stretching his shoulders, Albrecht half-

turned his head to say:

'I shan't want that.'

This I took as announcing without excess of chivalry that I was to occupy the other room; and there I quickly returned, carrying back my case. The proprietor followed, now bearing Albrecht's case, which he presented to me with the devotion one discovers in abnormally stupid dogs; and he was still wearing that look of brainless loyalty when, on Albrecht's arriving to demand the return of his case, he seized and gave him mine. No word was exchanged. For some time the two of them were locked in a sour incomprehension, each—I could see—convinced that the other was deliberately misunderstanding him. For my part, I was so exasperated by this irrational performance that I had not the self-command to intervene: it was all I could do to hold back childish tears until these blunderers had so far come to terms as to leave the room and let me go to bed.

Actually I did not even take off my shoes. Having locked the door and then switched off the light I simply lay down on the coverlet. Hours later, when I woke to see a thread of daylight showing through a crack in the shutters, I had scarcely moved.

For some time I continued to lie still, trying to believe there was nothing dangerous in my situation: the wilful and erratic man who had undertaken to drive me to Holland might well have remembered other business requiring his urgent attention and have changed his plans without pausing to think of my convenience. I had almost accepted this home-made reassurance when (as I suppose) a shift of wind outside brought me once again, from some way off, the noise of a train. The sound was enough to recall the terror which had seized me the evening before as I stood outside this building, and instantly my defences fell apart: it was useless now to pretend that this lodging had been picked at random, that I had been brought here with no special intention.

'*These things are not to be forgotten. I tell you, I will not let anyone forget them.*' As Albrecht's words echoed in my mind, like the sound of bombs falling in a neighbouring street, the shape of his mission began to be faintly visible: he wanted evidence against me, and where should he find it except in my own recollections! I was still convinced I had not been in this house before, but the feel of it was no longer separate from all other experience; the paralysing moment of the previous night had not (I thought) resulted simply from the fatigue that follows a day's dismal travelling, its source belonged to a time left far behind, and the vaporous country I had once fled from, haunted by spectres of cowardice and degradation, was closing about me once again. With that belief came a surge of curiosity: if indeed this place was one I had been to in the buried years, one glance outside might bring a large enlightenment.

I did go to the window, and was about to raise the shutter bar when a fresh wave of fear stopped me. Retreating, I went to the door and turned on the electric light.

This brought full wakefulness. And now my intelligence argued more and more persuasively that the course of good sense as well as courage was to find out where I was and then go boldly to meet whatever ordeal awaited me. But simultaneously I realised that to yield to such enticement would mean surrendering the citadel I had raised and so long guarded with fierce resolution. So began a struggle between instinct and reason which was to go on all day.

An hour or two must have passed when someone knocked on the door. I did not answer. But when a woman's voice called, 'Gnädige Frau! Are you all right?' I went and turned the key.

The door was pushed open by an elderly servant who, standing just inside the room, peered at me in the stolid way of her calling. She said:

'I thought you might be oversleeping. Do you want your breakfast kept?'

'Breakfast? No,' I said.

'Would you like it brought up?'

'No, thank you.'

She asked then, 'Shall I put back the shutters?' and without waiting for an answer would automatically have swept past me to do so, but I stopped her with a hand on her arm, saying sharply, *'Please leave them as they are!'* To cover this odd command I added, 'I prefer the indoor light. It suits my eyes better.'

She nodded: I expect she had served in that pension for many years, and the crotchets of its patrons no longer rippled even the surface of her mind. At once her simplicity had a sobering effect on me: I saw it was absurd to refuse the help of so harmless a creature, and now my body was reminding me that I had eaten no full meal since the previous midday. As she was about to leave the room I called her back.

'Please—I think, after all, I should like something to eat, if you will kindly bring it here.'

'But of course!'

It took her only five minutes to assemble a tray of bread, coffee and Rinderwurst which, returning, she set on a chair beside the bed. Formally she wished me good appetite, and then stood by to watch me as I ate; her face, now, wore the kindness (but also, I thought, the firmness) of a children's nurse. I said, to get rid of her:

'Thank you—I think that's all I shall want.'

She smiled but did not go. I saw from her brow that some thought was stirring, and presently she said, 'The gentleman left a message.'

'The gentleman?'

'Herr Weckerlin, I think his name is. He's had to go out. To make his business calls, I think he said.'

'I see, yes. I understand.'

'He said he might be back tonight, or else he might be staying at another place where he's got to make his calls.'

'I see.'

'I was to tell you he hoped you'd go out and have a walk round.'

'Oh, yes. Thank you,' I said.

Still she did not move; now she was staring at my face with an old sheep's inquisitive eyes, and presently she said naïvely, 'I thought you might be someone else. Your face is like a lady I used to know.'

At that all my nervousness returned. I said quickly, 'There are lots of women very like me to look at.' And when she continued staring I was obliged to speak with greater emphasis: 'Well, I mustn't keep you here—I expect you have work to do.'

Then at last she left me alone.

I remember how as a little girl I used to hear the story of Lot's wife with a feeling of superior virtue, thinking, 'Had I escaped from a doomed city, and been ordered by angelic rescuers not to look back, I, with my father's sense of discipline, should certainly not have yielded to a foolish curiosity.' What innocence! During the hours of solitude which followed the chambermaid's departure my situation was not far from that legendary woman's. In the years behind I had fought a dogged battle of disengagement, holding off the pursuit of memories, till I had almost seemed victorious. And now a distant rumble, a whiff of flowers in the night wind, had shown the victory to be illusion: I was still craving for one backward glance. Perhaps the force of curiosity alone would not have undermined a resistance which the years had hardened. My new surroundings were reawakening a sense of my own responsibility, I faintly realised that the dark besiegers were creatures I myself might have helped to fashion; and while one of my inward voices cried, 'Hold fast! Surrender nothing! Never look behind!' another was insisting, 'Here is a summons not to be evaded. You will have no peace till you know the shape and limits of whatever suffering you have to face.'

As the struggle in my mind became a war of attrition I grew more frantic in my longing to get away from the place which had occasioned it. But only the person who had brought me here could grant me that release. What had I to

172

offer Albrecht in persuasion? No verbal argument would count with a man so rigid in his attitudes, and I judged that even had my body been young and desirable he would have been proof against carnal bribery. All that was left, then, was to throw myself on his mercy. He had given me some glimpses of the austerities within his nature; but few men—except in times of ill-temper or their own distress—are entirely unaffected by women's tears, and it would need no play-acting to convince him of my despair. There was still a chance that in a moment of revulsion he would yield and set me on my way to Wilpenschoen, as he had promised first of all.

So, in a fashion, the day became one of longing for Albrecht to return. When some hours had passed the maid came again, bringing more food. I asked her, trying to make my voice sound casual:

'Herr Weckerlin isn't back?'

'No, gnädige Frau.... Shall I open the shutters now, just for a while? It feels stuffy in this room.'

'That doesn't matter!' I said firmly. 'Please leave them alone.'

At some time in the evening the performance was more or less repeated. On this occasion the old woman deemed it necessary to reiterate the instructions she had delivered earlier in the day: Herr Weckerlin might not be back at all tonight, he had hoped I would amuse myself by taking a walk in the countryside. And again, as she rehearsed those messages, she gazed at my face with a timorous rustic curiosity, as if I might be a dangerous person in disguise. There was no hostility in this—in memory I see her as a woman of good nature though of scant intelligence: and now I would have kept her with me on any terms rather than face again the protracted strain of solitude. But this time it was she who presently remembered that she had more urgent business than to garrison a single egregious visitor; she mumbled something about setting tables for next morning, and after delivering one sapient observation—'These travelling gentlemen, they come and go just as they please'—withdrew to her own part of the house.

Now the hours dragged like the last days of a pregnancy. My ears strained after the smallest sounds, and almost everything I heard—a car slowing up, the front door opening, the cough of a man on the stairs—raised some fresh hope that my vigil might be at an end. I walked up and down the narrow space which the furniture left free. I stood with forehead pressed against the wall trying to turn myself to a block of senseless matter, I paced the room again like a condemned man watching out his final hours; and my state was more tormented than that prisoner's, for one under sentence of death may concentrate his courage on the certain destination, while the punishment awaiting me remained shapeless and unknown. There is a limit to endurance. At midnight a clock striking somewhere in the house sounded in my ears like a prelude to eternity; I controlled myself for an hour more, but when it struck again I was certain Albrecht would not return that night and with this conviction came a swift surrender. Taking my handbag, I went out to the passage and then to the head of the stairs. From rooms about and above me came sounds of snoring, but none of movement or speech. The light from a feeble bulb in the hall just reached the street door, and now my immediate impulse was to see if it was locked as a prison door would be. Keeping close to the wall, where I thought my weight was least likely to make them creak, I went down the stairs one at a time.

The door was held at top and bottom by heavy bolts; the top one was only just within my reach, and very stiff, so that when I nervously tried to work it free it held fast for a time, then yielded with a noise like the firing of a gun. In the sleeping house the reverberation of that report so scared me that in one frantic moment I had drawn the lower bolt, opened the door, slipped outside and pulled it shut behind me.

Standing in the empty road, I had no sense of escape. Even then I must have faintly realised the truth: that in a matter

174

of seconds I had pierced the ramparts on which, for years, I had depended for my mind's safety.

I think of a newborn animal finding its way to the mother's teat as if it had made the journey many times before. Can it be conscious of a mysterious familiarity? Does it forget at once the darkness of the womb, as in dreams the waking life and on return to wakefulness the deeper dreams are instantly forgotten?

The feel of those few moments when I was walking down a country road returns to me distinctly: the earthy fragrance of the night air and its coolness on skin staled by many hours in a stuffy room, the noise, unnaturally loud, of my feet on the asphalt, the pumping of my heart as if I had climbed a long steep hill—those sensations, perfectly coherent, framed by the wall which my right hand used for guidance and by distant lights which alternately showed and vanished in the darkness ahead, belonged to no dream. But I had curiously lost connection with the hours which led towards them. In that interval the shape and smells of the *Fremdenheim*, the look of the old maidservant and the room I had occupied, had fallen so far out of my mind that I could not have answered any question about where I had come from. Nor could I have said where I was going. I only knew that the struggle was over, the city wall surrendered: I was going where I had to go.

Sometimes the body seems to work from its own volition, to have a knowledge of its own. The hand which felt along the wall was searching for a gate; the gate had gone, but a post still bearing hinges came where the hand expected it; turning there, my feet went down two steps as if those steps were clearly visible, then made their way with a curious confidence along the gravel path below. This was in bad condition, broken by frost and weeds; from either side the shrubs had so rampantly invaded it that in places I had to push them back to make a passage. And yet I knew just where it would turn, and where it would join a broader path that led to an upward flight of steps with a stone balustrade

The sadness which filled me now was woven with bewilderment: I could not understand why the house I had come to—the pillars of its wide porch just visible, its dormers silhouetted against the sky—should show no light, no evidence of habitation. I tried the door, it was locked, and when I searched my bag I found no key. I started walking towards the gable end, and came on scaffolding: some work had been started. But why? I could not remember giving orders for repairs or decoration, or hearing that such orders had been given. 'They leave me out,' I thought, 'they tell me nothing.' The feeling grew that here I was distrusted; it brought a new apprehension of guilt, since there must be some reason (I supposed) for this distrust, and it so increased my wretchedness that I almost turned to retreat. But if this house offered me no welcome, where else could I expect one? I continued my circuit, catching again the scent of phlox and now of roses, wondering what the time was, seeing time itself as an opaque and almost tangible cloud which, as I pressed my way through it, closed instantly behind.

The garden door which I sought at the end had been boarded over, but a window near it, left unfastened, allowed me an easy entrance. In the long drawing-room the floor seemed to be covered with planks and buckets, and I had some trouble picking my way to the far end, where my fingers found the electric switch instantly but without effect —it gave no light. The hall, too, was cluttered with builder's gear; I collided with a ladder, hurting my knee and forehead before I reached the staircase. Now, as I dragged myself up the carpetless stairs, a mounting lassitude eclipsed the sense of desolation which the bareness and alien smells of the house had started; I should not have minded stumbling against boards and trestles in the big bedroom could I have found clear space to sleep in. So compelling was this desire for rest, for escape from all responsibility, that when I returned to the landing I might have sunk down and slept there, if the mantle of silence had not been torn by a voice which issued from the darkness:

'I tell you I've got permission—let me alone!'

Some familiar note in that palpitating voice may have helped me to determine where it came from: after only a moment of hesitation I felt my way along the passage which went leftward from the stairhead and pushed open the door at the end. It was curious then to hear my own voice asking, as if in independence:

'Are you there, Berta? Are you all right?'

For a while there was no answer, only the sound of stertorous breathing somewhere near my feet; then came a few more words, sleepy and indistinct: 'They said we could stay—the builders' men. For a time, they said.'

Muffled as it was, I could not doubt that I had rightly identified the pinched and tremulous voice in which those words were uttered. It stirred me to say, with some attempt at authority, 'Tell me, Berta, where are the children sleeping? What have you done with them?'

Again the answer came slowly, with what sounded like a note of feeble protest: 'Children? She's with me here, the little girl. My little girl's all right.'

In this room the window was uncovered, with the faint light it gave I could just discern a dark cocoon of blankets where the woman lay on the floor, a blob of paleness showing for her face. Now a small movement drew my eyes to another bundle, close to the farther wall, and this seemed to confirm what she had said about 'the little girl'. But her words had explained nothing, and my own mind, sunk in drowsiness, would make no sense of the situation.

'I shall want to know what's happened,' I said weakly. 'You'll have to tell me in the morning.'

And with that I left her and returned to the landing.

Groping at the farther side of the main stairs I found two or three doors locked; but fortunately one was open, and my hands, searching the small room it led to, came on two things which would serve my immediate needs completely—what felt like a horse blanket, and a bedframe of the rudimentary sort which is commonly issued to soldiers. This furniture was a persuasion strong enough to silence all misgiving: as if at a word of command I dropped on the wire netting and pulled the rug up to my chin.

As I lay with my body comatose, sensible only of the wire pressing on ear and cheek, I passed from perplexity about the children, and Berta's resuming her old situation, to wondering why Josef was not at home. Of course he was often away: if important news broke late in the afternoon he would stay at the office all night, ready to guide his hard-pressed editors and share their labour. Again, it was not unlike a man so impatient of disorder to keep clear of a house under repair. But surely, then, I should have had some word from him, a note by messenger or a call from his secretary on the telephone? With my mind refusing to focus on the preceding hours I did not know at what time he had left in the morning, whether he had kissed me as usual or had hurried speechless (as occasionally he did) from the breakfast table to the waiting Mercedes, his mind and briefcase crammed with business; and out of this uncertainty grew the fear that his absence resulted from a quarrel between us. A quarrel with Josef? Could any disagreement have dulled for me the wide, still splendour of those serious eyes, the lambent humour in a mouth that Luca della Robbia might have carved? Could some irruption of callow pride have denied me for an hour the refreshment that came from the subtle modulations in his voice and mind, the power and softness of his adoring hands? At times, perhaps, he had treated my vanities too cavalierly—the pleasantries you tolerate from a lover may grow hurtful when they are part of a husband's stock-in-trade. 'You must remember,' he had once remarked, smiling, to a generously bosomed girl beside him, 'that my wife belongs to the military caste,' and to me the words had sounded like a betrayal. Had I said something to earn such a

178

snub? That small dinner was one I had planned with care, for the Niedelbaums were noted gourmets; and now, as I listened to Isaak Niedelbaum's dulcet voice turning all the small change of Charlottenburg to a stream of sardonic observation, as I watched the play of candlelight on the swarthy skin, on the spoilt mouth and handsome, con-tumelious eyes, I was wondering why I had to put myself to such pains for people so alien to all my sensibilities. 'Soon,' Isaak said, 'we shall need another war to show the taxpayer what he gets for his money—else he might start asking why we need an army at all.' And I found myself rejoining in sudden anger, 'I should say we need an army, Herr Niedel-baum, to guard us all—us Germans, and those who've settled under our protection.' In the glacial moments following that bêtise—with the suave Mischa Lohmann quizzically smiling, with old Frau Rosenbach glaring as if she would seize and screw my tongue—it was surely Josef who should have contrived some disengagement. But no, it was left to Tama Niedelbaum to mediate, addressing her husband: 'Isaak, my sweet, you bore our hostess with your student oratory!' And now, as if I had heard it practised over and over again, came that utterance of Josef's, cool, precise, delivered with only the faintest note of levity: 'You must remember, Tama dear, my wife belongs to the military caste.' He said no more. Like a creature trapped I glanced right and left, expecting to read amusement or contempt on the shrewd faces of Josef's friends. But our servant Raschke was removing the candles, drawing a shadow over Martha Rosenbach's gleaming shoul-ders and the pyrotechnic ornaments on Tama's wrists, and now that even the parade of glass and silver on the polished oak was no longer visible I could safely give myself to tears. It was finished, then, the party which had seemed to go on for ever, the blare of laughter and high-pitched voices was stilled, the sheen of jewellery and flesh all gone; when Josef came to bed he would realise he had been disloyal, and a new tide of tenderness would obliterate the hour of estrangement and humiliation. But another cloud intervened: I was freshly conscious of my physical discomfort, the harsh pressure of the wire, a chilliness about my feet; I could not imagine Josef consenting to share a bed like this, and the disappointment led me to wonder how long it was since we had last been together in perfect understanding. Something I had done must gravely have offended him—a few foolish words could not have brought about this dreadful separation. As I lay in the bonds of a curious inertia, straining my ears for the double note of the car's horn which would signal his return, the recrudescent sense of guilt was the more tormenting because it was still undefined. It was like those memories which come from earliest childhood, nebulous, charged with menace; or like listening as the night sky fills with the bourdon of an aerial armada, wondering how near you are to its objective, whether you will be able to meet the whine of falling bombs with any show of courage.

In the room which the first daylight formed about me the floor was strewn with remains of polishes and cleaning rags such as soldiers use; a trestle table beside the bed was of the military sort, while a soldier's belt and a rifle-sling hung in a drapery of cobwebs on the door. I had so far lost my hold on time and place that these trappings did not disturb me, and I felt nothing but a slight impatience when, with the light strengthening, my drifting eyes rested on other things which seemed to have no link with soldiering. The wall nearest where I lay was adorned with scraps of stained and curling papers on which typescript was still faintly visible; elsewhere it was thick with grime, but behind these accretions a pattern showed which, with the colours faded almost to uniformity, was yet familiar—a design of musical instruments grouped as a delicate motif. In a corner of the room was a wardrobe with its doors broken off, the shelves full—as far as I could see—of soldiers' leavings; on top of it lay the red and yellow model of a railway engine, and beside that toy a violin case with the top half missing. It was the case which took my mind in sudden flight to a furniture shop in Bremen; to a moment so vividly recalled that it brought me the exact tone of Josef's voice exclaiming, *'Johanna, look—that wallpaper with the flutes and viols—wouldn't it be perfect for Felix's room!'*

So Felix must be away, I thought; perhaps Josef, indulgent as all Jewish fathers are, had taken the child on one of his journeys. And there must be some simple reason for my sleeping in Felix's room instead of my own.

For a long time I lay with my face towards a gap in the wall where a tall window should have been, watching through a grid of scaffold poles the lazy stirring of the deodar, smelling with old appreciation a resinous aroma in the soft autumnal air. The lethargy which had fastened on my body seemed to give me some protection: palpably I had been through a serious illness, and people would excuse me from actions or decisions when they realised I had scarcely the strength to leave my bed. It troubled me a little that the things around me would not fit together comprehensibly: I could not see why Felix's room had been used to billet soldiers, for the War, I thought, was a circumstance of my own childhood, not of his. But no one was asking me for orders or explanations. I had an idea that the future held something which would hurt me cruelly; but I reasoned, 'If I keep quite still, putting no questions, making no demands, I can avoid the future indefinitely. Time, travelling forward, will leave me behind in a pocket of safety.'

When first I heard a man singing I thought it must be one of the gardeners, though I did not recognise the raucous voice. The sound came nearer, and presently I could tell that the singer was climbing up the ladder outside. A head appeared, square and red like a piece of raw meat, garnished with two draggled wings of moustache and what might have been a skull-cap of soiled and ragged cotton wool: it was not a head I knew. As I focus him in retrospect, this ox-like individual in undervest and military trousers exemplifies the old-style Saxon craftsman, innocent of polite ambitions, proud and diligent in his trade. Kneeling on the stage, starting to work without the smallest delay, he did not even glance inside the building, and if I had stayed silent he might have been there all morning without observing that the bed a few feet away was occupied. For me, however, this was not a congenial situation, and I presently called to him:

'Mr Builder!'

He started, but at once recovered. Resting his trowel, and with his light blue eyes fixed on me in mild remonstrance, he said:

'You, what are you doing there?'

I saw no reason to take any notice of that intrusive question; instead I asked him temperately, 'How long is this work going to take, can you tell me?' adding, 'My husband's away—I'm not sure exactly what instructions he's given.'

My enquiry seemed to confuse the simple man. 'Your husband?' he repeated. 'Herr Paulig?'

I said—no doubt with some impatience—'I am the mistress of this house. I want to know what orders my husband has given—I've been unwell, and it's difficult to keep track of things.'

'I don't know about your husband,' he answered stubbornly. 'It's Herr Paulig who gives us the orders.'

'And who, please, is Herr Paulig?'

'Why, Herr Paulig acts for the Council.'

He spoke as if I were a person of lame intelligence, while for my part, as our conversation proceeded, I saw him as a singularly childlike fellow. He had formed the idea that the District Council were owners of the house, which—someone had told him—had been left empty before the War. During the War it had suffered damage, and later had served as a billet for troops; now the Council were putting it in order, for use, he understood, as annexe to a nearby hospital. Whatever the source of this astonishing story, he himself undoubtedly believed it; and in the languor that follows illness I saw no point in disputing his assertions. What did it matter if this worthy labourer imagined that my house had passed into public possession!

None the less I was disturbed by his palpable curiosity about myself, and relieved when our desultory exchange was interrupted. The door of the room had opened a little way; I realised all at once that a small girl with straight, fair hair and a grubby pinafore was standing near the wardrobe, regarding me with the startled eyes of a baby seal. Spontaneously I said:

'Well, Ruth, how are you this morning?'

Her response was to edge away, still staring and keeping a thumb in her mouth: I might have been a wolfhound, uncertain in temper and insecurely chained.

This came as a shock to me, for it showed that my illness had been severer and more prolonged than I had realised hitherto: plainly the shy creature did not recognise me even as someone she had seen before, while I myself found her face so different from the delicate shaping of my mental portrait that I could hardly believe she was my own child. The bricklayer's presence put me at a disadvantage—with my brain moving so sluggishly I could not catechise a six-year-old in his hearing; so when she and I had for some time watched each other in mutual constraint it fell to him to break the silence.

'You, Mädel, you've no business in here!' he said to the child; and to me, 'She belongs to Fräulein Muller.'

Those words recalled my fleeting encounter with Berta a few hours earlier. I said, 'Yes, Fräulein Muller ought to be looking after her. But I expect she's busy.'

'You know Fräulein Muller?' he asked, in fresh perplexity.

And when I answered, 'Why, of course—she's this child's nurse,' he faintly smiled, glancing at me sidelong, with the raw sagacity of his kind.

'Her nurse? Good enough!' he pronounced; and then, 'She worked here once—so she says. Well, she's no business here now. But Herr Paulig says she can stay till we start on the room she's been using—she does no harm.'

Again his chatter made no sense to me, only the remark 'She worked here once' was meaningful, reminding me that I had given Berta notice—on account of her stupidity and laziness—some time before. Then had I re-engaged her? Or had she taken advantage of my illness to slip back into my service?

'All the same,' he continued, 'that's not to say just anyone can use this place for a doss. Herr Paulig will be round sometime. What's he going to say!'

His ponderously marching voice was still good-humoured, but I saw I was meant to take him seriously: ingenuous and dutiful, perturbed at finding someone unknown to him in what he had supposed to be an empty room, he truly thought it his business to set the matter right. Meanwhile the child, motionless and dumb, continued to gaze at me as if she had been posted to report my movements; and I think it was a gust of impatience with her stolid demeanour rather than any reasoned policy which made me say abruptly:

'Ruth, darling, find Berta, will you, and say I'd like her to come here as soon as she can.'

For a few seconds there was nothing to show that she had grasped that simple instruction; she only stared harder, still sucking her thumb. Then, as if bored with my society, she sauntered out of the room.

It seemed unlikely that the message would get through, but in my feeble state I could think of no other plan for escaping an absurd predicament. I shut my eyes, overwhelmed by a resurgent sense of loneliness and desertion: how could Josef have gone away when I was ill, telling me nothing about his orders to the builders, allowing me to be treated as a trespasser! (Had I, in some thoughtless way done him a serious injury? How could I possibly have earned such punishment as this?) In flight from a new distress I sank into a layer of darkness, and the sounds which presently reached me came as if from a long way above my head There was the child's insipid, adenoidal voice: 'She calls me Ruth, she said you were my nurse,' followed by the workman's cautious undertone, 'I found her when I came.... She talks in a funny way.' Then I caught the voice I had quickly recognised before, the anaemic, fluttering speech of Berta Muller:

'Why, it's the lady that lived here. It's Frau Schechter, who I used to work for.'

Strangely, I found a breath of comfort in that garbled utterance—as if it were a life-line drawing me back to the only world I could accept and sufficiently understand.

Cesar, that was what the workman was called. It must have been he and his mate—an aged creature like a squirrel, always addressed as 'Junge'—who carried me down to the denuded morning-room, and there it was Berta, I suppose, who put me properly into bed, in a patched nightgown which may have been her own. In the succeeding hours her face was foremost among the objects which, like the projections of delirium, were sometimes close and sometimes absent at the times when my eyes were open.

That interval—I have no means to tell how long it lasted—served me as one more respite. The stillness I lived in was like a bubble floating above the stream of ordinary happenings, its wall was fragile but I thought it would hold me safe so long as I myself remained incurious about the future, keeping mind and body motionless. The room itself suggested permanence, for although its furniture had gone it retained some features—the florid moulding of architraves and cornice, the spade-shaped patch of damp on an outer wall—which were part of my inveterate experience in the way one's mother's jewellery belongs to the frame of childhood. In the view through the tall south window I was conscious of a sad disorder: a tangled growth of snowberry and lilac had encroached on the broad walk, where the gravel was already overlaid by a carpet of hawkweed and groundsel; even the greenhouse was half hidden by this inundation of foliage. But the lovely bronze of Ceres which Josef had brought me from Dresden was always visible among the rioting syringa, and the pear trees standing in lank grass still made me think of a group of peasant women with their skirts flying about their heads in a gay, tempestuous dance. With the sun's movement the aspect of that tousled scene must have altered from hour to hour, but in memory I see it as unchanging, drenched in the pale gold of late September, an assurance that some part of life's goodness is proof against destruction: I needed only to confine my spirit within this nucleus of calm, satisfied with its fragile comfort, refusing to recognise the flow and menace of time. For a long while, then, I asked no questions, made no attempt to reduce the gap between myself and the figures which materialised beside the bed and presently were gone: I saw them as perhaps a captive fish sees the human visitors to an aquarium—presences confusing to its vision and outside its field of intelligence. Nor, any longer, did they question me. There must have been anxious commerce between them: I retain in memory a faded picture of 'der Junge' peering at me like a puppet doctor fearful of catching his patient's disease, while behind him Cesar's bucolic face, racked by severity and kindness, is yoked with the moonstruck face of Berta as they two continually discuss the situation in a rustling undertone. I realise now what gratitude I should have felt for their forbearance; at the time I only thought of them as trying to stir my curiosity, to draw me away from the quietness where I had taken refuge.

Even so, the malaise which faintly chilled my spirit did not begin with them. It came from the child, who on her repeated visits ventured only just inside the door and would say no word to me. A dozen times I appealed to her, 'Ruth darling, come and give me a kiss!' but without the smallest effect: she might have been deaf and blind.

Had she forgotten her name? That Berta called her 'Eva' was nothing strange: it pertains to the possessive nature of nursery-maids to use such sobriquets for children in their care. But a change so radical in Ruth's behaviour, as well as in her appearance, could only start a current of suspicion: had that insidious woman taken advantage of my illness to

186

appropriate my child, transferring to herself the love and loyalty which belonged by right to me? The worst aspect of the estrangement was that I felt increasingly cold and even hostile towards the child herself. At this stage nothing in her looks recalled my own, and her habitual expression, so far from suggesting a mind like Josef's, seemed to exhibit a coarse and meagre intelligence; moreover I seemed to detect a certain slyness, a callow contempt, in the moistly staring eyes—as if she thought me foolish to be lying ill while she was living her normal life. Had I once loved her, this gauche and wet-mouthed little thing, as any normal woman must love the creature she has given life to? I tried to picture the Ruth I had known before my illness, but nothing in these commonplace features helped me to penetrate the cloud which obscured my memory; there were only the child's fair hair and her familiarity with our surroundings to persuade me they belonged to the same being.

Perhaps it was that I had always left Ruth too much to her nurses, finding in her brother more to engross my mind and heart; for Felix in his earliest years had appeared to me a reproduction of his father, endowed with an intelligence— grave, speculative, sometimes frivolous and mocking—which seemed almost too robust to be framed by the slender features of a handsome little boy. Again I was puzzled: where was Felix now? It was nothing unusual for Josef to be absent—his work took him often to the capital, sometimes to Zurich or Wien—but I could think of no reason for Felix to be away from home when not on holiday with me. At some time there had been a passage of arms between us—he had wanted to play the violin in a period I had set apart for his reading lesson—but so trifling a collision would hardly have made him take to flight. A later memory came to the surface, shadowed and indistinct: I had caught a glimpse of him among a crowd of people on the deck of a canal boat, starting (I could only imagine) on some school excursion. Should he not long since have returned? From that uncertainty came a deepening disquiet which drove me at last to break my silence; when next I found Berta beside the bed, holding a cup of soup and eyeing me as always with a senseless curiosity, I gave her a simple order:

'Berta, I should like you, please, to send Felix to me.'

She made no answer. Her expression changed to one of feverish embarrassment, as if I had thoughtlessly touched a subject abhorrent to us both. Without meeting my eyes she put the cup on the floor and in a moment was out of the room.

That might point to nothing but the common foolishness of servant girls: Felix was being punished, perhaps, for some piece of naughtiness, and Berta was too timid or else too inarticulate to tell me. But I could not rest on so frail a supposition. Now I started wondering if the whispered conference between Berta and the workmen had been concerned with him. He might be ill or in some serious trouble. Possibly Josef had removed him to be reared in a wholly Jewish household, or he had been knocked down and killed in the road.

Thereafter I could not go back to the vaporous harbour where I had found a brief tranquillity, for now it seemed that the things about me, though superficially familiar, were so far changed that they ceased to fit together. A home is a living thing; this was one with the lifeblood gone. Yet my mind still lacked the strength to venture in a wider country. There was a time when I noticed Cesar cautiously observing me (as he often did) through the open window and when I saw such gentleness in his stolid face that I almost made an appeal to him: 'Why is everyone so silent? Come, tell me what is wrong! How can you do things to my house without my orders or agreement? And what has happened to my little son?' But because I could imagine no comfortable answers those questions remained unspoken. The current of despondency which chilled me now was akin to the fears of childhood; as if I were being pressed towards a grown-up world with only a child's powers of comprehension.

The sense of incongruity, of events escaping the rule of time, was heightened by a new female voice, which I heard first from the borderland of sleep:

'Yes, it's her, no doubt about it. I thought as soon as I first saw her—over there—I thought she was a lady I'd seen before. . . . It shook me, I can tell you, when I went to take in her tray and found she was gone.'

That voice gave way to Berta's: 'There's one thing certain, she can't be moved, not yet.' And then it came again:

'Soon as I can, I'll bring her some dinner over. After all, it's being paid for.'

I seemed to know it well, that menial, rather prim enunciation, but it had no place in the stage of life I had reached; and when I opened my eyes the face I saw presented the same disconnection—as when you meet in a feverish dream someone who has belonged to a closed period in your history. There was nothing remarkable in the features themselves—those of an elderly housemaid, moulded by virtue rather than intelligence; but the way in which she peered at me, like a ewe in helpless agitation over a sickly lamb, was at once acutely familiar and, in a sense, unreal: here was a domestic I distinctly recognised, but not as one in my own service; and while she obviously knew who I was she was not behaving as a servant towards the mistress of the house. If my thoughts had been articulate the words would have been, *'This cannot be happening to me! Not here. Not yet.'*

At that encounter there was, I think, no speech between her and me, and I remember supposing afterwards that her visit had belonged to some kind of illusion. But she appeared again, and soon the regular arrival of this old-fashioned figure, with her artless but individual dignity, became a part of the simple structure in which I was living.

In time she grew vocal, in the arch manner of a nursery governess trying to rouse a dull child: 'Well, you *did* make up your mind to have a walk then! But you didn't get far! . . . You ought to eat your supper, Frau Schechter, or how can you get back your strength! . . . Is it a pain in the legs, or just feeling tired?'

I paid little attention to her chatter, which, though it sounded almost meaningless, had a quality that disturbed me: it gave me the sense of living within a revolving drum, so that all experience had to keep recurring, and this commonplace illusion can be oppressive to one whose life has not been tranquil. Indeed, I had grown acutely impatient at the constant attendance of this honest creature when one short speech of hers entirely changed my feelings. It was as she was leaving the room, bearing the plentiful remains of a meal, that she turned to say nonchalantly:

'The gentleman's been on the telephone—he's going to be back tomorrow night. He said he was sorry he couldn't get back before—he's been delayed, he said.'

Elliptic as it was, I found nothing obscure in the core of that message. Tomorrow Josef would be back; and beside this dazzling prospect the sulphurous mountain of my fears and sadness dwindled to insignificance. He was on his way, Josef was coming home! Whatever dissensions had set us apart could only melt away in the warmth of our reunion. I thought of the gentleness which a few tears were enough to animate in Josef's eyes and voice, of how easily his gusts of anger or resentment would subside, giving place to an understanding so large in tolerance, so delicately tuned, that you felt as if an Italian sunlight were flooding into every crevice of your body and mind. With Josef at my side the lesser pains and obscurities would all dissolve: he would tell me what was happening to Felix and arrange his early return, he would lighten my concern over Ruth by sending Berta away; then he would so galvanise the workmen that the house would quickly resume its former state—soon it would be carpeted and furnished, warmed by the radiance of family meals which lengthened into hours of lazy gossip and effervescent laughter with the warble of a violin filtering from the children's room. The mere thought of such a restoration, of a life once more vested in other lives, drawing its meaning from a fabric of affections, was enough to ease a little the weight of lethargy which bound me to the bed. I

:emed to breathe more easily; and the tingling in my veins
·as as if my blood had begun to sing.

There remained a shadowy misgiving: I thought that in
ne period screened by my illness—how long lasting and how
ır behind I could not tell—I had done some foolish,
nnatural thing which had injured Josef's confidence. But I
ould not give rein to such vague apprehensions. 'He is on
is way!' my inner voice reiterated. It was like hearing in a
arkened city that the electric fault has been discovered and
ll the streets will soon be ablaze with light.

was without a looking-glass; that was one of my minor
:oubles, but it came to assume a large importance. Although
ɔsef had surely heard about my illness, and would not
xpect me to look my best, I could not bear that he should
nd a scarecrow when he came.

That day—the day which should end in his return—was
ne of incessant calculation. I wanted to do things which
ould please him, to put some part of the house in acceptable
rder, arrange a meal he would enjoy. But those ambitions
vere far beyond my powers. To be up and dressed, able to
valk a few paces to greet him, was the most I could hope for
fter lying for some months (as I now supposed) in bed; and
s I struggled against fresh waves of lassitude I began to
:ar that even that small accomplishment would be beyond
ıe.

I had only Berta to give me any help.

'Berta, there must be some other clothes,' I said, 'some-
·here in the house. I must have something slightly more
resentable than this old dress.'

The request brought nothing but a blank stare from that
voman of exasperating limitations. When I repeated it—
erhaps more than once—she spoke in a rambling way about
he soldiers', echoing Cesar's story that the house had been
sed for billeting and in consequence despoiled. I refused
hen to waste my scanty forces in sterile discussion. At least

she showed some capability and patience in getting me int
the clothes I had. When that was achieved I sat on a cha
they found for me; the elderly woman whom I could n
identify brought me food again, and the child I still calle
Ruth—though I had come to think of her as an impostor-
presently took up her usual station, gazing at me with th
mindless intensity of a young student who is told to copy
work of art. For myself, I felt no masterpiece, but rather as
I were imprisoned in a body where the nerves and sinews ha
died.

By late afternoon I had regained sufficient energy to wal
the few paces between the chair and the door, and when th
day began to weaken I thought I was equal to a further effor
This room, carpetless, with a tumbledown bedstead in th
middle, with clothes and crockery heaped on a broken chai
presented a scene so squalid that I could not face the prospe
of being found here. I thought of the attic room which Jos
used when he had work to do at home, and where I ofte
joined him late in the evenings; secluded from the traffic
the house, it was always a place where he and I felt close an
content. When Berta came again—it was nearly dark—
said:

'Berta, I think I'll go to the attic. I'll sit in the He
Direktor's room and wait for him there.'

To this she responded with her usual look of foolis
incomprehension, and then she raised objections: it was
long way up there, and the room I spoke of was probably i
great confusion like all the others. I was firm, however:

'I may need a little help going up,' I said. 'But first of al
will you have the kindness to go and see what you can do
put the room right.'

With conspicuous reluctance she did as I asked.

It was quite dark before she returned, accompanied by th
two workmen, 'der Junge' bearing a candle in a medicir
bottle. Now it was Cesar who, with masculine presumptio
put himself in charge of the movement I had ordered.

'You wish to visit the attic room?' he asked magisteriall

192

as if I had demanded a tour in the less reputable streets of Hamburg. And when I nodded he said, 'Then der Junge and I will have to carry you.'

'Thank you,' I answered, 'but I can manage perfectly on my own feet.'

In fact I nearly reached the first landing without support: I had only two more steps to conquer when the connection between my will and body seemed to break, and I dropped like a felled tree into the arms of Cesar, who was closely following me. From that point my independent climb was mere pretence; I was on my own legs, but Berta held me by one elbow and Cesar, with his huge hand in my armpit, bore most of my weight. 'Der Junge' followed with the candle, and I remember how on the sloped ceiling above the attic stairhead our shadows, enormous and grotesque, appeared to portray a draggled female under arrest. Apart from the noise of our feet, reverberating in the stripped house as in an empty courtroom, it was a silent passage: my escort wore the demeanour of bearers at a funeral, whilst I, irrationally frightened by their solemnity, could ward off hysteria only by remaining speechless.

As Berta had supposed, the attic room had not escaped the mischief wrought by some licensed invader in the rest of the house; here too were the dismal flavours of barrack living—of bareness garnished with martial debris, a lingering taint of polishes, stale food and sweaty clothes. But the task of moving the larger furniture from a room so hardly accessible had been too great for the vandals, or else someone of status had retained it for his own comfort: the large table which Josef used as writing-desk was standing, bare, at the far end, while the biggest bookcase, glassless and empty except for rubbish, was actually in its old position against the higher wall. Doubtless the lack of light served to disguise an accumulation of dirt and a hundred defects of every kind, but Berta must have taken some trouble to fulfil my wishes, for at least the room's remaining contents were placed in reasonable order: the desk chair which Josef generally sat in was beside the table, and I saw with instant satisfaction that the small upholstered chair which came from my childhood home was in its proper place in the recess facing the window I had been right to come up here. There was in this assemblage of familiar things a tincture of unreality, as in period rooms refashioned in museums, and yet it spoke of Josef as one of his old suits returning from the cleaners would: the hours which he and I had shared here, scanning the day's events in drifting talk and grateful silences, the ingenuous embraces following our sharp disputes, with Josef's laughter sounding like the fall of waves on a shingle beach, all that revenue of sweetness had given to the space within these walls a personality which no change, no ravages, could ever efface.

'This is the room you meant?' Cesar asked. 'You wanted to come here?'

I nodded, and he led me, rather officiously but not without kindness, to the little chair. There I gratefully sat down. To Berta I said:

'Will you please tell the Herr Direktor as soon as he comes that I am here. And will you explain to him, please, that I'm not coming downstairs to greet him because I haven't been well.'

She mumbled some answer I didn't catch, glancing sidelong at her companions as brainless children do in school. Now they stood almost in a line, those three, their mouths agape, their rustic eyes turned towards me in such a way that I felt as if my own face were exhibiting some dreadful abnormality. So, having thanked them for their service, I asked them almost brusquely to leave me. Obeying, they put me in mind again of undertakers' men—of those who have lowered the coffin into the grave and now withdraw—except that they gave me a faint impression of anxiety: I might have been an infant who if left alone for a few minutes is bound to do itself some harm.

Later I wished I had not been so anxious to get rid of them. To be all by oneself, and feeling the chill of autumn, in

194

a tarnished room where the candle has burnt far down is to watch one's hopefulness running to waste. I grew afraid, thinking, 'Illness must so have altered my appearance that he will not recognise, much less be fond of me.' Now the words I should use to greet him became a problem, complex and insoluble. I seemed to have lost my grasp of time's progression; for I could not, could not determine when—or why—he had gone away.

I must have been awake before the door was opened, for besides hearing a man's deliberate tread on the stairs I remember watching a strip of light which appeared and grew in strength between door and lintel. But in the moment which followed—the moment which hung motionless like the images of an arrested film—I felt as when one first returns to sensibility after the near explosion of a bomb; when one cannot tell the size or distance of objects coming into view, and faces familiar in themselves have no relation to each other or to one's shrunken field of recollection. This man standing over me with a torch pointed at my body, I knew his features as intimately as if we had been talking together only a few minutes before, but some seconds had to pass before the neat small head, the fair hair, the over-knowing smile, evoked a name. Involuntarily I said that name aloud, 'Herr Weckerlin!' And the sound of it was enough to set in motion the wheels of recent memory—the birthday party coming to a ragged end, the long drive in rain and cloud, our dark arrival at the *Fremdenheim*.

Memory? Not the resurgence of a protracted dream? No, no dream remains so entire, so tangible. And yet the things about me were not less real: this was Josef's room, even in the meagre light I could not for an instant doubt the evidence—the shape of a roughly fashioned tie-beam, a wall which leant a little inward, the peculiar carving of a chair within my reach. It is no flight of fancy, nor just a whimsical use of words, to say that in the moment of recognition I

195

experienced simultaneously two separate lives, one in the near, one in the farther past. That was an unendurable disjunction; and even now I hear again the high, unnatural voice in which I cried, 'Herr Weckerlin, you've no business here! This isn't where you belong!'

Probably it was Berta who brought up a second candle, and I think it was she who arrived later on with coffee and with things to eat, which had probably come from the pension. But her face shows nowhere in my recollection of that hour. At the fringe of the candle's light I see Albrecht leaning back with his elbows on a bookshelf, a tired small man who appears to be attending to some business from a sense of duty, without enthusiasm or personal concern. I see him stifling a yawn as he says, with what sounds like a note of apology:

'I didn't expect to be away so long. There were two men I wanted to talk to. I had a lot of trouble getting hold of the second one.'

My state was such that little of what he said stirred my intelligence: from his quiet opening a sentence here and there left an impression like that of the electric signs which catch your eye as you are driven at night through a foreign city; that was all.

'... You went for a walk, Erna tells me. Perhaps you were surprised to find a house you knew? It must be confusing—of course it's quite a time since you were living here with your husband and the children. There's a gap we shall have to fill....'

Had his manner been hostile I believe he would never have loosed the paralysis in which the shock of his arrival had left my mind. But at that stage he appeared as one whose first wish was to help me in my bewilderment, and because I had been so long without anyone of my own sort to speak to I was susceptible to any hint of sympathy. Moreover, though he was not a man I cared for I felt I could rely on his rectitude.

he stillness within the house and the gentle stir of leaves
utside the window, the sick fatigue which held my body in
he chair and the narrowness of the pool of light which
nclosed us, all conduced to a sense of privacy and trust. In
his room I was at least a person with some rights, holding a
recognised position. Or so I still imagined. On that assump-
on it seemed just possible that this quiet, reasonable man
might steer me to some highroad in the mapless country
here I was wandering. '*There's a gap we shall have to fill.*'
That at least was common ground. In my clouded state I was
till nursing the hope that Josef would be back that night—
his Albrecht Weckerlin, I thought, might have come to
xplain why he was late. And after a while, with my mind
losed to whatever Albrecht was saying, I found myself
peaking independently, with some pretence of dignity and
alm:

'I'm expecting my husband presently. You know my
usband, perhaps—Herr Dr Schechter, Director-in-Chief of
he Schechtergruppe?'

Although I put the question so quietly it seemed to affect
ny visitor as if a shot had been fired outside the window. He
ell silent, and the silence lasted so long that I wondered if he
had forgotten I was with him. At last, with an air of studious
ircumspection, he said slowly:

'Your husband? No, I never met him. I know a good deal
bout him. I mean, in recent years I suppose there's been no
ne in the newspaper world with a name standing as high as
his.... You say you expect him home this evening?'

'Yes. Well, probably.'

'He's been away some time?'

'He's often away,' I said briefly.

'On business?'

'As a rule.'

'And this is one of his business trips?'

I let that question pass. He persisted:

'You're worried about him?'

'Well, naturally I always want to see him back.'

At this he nodded gravely. 'I should like to help you,' l
said. 'Perhaps I could make some inquiries through busine
friends of my own. But first I need to know where he
gone—where he was when you last heard from him.'

'Thank you,' I said, 'but I shan't put you to so muc
trouble.'

I seemed to have sunk further into darkness, with r
foothold, no sense of direction; I only saw that it wa
Albrecht, once again, who asked the questions, I who wa
obliged to answer them; and though his manner was sti
friendly I began to suspect that he was leading me—as l
had done in some earlier conversation—towards the places
had no wish to explore.

My rebuff was ineffectual. Hardly pausing, he said plea
antly, 'It must be interesting, being married to a man in h
position. You yourself must know a great deal about new
paper work.'

'Scarcely anything,' I said.

'But before your marriage you were working in you
husband's office—isn't that so?'

'Only in a very junior capacity.'

'All the same, that must have given you some insight int
the way newspapers are conducted. It would make it easie
for you to follow your husband's talk about his work.'

'He hardly mentions it,' I said. 'When he wants to tal
business he can do so with people who thoroughly unde
stand it. He and I have other things to talk about.'

That was no more than a half-truth; even as I said it
recalled a conversation which had taken place in this roo
on a night when Josef's sister had been our guest. Josef ha
read us extracts from a series of articles by Georg Langke, hi
chief political contributor, which obliquely criticised th
current régime. I had begged him to suppress these essay
arguing that they could only lead to the proscription of th
journal concerned and perhaps of our other publications a
well; while Sara, taking the other side, had asserted that onc
a newspaper shrinks from its critical functions it loses i

198

right to exist. Now it almost seemed that Albrecht was reading my mind; for his next words were:

'I should have thought any man with a wife of outstanding intelligence would sometimes turn to her for counsel. At any rate he'd want to know her views on problems which were going to involve them both in the end.'

Again I was silent, since another picture had risen in my mind: once before I had been subject to such suave persuasion as this—someone had tried to disturb my loyalties by soft, persistent questioning. That reminiscence, faint as it was, served as a fresh warning; and when Albrecht leant forward to speak again I said sharply:

'Herr Weckerlin, I've been through a serious illness—it has left me far from well. I'm afraid I must ask you to leave me now.'

He did not move, he only observed me with fresh concentration, as a doctor might.

'In fact, you don't want to take me into your confidence?' he said soberly. 'But perhaps I should take you a little into mine. I should have told you that I too have a connection with the Schechter family.'

'That doesn't interest me,' I said.

'Indeed,' he continued, 'that connection was—and is—the most important thing in my life. Now look: I have here some old issues of the *Helstadtsanzeiger*, with some articles which created quite a stir when they appeared. You may remember that?'

'No, I do not remember.'

'Then perhaps you'd like to read them now?'

'Thank you—no. I'm not well enough to read anything.'

'But I think you'd very quickly remember all about them. I've been told that Josef Schechter was in some doubt whether to publish them, and that his wife—that you—tried to persuade him not to.'

'I have no wish,' I replied, 'and no reason to discuss my family affairs with you.'

He nodded pensively. 'You don't believe me, then, when I

tell you that I myself have a connection with the Schechters?' His eyes were still fixed intently on my face, as if searching for the diagnostics of some suspected disease. 'Listen, I'm not blaming you for what you did on that occasion—for trying to stop the publication of those articles. You may have been thinking only of your husband's interest —his political safety.'

I said, 'I'm not going to discuss that.'

'And some people,' he added, 'would say it was unfortunate that he didn't listen to your pleading. In view of what happened, I mean.'

I said, 'I don't know what you're talking about.'

A few moments earlier those words would have been true. I think it was not what Ælbrecht said so much as what he held in his hand—the copies of the *Helstadtsanzeiger* with the familiar name block on faintly greenish paper—which carried me backward, as a tune heard through the noises of a street will revive the tissue of sensations, the very taste and climate, belonging to an hour lost since childhood. Now I felt again the raw chill of the February morning when, starting in darkness, I had driven in a hired car to the Salzendorf airfield; there at daybreak Josef and I had waited in a corner of the hangar, a cold breeze whipping about my ankles and the smell of oil filling my nose, while out on the frosted turf a small machine, freshly brought to life, roared and quivered as if it would break loose from the men who leant on its tail. Impossible, in such an arena of din and discomfort, to imbue that parting with the essence of our coupled lives—their rhythm of ecstasy and dullness, their enlargement in the birth and growing of our children, the moments of passion which would always obliterate our failures in understanding. Distraught by anxiety, I had stupidly reproached him for rejecting my advice about Langke's articles; while he, not listening, taking refuge as men do in practicalities—the setting of his watch, a rapid check of the papers in his briefcase —had denied all entrance to emotion, his or mine. 'This fuss will all blow over,' he had said in his business voice. 'For me t's just a case of staying at Zurich till there's a change of government. Hoffmüller will give you an address to write to—but don't post letters anywhere near home.' His last kiss had been no more prolonged than the one he gave me on any ordinary morning. Then I had stood alone, shivering, watching the ugly unbirdlike thing which contained him as it climbed and made a clumsy turn to disappear in the low awning of cloud. In the shred of time it occupied, that reprise of misery was more real than my physical surroundings; against it the intruding voice of Albrecht was meaningless, like a message for someone else flashed on a cinema screen. But he would not let me ignore him.

'I think you know what happened!' he said for the second time. And when I made no reply the insistent voice went on: 'You know that he chose to disregard your views, to go his own way. He did publish the articles—because he considered it his moral duty, whatever the cost. And you remember what that led to.'

Again he waited for my assent, watching my face with eyes I couldn't escape. I said, no doubt with tears fluttering my voice:

'I simply don't see what it's to do with you, any of this—what it's to do with anyone but him and me! You can talk to my husband when he comes—though I don't know what right you have to question anyone.'

He nodded as electric dolls do, his eyes motionless; asking, 'And when is he coming?'

'I've told you, I expect him any time this evening.'

'You *really* expect him? How long did you say he'd been away?'

'I don't remember. I've told you, I've been ill, I can't remember when things happened before I was ill.'

'I think you could remember a great many things,' he said, 'if you set your mind to it. For example, where your husband was going when he went away.'

'I don't know. I don't remember.'

'Well, I can tell you about that. It was Switzerland—first of all with a cousin at Zurich. You remember now?'

'No.'

'But the letters he sent you—you must remember those? Look, here's one he sent to his sister. Don't tell me you've forgotten the look of his handwriting!'

'I tell you I've been ill. I don't remember things.'

'Excuse me—I think what you really mean is that you refuse to occupy your mind with anything difficult or painful. Let's consider for a moment what has happened to your two children—they were with you at the time your husband went away. Felix and Ruth, I mean. I'm asking you to be honest and think about what happened to them.'

Then I shouted at him, suddenly and with a force which both astonished and physically hurt me: 'What business have you in my house! You're to leave at once, do you hear! Go away! *Go away!*'

He turned as if to obey me. But he paused at the door to say austerely, 'I have some old acquaintances of yours downstairs—they can recall the time just after your husband went abroad. I think if you spent a little while with them it would do a good deal to clear your mind.'

Yes, it must have been before then that Berta came with some food, for when Albrecht had left me I found my eyes dwelling on the remains which lay near my feet—cups with coffee grounds and crumbs on a yellow plate. It hurt me to see such untidiness in Josef's room when I had not the strength to deal with it, and I spent some time composing an excuse: as soon as he arrived I should explain that the builders' men were still about and that everything would be put to rights as soon as they had gone. But once more I had forgotten what sort of repairs was being done, and which of us had ordered them; and from this new wave of uncertainty came the fear that I might be mistaken in expecting Josef home at all. Perhaps he had come already and gone off again—perhaps it was he whose feet I had recently heard descending the stairs.

It is frightening when your hold on time becomes uncertain—as if, on a river voyage, you were to find appearing on the banks distinctive farms and mansions which you had passed some distance farther back.

I had not moved, but one candle was out and the second had burnt low, when I saw a pair of boots and then trousered legs close to where the cups were standing. As my gaze lifted it took in a seated figure, not Albrecht's but that of someone else I seemed to know, a man with ill-fitting clothes and overgrown grey hair; I think what specially distinguished him was the scant eyebrows over unnaturally small, pale eyes —eyes which continually watched me yet managed never to meet my own. I could not have identified this man, but in spite of his changed appearance (for hitherto he had always been in uniform, with darker and shorter hair) I seemed to know at once what he was there for, and without even waiting for him to speak I said tremulously:

'I've had no word from my husband. I've still no idea where he's gone.'

That seemed to take him by surprise; he glanced over his shoulder, and now I saw that Albrecht was back in his former place by the bookshelf, while a third man stood in the near-darkness beside the door. It was Albrecht who spoke:

'Frau Schechter, if you think for a moment you'll remember you told Fischer here some time ago where your husband had gone. Isn't that right, Fischer?'

The man nodded acquiescently.

'Speak up!' Albrecht commanded.

'Yes, she told me,' the man said. 'It was Switzerland he went to.'

'Just so!' Albrecht said, and then addressed himself to me again: 'You see, I've taken a lot of trouble to get hold of this man—and the Captain here. I've brought them to assist your memory.'

I scarcely heard him. I was thinking, 'Surely my dealings with this Fischer are over—surely this is a battle I fought and lost long ago.'

'I know you don't wish to remember,' he pursued, with a new hardness in his voice. 'But I'm tired of that—people using forgetfulness as a smoke-screen, running away from their responsibilities. There comes a time when they've got to face the truth about themselves—themselves, and what others have had to pay for their evasions.'

That sententious speech—which I think I have recorded with sufficient exactness—sounded as if he had rehearsed it, but nothing in the cold voice suggested a hollow rhetoric. For myself, I did not need his warnings: the person of Fischer, sitting as he had always sat in these dreaded interviews with his podgy hands on his spread knees, would alone have convinced me there was to be no play-acting here; no compunction for a sick woman's weakness; no possible escape.

'Now let's get on with it!' Albrecht said. He was speaking to Fischer again, as if to a servant (and one he did not trust). 'I want to hear Frau Schechter's answers to your questions.'

'The questions, yes!' Fischer said hastily; and for a moment I had the notion that he himself was being driven back to a duty he was tired of. To me he said mechanically, 'I've got to ask you once more—where is your husband *now*?'

And just as automatically I answered, 'I've told you, over and over again, I simply don't know.'

At this he pulled his chair a little nearer to me—it was what he always did, he was a man of stereotyped behaviour. He said:

'You know very well that isn't true.'

I repeated: 'I've told you—I've no idea where my husband is now.'

What did it matter! I knew it all, the exhausting battle-dore-and shuttlecock of reiterated questions and empty replies. I knew, as well, that in this merciless engagement I was matched not merely against a stubborn policeman but against the whole invincible machinery of political investigation.

'I must ask for your serious attention!'

How familiar was that phrase, uttered quite vacantly, how invariable the way my inquisitor stretched his hairy neck, much as a threatening goose does, to bring his sallow face still closer to mine and a whiff of schnapps to my nose. He had a hand inside his coat, and now, with the histrionic flourish of a third-rate actor, he produced a sheaf of *Helstadts-anzeigers*—no doubt the ones which Albrecht had shown me already.

'This is one of your husband's publications, is it not? You've seen these articles by a person called Langke?'

I said, 'Yes, you've shown them to me before.'

'Don't quibble! I'm asking if you read them when they came out.'

'Very likely I did.'

'And you approved of them?'

'As I said before, I don't remember. It was nothing to do with me, what appeared in my husband's papers.'

'But you knew they were subversive articles?'

'I didn't think about it—it was none of my business.'

'But it was your husband's?'

'In a sense I suppose it was.'

'*In every sense!*' He had reached that stage of puerile anger where the eyes seem to dilate and the lips to whiten. 'There's no "suppose" about it!'

'No?'

'Your husband arranged the printing of this seditious poison—you know perfectly well he did. And then he ran away, like any Jew would. He couldn't face the consequences. And so long as you cover up for him you're just as much a traitor as he is.'

The man himself must have known that this was vaporous bombast; indeed, he had then the manner of a child practising a recitation with a prompter at his elbow. Yet I was frightened now. For one's fears are seldom wholly rational, they come from the haunting menace of dark avenues, from submerged memories, the mere shape or smell of things which long ago brought pain or humiliation. I had no one on my side. And while I was searching for some answer to my persecutor there came to my ears from the other end of the room a voice I associated with surrender:

'But what for? I've told you already what she did.'

That was said in a whisper; and the answer which came from Albrecht was only partly audible: 'Look, I haven't brought you here for amusement.' Then, '... or else I send your own dossier to the Department of Justice.'

All this time I had been just conscious of the person standing by the door, and in reminiscence it seems that long before he spoke I had been awaiting his intervention: certainly it came as an expected thing, the sound of that peculiar voice, derived from the old Cadet Schools but distinguished by a mannered slurring of the consonants; and though, to me, the accent was not outlandish (since the young officers I had known in my girlhood had all affected it) the curious lisp infused it with menace. The fellow who had been trying to bludgeon me into submission was one of circumscribed intelligence; not so the lean and wanly handsome man who came, now, to stand beside him. He too surprised me by his colouring—in the wavering candlelight it looked as if his blond hair had suddenly turned to silvergrey—but otherwise I noticed little change; here as always were the languid, slightly foppish airs of a spoilt cavalryman, the thin, covertly humorous mouth, the feminine brows surmounting vagrantly inquisitive eyes; and when he said pleasantly, 'Well, Frau Dr Schechter, we resume our little talks!' I felt as if there had been no more than a brief intermission.

It came to me naturally, then, to answer much as I had done on earlier occasions: 'Herr Hauptmann von Kleinen, I've told your agent here that I have no information to give about my husband. Really it's quite useless—'

He cut me short: 'Oh, but Herr Fischer is not my agent! We don't even belong to the same organisation. He's concerned with security matters—that is so, Herr Fischer?—while my business is simply to give what help I can to people who find themselves in special difficulties because of political developments.'

I answered with bare civility, 'That is what you've always told me.'

My coldness seemed to take him by surprise; he blinked, showing a faint embarrassment, and half turned his head as if he sought some new direction. Fischer meanwhile sat still, relaxed, like a mastiff called to heel by its master; Albrecht too was motionless, but I had an impression that he was closely watching the other men, as if they were a pair of athletes under his training. Again I had forgotten how I came to know him; and one of my inner voices kept saying, 'He shouldn't be here, this Albrecht Weckerlin. This part of my life is no concern of his, he doesn't belong to this place or occasion.'

Patiently, and as though with some reluctance, Kleinen began again. 'Whatever you may say, Frau Schechter, I believe in many ways you and I understand each other. We come, after all, from the same part of the country—at one time we probably had many friends in common. I should say we were brought up with much the same outlook on public affairs—perhaps a rather narrow one. And having some intelligence we've both, I suppose, become a good deal less provincial in our views since then. For example—'

'If you're talking of anti-Semitic prejudice,' I said, wearily, 'we've obviously moved in opposite directions.'

He showed no impatience, only a faint distress. 'Now wait a minute—I think you're taking rather too simple a view! I myself have no anti-Semitic feelings—quite the contrary. I merely think that our Jewish friends have a certain romanticism in their outlook which often makes it difficult to fit them into the realities of the European situation. For instance, if one takes a perfectly objective view of those articles in the *Helstadtsanzeiger*—'

There I tried to stop him, saying, 'Herr Hauptmann, I am not going to discuss my husband's professional affairs with you or anyone else.' But he was not to be suppressed.

'Listen!' he said. 'I perfectly understand your feelings, and I have the greatest respect for Herr Dr Schechter's personal integrity and professional brilliance. But I must remind you that the most gifted men can make errors in judgement. My own view is that he should have sought authoritative guidance before publishing those articles. Of course you won't agree with that. But I think you must realise now that he made a serious mistake in going abroad—surreptitiously—just after the publication. It was tantamount to a confession that he had *knowingly* acted against the national interest. You see what I mean?'

I had heard it all before, and I knew there was some faulty reasoning in that specious pronouncement. But I was in no condition to open a debate. I said nothing.

He went on: 'You see, we're constantly up against this kind of thing in dealing with the Jewish temperament. Well, you must have run into the same sort of trouble yourself—our Jewish friends have marvellous gifts, and remarkable virtues, but they're congenitally secretive. They make some bold move—relying simply on their intuitions—and then they lose their nerve and run away, leaving other people to face the consequences.'

His voice had become gentler, more confidential, and now in a fatherly way he put a hand very lightly on my arm.

'If only Dr Schechter hadn't gone,' he said, 'I believe all this trouble could have been cleared up in an hour's conversation. As things are—as he isn't here to answer questions—the security people are bound to react unfavourably.' He looked sidelong at Fischer, with apparent distaste. 'All they can do is bring their whole pressure to bear on his closest connections—in other words, to make things intolerable for you.'

I, in turn, glanced at Fischer, whose face showed only the sulky boredom of a child retained in school: no, it was not that lacquey who troubled me now. Soon, in utter weariness, I let my eyelids fall and sank into a physical quiescence which nearly resembled sleep; but I still felt the kneading pressure of Kleinen's fingers, and there was no escape from his insidious voice as he patiently developed his familiar theme—the need to persuade my husband, for his own good, to return and clear up the misunderstanding between himself and the authorities.

'... The letter must come from you. You can give him my personal assurance that he takes no risk of any sort in returning here for consultations—but naturally he won't accept that unless it's you who tell him.... It must be in your own words, of course. You must tell him of the friendly conversations you've had with me, and that I personally represent the Department for Press Affairs. You must make it absolutely plain that there's no danger of any sort in his returning. He will be treated with every consideration—we simply want to talk things over and arrive at a rational solution....'

Yes, even with my mind almost closed I knew this man was lying; but one may reach a state of exhaustion where the difference between truth and falsehood seems hardly to matter. That tireless voice had the quality of vulgar music; as if, lying in a sickbed, one heard incessantly the sound of a street organ—a single tune in a key which galls the ear, a beat as crude and relentless as the thud of a printing press. The tone grew more and more insistent, the phrases altered but their burden was always the same: a letter: a letter had to be written: I must send a letter to my husband begging him to come home without delay, for my sake and for that of his own reputation. Like a physical pain this merciless re-iteration brought with it a sense of infinity; I saw myself as a city whose entire history was of hostile encirclement, one which having long since capitulated was again besieged and for ever under fire. How long in fact that night's attrition lasted I have no means to tell; but I remember how, when my nerves at last gave way, I uttered a cry which barely escaped the onset of tears:

'I want to sleep! Why won't you let me sleep!'

My appeal should have moved a Torquemada; it did win

me a few moments' respite, in which I was conscious of the men whispering together. But the question came once more: 'Listen, Frau Schechter—when are you going to write that letter?' And it was then, without will or reflection, that I found myself hurling back an answer:

'I've done it already! You know I have!'

The convulsive agony of that admission gave way to darkness; I believe that Kleinen's hands saved me from falling out of my chair. In the last moments of awareness I heard, as if from far away, a different voice of his, a blend of servility and truculence: 'Is that enough for you?' and Albrecht's laconic answer, 'It will do.'

Above the mists which drifted through my mind as it returned to wakefulness one truth was visible: at some time in the past I had given in to these jackals, at their dictation I had written a letter of spurious confidence which could bring Josef into the gravest danger. But with this knowledge was confused my lingering fancy that he was due home that night. In consequence I imagined that at any instant I should hear the familiar sounds of his arrival, and as soon as he entered the house the trap these men had prepared for him would close. With the thought of such catastrophe came a terror like that of fire. Inert as I seemed to be, I was ready to struggle to the window and scream a warning to keep him away.

The conceit belonged only to the first movements of recovered consciousness; as the inward haze dissolved I realised it was founded in illusion.

When I opened my eyes a new candle was burning, but to little purpose—nothing but a lean corona surrounded its flame. In the pale, uniform illumination of earliest morning the room might have been a different place from the pattern of light and darkness which had framed the hours of questioning. The faces had receded. With a cigarette drooping from his underlip the agent Fischer, now visibly of a sort whose modest gifts earn miserable wages, was kneeling to re-tie a bootlace. The Captain, resting with his seat propped against the writing-table, was smoking too, but without the appearance of relaxation: observing him afresh, I saw that he was a creature of poor physique, with a hollow chest and match-stick legs, that his clothes had a makeshift, war-time look. These were small men, suited to the drab reality of a court-room where the case is over, of the operating theatre when the patient has been wheeled away. Albrecht alone, though white and heavy-eyed, was undiminished in presence. As far away from me as the room allowed he stood grasping his lapels, chin lowered, feet slightly apart; his mouth was shaped as if he were faintly smiling at some distant memory, but there was nothing light-hearted in the glance he gave me—retrospectively I see him as a hunter about to despatch, with cool compunction, some small animal which his hounds have caught and torn. For the rest, I seemed to be a thing these people were no longer much concerned with: they were male beings, by nature interested in the machinery of action, with little time for anything so incomputable as human feeling.

The first daylight as it takes possession of a house is colourless, it projects no falsifying shadows, dissolves the stubbornest illusions. In the past hours the bareness and disorder of the room had come to seem normal; now the symptoms of dilapidation, faded paintwork, stained and peeling walls, spoke even to an intelligence as dulled as mine of some larger happening than a brief invasion by soldiers or builders' men. It was first the men's faces that led towards enlightenment, insinuating that the long winter in my mind had blinded me to the passage of time outside. Starkly revealed, this face of Kleinen was not the one I knew; the lymphatic eyes which appeared to have slipped in their sockets, the crimped forehead, a fringe of grey on the lavishly bolstered chin, revealed more flagrantly than his grizzled hair a disconnection between the man who had just been plaguing me and the one who, long before, had done so with the same arguments, almost in the selfsame words. Were they in truth one person? Because I had been living in a private world I failed to see the reason for this incongruity. Fleetingly I thought the night's ordeal had been hallucination, but in Fischer's nervous coughing, in the looks and smells one associates with long, crowded journeys, there was nothing of fantasy. I found myself watching Albrecht's face again, and here was change of another kind, brought not by time but (as it appeared) by a ripening of his mood. *'I'm tired of your forgetfulness'*: some such words he had used in committing me to an insensate persecution, and then, *'These men may help you to remember things.'* Now I was near to understanding both his bitter purpose and his arduous contrivance; how, to bring me to self-judgement, he had made me live a second time through the cruel hours I had sought to obliterate. In effect he had cut an opening for reality to enter with the force of a dammed stream, sweeping away the wretched structure which had served so long to make the hopeless days seem bearable to me.

It is not a simple or easy passage, crossing from a region the fugitive mind has fashioned to one ruled by actualities: it compares with the feel of emerging from some kinds of anaesthesia—a hollow uproar in the ears, a light like a distant firework rising in the cavernous darkness, discovering fluid shapes which turn to familiar things, (the white pavilion framing a nurse's head, a red explosion of tulips, the furrowed hillside where your legs are entombed), objects that slowly coalesce to restore the intelligible world till nothing is left of the abyss behind you but its enormous pain. From the dull traffic which surrounded my awakening, that early morning, one spectacle remains in vivid focus: I see the door slowly opening and a small figure, that of Berta's child, standing there in a skimpy nightgown, her knees bent inward, bare feet wide apart; with her thumb, as always, between her teeth, she slowly turns her eyes to absorb the scene that offers, exhibiting a curiosity untroubled by intelligence. 'How,' I thought, 'could I ever have taken this sorry bantling for my own child, even if the emptiness which separates me from Ruth's image has expanded from days to years!' Perhaps it was that reflection which first made real to me the distance I had travelled as a sightless exile. But the child herself was far from the centre of my attention. Among the thoughts which overran my mind like an invading army, marching with alien music and derisive flags through broken and deserted streets, one grew dominant, as if it were a notice of my own execution: that I need no longer strain my ears to catch the first sounds of Josef's return. For at last I realised what I had done with the precious core of my existence; that long ago I had surrendered him to murderers, that I was not to feel his hands or hear his voice again.

I had presumed that at least when Albrecht's puppets were dismissed I should be spared another bout of cross-examination. That was too sanguine. As tufts of smoke continue breaking from an exhausted fire his questions pursued me long after he had manifestly achieved his purpose.

'But you knew Kleinen was lying?'

'I suppose so.'

'And you knew the letter he made you write was meant to bring Josef within his reach?'

'I suppose I must have.'

'You didn't even wait to see Josef if he came home?'

'No.'

'Or try to warn him? Or to get help from his friends?'

'I was frightened.'

'What—you thought you'd be arrested too?'

'I was frightened.'

'So you solved all your problems by running away?'

'Yes, I was frightened, so I ran away.'

But this harrying did not deeply trouble me; for such shock and humiliation as I had suffered will presently benumb one's moral sensibility. We were in the car again, passing through a shallow combe where loaded pear trees stood among the stubble: I can imagine the lovely variations of pale yellow and gold which other eyes would have seen there, but to me the countryside was colourless, as in a photograph. Not that I looked much to left or right; my body was like a sack of corn dumped on the seat.

'In your heart of hearts,' Albrecht said, 'you were angry with your husband for being so stubborn. That was how Sara saw it. You thought what happened to him was all his own fault because he wouldn't temporise—because he wouldn't listen to your advice.'

I let that pass.

'The truth,' he insisted, 'is that you thought he should defer to you because of your social status. You felt that as a Jew he was under a special obligation to a woman of Junker lineage who'd condescended to become his wife.'

Yes, in those two sentences he affected to draw the pattern of my marriage with Josef; as if the elements encompassing the life we had shared—my family's reproaches supporting my mother's rancorous opposition, the struggle to acclimatise myself to traditions incongruous with mine, a faint continuing current of distrust which all Josef's goodness could not entirely dispel and which vanished only in our climaxes of passion—could all be traced and rendered in a simple diagram. What use to argue! I only said:

'I expect your wife had interesting theories about her brother and me.'

At least I had lost all fear of him. His determination to make me suffer in return for what he had suffered—as if my responsibility for Josef's fate made me somehow chargeable for Sara's as well—had previously turned this single-minded man into a figure of prodigious menace; now, in the afterglow of his easy victory, I saw him in his natural proportions: a creature of nimble intelligence but of no moral stature, a tenacious meddler who would always prosper in some employment which needed no largeness of mind, only a fretful application. He showed, I think, no more than the common curiosity of little men when he questioned me, some

214

way farther on, about what I had done after my flight from home:

'Where did you go to? How did you live?'

In my weariness I found no answer which would convey reality to an understanding so circumscribed, so masculine as his. I said apathetically, 'There were jobs I could do—hotels take anyone for kitchen work, they don't ask questions. That was at a place near Stargard, and afterwards in Bremen. Then we were bombed—I had to be dug out from a cellar. Then I was drafted into munitions. And later on I was a sort of Putzfrau for the Americans.'

'So you were always busy?' he said flatly, as if interviewing me for further employment.

'Yes, nearly always.'

'With no time to think of Josef? Or your children?'

So senseless a question could not be treated seriously. Instead, I used off-hand a dictum of Herr Oestmann's which alighted in my mind. 'No one would complain of hell,' I said, 'if it gave you no time to think of things.'

For a while that silenced him, but later on he pressed me again about the children: had I simply left them, making no provision? This further scrutiny took place in a village of heavily timbered houses where we had stopped for some repair to the car; to Albrecht it made no difference that a bearded engineer lay immediately beneath us singing artless ballads in a lavish baritone, while an audience of inquisitive old men and toddlers crowded about us, even flattening their faces against the windows.

'You didn't stop,' he pursued, 'to wonder what would become of Felix and Ruth? Or what their feelings would be when they found themselves alone in the house?'

His fresh assault waked in my mind a picture far more vivid than the ring of bucolic faces in my field of actual vision: I saw, as I had seen them on the dreadful night of my departure, Ruth's pillowed cheek and forehead, moonlit, as she slept in childish tranquillity, and as if in the same frame I saw Felix's smile, unnaturally mature, shaped by a calm

215

affection. ('Yes, Mutti, I understand,' he had gravely told me. 'We'll wait and do what Tanti Gertrud says.') What, of that agony, could I convey to the stolid examiner at my side, while the voice from the car's bowels, chanting, *'Mädchen, die mit keuschen Trieben. Nur den braven Burschen lieben,'* seemed to swamp the glass box which contained us?

I said, 'They weren't alone. There was a governess, and other servants.'

'So you left it to servants to do what you were frightened of doing—to protect your own children?'

I started trying to explain how things had been—how highly placed friends had secretly advised me to make myself scarce for a few weeks only—but the mechanic's voice obliterated mine. *'Männern, die das Herz uns rühren,'* he roared, *'Uns den Pfad der Weisheit führen.'* In a gust of impatience Albrecht gripped my shoulder, forcing me to look him in the face.

'Is that what you did?'

'I telephoned to an old friend, one I trusted. I asked her to go as soon as she could and take the children to her own home. She promised she would.'

'And did she?'

His words, in turn, were almost lost as the maddening singer came to a fresh climax of emotion: *'Wo sich Brüder froh umarmen. In dem Hain Elysiums.'* I had to wait for a momentary lull in which to make my simple reply:

'I heard—afterwards—that she got there too late.'

I think this statement, sounding in my own ears as dispassionate and final as the dates on a tombstone, put an end at last to the unconscionable trial; I know that in making it I felt a certain relief, as one who had reached the limits of moral nakedness. Yet paradoxically that feeling had no relation to anyone who might have overheard my ultimate admission. The judgement of Albrecht had ceased to count. Among the clustering villagers I retain a sharp impression of an armless man leaning across the car's bonnet to stare at me brazenly through the windscreen, of another whose birdlike

216

eyes, closely hooded by the peak of an ancient military cap, were pointed like arrows at my face; but these I saw as if, from a long way off, I watched them through a giant telescope; for the world those people lived in—of gossip and ritual chaff, of common affection and instinctive understanding—was one I could never return to. I remember how the midday sun, emerging suddenly from a bank of cloud, lit the street as if a battery of lamps had come on at the turn of a switch, and how as the light poured on to my own cheek and neck my body still felt like a block of ice.

Farther on, where the road was carried on a lofty viaduct, I roused myself so far as to ask Albrecht where he was taking me. He answered:

'Why—to Wilpenschoen. Isn't that where you wanted to go?'

Although that name was perfectly familiar I could not bring my mind to bear on where it was or what it meant to me. This, however, was of no importance. Hell is borderless. There was no imaginable reason for me to be in one place rather than another.

4

On the day of my return to Coenraad's Lodge I went for some small purpose to the still-room, where I found Mejuffrouw Potgieter weighing out minute portions of butter-substitute. As I stood near the door, swaying a little (for at that time my legs still felt like thin canes), she tilted her eyes and perhaps a quarter of her mind towards me. 'Oh, Fräulein Leezen,' she said, 'I'd be glad if you'd have a look at Rosa Kossuth—she's supposed to be turning out the recreation-room. She does nothing unless some older person is there to keep her at it.'

Surprised by this greeting after my long absence, I could think of nothing to say, except, 'I should like you, please, to call me Frau Dr Schechter in future. That is my real name.'

'As you wish, Fräulein Leezen!' she answered, and went on with her weighing.

In so far as I had any feelings then, I was grateful for that somewhat uneffusive welcome: in those days the last thing I wanted was ceremony or emotion; my only solace lay in familiar patterns—in objects found where you expected them, the narcotic of a dull routine. The white collar and cuffs, neatly darned and admirably laundered, of Mejuffrouw Potgieter's brown serge dress, her flat Friedland voice, the grey down on her high cheeks and pointed chin, together presented an appearance of immutability—you could neither picture her in girlhood nor imagine her enfeebled by old age. Perhaps the military straightness of her shoulders had slightly relaxed, perhaps I should have noticed then—as I was to realise later—that the eyes were slightly filmed with weariness, that the busy hands had lost a little of their certainty. But even now I think of her as I think of a rock which towered above the village where I had spent my childhood, dominating the landscape, indestructible. If, at that encounter in the still-room, I had told her the truth about myself—'See, Mejuffrouw Potgieter, here is a woman who betrayed her husband and deserted her children'—I believe those words would hardly have stirred her. 'That,' she might have said, 'is no concern of mine. There is nothing in the House Rules about betrayal or desertion.'

Yes, when I re-entered that small, populous kingdom I found it at least a place of safety, as a dungeon or tomb would have been. The corridors in which a ceaseless hubbub swelled and rebounded, the linoed staircase where colliding draughts mingled the kitchen smells with those of over-crowded bedrooms, were like the clothes you unearth for a rustic holiday, yielding the comfort of long use, a sense of irresponsibility. As for my fellow-inmates, they were as little stirred as the housekeeper by my return—only one or two seemed to have noticed I had been away. Their minds were occupied by more momentous business.

'Of course Elena's just an awful fibber. It couldn't be true, could it, what she says about that thing of Teresa's!'

Those allusive words, uttered in a flush of giggles by Rosa Kossuth as she rested her unwieldy trunk on the handle of her mop, were probably the first I heard on the subject of Teresa Voltesova's opal pendant. I cannot have shown much interest, but Rosa was never acutely sensitive to the feelings of her audience. She chattered on:

'I mean, it does seem rather queer. I mean, Anna Wiedlich did ask her—the first time Teresa had it on she said, "Oh, Teresa, where did you get that gorgeous thing?" and Teresa seemed as if she didn't understand, and then she started crying.'

Soon I found this topic pervading the house as the smell from a brewery will filter through the streets all round. It seemed that wherever I sat at meals two girls would be talking across me in those theatrically furtive tones which afford as much concealment as barège.

'You heard what Elena said!'

'That isn't true—it can't be!'

'Well, Elena heard it in the camp they were in—from a woman who'd known Teresa for years and years. And then Gabriele says she saw a photo—it fell out when Teresa was making her bed—and it looked like her doing just what Elena said.'

'You mean—?'

'Well, of course! And have you seen the drawing Anna's done? Oh, you should! She keeps it in her belt, she's terrified Ludmilla might see it—you know what Ludmilla's like about Teresa! Of course it's an awful picture—Anna can't draw for nuts. But it really is rather good—it does show just what Teresa must have looked like doing it, if she really did.'

Some of the women taking part in those harmonious exchanges were recent arrivals, but because the ethos of the Lodge gave a certain sameness to its shifting population I felt as if I knew them all. The subject of their conversation was probably in the middle thirties, a creature one distinguished from half a dozen others by the extreme emaciation of her body and the many rats' tails in which she wore her sparse, grey-yellow hair; of her face, all I can recall is the damp, protuberant eyes, those of a backward child. I saw just once the pendant which had prompted so much speculation; it might have come from any tourist shop, but the large blue stone did give the impression of opulence, the more remarkable when seen against the drabness of her dress. Someone had asked—perhaps with kindly interest—how she had come by this trinket, and she, equipped with no more than a few lame words in either Dutch or German, had made a confused reply; this had led to the rumour (of a sort common in our society) that she had stolen it from a fellow-refugee, and when that was angrily denied by her compatriot Ludmilla Schiborska the way was open for the more ornate theory, launched by Elena Kral, that during the wartime occupation of Slovakia she had danced naked before Gauleiter Heydrich and received the pendant as reward.

Did anyone believe that legend? In the boundless vacuum which expatriates inhabit there is room for every dramatic invention, and fables, like climbing weeds, grow strong and solid as they spread. 'I'd have thought that Heydrich would be more particular,' an old Magyar woman said bleakly. 'For men, surely, you need some sort of figure.' But the mere fact that Teresa was increasingly morose, and would burst into tears when she came on one of Anna's ribald drawings, was taken by the mindless as convicting evidence. In the swarming barracoons where many of our number had previously been quartered a peculiar blight withers the human sensibilities, and for those conditioned to feline amusements Teresa, limp, innocuous, lachrymose, was a natural quarry. Her friend Ludmilla's strident patronage appeared to add some piquancy to their sport; in which, with trivial variations, the procedure was always the same.

'But where's Teresa today?' someone would ask, in Ludmilla's hearing, at a meal when Teresa was not in her usual place; to be answered by an outwardly demure Romanian at the far end of the table:

'Perhaps she's gone to her dancing lesson.'

A ripple of laughter ran along the line of heads like a breeze through standing corn. That was enough. Instantly Ludmilla was on her feet, with her massive fists clenched above her shoulders.

'All of you are great dirty sows in a filthy pig-house,' she proclaimed in her own rendering of Standard Dutch. 'You, Gheorghia, you have a pimply face and you do not wash your underclothes.'

'What's all this noise?' Mejuffrouw Potgieter demanded, coming in from the kitchen. 'What's the matter?'

That was a cue for Anna Wiedlich. 'Matter? Nothing, Mejuffrouw. Ludmilla Schiborska says Teresa's staying in bed today while she washes her smalls.'

'That is one big bastard lie!' Ludmilla announced. And fortune seemed to be on her side, for at that moment Teresa herself arrived. 'See there, my friend is not in bed at all, and she is wearing all her clothes!'

In the wake of her conspicuous triumph came a few seconds' calm, ruffled only by the voice of Elena chanting softly, as if in private devotion, ' "*Alas for her, poor maiden, her dancing days are done.*" ' But now the lumpish Rosa was moved to take a hand:

'Ludmilla, is it true that in Moravia you wear riding-boots for dancing?'

Ludmilla pounced again: 'You're stupid—you're nothing but a jack-ass girl! Of course we take off our riding boots when we dance. Everybody! Always!'

'What was that?' Anna asked. 'I didn't hear.'

'Ludmilla says that in Moravia they take off everything for dancing.'

'What—their pendants too?'

It was time for Mejuffrouw Potgieter to intervene: 'That's enough! You're all talking very impolitely.'

The reproof seemed to be effective: Elena gave her a startled, shamefaced glance, then lowered her eyes. 'But we do want to learn,' she said humbly, 'about other countries. I mean, things like when they wear their riding-boots.' She leant once more towards Ludmilla, to remark with studied gravity, 'I suppose there was a lot of difference between the Protectors your country had in the War. They say Herr Heydrich was nicer, really, than Herr Frick.'

Involuntarily I looked at the big Slovak girl, and saw her neck and shoulders tighten as if from an electric charge. She said, with her voice barely under control, 'Frick? "Nicer than Frick"? What is the difference—you tell me—between such German swine!' Then, her eloquence exhausted, she turned to her compatriot. 'You hear that, Teresa? Elena says that Heydrich was a nice man!'

Pronounced with vitriolic loathing, the name Heydrich was enough to rouse Teresa from the torpid state which generally gave her some protection. She said excitedly, 'Heydrich? What do they know about that fiend incarnate!'

Someone murmured, just audibly, 'Only that he gave nice bijoux to his popsies.' Then came the voice of Gheorghia, low, rich, a trifle saccharine: 'Do tell us, Teresa, what he was like when a person really knew him?'

Again Ludmilla leapt to her feet, thumping the table as she did so, crying, 'You, Romanian sow, shut your dirty jaw!' But by then Teresa, with her knuckles pressed into her forehead, was stumbling out of the room.

Among the older residents were some who tried spasmodically to quell this persecution. I myself must have been alive to its cruelty, but I made no protest. To preach, to indulge in moral gestures, is a privilege of the innocent. As far as I could tell, the truth about my history was still unknown at Wilpenschoen; in reason there was nothing to prevent my crying out, *'Why do you make that sad and helpless creature the object of your spite! How can you invent such senseless lies, adding to the misery of one more wretched than yourselves!'* But in imagination I could hear a crushing riposte: *'And you, Johanna Schechter, have you always stood firm against injustice? In the case, for example, of the man you married? The hell your defenceless children endured, was that nothing to do with you?'* No, I could no longer see myself as foreign to this community, living outside and above its bleak deformities. Before, I had clung to the remembrance that at least I was the daughter of an able and highly regarded soldier, from which it seemed to follow that only some malign conspiracy had brought me to so desolate a place. That comfort was extinct. For a while I nursed a hope that I should return to my former state—that my mind, crippled by the load of memories, would once more stoop and let them fall away. But such deliverance was not to come a second time. By degrees I saw that this house, devoid of every loveliness, peopled by the derelicts of Europe, was to be the permanent frame of my existence. Here, while my body remained alive, I should make a pretence of living; swallowing the tasteless food, watching from a small bed the passing of interminable nights; fearfully guarding the real facts about myself; waiting through year after year of stagnant loneliness for the final darkness to fall.

I shared a third-floor room with an elderly woman from a Russian labour camp. To occupy my hands I took on more domestic work than in my previous sojourn. In the Superintendent's office I was no longer needed, since the jobs I had done there were in the hands of one Lore Schutze, a Viennese girl of signal intelligence. That accorded with my own wishes. In my new situation I had no desire to mix with people of superior status; least of all to pursue my former association with such a person as Mijnheer Dekker, as if I pretended to a probity like his.

Someone told me that this Lore Schutze, for defying a Gestapo lieutenant, had suffered seventeen months of solitary confinement at Haugsberg. I should not have guessed that from her appearance: in her delicately sculptured face the marriage of perceptive eyes with a supple, feminine mouth suggested one too pliant, too humorously wise, to have been involved in the violence of our day. The first time I saw her she was coming out of the room which I myself had formerly shared with Tilka Zamoyska. The open-hearted smile she offered as we passed was enough to show me that here was a woman distinct from most of my fellow-inmates, in intellect and charity. And yet I took pains to keep at a distance from her; for I knew that any conversation between us must soon lead to the subject I was most anxious to avoid.

A vain design! Inevitably the day came when, at supper, the place beside mine was empty and when Lore arrived in the dining-room a little late. As soon as I caught sight of her I sensed that she had seen the vacant chair and was wondering if she could bear to sit next to a person so unpromising as a near-elderly woman, devoid of physical charm, who never smiled and scarcely spoke to anyone. Her hesitation was but

224

momentary. As if I had beckoned her she flashed her smile at me and then, holding her plate of soup high as waiters do, and with a grace that just a few women achieve in crowded rooms, steered her thin-boned body to my side.

'Is this place being kept for anyone?'

'No. No, I don't think so.'

She sat down. I still hoped that instead of talking to me she would occupy herself with the Slovene on her other side, a youngish man of engaging courtesy who (apart from a foolish intermittent belief that he was St Augustine) was gifted with a fine intelligence as well as learning. But no, it was my attention she gently demanded.

'Mijnheer Dekker was telling me you used to do the office work which I've taken on—you were his confidential secretary.'

I uttered a quiet contradiction: 'Oh, I only filed letters, that sort of thing. I couldn't do it now—my sight was better then.'

My off-hand tone should have discouraged her, but she was one whose natural warmth seems to cancel the coldness of others. 'All the same, you must think me rather a usurper!' she said lightly. 'Because I'm in the room you used to sleep in too.'

To which I answered briefly, 'Really, where I sleep doesn't matter to me at all.'

That was a shallow statement; and suddenly the curiosity which had tormented me since my return to the Lodge became too powerful for further restraint. It was I, then, who introduced Tilka's name. 'There was a young Polish woman —Mme Zamoyska,' I said, preserving a show of detachment. 'She and I used to share that room.'

Lore nodded. 'Why, yes—I sent you a letter from her.' Then, 'She is still there, in the other bed. But not for long, I'm afraid. She's very weak now.'

The news that Tilka was alive, which I had both dreaded and longed for, had the effect of suspending my power to swallow—I had actually to empty my mouth into a hand-

225

kerchief, and to leave untouched the rest of what was on my plate. Lore, I think, must have seen and in some sense understood my malaise, for she did then turn to Dr Sesnik, and for a while remained in conversation with him. Only after giving me ample time to recover did she speak to me again:

'You know, of course, that you're free to go to your old room whenever you like?'

'Thank you,' I said.

'I mean—if you'd like to visit Tilka, I know she's longing to see you.'

I said, 'You're very kind, but I think I'd rather not—not at present. I'm not much use with sick people.'

It spoke well for Lore that she seemed to meet this childish evasion with equanimity; all she said was, 'Well, do let me know if you change your mind—if you want to see her at any time. Then I'll tell her you're coming.' From her easy tone one would have thought the question was neither urgent nor of any moral consequence.

In a curious way that ragged exchange seemed to relieve the bareness of the future: now I could tell myself, 'Possibly there is still some gleam ahead—an hour, perhaps, in which my existence will not be meaningless. Once my body feels well again I shall pay a visit to Tilka.' Yet I made no move to turn this prospect into reality. Was it merely that I feared what I might find—an unbearable spectacle of suffering, the terribly distorted image of a face I had loved? No, I think the larger hindrance was a dread of meeting her without my old disguise. There are those whose friendship will subsist on half truths, on comfortable pretences. Tilka had never been that kind of friend. If I meant to find my way to our old companionship I should need to tell her, to the last particular what sort of person I had lately found myself to be; and for the time I felt that such an ordeal would be harder to face than death itself—hers or mine.

Meanwhile I was not quite friendless. It was characteristic of

Dr Hofdijk that as soon as he heard of my return he asked where I was, and eventually found me sorting linen in the old coachhouse we used as laundry. I remember how a burst of sunlight seemed to fill that cheerless building when I looked up and saw his enormous figure filling the doorway, his big schoolboy face broken up with laughter.

'At last!' he trumpeted, as he came and put his hands on my shoulders. 'At last we have our dear Fräulein von Leezen in our midst again—to do all the chores the rest of us shrink from, to bring her German sense of order into this decrepit institution!'

Perversely, in the face of that genial greeting, my mind went back to a different encounter—to the implacable face of Albrecht, the sullen looks of his tame informers; and in a wave of shyness I answered with ridiculous formality:

'Goede morgen, Mijnheer Dokter. I must tell you that I am not really Fräulein von Leezen. That was a mistake—my memory was clouded by the War, and other things. I am really Frau Josef Schechter.'

But Hofdijk would have none of this grandiloquence. 'Then I as a seasoned widower shall take the liberty to call you Johanna,' he said boisterously. 'At my age I can't learn new names—and what is marriage but the mainspring of all social confusion! Now tell me—how are you, how have you been keeping? Give me a list of your current diseases and I'll look up the remedies as soon as I get home.'

His heartiness worked on me slowly. I told him very little at that meeting; but later on I did draw his attention to a rash on my cheeks and forehead, and thereafter he took a good deal of trouble over this complaint, giving me first one ointment and then another to try. Those consultations at least made a welcome diversion from the grey routine of the Lodge. Perhaps I did not entirely trust him—one could not be altogether blind to a professional strain in his bonhomie. But in a world so small as ours, so suffocatingly provincial, the panache he achieved with his florid ties and crimson waistcoat, his loud laugh and romping speech, his trailing

227

odour of cigar ash mixed with English soap, served to remind
me of less sterile ways of living, of experience at once more
vivid and more real than watching the languid passage of the
hours. For all his vernal ebullience Pieter Hofdijk was adult
in the way my friends at Tübingen had been—professors and
students alike. Inevitably I came to look forward to our short
encounters as a prisoner in close confinement must long for
the daily hour of exercise. I saw hardly anything of Mijnheer
Dekker, who seemed to have grown much older, more
impersonal, in my absence; so the doctor was the one person
I could talk to now and then on terms of equal understanding.

I was helping him one morning when he had to treat a
ulcer on a girl's neck—he liked to have someone standing by
to hand him instruments and to keep a kettle boiling. When
the patient had gone and we were tidying up he made
characteristic remark, at once frivolous and humane:

'Really it's a waste of time! Simply because that woman is
in Wilpenschoen when she longs to be in Buda she won't take
sensible nourishment, whatever I tell her. So she'll just go on
getting one ulcer after another.'

This prompted me to say, without reflection, 'Yes, Mijnheer Doktor, we're all a great nuisance to you, we foolish
females who can't reorganise ourselves.'

'Ah, but you, dear colleague, are altogether different!' he
answered, with a gallantry in which the note of persiflage was
barely audible. 'You follow my prescriptions with perfect
fidelity, with specialised intelligence. With what result? The
rash you complained of—vanished, gone for ever!'

Those words, spoken so easily, came as a shock to me. I
said, 'Gone? I wish it had!'

'But it *has* gone!' He was serious now. 'Haven't you seen
that for yourself?'

I said, 'I don't spend my time in front of a looking-glass.'

'No more do I! he rejoined. 'And yet I can tell you with
absolute assurance that I haven't a purple moustache.'

He had taken hold of my arm, and as he spoke he
228

propelled me towards a small glass on the wall.

'Now look!' he commanded. 'Do you see any rash at all?'

'No. But it's still there.'

'What on earth do you mean?'

'I can still *feel* it's there,' I said.

For a second I thought he would explode, with mirth or with indignation. But he controlled himself. 'I'm late,' he said, with a tactical glance at his watch, 'I should have been at the hospital half an hour ago. Look—I'll be in again on Monday, let us continue our researches then.'

In the event I did not see him on the Monday, and I think a week or more had passed when we met, again in the surgery. On this occasion he asked, when the work was done, if I would beg him a cup of coffee from 'Our Fairy Queen' (as he called Mejuffrouw Potgieter), and of course I quickly made it for him myself. He seemed to be more at leisure than usual; as he sipped the coffee he gossiped about Nicolaas Dekker, who he said had become sadly absent-minded and forgetful through overwork, then about various people who had been at the Lodge during my earlier time there. Still talking discursively, he said:

'There used to be more Jews than there are now. I suppose the way has cleared for quite a number to go back to their old homes and occupations.'

I said I had not noticed this difference.

'No? But I had the impression,' he said, 'that they used rather to get on your nerves.' And when I let that pass he continued tolerantly, 'At any rate you have fewer anxieties now—isn't that so? I think you used to be a little fanciful—you imagined this town was full of people planning to arrest you for some kind of political misdemeanour. Or simply for wearing a fashion in shoes they didn't care for!'

His tone was half-playful, touched with a semblance of affection; but it was startling to find that he, who appeared to concern himself so little with the real lives of those he met professionally, had learnt and remembered so much about my former state of mind. I had still nothing to say, and he took advantage of my silence to develop a sophistry of his own:

'Well, we grow out of such vagaries, we who boast an adult intelligence. Some of our physical bugbears too. That skin infection you were bothered with, I think it belonged to a period of readjustment. I claim no credit at all for curing it—the cure has come from your own good sense and resolution.'

The flaw in these blandishments was that the rash had not healed at all—invisibly it had been gaining ground. Now, guessing what his words implied, I felt a sudden resentment that he should presume to know more about my private interests than I did, and I found my voice trembling with stifled anger when I answered:

'Yes, of course you put all my troubles down to feminine fancies—you think I've never had any real reason to be frightened of anyone. You imagine—'

He started to protest: 'I wasn't suggesting anything like that. I only—'

'Listen!' I said fervidly. 'You know nothing—absolutely nothing—about my history. If you'd been with me on a journey I made not long ago, if you'd heard the charges brought against me—charges I couldn't answer, because they were true to the last detail—you wouldn't be saying now that all my old fears were nonsense! Oh, I'm not blaming you—I know this godforsaken hole is lined with hysterical women! But that's not to say we invent our misfortunes. It doesn't mean I've never had anything to be afraid of except what comes from my own stupid imagination!'

It brought me some relief, the delivery of that tirade. But anger depends on nourishment, and the face of Dr Hofdijk gave my indignation nothing to feed on. True, his expression of genial patronage had gone, but he wore in its place the looks of a patient judge receiving evidence—serious, humane. And having waited passively for my eloquence to peter out he said with a sad simplicity:

'So, there's no way I can help you—there's nothing to be done.'

He had put down his cup, I thought he was going to slip away. But now, impulsively, he faced me again, and with something like a lover's darting gentleness he took my wrists in his long, muscular hands.

'To you I'm a foreigner,' he said, 'and also a sort of official personage, because of my appointment in this place. So I can't expect you to confide in me—it wouldn't make sense. All the same, it hurts me—I feel it can only be harmful, bearing a load like yours entirely alone. I wish to God there was someone for you to confide in.'

Those last words, spoken almost harshly, were addressed rather to himself than to me. Already he had let go my arms, and now, to show the interview was over, he turned to pick up his things—the worn attaché-case in which he kept his tools, his huge green umbrella and Tirolean hat. So: he had not explicitly invited my confidence, and I was past the age when a sickness of the heart can be relieved by emotional scenes. Here, though, there was small risk of that indulgence. This room, with its pitch-pine chairs and cracked hand-basin, its radiator shuddering and thumping to promote a fitful current of tepid air, was not a place where you feared the indignity of sentimental tears; in the bald light from its high window one's natural talk was of practical affairs, and I could hardly have looked for a less emotional confidant than the sturdy pragmatist who was about to leave me. He had reached the door and opened it when I asked spontaneously:

'You're in a hurry?'

'Today—no,' he answered. 'My next patient is one who always gets on better without me.'

He shut the door again, put down his impedimenta and sat on the edge of the table. One cannot withstand such complaisance. I had yielded to instinct, and now I could only go where the current carried me.

'I think you'd better know the whole thing,' I said with resignation. 'I mean, the reason I don't fit in here. Or anywhere. Since you've been kind enough to show an interest in my worries.'

He shrugged his shoulders in the peculiarly Dutch way which means, 'I should be at your service if I knew how.' And to round off that gesture he took a carton of cigarettes from his pocket, put one between my lips and lit it.

'You had a husband,' he prompted. 'That much you've told me. And your marriage was not plain sailing—that I know, because marriage never is. Yes?'

'My husband's dead,' I said. 'He died during the War—probably at Dachau.'

'I see. And because his death was a monstrous tragedy you're troubled now by a sense of failure: you feel you could have done more for him in his lifetime—you could have given him greater happiness by taking more pains, making better use of your gifts. Is that how it is?'

I shook my head. 'That's the smallest part of it,' I said.

Then, because this man was at once so impartial and so *gemütlich*, I told him what my brother-in-law had zealously brought back to my memory. I related how, under inquisition, I had betrayed my husband to the hunters; how, in flight from the consequence of my own infamy, I had surrendered my two children as well. It was not done fluently: I passed at random from one fact to another, like a child displaying his toys. But I did control my voice—I might have been recounting the doings of some woman in whom I had only a transient interest. And I left nothing out.

Two or three times as I was speaking I dared to glance at Hofdijk's face; always he was listening with an air of rapt intelligence, as if I were reporting on some scientific experiment. When I had finished he said earnestly, 'Yes, you've been through a dreadful time. I appreciate your telling me. Now you must try to put the whole thing behind you.' Nothing more. I wondered, when he had gone, if he thought I had imagined the entire history, in the way that volatile adolescents do.

As to that, my doubts were presently satisfied. A day or so

later he sought me out in my room, where I was side-to-middling a worn sheet, and deposited his great body—as if at a picnic—on Sofya Pantaleyevna's bed. From that position of lazy comfort he ordered me to turn my face towards the window; then, instead of making any reference to the rash on my cheek, he said pensively:

'I wonder if you and I had the same sort of moral upbringing. It's not unlikely. My parents were disciples of Kuyper, my father's religion consisted mainly of a Calvinistic puritanism. So I was taught to examine the moral content of every tiny action, and it took me half a lifetime to get that melancholy way of thinking out of my system. Were you indoctrinated in the same fashion?'

I answered that I had been brought up a Catholic. Yes, my mother had been exceedingly strict with me.

He nodded, as if he had already seen that information printed in large letters on my forehead. 'And from such an education,' he said, 'we may suffer for years, setting ourselves a programme of virtue we can't possibly keep up with—because we happen to be neither saints nor fakirs. Nature has her own programme for ordinary people like you and me. Sometimes she requires us to overeat, or to drink too much, or to forsake the occidental man-made codes of chastity. There—now I've shocked you!'

I gave him some lame answer, to the effect that life would be shapeless if one merely followed one's instincts, making no distinction between good actions and bad.

'Why, yes, I agree!' he said lustily. 'We need certain principles to set our course by—the journey, as you say, would be mere vagabondage without them. Even so, a sensible traveller knows he won't get to his destination without making mistakes, wandering into blind alleys. Perhaps the trip would be rather a dull one if he did.'

It crossed my mind, as he said those words, that this tolerant, sagacious man would be a comfortable one to travel with. The lazy gestures, the eruptive laughter, were the outgrowth of a personality which multifarious experience had shaped and reason tempered. Moreover he himself would never stray too far from any course he had planned.

'At least,' he went on, 'we need to be realistic about our own limitations—to remember they're built into us. You get a soldier who fights with marvellous bravery all through a long campaign. Then some odd thing happens—the bursting of a stray shell nearby, the sight of a friend's arm dangling loose from the shoulder—and all the fear he's been refusing to recognise is suddenly released, he drops his rifle and runs. You can say then—in the strictest scientific sense—that his action is outside his own control. You see what I mean? But it's not only in fighting that such things happen. You and I have been conditioned by a highly developed civilisation—we were reared at a huge distance from primitive ways of living. Then in the middle of our lives all the things we'd learnt to depend on disappeared. You won't think me offensive if I say that in your country you had the first shock, and it must have been overpowering. You were used to a government—legislators, judges, police—which everyone could rely on for their protection. All of a sudden that was gone, the high places were taken over by a scum of beerhouse politicians, lunatic adventurers. To people of culture—people with a sense of their national inheritance—it must have seemed like a cosmic explosion. All the certainties of life had cracked and crumpled overnight.'

He paused and cocked an eyebrow, inviting my agreement. I nodded, though in truth what he said was little more to me than a string of phrases: the kind of language historians use seems to fit so loosely the history you've encountered at first-hand. Perhaps he saw my hesitation, for now he descended to simpler and more personal terms:

'Listen, dear lady! If you had lived at some other time you'd have been a woman of distinguished reputation—one noted for her goodness and wisdom. I'm certain of that, simply from knowing you as I do. But fortune treated you shamefully. You were brought to a desperate situation, it called for virtues you'd never cultivated because they'd never

234

before been needed. So of course you made wrong decisions, of course you failed to live up to your own exalted notions of honour and courage! A shattering failure—one that was bound to leave a permanent scar—but not, in sober truth, one you had any chance to avoid. I want you to believe that, because I speak from a scientific knowledge of how human beings behave under peculiar stresses. I'm not asking you to forget about the past—that's something you've tried already, with far from happy results. What I'm saying is that you must stop thinking of yourself as a guilty person. The idea of guilt is really a legacy from old-fashioned theology—something which sensible people have long since discarded. You—with your exceptional intelligence—you can discard it too.'

He had spoken with unwonted earnestness, but as he uttered those last words his smile returned, as if the growing heat of his sincerity were suddenly transformed into light. I saw he was trying to give me not counsel only but a measure of his own spirit—his resilience, his steadfast hold on realities, the informed assurance which kept him immune to common fears and griefs. And of course my heart responded. I wanted to accept the relief he offered, I realised how all my wretchedness would turn to tranquillity if once I learnt to see the past with a vision as dispassionate as his. Watching his seasoned face, the intensely sympathetic eyes, I felt a glowing gratitude.

But simultaneously I knew that for me there was no sort of truth in what he said.

You cling to life, when it has lost all purpose, simply because it is the one state you know; you school yourself to its increasing narrowness, its vacancy, as the great Belgian horses were schooled to plod almost unconsciously through our interminable Luneburger plough-lands. By mid-winter my routine had crystallised—kitchen work on Tuesdays, on Wednesdays laundry, other chores for each day in the week—and these pedestrian activities were enclosed in a padding of sensation which varied hardly at all. Every morning I was wakened by a chortling noise in the pipe above my bed—it brought the sterile information that Agatha Lange had arrived in the adjoining bathroom—and almost immediately my nose would pick up the herbal smell from Sofya Pantalayevna's first cigarette. In the passage leading to the dining-room I encountered with tedious regularity a goat-faced man who felt himself at liberty to squeeze my rump, crying in his high pseudo-Dutch, 'Hoe gaat 't? You German girls are thin these days!' At every hour I would hear when I passed the recreation room the same eerie cries from the communal radio, as Gheorghia Petrescu tried with uniform incompetence to bring in Bucharest. To say I found contentment in being tied to an endlessly revolving wheel would be absurd; but the monotony of that routine did become an anodyne, dulling the edge of insistent mental pain.

Such isolation is never secure where there are things like roads and telephones: sooner or later the domain I had forsaken was bound to make its signals heard in the one where I had taken refuge. A letter came, and presently another, from Luise, asking for my news. I briefly answered the second one, saying that my plans remained uncertain. Then one day in (I think) December the Superintendent arrived in the dining-room during the midday meal with an envelope which he ceremoniously laid beside my mug.

'For you, Frau Schechter!' he said with a shambling benevolence. 'I hope it may bring you good news.'

There was no precedent for this—as a rule incoming letters were put on a rack in the entrance hall. And when he hung about, plainly hoping to hear something of what the envelope contained, I was faintly offended by his curiosity; not less because it was blended with a kindly patronage. Having seen the Astelbrucke postmark I put the letter under my plate, to be read in private later on.

It came from Walther; and the carefulness of the shaky handwriting told me something of the heroic labour which must have gone into its composition. He wrote:

'Gnädiges Fräulein Johanna von Leezen!

'I venture to send you a brief letter, to express the hope that you are in good health and receiving benefit from the goodness of those people, happily known to myself also, who are managers of "Coenraad's Lodge". Also to tell you that here at Astelbrucke my good Wife and I greatly miss you, remembering the care you have always so graciously given us. We continue in our heartfelt gratitude to "Herr Franz Weckerlin" and his Wife for the home they have provided for us, also to "Fräulein Agnes Weckerlin", who gives much domestic help, but these young people have their time filled with many occupations, also it is not easy for such young people to completely understand the needs of a lady of many years such as my good Wife has become now, and who is accustomed in better times to high honour. My Wife is in fair health, but she no longer finds it easy to be patient with those surrounding her, not understanding why she cannot return immediately to her old home, with all its comfort and glory. For this reason I take the liberty to let you know that your return to Astelbrucke, whenever it is possible, will be much welcomed by my good Wife, and will call for the highest gratitude from myself. Because I venture to tell you, gnädiges Fräulein, that every day I am often in despair how to look after my good Wife with all her memories of the life of grandeur she used to have, and also her bodily ills. I send you on behalf of us both our most heartfelt wishes for your continued good health, and this expression of our hope that we may perhaps before the winter is much more advanced have the delight of finding you again beside us in this household.

'Believe me, gnädiges Fräulein, your very faithful and wellwishing old servant-friend,

Walther Stahl.'

That letter was meant, of course, simply as an appeal to

my supposed good nature. How astonished the old man would have been had he witnessed its catastrophic effect; had he realised how, at a stroke, it would demolish my sedative pretence that I could go on living as if in a different universe from his!

I read it sitting on my bed, alone, with a moan of trams from the Veerestraat and a charivari of foreign voices percolating the sparsely furnished room; and despite its artlessness it brought me a living picture of the Warren: of Debora waddling out to the courtyard to catch the morning sun, the tired evening chatter in the kitchen, Franz's large hand resting for a moment on my wrist—the entire complexion, the very breath and tingle of those months which I saw now as faintly coloured with happiness, as the last which counted for reality. And surely the warmth in the old man's laboured phrases should have waked a reflection in my own spirit! Yet in truth I felt as one who, wintering in arctic regions, wakes to find his cabin door stove in by a vicious wind. Of course I wanted to return! How painfully I longed to offer Josef's mother some fraction of the service I had once owed to her son! But of all places Astelbrucke had become the last I could think of living in, or even visiting. For how could I bear to look into the face of Ruth (as my mind had already learnt to call the timid Agnes) now that I knew what had brought her to her present state; or how, exposed by the harsh daylight I had come to live in, could I speak to my child Felix while he surveyed me through the man Franz's coolly penetrating eyes! With him, if we met again, pretence would be impossible, on my side or on his; and even if he proposed to annul the past, to forget that the crippling of his life resulted simply from my dereliction, I could not imagine myself accepting such forgiveness. Here was a predicament I could not escape from: the urge to go back would not weaken, for no home except my children's could ever promise the web of familiarities—the small coin of gossip and raillery, swift gestures of understanding, accepted silences— which is all the sweetness and the wealth of living; but I knew that those riches are not for the guilty, that without the shelter of amnesia I could not enjoy an hour with those who were dearer to me now than anyone alive. This was no new-found misery: what Walther's letter did was to bring to the lighted centre of my mind the truth I had so far kept in its outer shadows—as one might hold a glass for a sick man to observe his own emaciation.

How to answer him, that was the first anxiety: it would be cruel as well as dishonest to let him believe that I should shortly—or ever—return to his assistance, yet a blunt refusal would hardly be less hurtful. And what excuse could I fabricate?

Weakly, I shelved the problem, and when there was so little else to engage my mind it expanded banefully, as the infection from an insect bite can spread and disable one's whole body. My own weariness, the tedium of living without an object, these I had learnt to bear, but now I was denied the solace of pretending that I suffered alone: at least one other person was patently concerned with my existence, and as long as I was known to be alive he (together with those about him) would be affected by the decisions I made or my failure to make them. Once more, then, I had come to a situation which could not be endured for ever; and now that I had lost the faculty of closing my mind to harsh realities there remained but one solution—to escape from life itself.

A man I once interviewed who had been rescued unconscious from the sea told me with conviction that drowning would be an easy death; you reach quickly, he said, the stage where you surrender, and then insensibility comes with the friendliness of sleep. It may have been that man's account which gave my thoughts direction.

But there are no simple ways. To be seen and intercepted, the act half done, what bitter humiliation! So I needed to select the time and place with the same minuteness that others give to a means of staying alive. I began to take the same walk every evening, making for the farthest corner of the Plein (the square we lived in), then crossing the iron bridge which carries Reinier-Pauwstraat over the Alphen Waterweg; from there I went along the farther bank, sheltered by high warehouses, and under the railway, returning by a narrow footbridge and a passage which led deviously back to the Plein. Below the railway bridge the hull of an old canal boat was moored against the bank, so low in the water that its gunwale stood only a few inches above the surface. The light from the nearest of the feeble lamps along the towpath hardly reached it: on a moonless night it would be possible to lie invisible on the floor of that boat, waiting till the towpath was certainly deserted, then—perhaps when a train was passing overhead—to slip almost noiselessly over the side, into the water and so into merciful extinction. That was how my design shaped, but only by degrees. Something of my father's disposition—he had been famed for his thoroughness in planning—may have worked in me to demand so careful a reconnaissance; but chiefly I recognise this circumspection as the disguise of cowardice. Again and again I returned to the footbridge, pretending I needed to perfect my scheme, in reality struggling afresh against a craven repugnance. There, leaning on the parapet, I could view the place I had chosen for my ending, a clot of denser darkness against the faintly glistening blackness of the water, a picture tautly framed by the stark abutments of the railway bridge and the lattice girder which strode between them; whenever a train went by its air of purpose and its lighted windows recalled for a brief interval the exhilaration of other days, then the curtain of uneasy stillness fell once more, narrowing my world to a fillet of ghostly lights which hung in the engine's smoke, the whisper of ceaseless dripping from damp walls, a stench of ordure and decay. This desolation, while it sustained my hopelessness, did nothing to fortify my resolution. In the business I had undertaken you are prey not only to the animal dread of death but to irrational sensibilities. Searching that stagnant water, I feared, besides its coldness, the foulness and the slime; absurdly, picturing the scene when my body would be dragged to the surface in the view of curious spectators (women as well as men), I worried about which of my few and uninspiring clothes I should wear to die in. And still I faintly hoped that on one of these timorous excursions a sudden access of boldness would master my irresolution; that in a single reckless moment the dreadful thing would happen, that after a few seconds the agonising light of consciousness would finally go out.

That alley was not much used at night, and as a rule the occasional passer-by paid me no attention: there was nothing remarkable in the sight of a middle-aged woman taking a rest against the side of a bridge. But this immunity was not to last. One evening a heavy-footed man approached from the direction of the Plein and as he came towards me slowed his pace; for an instant I was in fear that he would accost me, but he evidently changed his mind, and went on towards the Merken quarter without looking back. Naturally I glanced after him, and even in the near-darkness I could not fail to identify the squat, frog-like figure: it was that of Mijnheer Dekker, going home. Apparently I had not been recognised, but I was in so nervous a condition that the incident weighed on my mind. I determined not to take that walk again without being sure that the Superintendent had left the Lodge and been gone long enough to have reached his Pastorie, about two kilometres away.

My calculations were defective. Two or three nights later, making my dismal promenade once more, I saw that the footbridge was occupied, and when I went nearer I again distinguished the Superintendent's wide, hunched shoulders and his toadstool hat. He was leaning on the parapet, just as I was wont to do, and keeping so still that I thought he might have fallen asleep; but when I tried to slip past unnoticed he turned and greeted me.

'So this is your regular walk, Frau Schechter?' he said, raising his shapeless hat and bowing amiably.

I replied that I came this way quite often, preferring it to the traffic-laden streets.

'And always alone?' he asked.

'Yes. Yes, I enjoy walking alone.'

With that I gave him a thin, valedictory smile and started to walk on in the direction of the Plein. Either because it was too dark for him to read my face, or else of set purpose, he turned and walked beside me. And now, with the loquacity which is endemic among Dutchmen, he spoke as if we were in the middle of a long discussion:

'In some sense I can sympathise,' he said judiciously. 'A certain times in life one values one's own company more than any other. It was like that with me when my wife died, many years ago—for a long time the only happiness I could find was in sailing my little *Jol*, and I was much put out if anyone wanted to come with me. And you, since you've taken a new name—or rather, returned to an earlier one—I suspect you are in a period of adjustment, not altogether unlike the one I went through then.'

It crossed my mind that if he truly sympathised with my desire for solitude he might be doing more to promote it; but all I said was, 'Mijnheer Bestuurder, I mustn't take you out of your way—you were on your way home, I think.'

He took as little notice of this interruption as if I had been a young and handsome woman protesting against a lover's attentions; he continued affably, 'All the same, one has to beware of turning a desire for solitude into self-indulgence. You see, it limits one's usefulness. For some of your fellow residents at the Lodge solitude is a thing to be dreaded—you must have realised that. They're rather simple people, they've always depended very much on having others of their own sort about them all day long—their families and a swarm of other relations, those who think and speak in their own simple patterns. All that has gone—in many cases gone for ever—and no one can make up the loss. But those with a larger mental equipment—yourself for example—could often help them in the way a foster parent would.'

I was in no mood to listen to such moralising as this, and

242

said—no doubt with audible impatience—'Yes, if I had a taste for philanthropy I might be useful in that way. Unfortunately I've no such virtue. To tell the truth, I take very little interest now in anyone's affairs but mine.'

'Oh, I know that!' he answered, in a tone of indifference. 'In my job one gets to recognise the symptoms of cancerous self-absorption—it's a disease of the soul.' He came to a halt, and perforce I halted too. 'Since your return here,' he continued conversationally, 'you've not once been to see Mevrouw Zamoyska. That alone would tell me you've given up trying to live with any thought of charity. Still, I always pray for you—my calling won't let me think of any sickness as incurable.'

I should have made a forceful protest against this oracular judgement had I not been utterly astonished. Of late I had come to think of this man as a cypher, a timid creature whose native benevolence was largely stultified by the vagueness of his mind. Here he spoke with calm authority, as if he had made a study of my moral condition and had the plenary right to pronounce his verdict. 'Surely, Superintendent, your language is rather old-fashioned!'—that was the best retort I could immediately think of; I delivered it with a fluttering asperity, and then I said, 'It's rather cold, standing here. If you'll excuse me, I think I'll hurry back to the Lodge.'

When I arrived there I went straight up to my room. I was now furiously angry. Long aware of my own deformities, I had needed no preacher to review them; least of all had I looked for instruction from a shabby pietist whose knowledge of life and whose imagination were encircled by the margins of a Dutch provincial town. My resentment was not softened by the suspicion that he had guessed my intention and set himself to thwart it: if I chose to devise my own punishment, and by the same act to relinquish a life of manifest futility, what right had he to interpose his own credulous opinions! Could he not see the cruelty of requiring me to start again on the agonising, hopeless journey! Such heartless

243

opposition (as I saw it) only made me more determined to do what I had planned. I could not return at once to the canal, for he might still be waiting to intercept me, but he would not be able to maintain his vigil all night long; I must wait for two or three hours and then, still riding on the crest of anger, I would go swiftly to the chosen place and achieve my purpose, proving at least that my convictions were not less imperative than his. With that resolve I got into bed still dressed and pulled the top blanket up to my chin, so that Sofya when she came to bed should think I was sleeping in the ordinary way. As it turned out, I did not see or hear her come: by then I had passed into a vivid dream where, without exertion or distress, I took my walk once more and reached the railway bridge as I intended; with equal ease I rolled over the side of the canal boat and into the water, which was warm and blandly comforting, so that I thought, 'Death, after all, is nothing to be afraid of, it is simply a restfulness safer and more profound than sleep.' It came as a harsh anticlimax when, brought by Sofya's snores to consciousness, I realised that the thing had still to be done.

Although the heat of my anger had passed, the sense of compulsion was unabated: as if under military orders I mechanically got out of bed, felt about in the darkness and put on my shoes. Perhaps I was not yet fully awake, but my memory of that interlude is oddly substantial and sharp-edged—the draught from the bare floor-boards lapping like icy water about my legs, the smell of a cheap hotel left by Sofya's vespertine cigarettes and ointments, a petrifying loneliness. I remember how, feeling about for my brush and comb, I knocked something on to the floor, and how Sofya alarmed me then by breaking into excited speech; my fear was groundless—she spoke in Russian, arguing, as far as I could tell, with some vaporous Isvoshtchik over a cab-fare—but now, contrarily, I longed to rouse her and make her talk to me, for when you set out on that forbidding voyage you need some fellow-creature at least to say 'Farewell'. I had left my coat hanging from a peg on the door; Sofya had put her jacket and scarf on top, and in the dark I found it no simple task, loaded as I was with weariness, to sort these garments, putting on my own and restoring hers to the peg. By then I was in tears, partly because of the complications dogging every stage in my struggle to escape from living, partly from a new, intensive vision of how my life had run to waste; for however widely my thoughts ranged they helplessly returned to what I and those dear to me had suffered through my hideous dereliction. In this extremity of sadness I might finally have surrendered; I could simply have gone back to bed and thereafter renounced all independence, content to drift through the years in the barren safety of the Wilpen-schoen routine. But the impetus from Mijnheer Dekker's reproaches was not exhausted. *Meine Nacht ist hier!* Some voice within my mind had framed those words, and now the message was recurring and recurring like an artless tune. 'My time has come!' My body seemed to stiffen in obedience to that decree. I ceased to devise new tactics for delay—searching for gloves, passing my hands with a sort of affection over my few small possessions. Still in fear that Sofya might wake, I opened the door with extreme caution, went out to the passage and shut it noiselessly behind me.

As I crept down the stairs I suffered the widely-known illusion (easy in this instance to explain) that I had returned to some earlier phase in my existence. As if I were passing through a valley of the restless dead the fragile silence in which I moved was ringed by a tangle of eerie sounds—a smothered chorus of snores and mumbling, the sudden cry of someone caught in a frightening dream. These noises were an irritation to my nerves, but I was wholly detached from the presences behind them. I had passed the point of decision: my body was carrying out my earlier command, now it would resolutely bear me all the way to the canal and there perform the final act which I had so meticulously planned.

That, I believe, would have taken place. But when I reached the lower landing a glimmer of light was showing through a doorway at the end of the corridor. The room it came from could never be without significance to me—it was the one I had shared with Tilka; and inevitably that glimpse of the open door brought back to me the Superintendent's cutting observation, 'Since your return you've not once been to see Mevrouw Zamoyska.' Clearly it was too late now to make amends for my neglect; but while I paused I was stirred by the kind of curiosity which makes you listen to any gossip about a former friend, and under this impulse I had taken a few steps along the corridor when Lore Schutze, wearing a coat over her nightdress, emerged and came towards me. Catching sight of me in the near-darkness, she stopped and peered ahead to see who it was; then, as if there were nothing out of the ordinary in this encounter, she said agreeably, 'Oh, Frau Schechter, you've come to see Tilka!' With my brain so numb I could construct no answer; in silent and sleepy acquiescence I let her lead me into the scantily lighted room.

The source of that meagre light was a single bulb, now muffled with a blue blouse, which hung between the beds—I myself had secured it there, long before, with a piece of cord attached to the wall. As I looked stupidly about me I had the impression that nothing had changed: the military chest containing Tilka's clothes was in its old place by the window, the same repulsive vessels stood on a decrepit writing desk, a forest of medicine bottles on the bedside cabinet was still surmounted by the Veit Stoss crucifix which had come from her Cracow home. And yet I did not feel I was back in a room I knew. The smell of this captive air was wholly alien; it had a strain of pungent sweetness belonging, I suppose, to the cosmetics Lore used, but uppermost was an odour I had been familiar with in the Bremen shelters, that of corporal putrefaction. It was almost without shock that, nerving myself to look directly at Tilka's bed, I saw there a face which might have been made from candle-wax in crude imitation of hers; and since the lineaments of death had long ceased to

246

disturb me I only thought, 'It was strange of them, and especially of this Fräulein Schutze, not to tell me she had died.'

When your mind and emotions are torpid, 'good manners' serve in their place: feeling that Lore would wish it, I respectfully went nearer to what was left of her friend and mine. This was a movement I should rather have avoided. At close quarters the odour from the body in the bed, even to one whose sensibilities were abnormally dulled, was grossly offensive, and in what I saw there was nothing to relieve the nausea it induced. Here was no more than a sordid caricature of the face I had known; the skin, which even in illness had been clear and beautiful, was blotched and ragged now, it seemed to hang like clothes made carelessly on features from which the wasting of flesh had taken all their grace; even the gold hair looked lifeless, sprawling thinly on the grey forehead and the crumpled pillow. No, there was nothing in this spectacle which tempted me to recall the Tilka who, through every hindrance, had found her way into my affections; and I remember wondering impatiently how long I needed to continue this vain observance, which was keeping me from the business I had set my hand to.

I had forgotten that in death the eyes are not naturally shut: what told me first that I had sprung to a false conclusion was a painful murmur which, though it sounded far away, could only have come from the object I was watching. Now I noticed the spasmodic twitching of a small muscle below one eye, and when I bent nearer I was conscious of a faint exhalation, sour and warm, from the just-parted lips. Soon there was a further movement: a hand—a tiny thing, reduced almost to a bird's claw—began to creep about the coverlet as if in search of food; instinctively I put my own hand underneath it, and it lay in that soft couch as a small, scared, puzzled 'animal might do. After a while I realised that the eyes had come open.

As I try to review that curious hour my thoughts go farther back, to Felix as I knew him in his earliest days:

often he would fall asleep when I was nursing him, I myself would doze for a while, and when I woke I would find that his eyes were open, watching my face. Watching? No, I was not long so naïve as seriously to think so. But within the dark pupils of that minikin creature, so lately a part of my own body, I in my first exuberant maternity had read not only a power to observe but an eager recognition, a whole gamut of feelings and intelligence. Something resembling that experience came to me now. At first the enfeebled eyes which lay a few inches below mine appeared to be lightless, showing no movement at all; then I thought they were stretching for some object out of reach, much as the wartime searchlights had probed the infinite darkness for craft flying far above their range. I bent nearer still. The straining ceased. And now, as if I looked far down into a deep, still pool, I suddenly caught sight of the Tilka I knew.

It seemed impossible that she with those nerveless eyes would ever recognise the face suspended over hers; nor could I believe that any words of mine would penetrate the cloud which extreme illness wraps about the understanding. So I did not attempt to speak, or to force a smile; I could only try, with a very gentle chafing of the hand which lay in mine, to let her know that someone who held her in affection had come close. But again I had judged her state too sombrely. Her lips began to move, and all of a sudden, as if it were under a ventriloquist's command, a small, distant voice said distinctly:

'Johanna, dear, you must go now! You'll miss your train.'

It came to my mind that she was thinking of our last parting, in the hospital at Utrecht; and I responded quickly, 'Oh, it doesn't matter when I get back.'

'But they'll be waiting for you,' she said, 'those people at that place—I can't remember—'

From behind me Lore (whose presence I had forgotten) said, 'Astelbrucke.'

And Tilka echoed, 'Yes, Astelbrucke. Your people will be waiting for you there.'

248

There was no clear way for me to answer her; I could only say feebly, 'There isn't any hurry. Really there's no hurry at all ' This brought us back to silence; but now her stiff, cold lips had shaped the beginning of a smile, and presently she was speaking again, first with a trickle of Polish words which I did not understand, then in the gracefully mannered German which reminded me of our earlier times together:

'Darling, I like you with your hair grown. So handsome, so feminine! ... And now you have a new name, Lore says.'

'Frau Dr Schechter,' Lore reminded her.

' "Frau Dr Schechter"—but how learned, how eminent! So you're married, after all! For a long time?'

I answered, 'Yes, a long time.'

'And you have children?'

I hesitated, and then I told her, 'Once I had children. They're grown-up, they don't need me now.'

At that she made a little movement, eager and impatient, with her free hand; saying, 'Oh, but they always will, they *must* need you!' Visibly that spurt of excited speech cost her some pain, but with hardly a pause she went on: 'We never had children, Wladyslaw and I—he was killed too soon. If we had, they would always have needed me—I'd have seen to that.' And now I could hear within her faint voice the old, effervescent laughter. 'Oh, Johanna, dear, you still need me to teach you things!'

Here Lore thought it time to interfere. Coming beside me, she said with a maternal gentleness, 'Tilka, sweet, I think we've had enough talking just for now. We're breaking Dr Hofdijk's rules, you know.'

But that was fruitless. From the grey mask dumped in the pillow, so still you could hardly think it breathed, the answer came at once: 'What, that muddle-headed Dutchman? How could we ever have any fun if we listened to him!'

When I remember how much younger Tilka was than I, and how little older than Lore, I marvel that with a voice which came so weakly, with such labour, she seemed to have us wholly under her command. Her ascendancy came, I think, from her stillness—not only the inertia of her body but the tranquillity of her heart and mind. She had passed beyond the uncertainties of living, there were no decisions left for her to make. Apparently she had no fear of the final voyage, though she must have known it had begun; and you felt that even the physical pain attending every speech and movement had ceased to count with her, so long had it been constant in her experience. In one sense she was unchanged: I had never known her as a whole and active woman, and for me there remained within this wasted shell the creature of lambent humanity, acutely feminine in her responses to absurdity or fondness, who had long ago enthralled my affection. Yet I recognised a new complexion in our friendship: as the younger of two sisters will sometimes outstrip the elder in school, she had attained a place of privilege which I could neither doubt nor define. Perhaps it was that in the long captivity of illness she had discovered insights not available to us others; or perhaps the discarding of almost everything which matters in ordinary life had left her with a more luminous vision of what remained.

It was Lore whose face, now, she sought and fastened on, asking, 'Is that you, Lore? Are you there?' And when I had moved a little, allowing Lore to bend closer, she said, with a child's eagerness, 'Lore, you know my old friend Johanna, my other German friend? She looked after me before you came. Oh, so good to me! So sad, and yet so kind.'

Lore said simply: 'Why, yes, dear. And now she's back with us—you'll be seeing her every day in future.'

Perceptibly, Tilka shook her head. 'No no,' she said decisively, 'Johanna has her children to look after. At a place called Astelbrucke. She's on her way there now.'

This aberration could not be righted verbally; but her spell so worked on Lore and me as to fuse our responses—Lore drew back a little, while I stooped to take her place again. And Tilka, as far as I could tell, was undisturbed by this change in her small scenery. With her eyes once more linked to mine, and smiling pensively, she continued, whispering, along the path of her erratic reflections:

'All my life there's been such happiness for me. We used to picnic in the birchwoods every day, and the country women wore such lovely things. Oh, and it was all so joyful when we lived at Lwow, the people we knew were so amusing. And when Wladyslaw came home from climbing, all streaked with mud and sweat and laughing, oh that was heaven!' She stopped, as if suddenly ashamed of her vivacity. Then, with a change of tone, she said, 'But you, Johanna dear, you were in the dark so long you've missed it all—all the joy there is, the foolish, funny things.' Her hand had strayed, but now the skeletal fingers were seeking my palm again. She said, 'You must tell your children—tell them from me—that they've got to make you happy. You see, I can't do it myself—I'm always so busy trying to die, which the turnip-head Dutchman won't allow me.'

Had I myself been in a placid state of mind I should simply have accepted her benevolence. But because I was distracted by a turmoil of emotions I felt I could not leave her with so false a picture of my deserts; and since there was nothing sensible for me to say I found myself answering in a kind of frenzy: 'That isn't what I want—I don't deserve to be happy. It's different for you—your life's been all goodness, nothing but goodness and courage.'

Those words seemed to shock her, almost as an insult would have done. She echoed faintly, 'Goodness?' And then she said, 'Lore, are you there? Lore, tell her! Tell her about the prisoners.'

Another woman would have gently led the invalid away from such excitement; but I see it now as a measure of Lore's stature that instead of pretending not to have heard that order she quietly fulfilled it. In a level voice she said, 'It's something Tilka won't let herself forget. She was nursing in an army hospital—at Lubartow—when she got the news of Wladyslaw's death. There were four prisoners there—youngsters from a crashed bomber—in a ward by themselves, which she had charge of. She went to them, she said "Your friends have killed my husband, so you'll get no more nursing". And she locked the door and left them to die. That was her revenge against the Germans.'

Tilka was lying with her eyes shut—I thought she had fallen asleep. But now she spoke again, with perfect clarity:

'Not just the Germans. It was my revenge on God. He had taken Wladyslaw—I meant to take four lives in return, I wanted to defy Him and insult Him.'

I asked spontaneously, 'You say they died, those men?'

She did not answer at once—it seemed that she was struggling to clear her mind. At last she said wearily, 'He met me in the passage and told me to give him the key. He said if I wouldn't look after the airmen he must do it himself, in spite of his condition—and you could see a trail of blood where he'd come across the snow. So I had to give in and nurse them.'

I could not follow this. I said, 'But who was it who wanted the key?'

Her eyes had opened, and she made a small gesture with her head, as if to point to someone behind me. '*He* did.' I turned, thinking for an instant that someone had entered the room without my hearing. But I saw nothing new, only the calm grave face of Lore, the pale figure on the ebony cross, a heap of Lore's daytime clothes on a backless chair.

I suppose that wave of fantasy would hardly have fluttered anyone who was quiet in her own mind, for the thoughts of the sick are often turbulent, opening the door to wild hallucination; but in those crowded moments I had not the composure of one who surveys from a state of health the lineaments of illness. The presence of Lore prevented that. Lore had been generous, inviting me to return into the friendship where she had taken my place, but now I saw that these two women had in common something I could not share: an attitude, a peculiar liberty. Apparently it did not matter that one of them had reached the crumbling edge of life: to them death, which I was seeking so laboriously and

Tilka with an angler's patience, was an event of relatively small significance, part of a mystery in which, together, they were involved already. In the pool of dingy light which contained the rococo bedhead, the garish colours in the bottles, the drooping counterpane, we three were very close; yet I had the impression that what I saw and felt was a fabric of illusion, while the other two had discovered a reality outside my understanding. No question they were happy. In each other's fondness? Rather, I think, in a common enlargement of perception, by which the bareness of our present lives, the fetor of the sickbed, the besieging pain, were lost in a wider landscape. Together, as I dimly realised, they had found their way to a countryside where the darker tracts of experience showed small against the vastness of the prospect; a spectacle whose calm and radiance were distantly reflected in Lore's eyes; while to me it stayed invisible.

I had been at that bedside long enough; but it was not easy, in my state of confusion and weariness, to find a formula for taking leave. In fact I did it clumsily, uttering vacant courtesies—'So kind of you.... You'll let me know if I can help in any way?' I had a desire to embrace Tilka, but it seemed better only to stoop and press my lips against the hand I had been holding. (To that there was no response; she was asleep again, or in that withdrawal which resembles sleep.) Lore and I touched fingers as I turned to go. Perhaps that did duty for a great deal of speech.

As far as the street door I went on with my expedition just as if it had not been interrupted, though I did not remember at that stage why I was making it: it was only while I was unfastening the door that the reason came back to me. My first thought then—it seems ingenuous when reduced to words—was that in a night so filled with other business I no longer had the energy to pursue my own. This was followed by a larger reflection: I had spent an hour—or perhaps only a quarter of that time—in the presence of one who was dying with perfect serenity, and against the splendour of that revelation I saw the clandestine and squalid death I had planned for myself as the shameful burlesque of a mystery; if life was meaningless, it was still ignoble to cheapen its ending—to surrender the final chance of dignity which natural death might offer even to me. Vague as it was, that concept had the power to turn my steps. All but asleep, like a clockwork toy which is nearly ready for re-winding, I mounted the stairs again, flight after flight, and returned to my own room. I remember thinking—as once more I found myself stumbling about in the darkness, hunting for a nightgown, still absurdly anxious not to wake Sofya—that the mere hope of enlightenment might after all redress the pain of staying alive; that there was some truth about the nature of things, some reason for existence, which others knew and I had yet to find.

I did not visit Tilka again. That is not a fact I am ashamed of If she still had any need for the human voice and presence there was no one else who could answer it as Lore did; I should have been no more than a prying tourist in a place whose language I had largely forgotten. Moreover, it was only a day or two later that my circumstances began to change once more.

A polite message summoned me to the Superintendent's office, where I found him in his sunniest mood, as friendly as in former days.

'I am bidden,' he told me, 'to attend a conference organised by my Association—a parliament of those misguided men who have charge of establishments like this one. It starts on Thursday—at Zutphen.'

I said I hoped it would be interesting.

'Yes yes, that is what kindly people used to say to prisoners on their way to the torture chamber. Now listen: I shall need a travelling companion to stiffen my morale on the outward journey, and it seems to me this might be a convenient way for you to start your German expedition. Our friend Dr Hofdijk tells me there are trains from Zutphen going on into all parts of Germany. Poor Hofdijk—I find him totally absurd in his philosophy, but in practical matters he's wonderfully intelligent.'

I interrupted: 'But Mijnheer Dekker, I have no reason for going to Germany at present. Or indeed at any time.'

'Oh, but there I beg leave most respectfully to contradict you. I had a letter from that old man—what is his name?— from Herr Walther Stahl, saying they really can't get on without you. Well, that may be an exaggeration. But I think you ought to see for yourself how things are in that household.'

Strictly, this was an impertinence, but the amiability which radiated from his chameleon countenance, his pretence of confidential partnership, were enough to overcome my resentment. I replied that I should like to think over his suggestion.

'Good!' he said (perhaps misunderstanding my imperfect Dutch). 'Well, we start after breakfast on Thursday morning. We go by road—the rail connections between here and Zutphen are quite impossible, Pietr Hofdijk says. I've already ordered a conveyance, there's a man called Asselijn who hires out himself and his automobile—you may have met him when you were here before. Not a person I could recommend for immediate canonisation—supposing that were my responsibility—but he lost his wife some time ago and he seems to need encouragement. Thursday, then, at eight-thirty. And I do appreciate your kindness, dear Frau Johanna—I shall face the ordeal at Zutphen far more bravely now I know I shan't be travelling there alone.'

Yes, I did remember the taxi-owner Asselijn; and I had not relaxed my resolve to keep clear of Astelbrucke. But once again the direction of my affairs seemed to have passed into hands more resolute than mine.

5

At least one satisfaction came from that unluxurious journey to Zutphen—the comfort of not having Albrecht Weckerlin as my escort. I looked back on my travels with him as on one of those dreams where all the objects that surround you, the blank faces, the sky itself, are taut with menace; by comparison the imperfections of Asselijn's vehicle, the volatility of his driving, were easy to put up with. For the rest, most of my mind was moving far ahead of the bald and frozen country which we traversed; I was trying to recall the faces in The Warren as I had last seen them, I was wondering how much my children knew—had always known—of what Albrecht had so drastically recalled to me. It was certain that the time ahead would be one of corrosive humiliation. Like a shivering infant ordered by her parents to bathe in a cold sea, I could not decide whether to feel my way gingerly into this ordeal or to accept the worst of its punishment in one reckless plunge.

Manifestly no serious apprehensions troubled my companion, who was like a boy excused from a morning's school; with his squat body wedged in a corner of the sedan, a black woollen cap pulled down over half his ears and an orange muffler lagging his chin, he exposed almost nothing of himself but two eyes of slightly fatuous benignity and a mouth fixed in a complacent smile. Once, in the first few miles, he criticised our driver: 'Mijnheer Asselijn, I think you should give more room to the bicyclists—they're easily frightened.' (This was when an old woman had ridden right off the road and pitched herself, approximately upside-down, on the lip of the dyke beside it.) But I judged that neither

Asselijn's eccentric steering nor the violent jolting which we suffered from broken springs was going to disturb his basic equanimity.

Not sharing his cheerfulness, I may have spoken coolly when I remarked, 'You're glad, I suppose, to get away from the Lodge for a while. We expatriates must be a troublesome responsibility.'

His answer surprised me: 'Comparatively—not at all. I have, as you may know, a congregation as well—they provide a sterner test of virtue. Oh, don't mistake me, they are good people! But also highly respectable. Week after week I see them sitting there in rows, clean, well-shaven, appropriately dressed, looking to me for a soporific dose of conventional piety, one to absolve them from the harsher obligations of discipleship. Which is just what I can give them with the smallest effort imaginable, and often—from sheer laziness—I do. Now one thing I cannot do with Anna Wiedlich, for example, is to smother her with unctuous platitudes. One may find Anna awkward now and then to deal with—the same thing applies to hedgehogs—but her temperament is totally exposed to us and her problems are real.... Yes, Constable, what may I do for you?'

We had been stopped—I think it was the second time—by policemen, and while one of them was taking particulars from Asselijn another, stooping to put his head in at our window, said, 'I'm telling your driver, it's thoroughly unsafe to have the tyres like these—two of them are nearly flat. They should be evenly inflated.'

'Indeed, yes!' Mijnheer Dekker said. 'I think my good driver was hurrying to the next garage to get them re-adjusted.'

The young policeman put his head a little closer, to ask in a low voice, 'Are you satisfied this man's quite fit for driving?'

'Why, certainly—he has driven me many times. He lost his wife some while ago, poor fellow—it has left him in a state of intermittent melancholia. But I'm sure his skill is just the same as it has always been.'

We were accompanied by a groom of sorts in the person of Gregor Vaclav, a man of extreme simplicity hailing from Moravska Ostrava, whom the Superintendent liked to have about him; and while this parley with the police was filling me with weary impatience it provoked Vaclav to ferocious loyalty.

'Do I punch the policeman?' he asked in his barbarous German (the only language he knew of besides his own).

'No no, Gregor. The policeman is most kindly seeing about our tyres and things of that kind.'

This was beyond Vaclav's comprehension. 'When you say, I punch him,' he pronounced, and the set of his wide shoulders made me glad not to be in the policeman's place.

Such interruptions were not enough to ruffle Mijnheer Dekker's sense of holiday; as soon as we were in motion again he resumed, smiling pensively: 'Yes, the Lodge gives me much to be thankful for. It serves to remind me of what my fellow humans are like in the natural state—I mean, when not upholstered with genial friends and gullible relations and a healthy balance in the Bank of Rotterdam. Most of my Coenraad customers have found for themselves that what the rest of us take for granted is only contingent: food, shelter safety—there's nothing you can rely on. They've had an extended view of life in what we may call its natural state. And as a result they've lost their own disguises.'

The turn his speech had taken, tolerant and discursive, had been reminding me of someone I could not bring into focus. Now all at once I knew who it was. Herr Oestmann, my invalid acquaintance at Astelbrucke, had exhibited no single feature or mannerism which matched my present companion's, yet these two men, alike egregious in body, shared too a certain attitude to their experience, a warmth of feeling strangely coupled with detachment. For myself, I could never have entered the mind of either, for they showed excessively the masculine bent for evading immediate realities; but I found myself envying Mijnheer Dekker's power (as I had envied Herr Oestmann's) to live outside the place and moment in which he was physically enclosed. 'They've lost their own disguises': I wanted to ask him what he meant by that. But now the wretched Asselijn, with his head half-turned towards us, was demanding to be heard.

'If this was a Mercedes,' he said, 'costing fifty thousand florins, we wouldn't be mucked about by snooping cops all the time.'

'Well, that is a point of view,' Mijnheer Dekker allowed. 'But I think, my friend, you should face the way we're going when the road's so crowded.'

In truth we were swerving extravagantly. 'Do I punch this driver?' Vaclav asked.

'I think not, Gregor. It would only magnify the existing hazards.'

'There'll be no justice in this country,' Asselijn explained, still showing us his profile, 'till we get a Marxist régime. Do you think Comrade Lenin would allow the police to persecute a poor man like me!'

'Comrade Lenin has been in Heaven for some time,' Mijnheer Dekker reminded him. 'Or so we must hope. Now I really think you should give attention to the steering.'

Asselijn's response was to lean further back, so that, aiming at the right-hand window, he could spit behind Vaclav's head. 'In this country nobody cares two cents about the workers,' he concluded.

By then I was inured to the man's inadequate performance, which—to speak fairly—seemed to cause little harm. I noticed only that more cyclists here and there dismounted and pulled their machines to the verge when they saw us approaching; there was some abuse from other drivers but (as far as I remember) no mechanical collision. In this matter I was happily without responsibility, and even my despondent thoughts about what awaited me at Astelbrucke could not entirely quench the elation which movement brings—the illusion of escape from all one's failures. It was cold; but as we entered the Province of Guilderland the haze above us

thinned, till the winter sun which seems to belong especiall
to the Netherlands, clean and complacent as the round face
of their women, lit all the countryside with a milky, operat
radiance. On a frozen lake at Vindenloo there were skat
shod grandmamas in decorous promenade among the wea
ing hordes of children, while in the farther reaches men an
girls in scarlet jerseys raced and swung and darted lil
swallows gathering to migrate; I thought of poor Avercamp
warm-hearted pictures, and in one enchanted instant I faintl
saw the goodness of life not as a Goethian invention but as
part of reality, a warm stream flowing constantly beside th
sterile vacuum of my own existence. My companion had lit
small clay pipe—the sort of thing that children use fo
blowing bubbles—and while he was suckled, so to speak, b
that slender object his face relaxed into a curiously pueri
innocence. It was hard to identity this genial creature with th
sacerdotal personage who had presumed to lecture me a fe
nights before; and no one could have nursed resentmer
against the man as he appeared that morning.

Somewhere in the region of heath and pine which coun
with the Dutch as hill country I asked what it was tha
seemed to amuse him. He said:

'I was thinking of my grandmother—how she would hav
laughed to find me in my present station. She used to say
was far and away the stupidest of her grandchildren—sh
had twenty-three. If she'd lived to see me in charge of a soi
of pan-European *béguinage* she'd have thought the worl
had turned upside down.'

'But you yourself,' I said with diffidence, 'you tell me yo
don't find the post too burdensome?'

He considered this question, his lips rolling over each othe
like puppies at play, and presently smiled again. 'Sometime
it entertains me,' he said, 'but more often I find it excessivel
humbling. And then again it always plays upon my curiosit
I can never understand how people who have lost everythin
—their homes and friends, all their possessions, even th
modicum of dignity which every human counts on—ho

they can *still* show so much virtue, such unadulterated goodness of heart.'

This quaint belief was so little in accord with the facts, as I myself had observed them, that I could not let it go unchallenged. I said, 'Perhaps you'd see things differently if you lived as close to these people as I do. What strikes me is that those who've been through vicious treatment will often take the first chance that comes to treat others viciously.'

'Ah, but that's only a passing aberration,' he said. 'Those who suffer unbearable hardships, yes, for a time they often behave callously. It doesn't mean they've lost for ever what I should call their portion of divinity.'

I said, 'What—you think there's "a portion of divinity" in Elena Kral! Have you ever seen her and Anna Wiedlich getting together to make the life of Teresa Voltesova more wretched than it is already?'

This protest was not ineffective—at least it drew a film of sobriety over Mijnheer Dekker's amiable features. 'Oh,' he answered, 'I'm not saying that such people miraculously lose the human propensity to wickedness. Elena Kral, yes, her cruelty to Teresa is beyond all bearing. But in her best moments she does *know* she's doing the Devil's work. Twice she has cut her wrists—though without much skill, as Pietr Hofdijk would explain to you. And once she would have starved herself to death, if that mystically dedicated woman Louisa Potgieter hadn't exercised her greater will-power.'

'And Anna Wiedlich?' I persisted.

'Anna Wiedlich is a child—though she is thirty-one years old. A spoilt child—what she suffered in the War was only a coping stone on the harm her rich and stupid parents did her. Still, no one is spoilt for ever. In time she will become grown-up—quite suddenly. And then we shall find that all the force, all the intelligence she gives to her present cruelties will be turned to a useful kindness. I've known enough people of her sort to feel quite certain that will happen.'

I could conceive no shred of reason to support his thesis; only his way of speaking was persuasive—the glow of confidence which had returned to his humorous eyes, his air of a professor who knows that every pupil of his will do well in the final examination. Not sorry to be diverted from my own despondent thoughts, I should have pressed him further; but once more a police sergeant, his big face and shoulders filling the window, was claiming his attention:

'Have you any reason for stopping here, sir?'

'To tell the truth, Mijnheer Wachtmeister, I hadn't realised we'd stopped at all.'

We were, in fact, halted almost a car's width from the pavement in the narrow street of some small town, thus impeding the movement of every other vehicle in both directions. Asselijn had left his seat and was nowhere to be seen.

'And where is your driver?' the policeman demanded.

'Well, when I last saw him he was in his usual place beside the controls. To be perfectly honest, I hadn't noticed he was absent.'

These sterile exchanges were still in progress when Asselijn appeared, wiping his mouth, from a crack between the houses; and when the car had been brought to the kerb the familiar, wearisome routine began again. The sergeant was magisterial, Asselijn self-righteous: every man, Asselijn said, had to yield to the demands of nature; it was no fault of his if a town had placed itself around his car at the moment when his entrails clamoured for relief. As usual, Mijnheer Dekker spoke in his support: Mijnheer Asselijn was a conscientious driver, but one whose physique was sometimes disturbed by emotional pressures; he had had the great misfortune to lose a devoted wife, occasionally the resultant grief affected his nervous system, and so forth. Some fifteen minutes must have passed before we were allowed to go on.

But while I was vexed by this recurrent foolishness I no longer felt the same impatience: anything was welcome now which might delay the final stage of my journey. It is usual, I suppose, to value places or people more highly when you are about to lose them. Provincial Mijnheer Dekker might be, even somewhat childish in his roseate outlook, but one came to draw from his glowing warmth, his ingenuous convictions, a peculiar sense of safety. In the season which lay ahead I should have no counsel but my own to rest on; I could not help thinking how much more easily I should face the future if I could argue each day's problems with this stunted, genial, single-minded man. Perhaps he had some idea of my feelings —he was not without intuition; for at Zutphen, where he and I had a final meal together in the station restaurant, he was intensely paternal, bathing my face with the ardent kindness of his eyes, cherishing my wrist in his capacious hand, while he told me again and again how much the Stahls would welcome my return. Yet I remained in great confusion. As usual, our conversation was interrupted by policemen, this time asking if we owned the ancient car which had been left in the very place where vehicles were most strictly forbidden to stand; and then I was suffering from the kind of despair which a child feels if she strays from her mother on a crowded pavement; with Wilpenschoen left behind, and with no claim to any rights in the place where I was going, I felt once more that I belonged nowhere at all.

Was it a sort of genius, or just another of his frivolous vagaries, which suggested to Nicolaas Dekker a way of distracting me from my dismal absorption? Just after he had got rid of the police he turned to me to say carelessly:

'Look, I think I'll send Gregor Vaclav along with you—one more railway fare won't break the Association's funds. He's fond of the Stahls, you remember—he'd do anything for the old lady. Keep him with you for a week, say, and see how it goes. He'll certainly earn his corn.'

I cannot remember exactly how I answered this surprising proposal: I must have tamely agreed to it. Vaclav himself, when it was put to him (in Nicolaas's rudimentary German), took it just as a professional soldier accepts a new posting. He was to go on the train with this Frau Schechter? To carry her baggage? To clean the shoes and wash the floors for the old German lady who had once been at the Lodge? 'Understood! Most happy!'

So I was not quite alone, that chilly winter evening, when I
stood at a lowered window in the corridor of the train, wait
ing to be borne away: square-shouldered, solemn as a young
cornet, Vaclav was posted dutifully beside me. Yes, and I was
grateful for his silent presence, suggesting as it did that some
part of experience was lasting, even if all the rest was to be
rolled away like stage scenery as I passed from one state of
life to another; for in the long final minute before the train
started the things I saw—a woman who stooped to tie a small
boy's shoe-lace, the garish picture of a workman grinning
through the foam of his beer—were already quite unreal.
Largely I kept my eyes away from Nicolaas's face: the sight
of it, grotesquely garnished with the cap and scarf, both set
askew, had the strange effect of making me want to weep. At
such times one's voice is unreliable; it cost me some effort just
to utter two words with force enough to penetrate the
clamour of the station:

'I'm frightened.'

He did hear me; and instead of answering as others might
have done that my fears were all illusory he said soberly
'Yes, I see no easy days in front of you, not yet.' Then he
added, 'I myself, I believe we can make an offering of
everything we suffer, all our humiliations. Quite honestly
I've proved that for myself. And then they come back to us
as something to be valued—if only to revive our courage.'

The train was already moving when he came out with that
characteristic *obiter dictum*. Walking to keep level he
reached for my hand; he held it for a moment, breaking into
a run, gazing up at me and fondly laughing, as if he and I
were bound together by some private joke against the world.
A much larger man stood in his way; I had a final glimpse of
the yellow muffler, and after that a sense of loss curiously
akin to that which a late miscarriage leaves behind.

It must have been long past midnight when the train reached
Astelbrucke. In that windy arena perhaps a dozen people

stood waiting to meet their friends, but no one I knew was among them. Afterwards I found that my telegram from Wilpenschoen had failed to get through; at the time, I took the default as proof of what I had more than half expected—that there was no enthusiasm (save on the part of Walther Stahl) for my return.

In dreams, as I remember now, I had more than once made the journey from the station to the Warren, with the faces of Ruth and Felix peering at me from high shadows, their lips remaining motionless when I begged them to tell me the way; and here again were the shifting perspectives, the silence of a planet deserted by all its inhabitants except Vaclav and me. I suppose the hidden moon was near the full, for the darkness was dilute; but a thin snow was falling, and the flurries of small flakes, whipped into spirals by a bustling wind, confused every aspect in this eviscerated town. I had made the passage only once before. Now, in tracts where nothing had been visible on the earlier occasion but tumbled masonry, square blocks were sprouting, some as high already as a church tower; the wooden bridge I looked for seemed to have gone, and when I had crossed the river by a steel construction two or three hundred metres away I found myself in a web of narrow streets where I had never been before. Here, as I turned this way and that, every egress seemed to be blocked by a building which had fallen. The houses leaning over me were broken and lifeless; when I heard the protracted whine of a door swinging on bent hinges, when a grey kitten ran suddenly across my feet, I was more than ever glad to have Vaclav at my side.

'Keine Mühe!' That was his constant answer when I murmured an apology for the hopeless march on which I seemed to be leading him. It was a favourite among his few German phrases, and you could never doubt that he used it sincerely; he was a man perhaps nearing fifty, but his pride in service was that of a schoolboy waiting on some athletic hero. On this disheartening walk he carried a case of his own as well as mine, he must have been as tired and cold as I, yet he never showed a sign of distress. When we found ourselves in a blind alley for the third or fourth time he said in Czech what I took to mean 'Funny town!' Then, 'No trouble!' he declared again, and laughed as a small boy will when you bo at him from behind a tree.

Was it his fortitude which drew a spark of courage from my own chilled spirit? Or was it a lingering warmth from something that Nicolaas had said before we parted? I know it was when I had almost despaired of emerging from that ghostly labyrinth—when I was actually crying from the pain in my frozen hands—that I came mysteriously to feel a new stability of purpose. Although the decision for this move had not been mine I recognised it now as the right one. I could foresee little joy in the years ahead, but those years would not be meaningless; whatever hardships I had to bear, I should be close to the only people whose lives still counted as part of my own. Yes, I would work for them, and I would not look for payment in the coin of affection. I was, after all, a woman: a man will think his life well used if he expends it in the capture of an outpost, the rescue of a shredded flag, since such romanticism permeates the masculine mind; but we are realists, we know there is but one object worthy of our sacrifice—the good of those who are dear to us, whether or no we be dear to them. When I live again through the discomforts of that hour—the rub of stays worn through the long journey, my nose incessantly dripping, snow blowing in my eyes as if purposely to hinder our escape—I know that in that extreme of wretchedness I was turned, at least for a time, from despair to resolution. This was no bravery of the hero's sort, only the stoicism which comes from believing in what one has undertaken. On the grinding march I had engaged in I could look for no tangible reward, certainly for no esteem; enough, that I should ask for no indulgence, yield to no weariness, never fall out.

Probably we were in that maze of ruins for several minutes more and only a distortion of memory makes me think that this sudden emancipation of spirit was followed instantly by physical release. All I certainly remember is that when a new play of the wind thrust the curtain of snow aside it revealed for a moment an opening between two houses which I had twice failed to notice; this was one end of a foot passage which led us shortly into a street I knew.

Because of its copious population the main entrance to the Warren was never shut fast, and a globe always burning above the Pavaakas' landing gave a light that reached, feebly, down to the hall. The feeling of that hall was slightly changed—chiefly, I suppose, by the command of winter over its dominant smells. But when I reached the kitchen I felt as if I had left it only a few hours before.

The question where Vaclav should immediately be lodged was settled by himself, with the sort of practicality one associates with old soldiers: while I was making soup for him and me with some stock of Luise's he quietly explored the room and its adjoining offices; discovering in one of these a space just large enough for a man of his build to lie between a pile of firewood and an old mangle, he exclaimed, 'For Vaclav—good!' and threw in his valise. Later I must have found at least a blanket or two to bring that berth closer to human standards.

But I cannot pretend I was capable just then of making sensible arrangements—I had reached a state of torpor not far from that of the haunting night when I had come (as it seemed) from nowhere to my own former home. The room was in more than its normal disorder; I recognised a stack of unwashed china as belonging to Frau Reuben, with some of Hanna's things mixed up in it; automatically I started to wash up those things, but soon I found myself moving fecklessly from one task to another, trying to clear the chaos on the big table, stopping to sweep a litter of peel and wrappings from the floor. More than once Vaclav asked by gestures where he should put my case, but I could not bring my wits to bear on this: my former bedroom might or might not be free, and the task of ascending several flights of stairs to investigate seemed, at that point, one equal to a mountain climb. In the end I simply lay down—still in my outdoor clothes—on the kitchen floor; and there fell at once into a restless sleep.

Had my intelligence been at work I should have thought it foolish so to plant myself, when I had told no one of my return.

And of course it was Ruth (I no longer thought of her as 'Agnes') who arrived in the kitchen first—she was generally the earliest riser in that household. When the electric light opened my eyes she was standing by the sink in her brown slip, apathetically washing her face and neck; obviously she had not yet seen me, and I was too sleepy to think how, without startling her, I could let her know I was there.

The result of my feebleness was that when, turning round, she saw the tousled shape of someone stretched on the floor she must have suffered at least as great a shock as a sudden utterance would have given her. She did, indeed, start as if at a pistol shot; but then, with the boldness which belongs especially, I think, to people of great simplicity, she came a little nearer and curiously surveyed me. Now I made a further mistake. I should have given her all the time she needed for examining the outlandish object I presented, to link it by degrees with the person who had entered her life some time before, who had stayed for a while and then abruptly departed. But my feelings were too strong for such forbearance. More than I had realised hitherto this stolid and shapeless young woman, always faithful as my under-servant, had become in our earlier association one I valued for her gentleness of spirit; now, as we faced each other, I wondered how I could have failed to see—above the barbarous flatness of the mouth, behind the ugly spectacles—a reflection of her father's quiet regard, his immutable honesty, the tenderness which his intellectuality could never hide; and the thought of her being his child and mine so stirred me that in a moment I was on my feet and crying artlessly:

'Ruth! Ruth, darling, how lovely to be with you again!'

I see now that it was the use of her real name (she herself had probably forgotten it) which put her in fresh bewilderment; as I pronounced it the dawning light of recognition faded in her eyes; sharply—as when one has bowed by mistake to some man who proves a stranger—she turned her head; I caught for an instant a look of disappointment, then she deliberately went back to her own room.

At least I had the sense not to pursue her. I realised even then that the ground lost by my blundering approach could only be won back—if at all—very slowly, with insight and with tireless patience.

At that hour the resolution I had felt the night before was dormant, and my dread of the first encounter with Felix had returned; none the less I was impatient to see him and to hear his voice, at the least to recruit the fragmentary image which is all that memory retains of those at the centre of one's life when they are physically absent. Pursuing sleepily the old routine, I prepared his breakfast and the packed lunch he would need; after that it was at once a relief and a grievous disappointment that he did not appear.

When I had given breakfast to Vaclav, and there was still no sign of Felix or Luise, I remembered that my cardinal duty was with the Stahls. Having made myself tidy, I went and knocked at the door of their room.

The voice which feebly answered was Walther's. Entering cautiously, I found him in his narrow bed near the window, with Debora nowhere to be seen. This was a reunion which both moved and shamed me. I had not switched on the electric light, and in such daylight as could penetrate the snow clouds and the filmed window it was some time before the old man saw who I was; when he did so he stretched out his hand (so much thinner than when I had last seen him, so

269

dreadfully cold) and grasped my arm, whispering:

'Frau Josef, I said you would come! Oh, I knew you would come!'

How little had I deserved that confidence! But to make disclaimers and excuses would have been pointless now: I simply said I was glad to be back, and asked conventionally about his health, at which he answered:

'Me? I am perfectly well, gnädige Frau, except for a little weakness in the small of my back—at the moment it stops me sitting up or using my legs. It's the cold weather, you understand—as soon as the weather mends I shall be getting up. No, it's Frau Schechter—it's my wife, I should say— who's poorly. Yes, for some time now. But now that you've come back, with all your gracious kindness, I shall have no need to worry.'

There was no pretence in that effusion: even as I scanned the ashen forehead, the scarlet mottling on the cheeks, the shaking hands, I knew that he truly thought of himself as one incapacitated for just a day or two. And what could I do but tell him—kneeling and placing an arm about his shoulders so that a little warmth might pass from my body into his—that he must not be in too great a hurry, that a few days' idleness would reward him with greater strength when he was on his feet again. The next thing was to straighten his bed, and to open an attack on the Augean chaos which had grown about it. The floor was strewn with newspapers and novelettes, with patent medicines of every pernicious kind; whoever had been waiting on the invalid had supposed that a liquid diet—soups, liquorice tea and other nauseous ptisans— must be supplied in reckless abundance, and now the vessels used (some of them still nearly full, some with seasoned stains) had strayed about the room to consort repugnantly with a great profusion of bed and body linen. To thin this harvest of noisome crockery seemed to me the prime necessity; I stacked as much as possible on a tray and carried it towards the kitchen.

But I did not get so far without interruption. In the

twilight of the corridor a horrifying figure was creeping towards me—it gave the impression of a sack of beets draped with a cotton nightgown and surmounted by one of those preposterous effigies which are borne in carnivals; of course I saw almost at once that this was Debora, but even when we were close she seemed to be less the woman I knew than a rubber model, grossly and unevenly inflated, so that the eyes stood out enormously over shrunken cheeks, the sagging breasts hung like the fenders of a ship. As I came into her range of vision she halted and stood still, holding herself upright in the cautious way a drunken man will do; a moment had to pass before the mechanism of her brain would operate, and then she said in a voice that was little altered:

'Ah, Hilde, dear, how nice to see you home again—I hope you enjoyed your holiday! And your dear distinguished father, I trust he is better now?'

I answered, to save trouble, that I was no longer in great anxiety about my father's health.

'Well, that is splendid news!' she said. 'I myself—just at present—am having a difficult time. My husband—a little unwisely, I think—has sent all the staff away for their summer holiday, except my chauffeur, and he, poor man, is not himself at all; I have to keep him in bed for the time being. Of course it's not a serious matter—I have really no wish to take drives in this weather—but his own sense of duty makes him a restless patient. Today I'm going to give him some gruel with a solution of asafoetida mixed into it— Johanna says it's just the thing for anyone in a run-down condition.'

I ventured a correction here: 'But you know, liebe Schwiegermutter, I am Johanna.'

'Why, of course you are, dear!'

Physically this was a comfortless interview, for my muscles were stretched by the weight of the tray while she too was burdened with a vessel of the humbler sort, yet in a sense I did not want it to end. She was leaning forward now, and as she peered at my face I could see far back in her terribly distended eyes—as if I looked through an inverted telescope —the real Debora, limitless in her endurance, burning with indiscriminate affection. Gradually, then, I retreated to the bedroom, and at her own stiff, nibbling gait she followed me, as if I were pulling a wheeled statue on a short string; there, having set down our loads, we continued our conversation while I helped her to dress.

'You must turn your head away,' she said to Walther, and to me, 'I have him in my own room for convenience—often he needs a digestive tablet in the night. And of course you couldn't find a more trustworthy man, he has been in our service many years and I've always found him perfectly controlled.'

She was pleased when I told her I had brought Vaclav to give some assistance with the rougher domestic duties.

'Vaclav? But of course I remember him well,' she said. 'He belonged to my maid, Gertrud Bergen, her parents had never told the poor girl the rules about procreation. Yes, Vaclav will be most useful, especially when I start my summer concerts again—he's an accompanist of quite remarkable ability. Hilde, dear, how wonderfully you organise everything for me!'

Yes, she had always been uncertain in her use of names, and she lacked the sort of brain which keeps its various business in orderly compartments. But I had come to value her for the warmth of her nature, and never was her cordiality more welcome than on that day, when I felt as a child might feel in starting again, by special indulgence, at a school she has been expelled from. It was not an idle morning. The lumpish Hanna was only one of the women who came (as they were now accustomed) to offer Debora some small assistance and who, finding me at work, were content to add themselves to the redundant furniture: how much more easily could I have brought the room to some sort of order had I been able first to clear it of this human encumbrance! But the presence of Debora herself, the in-

creasing elevation of her spirits, so heartened me that I was
scarcely conscious of the drudgery. In recollection I see her
resting, a shapeless bundle of clothes plumped on a little stool
beside the oilstove; I hear the scraping bronchial noises, the
laboured breathing, as she tries to infect Frau Reuben with
her own soaring gladness:

'For me, Frau Balaam, such a happy day! My daughter, as
you see, my dear daughter Hilde is back from her trip to
Wien, she's taking over all the household responsibilities.
And then dear Stahl, my excellent chauffeur, today he's so
much better—look, turn him over and you'll see what a
much better colour he has today. Of course he can't drive me
for the present, he's not well enough for that. But Johanna
has most thoughtfully brought me poor Gertrud's child—
such a clever boy, I expect you've heard of his fame as a
musician—and no doubt he can manage the motor as well as
anyone.'

Repeatedly she struggled to her feet, to seize and cling to
my hands; then, with the exuberance that belongs to Jewish
women, she would moisten my neck and cheeks with maternal kisses. Once, clutching my arms almost fiercely, she
surveyed me for perhaps a quarter of a minute with steadfast
concentration, while I, suffering that gaze, was reminded
once again that only the years, only the immanent sadness of
those who survive their generation, had dimmed in this
benign woman a lively intelligence. In that brief lucid
interval it seemed to me that all the barriers had fallen
between her mind and mine; and as if to establish this
recognition she said spontaneously:

'Yes, Anna dear, I see now why my son Josef had to marry
you! I used to think you were simply one of those North
German girls, made to a pattern, handsome and cold as the
snow out there. Now I see that God always meant your heart
and body to be beautiful.'

With that she laughed, and kissed me again, and trudged
away to the kitchen to prepare some fresh concoction for
Walther. A little later she was telling me she had arranged a

concert in the Palmengarten hall at Frankfurt, at which my son Bruno Vaclav was to be the chief performer.

Grateful as I was for Debora's amiability, and the simple, unquestioning way in which the other women received me, I could not silence the small inward voice which insisted that these encounters hardly mattered: fearfully, impatiently, I was still waiting to face the farouche, mercurial creature once known to me as Franz Weckerlin, now the only living person who—if he were generous—might restore to me some part of the life I had thrown away. Presumably he had gone to his work before I was up, and would not be back until evening; yet while I listened to Hanna's raucous gossip, to the twittering of Maria Pavaaka as she stood with tedious humility just inside the door, my ears continually strained for a limping footstep, for the gusty laugh, the deep, flexile voice of the man I ached to greet as my son.

It was not till late afternoon that I came across Luise. I had taken some rubbish to the incinerator on the far side of the courtyard (now carpeted with snow) and on my way back I saw her coming towards me on a similar errand. Wearing a thin, short frock and indoor slippers she made me think of our first meeting, in the lobby of a Utrecht hotel, when she had seemed so much too childish for the married state; but then she had been alert and gay, and there was nothing vivacious in the white-lipped, shrunken being who stopped before me now. When I bent to embrace her she received my kiss quite passively. At a loss, I said:

'Perhaps you didn't know I was coming? Perhaps you didn't get the telegram?'

To which she answered, unsmiling, 'It doesn't matter. Really it doesn't matter at all. The room you had is empty.'

That bleak reception hurt but did not surprise me. Her pregnancy was finished; and even without the memory of my own experience I should have known from the desolate look in her eyes that she had miscarried, or else that her child, if born alive, had shortly died. All I could do just then was to take the box of garbage from her hands, saying, 'Luise, you

oughtn't to be out of doors without a coat. Go in—please go
in quickly and get yourself warm.'

Later I had the facts from Hilde Oestmann. The child, a boy,
had been born alive, after a difficult confinement; he had
been a little undersized—two and a half kilograms—but
apparently sound in body, with his features exquisitely
formed. His life had lasted just five days.

It was also Hilde who told me that 'Franz' had been sent
by his employers to Kassel, and would not be back for a
month or more.

For such a loss as Luise's there is no sort of consolation.
Kind words are hard to bear. You keep seeing some part of
the layette, or else, if thoughtful people have put it out of
sight, you keep noticing with a sadness not far from resentment that it has gone. So I did not try to commiserate with
Luise; I only did my best with looks and the simplest gestures
to show myself involved in her distress.

As far as I could see she desired no sympathy at all,
preferring the more astringent medicine of loneliness. She
went on with her domestic duties, shopping, attending to
meals, but with such a listless air that I felt as if some worn
machine occupied her body while her spirit was elsewhere.
This made it difficult for me to be of practical use to her, as I
had been before. The only company she accepted with
obvious content was that of Ruth, who was very often at her
side. If Ruth did not fully understand what had happened,
some intuition worked for her instead; with a range of facial
expression at which I marvelled she showed her sister-in-law
a constant tenderness, and it seemed to me that Luise
accepted from a barely articulate young woman a condolence
which no one else knew how to offer.

I bided my time, and the evening came when, seeming
unusually tired, she went early and supperless to bed. After a
few minutes I followed her to her room, where the light was
on and I found her still awake. I put some soup I had made

beside her; she said she was not hungry, but when I had talked for a minute or two, suggesting she should stay in bed next day, I noticed she was nibbling at the pumpernickel I had brought as well. Now once more I saw her as a child, one who needed an adult woman's care: and riding that wave of sentiment I said:

'Dear Luise, I do hope you'll let me live here at least till Felix comes home. I know I've no claim to be here at all—it wasn't my own idea to come. But I think I can be quite a lot of use—with the grandparents, for one thing.'

I looked for a little warmth in her response—it seemed absurd that she and I should be holding cautious conversation, as strangers do in a railway-train. But I had to be content with an answer in which I caught no note of feeling: 'Oh, there's no need for you to go before Franz comes back. Yes, it's difficult with the grandparents, they need a lot of looking after.'

'And you yourself,' I pursued, 'I feel you ought to get more rest than you do, until you're really well again.'

'Oh, I'm all right.'

'And Felix comes back when, do you know?'

'In about three weeks. Three weeks and two days.'

She was sitting up now, and absentmindedly she had begun to take the soup. Accepting that as a breath of encouragement, I said, 'It's hard for you, having him away just now.'

'Yes, I suppose so. Yes, he didn't want to go. But I thought he should.'

'What—it's an important job he's on?'

'It isn't a job. It's training.'

She explained then that his employers had come to realise the prodigality of using so clever a man for purely mechanical work; they had taken him into the drawing office, and then had sent him on one of the short courses in engineering organised by the Department of Reconstruction. As she dilated on her man's advancement something of her old animation returned.

276

'Of course I knew,' she said, 'that he wasn't going to spend his life as a mere labourer—I knew he would be successful, as Jewish men always are, and Franz above all others, whatever he did. Quite soon he'll be very important, then we'll try again and have a lot more babies—the money side won't matter. Already I don't have to work because Franz earns so much more.'

So far had she relaxed her stiffness that I thought she might come with me a little way into the field of my own anxieties; and when she told me that she wrote to Franz every day I ventured to ask, 'Have you let him know I'm back?'

'Oh yes. Yes, I tell him everything.'

'And does he mind my being here?'

'He hasn't said.'

I had to be still bolder then. I said, 'I suppose you've heard what happened when I went away with Albrecht Weckerlin? He must have told you all about it.'

'Well, not everything, I don't suppose.' Now she spoke warily, as I had expected. 'He told us you'd been to your old home. And you'd got back your memory. I mean, about what happened to Franz's father, and what you did afterwards.'

'But those are things which you—you and Franz—have always known?'

'Not all of it. A little. I think Franz knew more than he told me. He only said you'd had an illness which made you forget things—things you didn't really want to remember. Well, I could see that for myself when I met you at Utrecht.'

I asked then, 'Has Albrecht been here again, since that day he took me in his car?'

'Yes, he spent a night here. He was in his angry mood, like always when he's thinking about what they did to his wife. He and Franz were up talking half the night.'

Now she was lying back, her eyes almost shut. Plainly I had catechised her long enough, but I was desperate for some light on Felix's present feelings. I said:

'Luise, do tell me, please: has Felix—Franz—has he talked

about me at all? Since Albrecht came again, I mean.'

In her tired voice she answered haltingly, 'He did wonder why you hadn't written, after you remembered everything that had happened. I think he thought you might explain things. He thought you'd give him some reason why you went away from your home that night, with no one left to look after him and Agnes but stupid servants.'

'And now,' I said, 'I suppose it's too late for me to try and explain anything?'

She was silent for a while—I thought she had fallen asleep. But then she said wearily, 'I don't know. I'm not sure if he would listen now. I don't know if he would even want to listen.'

Those last words of Luise's were to haunt me : it was rather as if a doctor had said, 'I will tell you in three weeks and two days from now whether the tumour I've found in your breast is malignant or benign.'

In no sense (I thought) would it be possible to remain in the Warren if Felix had finally turned against me; and even apart from the tug of my emotions I saw already that this jejune demanding household was the only one I could live in as a whole being. Beyond the satisfactions of familiarity— which Coenraad's Lodge had also offered—it gave me, in this second sojourn, an unexpected feeling of membership; for I realised by degrees that the barriers which an ailing mind had once erected between myself and the other inhabitants had dissolved as a mirage does. These people, if they knew even a little of my past, cannot much have esteemed me, and for some time a gnawing shame kept me to that part of the house where my own kin was quartered; but I no longer saw in them, or imagined, any trace of animosity or contempt.

I think most gratefully of Klara Kilreuter's goodness. She never bore down upon me with her friendship, in the way some women do; on the several occasions in the first week or so of my return when we chanced to meet she was content to bow, with a smile almost as bashful as my own. But on a later evening, when we were about to pass at the first landing, she diffidently stopped me.

'You are very busy, Frau Doktor Schechter? I wondered if you could spare the time to visit me in my room—I've had a parcel with some really drinkable coffee, I want some of my friends to help me enjoy it. One or two of the others are coming, at round-about nine.'

I had, in fact, other things to do—evening was the only time when I could find leisure to wash Debora's linen—but no one could have resisted so amiable an invitation, delivered with such modesty. The small room which Klara slept and lived in was on the second floor; there, arriving a little later than the time given, I found the Szamuelys, an old Hungarian couple who lived in the coach-house, seated primly on a shallow settee; at my entrance they rose together as if they were Siamese twins, together bowed, and with kindly, coalescent smiles sat down again. Klara herself, to play the hostess's part, had added a silver-brocaded stole to the black jersey dress she always wore and had combed the hair from her forehead into a mannishly recumbent wave, dull-black with strands of grey; by accepted standards her face was too heavily made-up, but in combination with her greying eyebrows the over-reddened mouth and whitened cheeks had curiously enlarged her dignity; tonight she seemed to have resumed her former consequence, and in this penuriously furnished room, with the signed portraits of Ernest Bloch and Rudolf Hindemith as its only adornment, I caught a fleeting aftertaste of flavours I had long forgotten—the clamorous lobbies of the Hochschule für Musik at München, a swirl of cigars and decorations among the vast bouquets in the artists' room of the Nymphenburg Festsaal. I am certain, though, that she did not mean to overwhelm us with her past glories; tired, and as always far from well, she was intent upon our comfort, constantly asking me if I was warm enough, then with equal fluency addressing the Szamuelys in their own tongue, while she delicately filled the borrowed cups she had ranged along the clavichord. By art or instinct this prematurely wasted woman gave me the illusion that the circle centred in her genius was one where I had long been intimately welcome.

When we were settled, and the talk wound to a topic I had no part in, she turned to say (with only a slight hesitation), 'Johanna, you must be longing to see your Franz again. Luise tells me he'll be home quite soon.'

'Your Franz': because it came without warning I was taken aback by that ascription. Yet such already was my faith in the friendship surrounding me that I found myself answering calmly, 'Of course! But whether he'll be glad to see *me* is another question. He's a young man of moods.'

It was Hilde Oestmann—by then she and her father had joined us—who said tactfully, 'Why, yes—Franz is at heart an artist, and that must always mean a certain variability of temperament.'

At which Klara interposed, 'You mean, dear Hilde, that musicians—like Franz and me—are never quite right in the head!'

I could not join these women in their levity, which belonged to a mutual affection. But their gentleness emboldened me to seek some further sympathy. I said:

'I keep hoping, now he's on more interesting work, it may do something to make up for all his disappointment. Do you think it ever can? When I was last with him it was still the one thing which mattered—that he couldn't ever be the musician he'd dreamed of being. And you know, I suppose, what that means between him and me—you know about my own responsibility?'

Again I was answered by Hilde, with a firmness which no one would have looked for in a spinster of such unimposing exterior: 'Your son, Frau Schechter, has far too much intelligence to spend his life mourning the loss of one faculty. Ambitious—yes, of course he is. For a young man of his sort—so marvellously gifted—success in life is simply a necessity. But then success is on the way already. When he's an engineer with a great reputation he won't be thinking about his childhood aspirations.'

How easy just to accept that reassurance! But inevitably I glanced with raised eyebrows at Klara's face.

'I wish I could agree!' Klara said. 'Well, Hilde may be right, I'm not a man, and nothing in the world bores me so much as anything to do with mechanics, so I can only see things with my own eyes. When I was put under "protective restriction" there seemed to be no point any more in being alive. I don't mean just because the camp was barbarous—there were still worse places where they sent some of my friends. No, it was simply knowing that even if I ever did get free again I'd no longer have anything to give to music. That was like dying without losing consciousness.'

I said spontaneously, 'But *you* at least had memories to live with. You'd achieved—if only for a time—what you wanted to.'

She made a small, sad gesture of contradiction. 'It amounted to nothing,' she said. 'Oh yes, people were pleased with my singing, there was plenty of applause—for a time I found it exciting. But that's the sort of thing they do in circuses. Music isn't an exhibition of gymnastics. It's a barefoot journey towards impossible perfections.' She paused, ruminating, and then she said, 'I've tried to give Franz the idea of getting his voice trained—he has a very unusual singing voice. I could give him some help myself in the early stages. But so far he won't take me seriously. He's enormously self-willed, and he thinks I'm only applying a salve to his wound.'

She moved to refill the Szamuelys' cups, and to give them—I supposed—a brief account of our discussion, which they received with sympathetic murmurs, nodding in unison; while a stertorous whisper such as a sleeping child will utter drew my eyes towards Herr Oestmann. He was sitting with his eyes shut in the armed chair which he had occupied at our first meeting (for the custom within that leanly furnished house was to take one's own chair when visiting) but now his

281

thin trunk was erect, and as stiff as a soldier's—it looked as if he had been fastened there by his collar and then fallen asleep. Suddenly he spoke, and though his voice was small and tired it had the old flavour of graceful pedantry:

'Dear Fräulein Kilreuter, whatever you say, I still look on you with envy.' His eyes were slowly opening; for an instant the light of raillery showed in the palsied, bloodless face, then he said gravely, 'If nothing else, you lived for a *numen* worthy of your dedication—almost the only thing of non-contingent value that we know. A Bach fugue is indestructible; whereas the things to which we ordinary people give our lives can perish before we do.'

Hilde said quickly, 'But Vati, surely you're not sorry you gave your working life to Law!'

'Indeed I am sorry,' he answered, 'that I based my career on ideas which turned out to be moonshine. I never thought of the Law as a mere machinery for settling disagreements, I saw it as a great citadel, built by wise and honourable men to safeguard the rights of people who were less learned, more vulnerable. I believed that in my practice as well as in my writings I was contributing something to that work of protection. It didn't occur to me that a few talking chimpanzees could wreck the product of centuries in a matter of weeks.'

'But not for ever—not beyond rebuilding!' Hilde said; and then: 'Almost everything I taught at my Oberschule went on the scrap-heap, but a small part must have found some refuge in my pupils' minds. Some day it will take new life.'

Her father looked at her with mournful affection. 'Truly I hope so!' he said. 'For myself, I've come to accept the fact of absolute failure. I've lived so long in total darkness, I don't want to be disturbed by those who say they see a glimmer of light.'

That statement might have reflected a passing mood; but in his face, where once I had seen a Greek refinement, I was now aware of altered and distressing contours—as if cruel fingers, gathering the flesh below his mouth and thrusting upward, had forced the lower lip to curl and spread. To escape this portrait of despair I turned once more to look at Klara, who was patiently reporting Herr Oestmann's words to the Hungarian couple; for a while my eyes were content to travel over Frau Szamuely's ragged shoes, the delicate veining of her wrists and temples, the many skilful patches on her husband's ancient suit, then they were drawn through an unshielded window to the ant-like figures which, in a distant pool of light shed by lofty arc-lamps, were swarming about an entanglement of cranes and scaffold-poles. That vision of a half-built factory on the site of the old Tersteegenhalle might have seemed unreal, but in the street below us—so quiet in the evenings of the past summer that the roadway would be sprinkled with embracing lovers—the lorries with their loads of bricks and sand were rumbling even at this hour, reminding me how thin a space divided the industrious world from our immediate peacefulness. Nor was this feverish action meaningless to me: it stood for the courage of my fatherland, its unquenchable vitality; indeed, a moment came when I felt it was my companions in this room, so incongruously stationed, with so little reason left for existence, who were the creatures of illusion. But almost instantly I saw afresh that my own being was joined with theirs; in poverty, in helplessness; by a rising warmth of gratitude.

It seemed significant that when Herr Szamuely launched himself into speech he was at pains to include me in the traverse of his eyes, so that I felt the cordiality which glowed behind their serene intelligence. His soft utterance, attentive to the shape of every word, almost persuaded me that I understood what he was saying; though in truth my knowledge of Hungarian was negligible, and I had always to wait for Klara's intercurrent translation.

'Herr Szamuely is profoundly moved by what you say, Herr Oestmann.'

'How kind!' Herr Oestmann said. 'Pray give my thanks to Herr Szamuely.'

A late echo came from Szamuely's wife, who believed

herself a promising student of German: 'Profoundly moved!'

'But he suggests'—Klara went on—'that you are taking too sombre a view of the situation.'

'Too sombre!' Frau Szamuely said forbearingly.

'He would like respectfully to remind you that all human law-making, in so far as it transcends the mere convenience of society, is derived from a higher code—the laws of God Himself. Those divine laws are not susceptible to change—they don't alter with the new ideas and modes of living we arrive at from one day to another. And because they are immutable, there will always be a trustworthy foundation for new legislation to build on. In the future, as in the past, some laws will be good, some mischievous. But for us there remains a stable point of reference—in the law entrusted to our keeping almost at the start of human history.'

'Agreed!' Frau Szamuely said fervently. 'Everything my husband states is perfectly correct.'

One saw that Herr Szamuely kept finding it hard to wait for his interpreter to finish; almost before her mouth closed the passionate conviction one read in his face erupted in another flow of words. And it seemed to me that by degrees Klara herself was caught in the heat of his sincerity.

'Herr Szamuely is altogether in agreement with what you say about music—it belongs to the imperishable things. . . . And that is supremely important to us, because we live in an age unique in its record of destruction. We see now that a whole town can be laid waste by one man pulling a lever in his aeroplane; as for human lives, men have learnt to organise extermination on a scale that was never thought of before except in dealing with a plague of wasps or locusts. We here, we belong to the fortunate minority—we've escaped, like Job, with the skin of our teeth.'

'You mean,' Hilde bleakly interposed, 'with nothing besides.'

'But that's what our friend is saying! And he asks how much we are worse off through the loss of our material possessions. We have still our faculties, we can still see the beauty of the natural world, we take pleasure every day in each other's voices. Those are possessions of the mind, which no one can steal from us. Above all—and he's sure Frau Schechter will take no offence at this—we have our spiritual inheritance. Through every trial, through all our agonies, we of Israel cannot lose our vision of the Eternal, the divine glory, the everlasting justice.'

From a faint embarrassment I had taken refuge in returning to the study of Herr Oestmann's face: it was as rigid as a death-mask, but the eyes, fixed on Szamuely, were critically alive; and when Klara paused to search for a phrase he said just audibly, 'Justice? Where does it show?'

I had the impression that in transmitting this protest Klara softened it. At any rate Herr Szamuely was unshaken; with a passionate assurance he delivered his answer, which Klara fluently translated:

'Yes, we may feel that in our own time Justice has finally deserted us. That's because our vision is so narrowly confined—our minds fail to operate even on the scale of history. And yet we can never forget that we are promised a Vindicator—we know, we're certain, his appearance will mean the reversal of our present situation, the end of all our suffering, all our humiliations. More than that, it will bring a huge enlightenment, we shall see a design of such immensity and splendour that all the miseries of our past will dwindle to insignificance.'

Motionless, attentive, Herr Oestmann had allowed his sober eyes to travel slowly to Klara's face and back to Szamuely's. Now he was staring at his own feet.

'But when?' he asked. 'Please tell me when!'

I saw that Herr Szamuely understood this dry question without its being translated. Perhaps it was only my imagination which read in his face a spasm of distress, but certainly the answer which came was tinged with weariness: 'The greatest prophets, honoured Herr Oestmann, have not been told the time of deliverance. And I am not a prophet—I am a wholesale draper from Debreczin. We wait as our fathers did, with the same hope and courage.'

It would be disingenuous to pretend I could enter the mind from which those words came: of the two old men engaged in courteous disagreement it was the gaunt Herr Oestmann whose thinking seemed to march more evenly with mine. And yet when I review that haunting occasion the voice and features of the aged Hungarian are always at the centre of the scene. Whether or no he had learnt something of my private history, he must have seen me as one whose traditions were as far as possible from his, and for that reason, I surmise, he took care to consider my feelings even when his own were ablaze with what he believed in. At his peaks of eloquence he always remembered to put in a word or two (certain to be faithfully translated) which should render it harmless to my sensibilities, and he would make small, tortuous gestures of apology, smiling with a warmth which seemed to include me in both the moral privilege and the transcendent riches he claimed for his own kind. Nor did I regard this dual demeanour as hypocrisy. We were five beings brought together by life's eccentric currents who had in common a consummate knowledge of its harshness. Our modes of thought, desires, convictions, all divided us; but in this narrow room we were physically close, and alike weary, with nothing tangible to hope for; so it was natural, perhaps, that what we recognised within each other was not our differences but our sameness.

Something of that sympathy would surely outlast the hour which shaped it; before the evening closed I was finally persuaded that the house enshrining so generous a friendship was the one place where my spirit might rest and grow. But equally I was still convinced that I could not live under the same roof as my son if he showed himself estranged and hostile. Thus the prospect of his return became more than a cynosure of my emotions; it would finally decide whether my existence was to be purposeful or sterile, whether I should spend it as a live creature or as one which merely went through the motions of living.

A curious encounter which followed the party puzzled and disturbed me. Leaving Klara's room before the others, I came upon Ruth—who was normally in bed at that hour—standing motionless in the middle of the dimly lighted passage. Hurrying towards her, I said anxiously, 'Ruth, darling—Agnes—what are you doing? Have you been hunting for me?' She waited only long enough to give me one swift glance, in which my troubled fancy read sadness and reproach; then, without answering, she turned and fled to the stairs where—a shadow among shadows—she passed out of sight.

At that time I was sufficiently collected (and enough my father's daughter) to consider lines of retreat. If my deepest dread should be realised, forcing me to leave this house, I should not be able to face the prospect of sheltering once more in the stark benevolence of Coenraad's Lodge. But where else would a woman of middle age without money or friends be received?

Searching my mind, I remembered a cousin who, married to a large landowner, had once been comfortably established in a country house not far from Pforzheim. During my student days at Tübingen I had often been her guest, and although she was some years older than I we had become close friends; later, almost alone among my relatives, she had loyally supported me in my betrothal and marriage. I had been out of touch with her since some time before the War, and now it seemed sanguine to expect that a letter sent to the old address would reach her; nevertheless I wrote, asking if at some time in the summer I might pay her a short visit. To my surprise I had a reply within two or three days, written with all the former warmth. She and Arnold, my cousin said, were living a more restricted life than in the old days, but they were still occupying a part of the same house, and could offer tolerable comfort to one or two guests. She begged me to go to them whenever I wished, to stay as long as I could.

It may have been the strain of uncertainty which led to a setback in my health: I was having bad nights, and the spots on my face, though still invisible in the looking-glass, grew troublesome again. Once, when there were only five whole days to pass before Felix's return, the torment of sleeplessness drove me to get up in the early hours of morning and go for a walk in the town; there I became confused and strangely frightened, looking in the darkness for landmarks which in fact belonged to Wilpenschoen. Again and again, in those last days, I told myself that my fears were irrational: however changeable in mood, Felix had shown me more than once a core of gentleness, a capacity for deep affection; he would surely see that I belonged to this house, where at least I paid for my keep in domestic service. Yet the doubt remained.

Almost every morning I sought some reassurance from Luise: 'You've heard from Felix today? From Franz, I mean.'

'Yes, Frau Schechter.'

'He's well?'

'Yes, he seems quite well. He has found the course interesting.'

'He still hasn't said anything about me—whether he wants me to stay here?'

'I don't think so. No, he doesn't seem to think much about anything that's happening here.'

Sometimes she seemed deliberately evasive; but when I troubled to look at things with her eyes I realised how small a place the anxieties of a mother-in-law must have in the view from her mind. She lived in a cocoon of lethargy, through which she stared at other people as if they were amorphous objects hung against the light; even her way of walking should always have reminded me that her thin, tired legs carried (as it were) a huge weight of emptiness. How trivial must *my* hunger for Felix's return have seemed to her, aching to start again on the wearisome journey which might bring her a son of her own!

Small use, then, to discuss with her the practical questions of the future—in particular the increasing burden of caring for the Stahls. Intermittently I took some comfort from that problem: 'They will have to keep me,' I thought, 'because no one else understands the old people as I do.' But the premiss was not entirely valid. Awkward as she was in her movements, Ruth was learning how to put a room in order; even her slowness, combined with her evenness of temper, made her such a person as Debora found easy to get on with. Then too Vaclav, now he had learnt the ways of the house, was immeasurably useful; he had the physical strength and—more surprisingly—the gentleness that were needed for nursing Walther, under supervision he could lift him in and out of bed, and would wash him all over, addressing him as 'alter Kerl' and then uttering in his own tongue a stream of encouragement, much as a mother does to an infant in arms. It was Debora, though, who stood once more at the centre of his devotion—there was never an order of hers that he would not cheerfully carry out so long as intuition told him what she wanted. She, for her part, accepted him with something more than her normal amiability: he could make her laugh with his clownish movements, but her overriding attitude towards him was one of proprietary affection. 'My steward,' she came to call him, and in her efflorescent mind the appellation promoted by degrees an image which owed little to reality.

'My steward is weak in language,' she once confided to me. 'That is due, of course, to his far-eastern origins. All the same, I can trust him implicitly with the arrangements for next season's concerts—with musicians he has no trouble in making himself understood.'

Some of Vaclav's duties were performed as Ruth's assistant, and it interested me to see how she managed him. Meeting a simplicity which far exceeded hers, she seemed to discover in

herself a buried confidence; with her limited stock of words—
'Vaclav, here please! ... Lift so ... Move that way'—and
with decisive gestures she controlled his actions almost as
assuredly as an army corporal drilling his squad, while he
appeared to accept her rule with the complaisance that
toddlers often show towards their elder sisters'. Indeed, their
ways with each other grew so harmonious that at times—
absurdly—I felt a kind of jealousy: so easily had this rustic
found a way into my daughter's understanding, while it
remained impervious to me.

The continuing estrangement between Ruth and me was
the more distressing as I became aware of a new growth in
her personality, a widening of her mental range. Although
her use of language remained largely childish she spoke more
often now, with a slightly extended repertoire of phrases and
sometimes with surprisingly ambitious constructions. ('Agnes
is too tired,' I heard her say one morning to Luise. 'Vaclav
will go instead.') Her face, too, had altered: much of the
surplus flesh had gone, leaving the cheeks more spare, firm-
ing the lines of chin and forehead, while her eyes—it seemed
to me—had lost something of their naïveté. Unhappily the
advance marked by those symptoms brought her no nearer to
myself. The expression she generally showed me was the one
she had worn on the morning of my departure in Albrecht's
car—the bewildered look of a childlike creature suddenly
deserted by a friend. Sometimes I caught her regarding me
sidelong with a searching curiosity; but in the instant when
our eyes met hers would become distrustful, and she would
quickly turn away, as if she had suffered some physical
cruelty at my hands and was fearful of being hurt again.

Though she and I exchanged a few words every day in the
course of our activities, I remember only one occasion in
those weeks when we held what might pass for a conversation. This was on a late afternoon, when I found her all by
herself in the kitchen. She was standing by the window, using
the last daylight to help her darn a stocking; its fellow was on
the floor at her feet, and as I watched I saw a drop of blood

fall beside it—she had pricked her hand. There are incidents which overcome the restraints of reason; to Ruth, with her poor eyesight and ill-coordinated muscles, any use of the needle was slow, exacting labour, yielding pitiful results, and the sight of this awkward young woman toiling so conscientiously in the grey loneliness which surrounds an injured mind brought me suddenly close to tears. I yearned to put my arm round her shoulders, but that would likely have dismayed her; instead, I picked up the stocking which had fallen, and finding a large hole above the heel I said:

'I'll do this one for you—may I, please?'

When she did not answer I pulled up a chair and sat where I formed an effective barrier to the position she stood in—she would have had to squeeze between me and the sink in order to retreat. I saw that this action made her uneasy, but in my heightened longing for her friendship I could not bear to let go the chance our encounter seemed to offer. She had her sewing things in a biscuit box beside her; I took what I wanted and set to work, in almost palpable silence.

After a while I said, as if casually, 'It'll be nice, won't it, to have Felix home again.'

At first she appeared not to hear me, but after a few minutes she repeated dimly, 'Felix?'

'I mean Franz,' I explained. 'He used to be my Felix, just as you used to be my Ruth.'

Naturally she could make nothing of that statement, and only shook her head. 'No,' she said. And then, ponderously, 'Franz has gone away. Franz makes engines—Luise told me.'

In a way those words were encouraging, for they showed that her intelligence, however modest, could reach a good way further than I had previously supposed. So after a while I tried again to lead her thoughts to where they might connect with mine.

'I had a son once,' I told her, speaking very slowly, like an old nurse reciting fairy-tales to her charges, '—a boy called Felix. And a girl, Ruth—she was younger. That was a happy time for me, with Felix and Ruth to look after. But then the

War came and I had to go away, so I lost both of them.'

She had kept her eyes on her work while I spoke, and I did not know if she was listening; I was startled when she said abruptly, 'I don't want it. I don't want the War.'

'Nobody does,' I answered. 'Nobody wants any wars. But that's all over now.'

There I made no impression: as if I were trying to outwit her she repeated obstinately, glancing at her stocking, 'I don't want the War.' But I could not so soon admit a total failure, and after letting a minute or two go past us empty I tried a fresh approach:

'Listen, Ruth—Agnes. Would you like me to stay in this house for always? To look after you?'

Her reply came almost at once: 'Franz looks after me.'

'But of course!' I said; and again I fell into the slow, pedantic speech of seasoned nursemaids. 'Franz, he's a wonderful brother. But some people like to have a mother as well. That's what I could be.'

Now, for the first time, she stole a glance at my face. That was enough to start a current of excitement which set my hands and my chin trembling. I waited in fierce impatience for some sign that I had crossed the threshold of her understanding. She had finished her strand of wool; with maddening deliberation she sorted out another and re-threaded her needle. Then at last she said something, but it reached my ears as a mumble in which I recognised only two words: 'Uncle Albrecht.' These I caught hold of—how else could I keep in touch! I said:

'Uncle Albrecht—yes—I know he was very kind to you. You've seen him lately?'

'Uncle Albrecht,' she repeated stolidly, and now her enunciation was just clear enough for me to follow. 'He says she's gone. She went away.'

'Gone? Who's gone, dear?'

No answer.

'You mean—your mother? Uncle Albrecht says your mother has gone?'

No answer still; but I took her silence for affirmation. I asked, 'But didn't he tell you she might come back again?'

'She's gone,' Ruth said once more; and then with a dreadful finality, 'He says she ran away.'

It was like climbing on shale—there was no hand or foothold to rely on, I was always sliding to the base of the ascent. In retrospect, I believe I should have done better to relinquish words, to follow my instinct and at least to take her hands in mine. But I was still afraid of scaring her by what might appear to be duress, and while I was searching for some other doorway to her mind our privacy was broken: some child—I think it was Jakob, always the most plaintive of Frau Reuben's progeny—arrived to pester me for a titbit, and by the time I had appeased him Ruth had made her escape.

I remember thinking then that one hope remained: Felix might bridge the chasm between her and me. In his own way he could surely persuade her—if he would—that the friendship I offered was sincere and would be faithful. But this notion brought me no more than a faint comfort; its chief effect was to exacerbate my hunger for his return.

The accepted stratagems for speeding time are useless: you try to narcotise your mind with industry, but your eyes will always stray towards the clock on the kitchen wall. (What—only an hour gone! Six more before this day can be considered over, two further days and part of another to follow empty!) In the endless term of waiting my mother-in-law was always demanding some unusual service, Larin Pavaaka kept me for half a morning helping him to pursue some wage dispute with the municipal sanitation office (which employed him now as a scavenger), all day long I seemed to be running to the aid of children who had hurt themselves or lost things. But those activities meant no more to me than files and ledgers mean to an office girl who is to meet her lover in the evening. The things which happened about me, events I was physically involved in, would remain outside my real life until the moment when my son and I were again face to face.

Beneath my festering impatience a terror grew like that of being marooned. In the formidable journey towards wholeness I had seemed to gain some ground; now I realised that if Felix refused me the amnesty I looked for I should be back in the haunted solitude where it had started, without strength or reason to struggle again.

You make a hundred pictures of a longed-for meeting—what he will look like, what you and he will say. The actuality never at all resembles what you have imagined.

On the day when Felix was due, Luise, naturally, was in a state not radically different from mine. When, meeting her in the hall, I asked what time she expected him she looked as if I had faced her with some abstruse problem in mathematics; it took her several seconds to answer hazily, 'Oh, not till this evening. I'll be going to meet him.' A return of shyness forbade me to press her. Thus we two who had both to endure the stubborn dragging of the hours were no help to each other. All I could do, when the day at last began to age, was to keep an unobtrusive watch on her movements, so I should know when she started for the station.

As soon as she had gone I put into effect a simple plan for giving Felix a welcome. Obviously he would want to spend the first hour or more alone with his wife, and even at the climax of my impatience I knew he would be more ready to take some notice of me when that wish had been granted. The kitchen at that time of day offered no more privacy than the Potsdamer Platz; so, having given Ruth her supper a little earlier than usual, I got her to help me set a tête-à-tête meal for the young couple in their own bedroom, using a table and chairs I had borrowed from friends upstairs. I had managed to get a few flowers from the sisters Essenschneider, and beside these—in case I should not be available when the pair arrived—I placed a note to tell them they would find a casserole in the oven.

That proved a sensible precaution, for the preparations were hardly finished when I received an urgent summons to wait upon Walther Stahl. The message, brought by one of the children, actually came from Maria Pavaaka, whom I found in a state of somewhat intemperate distress, standing beside her Larin in the passage which led to the Stahls' room.

'Pavaaka has been a stupid,' she informed me.

'What can I do!' Pavaaka retorted. He was in his working clothes, tired, resentful. 'The old ladyship commands me—I must seek her a droshky—no delay. How will I say "Rubbish!" to such a lady?'

In the bedroom I was greeted first by Hanna. She too was in that overcharged condition which often makes Baltic folk so trying to deal with; as soon as I entered she came to plant her puff-ball body in front of mine and addressed me as if she and I were persons of equal responsibility. 'Now this old man will be dead quite soon,' she said dogmatically. 'I tell him, if that old Jezebel goes parading like the queen-whore in this motor Pavaaka brings up now, any smart old man will keep his bum inside his bed.' Her slipshod elocution made this announcement all but meaningless to me; without much formality I stepped aside to see for myself what was happening.

In the angle between Debora's bed and the washstand Frau Reuben and Vaclav faced each other, bending forward, like Gothic angels on guard at either end of a pretentious tomb; she with that sweet, besotted look of resignation which never ceased to irritate me, he fatuously giggling as he was wont to do when any situation baffled him. Between them Walther, with a pair of trousers pulled on over his nightshirt, was seated on the floor, leaning back against the cabin trunk where Debora kept her clothes. It was some days since I had shaved him (for of late he had become hypersensitive about the operation), so his lower face and neck were coated with a grey down; elsewhere his skin, appearing almost translucent in the artificial light, and the eyes which feebly sought to identify my face, so pointed his extreme age that in that company he seemed a little unreal, like an ancient farmhouse left standing among the suburban villas of an expanding town. To me, however, this incongruity was far from pitiful, since the old man's expression showed nothing of self-pity: if his eyes were dim, the set of his lips and his clenched hands were alike signals of a measured purpose, while the cirrus of fine white hair which framed his forehead gave him something of the nobility that Michelangelo reveals in the aged. Here, I thought, was a person of greater stature than I had realised hitherto. From close behind, Hanna continued her efforts to instruct me: 'He's lost himself, that old rooster—his brain is gone.' Ignoring her impertinence, I stooped to speak to him:

'Walther, dear friend, it's Frau Josef here to help you. What is the trouble?'

I think he knew my voice at once, but he did not answer my smile; he only said, 'I tell you it's wrong. The Mistress isn't fit to go alone.'

'Go where, Walther?'

'She's going to see about her house. At Eisenach. She doesn't realise what it's like there—she won't believe what those Russians have done to the place.'

'Well, I quite agree—it would be foolish for her to go just yet,' I said.

Either he did not hear or he failed to understand me. With a slight change of voice he said earnestly, 'If you will be so gracious as to help me, Frau Josef, with my collar and tie. And I don't know where my coat has got to. All I need is to finish dressing, and then perhaps the boy here will give me a hand to the car. After that I will be all right.'

He was struggling to stand up; I motioned Vaclav to help me, and together we presently had him on his feet.

'Listen,' I said quietly, as he stood swaying with nearly all his weight on my arm, 'there's no need to think of any such journey for the time being. To begin with, there are no cars available, with the present shortage of petrol.'

But this convenient falsehood brought a sharp contradiction from Hanna: 'All the time that crazy Pavaaka has a car that waits outside.'

Till then Debora herself had not interfered. Most of that day she had stayed in bed complaining of 'my old protein trouble'; now she was sitting in her blue nightgown on the bedside chair, observing us with that air of sublime detachment which the highly-placed instinctively adopt in the face of minor hindrances. Her old valise was on the bed beside her, and I should have seen that travelling was in her mind because she had donned the flamboyant hat which embellished all her journeys. It was Hanna's words, I think, which disturbed her recession; for at the mention of the car she stood up on her bare feet and, with that dignity of carriage which she could still achieve to meet a crucial occasion, came to stand at my side.

'Jemima, dear, there's a small difficulty,' she said. 'The owner of this conveyance I've ordered wishes to be paid in advance—of course, in a small place like this they don't know anything about Herr Schechter's standing. So I thought if you'd be good enough to lend me a hundred marks just till tomorrow that would be the simplest solution. And after that I'd be glad of a little help to fasten my outdoor shoes.'

Before I could think of an answer, Walther was reaffirming his opposition: 'It's not right for the Mistress to go,' he said decisively. 'At Eisenach there'll be nowhere suitable for her to sleep, and all the contractors will cheat her.'

His protest won no more than a cool, swift glance from Debora, who now put her mouth as close as possible to my ear. 'Poor Walther is getting old,' she explained, 'he forgets nearly everything I say. I've told him quite distinctly I've arranged for another chauffeur to take me to Eisenach—it would be quite wrong for him to drive me when he has a temperature.'

Here was my chance to show her a measure of unanimity. 'Certainly Walther's not well enough to travel,' I said. 'But then I think, liebe Schwiegermutter, the expedition would be much better postponed altogether till the weather is warmer. For one thing, the people at Eisenach will want time to arrange a proper reception.'

'But my dear, the motor is waiting outside there now.'

'Then we'll get Herr Pavaaka to send it away.'

I had spoken a little too loudly. From Maria Pavaaka, standing in the doorway, came a thinly voiced but resolute demurrer: 'The man has been here already half an hour—the man with the cab. If no one will pay him he says he takes hold of Larin's neck and kicks his insides into the highway.'

'Just so!' Hanna pronounced, in fluent sympathy. 'And without his insides this Larin will look like nothing but a gutted sheep.'

But the tiresome inconsequence of these women was the least of my troubles. At that juncture I wanted to divide myself into three—then I could have treated both the Stahls with appropriate consideration and simultaneously got rid of the droshky. As it was, I could only reiterate to Walther that I was assuming his responsibilities, and then instruct Vaclav to help him back into bed while I did a like service for his wife. For the moment my strongest feeling was for her. The brave notion of a visit to her former home had evidently ruled her thoughts for some time past; she had made a rudimentary plan, had shrewdly recognised in the stolid Pavaaka the one person who would consent to forward it, and now the wanton obstruction of her retinue (as it must have seemed to her) had brought her brilliant hopes to ruin. So, when I had coaxed her between the bedclothes, and cleared the room of sightseers, I sat beside her for a while, praising her patience, talking speciously about the greater pleasures of travelling in summer. But already her impetuous mind had found a new cause for concern: she feared—she told me in a throaty whisper—that she had spoken over-hastily to her chauffeur, and nothing was more shameful than to treat an old servant with any lack of courtesy.

'I should like you, dear, as soon as you have leisure, to

interview the poor man and make a full apology on my behalf.'

I assured her that this could be done without delay, and I crossed the room at once to carry out her wish. But Walther, lying with his eyes shut, would pay no attention to the message I brought; realising that the expedition to Eisenach had been abandoned, he had suffered a revulsion of feeling and was dwelling now with acute distress on Debora's disappointment. Perhaps he should not have interfered? Would I be good enough to speak to the Mistress, to tell her that he himself would make all the needful arrangements for her journey as soon as he had thrown off the small bronchial trouble which had temporarily made him unsteady on his feet. The effort and excitement of the evening had left him exhausted, his voice so feeble that I had to keep my ear close to his lips to make out what he said. Thus absorbed, I hardly noticed the sound of someone entering the room—I vaguely thought it was Vaclav, who habitually came and went with no more ceremony than a ward maid in a hospital. When I turned, however, I saw that a man I did not know was bending over Debora's bed.

It cannot have taken me more than a fraction of a second to realise who it was, yet I distinctly remember how my mind went through two stages before it arrived at that recognition: I thought first, 'This uncommonly handsome man must be a doctor they engaged to attend the Stahls while I was away,' and then, 'But this is Josef—Josef as I saw him at our first meeting, when I was summoned to his office desk.' That mental graduation is simply explained: Felix had taken off his heavy beard, and so presented—to my first glance—a different shape of head; moreover, the major change was supplemented by a general neatening of his appearance—his hair had been respectably barbered, he wore a dark suit of a kind appropriate to office work. Those were details I appreciated later; when I caught sight of him at Debora's bedside I had only a general impression of familiarity transmuted, of a presence which far surpassed the image on which I had been depending. Yes, the moment I had so long lived for was in fact more convulsive than anything I had imagined. If Josef himself had quietly walked into the room I could not have been much more violently startled or stirred to fiercer longing.

I stood up and made a movement towards Debora's bed, letting fall some trite phrase like 'Ah, Felix, so you've come!' At this he turned his head and very slightly bowed. Then he continued his conversation—I remember him saying, 'Yes, liebe Grossmutter, next time I go on such a course I'll take you with me as my secretary!' and how she, laughing like a girl, pulled down his head to kiss him again and again. At that point my body would answer to none of my commands; but I suppose no more than a few seconds passed before I recovered sufficient control to get myself out of the room.

To go to bed without seeing him again—with nothing settled, nothing even discussed—that was unthinkable. But how, in this house which resembled a fair-ground, was I to get him by himself?

From a dark corner on the first floor landing I heard him come out of the Stahls' room and go to his own. I followed, to listen outside the door, and so learnt that Luise—as I had expected—was with him. As a rule she went down to the kitchen fairly late to see about the next day's meals; if she followed that routine tonight it would give me my chance. I returned, then, to my hiding-post and stood there shivering in the cold. I had to wait a long time: I think it was some-where about eleven that Luise did at last emerge and I had a slanting glimpse of her going downstairs with a bundle of linen in her arms—I guessed it was mainly clothes which Felix had brought back and which she meant to wash immediately. That would entirely suit my purpose. As soon as my ears told me she had reached the kitchen I slipped across to her room, knocked and went in.

Amid the aftermath of unpacking—clothes, papers, shoes —Felix lay across the bed with a book under his chin; his eyes, raised as I entered, showed him occupied with other things than me. Shutting the door behind me, wasting no time on protocol, I delivered the sentence I had been rehearsing:

'Felix, I'm sorry to intrude—I just wanted to get one or two things settled.'

'Oh—yes.'

He shut his book and rather awkwardly slid off the bed to stand beside it, facing me with the stiff politeness of a shop-assistant who recognises an exacting customer. I, in turn, moved to where I could grasp the rail at the foot of the bed—it was of great importance that I should have something fixed and solid to hold on to.

'Yes?' he said.

'Well, first about Vaclav, this man I've brought here—Luise will have told you. It wasn't my own idea—the superintendent at Wilpenschoen sent him, he thought he'd be useful to the Stahls. He has a special devotion to your grandmother.'

'Yes, Luise has told me.'

'But of course it's an extra mouth to feed, so I thought you might really feel he ought to go back. You only have to say so and of course I'll arrange it straight away.'

He considered this, and then he said, 'I think Luise wants to keep him for the time being.'

I nodded. 'Very well!'

'And there was something else?'

It was uncanny, as he said those words, to see an expression of his father's reproduced with perfect fidelity. So often, when Josef had been merely my employer, I had gone to his office with some problem and found him submerged in weightier affairs; always he had listened to me with the most courteous patience, always I had felt as if he were looking through the back of his head at the electric clock behind him, calculating how many marks the interview was costing the company as every minute passed.

'Well, it's about myself,' I said—and I was astonished that

301

my voice did its work so well, issuing almost as evenly as if I spoke of some trifling technicality. 'I mean, I'm another *bouche inutile*, and you have a wife to support, and Ruth as well, and the old people. I think I can probably find some paid work in the town—office work or something. But in the meantime it's perhaps hardly reasonable that you should be expected to keep me.'

That speech left him silent for a few moments. Then he said, 'I see what you mean.'

We were avoiding each other's eyes. It was a curious interview, sedate and circumspect; to me unreal.

'As a matter of fact,' he continued soberly, 'you're saving me a certain amount of money. The state my grandmother's got to now, she—and the old man—they're too much for the girls to look after. One can't altogether rely on Ruth, and Luise isn't really well. If you weren't here I'd have to pay someone.'

'So it would suit you if I stayed for the time being?'

'Yes.'

'On the understanding, of course, that if my services were no longer needed I should find somewhere else to go?'

Again he hesitated. His hands were moving restlessly along the quilt, freshly drawing my attention to the dreadful gap in the left one. I noticed too that his eyes were puffed with fatigue.

'You mean,' he said, 'would you be turned out if Grand-mother died, for instance? Well, no—I'm sure that isn't what my father would have wished. That's to say, you're free to stay here whatever happens. You will always be provided for. Always.'

So, I had my answer. The question how I was to live was settled: I should be maintained, as long as I wished, by my son's philanthropy. Logically the interview was at an end; only the physical difficulty of letting go the bed-rail and taking three steps to the door made me stay to raise another question.

'Luise tells me,' I said, 'that you've been seeing Albrecht Weckerlin again.'

'Yes, he was here some weeks ago.'

'And he talked about me?'

'Well, yes, naturally.'

'But he can't have told you much that you didn't know already.'

'No, but he had it in more detail. All the things we weren't certain about had been cleared up—well, you know how. I mean, it's proved now that my father would never have come back from Switzerland—never been caught and "liquidated" —if you hadn't sent him a deceitful letter. And then, your running away, leaving Agnes and me to the mercy of those bastards—well, unfortunately there's no doubt about that either. Not now.'

The bed was shaking violently. I suddenly became aware that the movement derived from my own body, and I had to slacken my hold on the rail. For a few seconds my voice was out of use; when it returned I said:

'You do realise, I suppose, that Albrecht has a special view of things. A special bitterness. Because of what happened to his wife.'

'Well, of course.'

'So he wouldn't be likely to say anything at all in my favour. To accept anything I said in my own defence.'

'No, naturally he wouldn't.'

'And you yourself—you don't want to hear my side, anything I could tell you about how things happened?'

I looked at his face as I said that, but his eyes would not meet mine. He began to answer, 'Look, I don't think there's much point in discussing—' and then stopped. Presently he started again, haltingly, as if he had to explain some abstruse subject in a foreign tongue:

'Gnädige Mutter, I've told you you can stay here, I've said we'll look after you. I don't think you can really ask for more than that. For anything emotional, I mean. Luise and I—all of us, in fact—when you were here before we felt for you

303

because in a way you were ill. That was what the man at Wilpenschoen told us in his letter—you didn't remember things. So we felt—in a way—as if you weren't responsible for what you'd done. That was how I looked at it—and Luise too. We made all the allowances. Well, that time's over. From what Albrecht says, you've remembered everything now, and it doesn't seem to make any real difference to you.'

One's mind moves erratically under certain kinds of stress. I remember thinking it strange to hear those words from a person I had first known as a presence in my womb.

' "From what Albrecht says",' I repeated. And then I heard myself asking, in a voice that still sounded almost normal, 'You yourself, you don't think I feel any different? You don't imagine those memories hurt me at all?'

'Well, really,' he answered, 'I don't want to go into that—I see no need to. As far as I'm concerned the subject's closed.'

A woman is at a disadvantage, always; her breaking-point is so much lower than a man's, and if she gives way to tears—if she even lets her voice escape her control—she is condemned for using tactics which are feminine, dishonest. My only refuge, then, was in silence. It is fair to suppose (as I do in retrospect) that Felix too needed to guard himself against the pressure of certain instincts—that when he spoke again the metallic coldness of his eyes and voice was partly a means of defence; because I do not see him—even then I did not see him—as a man who would ever practise cruelty for his own pleasure. He must have thought beforehand—perhaps on the journey home—of phrases he would use at a meeting with me, for parts of what he said came with a chilling fluency; but other parts were delivered less glibly; and I know it is often when men are unsure of their own position that their voices become grinding and inhuman.

'I rather wish,' he said, 'that we hadn't needed to discuss this at all. You're my mother, but I just don't feel the relationship—not any more. As a child I suppose I did. It's just that I don't belong to the kind of people you do. You spent your early life—the part that counts—in a sort of imitation world, from what I've heard of it. A sort of dance, in which everyone knew their special routines. Mine's been different. All I've ever known is two sorts of people—one lot which goes through hell, the other lot that makes them, or else just stands back and does nothing. Well, you can't belong to both those. And I know which I belong to.'

He turned away then, to busy himself (or pretend to) with shifting things from an almost empty suitcase into a chest of drawers. I thought his effusion had come to its end. But he added, without facing me again, 'All the same, I don't mean—as I've told you—that I'm asking you to go away.'

Of the dozen answers which all at once crowded my mind none took on the shape of words. It must have been just then that Luise returned. And I released my hold on the bed-rail and left the two of them together.

When I had gained my own room it did not take me long to pack my things, since they were few. I had then to wait for a while, not wishing to meet anyone on my way downstairs with a suitcase—that would have meant talk and explanations.

As soon as the lights were out in all the windows which I could see from mine I thought it safe enough to go. But now I was suffering from a familiar kind of fatigue in which one's muscles refuse to respond to orders from the brain. For a time I sat on the bed, and then I lay back against the pillow. My own light was still on and I thought it would keep me awake; but I must have slept for at least a few moments, for I thought I saw Nicolaas Dekker kneeling at the end of the bed, and that manifestation (which has since impressed me as an odd coincidence) can only have come from a dream. From then I was continually conscious, though the heavy stillness of my body made me feel as if it were independently asleep.

I could afford to rest for an hour or two, so long as I was clear of the house before anyone was stirring: the important thing was that my severance from this place and all it meant to me—the emotional ties, the sanguine illusions—should be sudden and complete. My further plans were nebulous. The very little money I had must be kept for food; begging lifts, I might make my way by stages to Pforzheim, and then my cousins would probably shelter me for a time. Possibly some temporary office jobs were to be had in Stuttgart; at worst, summer would bring a demand for extra staff in the Schwarzwald hotels.

In truth, the question of livelihood did not trouble me severely in those hours. When your emotions have been over-taxed you come to a state of tiredness where your thoughts seem to be loosed from the ties which normally confine them; once again I reviewed the plan I had made some time before to bring the wretchedness of living to an end in the Alphen Waterweg, but now I realised afresh that an enterprise which had proved impossible, demanding a resolution far firmer than mine, was not the only means of release. Detachment: that was an operation which the mind could manage with its own resources. The past, I thought, need not command us. The burdens which arrived each day—the stress of fending for oneself, the pain of watching in the glass a creature who will presently grow old and useless—these should suffice to fill one's mental horizon: only perversity would make one look backward to revive old causes of distress. Yes, I needed to be vigilant; but now it occurred to me that I was expert in such vigilance already—I had only to re-employ the faculty of suppression which I had wantonly discarded. Distantly a murmur of disquiet sought to remind me that such annul-ment of the past was never harmless; but I had no ears for that disturbing voice.

I must have gone some way towards achieving the detach-ment I relied on before I left the bedroom, for although I have a distinct memory of going downstairs—the pull of the valise on a numbed arm, the shadows of the balusters and my own floundering shadow on the dingy walls—I did not con-

nect that passage with any thought of people living behind
the doors which at every stage came dimly into view. This
was no more than the carcass of a house I had once known as
a living presence. None the less I enjoyed a sense of deliverance when I was out of the building: I was at least free from
an environment which would always have threatened my
inward security.

Knowing only a small portion of the town, I had an idea
that the main southward road would start from the other
side of the river, so from the street in which the Warren
stood I turned to retrace if possible the route by which Luise
had brought me from the station at my first arrival. This—as
a more recent transit should have warned me—was not a
simple project. From the sky, thinly hazed, there was light
enough to guide me from one street corner to the next, but in
the largely mediaeval district which gathered about me the
houses with their steeply pointed gables, their small windows
almost hidden under beetling timbers, were at night so
uniform in aspect that every street seemed a copy of its
neighbour. Here was the squat, cone-capped tower of a
church which lacked its roof, here the hollow façade of a
Volksschule: moving slowly, with tired and inattentive eyes, I
could not tell if features such as those were duplicated or if,
having lost direction, I was passing the same ones a second
time. From the rub of the shoe on my left heel a small, insistent pain kept me aware of my body, which, long after my
mind had lost its hold on the purpose of this expedition, continued its lame, dogged march; now I saw like the projection
of a lantern slide a huddle of youths playing cards, now at
the level of my eyes a woman stooped over a tousled heap of
bedclothes where a child lay with his bare arms stretched
above his head, and although I had lost connection with my
surroundings those glimpses denied me the tranquillity of
total isolation—they seemed to argue that the material world
existed and was something to which I still belonged. There
were, indeed, those who would have helped me—an old
woman who called from a high window to ask if I was ill, a

workman of some kind who offered to carry my case—but I thought those people might have some link with the ones I was determined not to think of, so I pretended not to hear or not to understand.

Recalling that night, I think of Jacopo Frugoni, the escaped convict who in the year 1605 stole a small boat at Livorno and hazardously sailed it to the Turkish coast; of how, in the market of Adalia, he thought that every face was one he knew, and became so frightened that he took to his boat again, only to have that grim experience repeated at every harbour where he went ashore. '*Each time,*' he tells us in his journal, '*I returned to my frail craft with inexpressible relief, recognising it as the one place in all the world which for me held peace and safety. Yet always, when the land drew out of sight, I felt a fresh and excruciating terror; not of the great seas which often threatened to engulf me, but of the unimaginable solitude, as if I had been coffined, still alive, for all eternity.*' As I wandered in that tangle of narrow streets my first sensation was just the relief Frugoni speaks of. Like him, I had recovered possession of a secret place just large enough to live in; I was back—as if there had been no interruption—in the course of life where a wall of darkness followed me, cancelling all disgrace, obliterating every name and image which stood for the agony of forfeited affections. But because this state was so familiar the relief quickly gave place to a peculiar distress. While the body lasts, the death of the mind is never complete. I realised that the safety to which I had returned depends on universal estrangement: you speak as little as you can to people who cross your path, knowing that any speech may stir them to a dangerous inquisition or else that they will try to weaken your resolve, drawing you back to the unbearable world of actuality; yet simultaneously you long to yield; for you never totally forget that all the riches which exist are stored within those beings, their thoughts, their braveries, their care for one another's suffering, and you cannot finally extinguish the desire to share in their circumstance. The thing was settled, however:

308

it was not conceivable that I should return to normal living a second time. Like the Piedmontese sailor I had escaped from one state of misery only to an infinite loneliness, and as the picture of that barren circuit grew larger in my mind the anguish turned to a mounting fear. There came a time that night when I found myself mouthing incoherent prayers as a terrified child would; but without the hopefulness of children; for when you cease to talk to fellow-creatures you put between yourself and any imaginable God a boundless and impenetrable silence.

Supposing vaguely that as night advanced the darkness would intensify, I was surprised when the shapes within my view grew more distinct—an object like a large box turned into a delivery van, beside it were the broad, shuttered windows of (I think) a café or some small hotel. I was sitting on a stone step: I must have stopped there to rest my legs some time before. It was a perch of little comfort, but I continued to make the best of it. There was no reason I could think of to hurry on.

One or two people were passing now, and after a while a man in uniform came to ask me questions—did I need help, and so on. This would have been alarming, except that the cold had made me too slow in mind to be greatly stirred by anything that happened. I told him with a reasonable calm that I had the Superintendent's permission to go about the town as I desired.

'The Superintendent? Please, what do you mean? Where are you living?'

'At Coenraad's Lodge,' I told him. 'I am one of the prisoners. But I am allowed out on parole, with special permission from the Superintendent.'

He did not seem to understand what I was saying; at the time I supposed that this was due to stupidity—he was an oldish man of the kind which is pushed into the Army in early youth, often to follow a military career consisting mainly of cookhouse fatigues.

'I have a document,' I said, 'to prove what I've told you. For the moment I'm not sure what I've done with it, but it's probably somewhere in my case.'

'Never mind, never mind!' he said. But he stopped and stared with a student's concentration at an old label on the case, as if that would help him to check my statement. 'Perhaps you had rather a nice party last night,' he suggested in a foolish, genial fashion.

I replied that at Coenraad's Lodge there was nothing much in the way of parties.

He must, after all, have been a man of natural kindness; there was quite a fatherly note in his voice when he advised me to be on my way. 'If I was you,' he said, 'I'd take the second turning on the left, and then the first to the right. After that you'll probably know where you are.' The confidence with which he issued those directions persuaded me that in fact he had understood me perfectly and knew the way to Coenraad's Lodge; walking on as he bade me, I expected presently to come on landmarks I should recognise, perhaps the tower of the Noorderkerke, or the road bridge over the Old Canal.

I had got very stiff, and I went through extreme discomfort before the act of walking had restored my circulation, but as soon as some warmth returned to my feet and hands my body began to draw a kind of contentment from the perambulation my mind was so little engaged in; however fervently you may want to be done with the physical world, your senses will always linger among flavours which once delighted them. The sepulchral light of earliest morning had turned to a pale sunshine, and I remember how, above a ragged silhouette of roofs and naked branches, the smoke drifting from a score of chimneys wrought a pattern of curious beauty on the hazed yellow sky. I think the wind must have veered in the night; its touch on my face was quiet now, with none of the winter's edge, and at the corner where I turned, as the Schupo had directed, it brought me a brackish smell, a whiff of high heathland, recalling for an instant the thrill of riding with my father on a morning in early spring. When I had made the second turn the endemic urban smells—of motor oil and refuse, of ironsmiths' furnaces—surrounded me again, and these too were grateful because of their familiarity. Where the street abruptly narrowed I caught from an old-fashioned bakery the most engrossing odour of them all: the homely smell of fresh rye bread, never exactly matched in foreign towns, will always recreate for me the strange last stage of that night's wayfaring, when, with my spirit sunk in the lethargy of total surrender, I found my nerves and organs responding to the magic of morning with an incandescent, pure delight.

It is harder to recapture the frame of mind in which I still supposed that town to be Wilpenschoen, when everything around me spoke of the strong and gentle culture of my own land; but others—soldiers, women working long hours in hospitals—have described to me the same state of exhaustion, where one's thoughts are no more ruled by logic than are the fragments of a dream. I know that when I suddenly arrived in the street from which I had started a few hours earlier—when I caught sight of two old men repairing bicycles beneath a name-board which said 'Rosamunde', and then the little shop I went to almost every day for groceries—I still failed to join my thought of Astelbrucke with this distinctive scene: I recognised it only as, in a sleepy afternoon at the cinema, one acknowledges a fleeting view of the Brandenburger Tor or the Parthenon—objects which meet the eye so often that the brain no longer troubles to attach their names. So it was that when I came opposite a high, square, shabby house, faced with much vulgar decoration, I saw it first as you see a hackneyed poster and then merely as one of the buildings in which—not recently, I thought—I had once been held as a suspected person. I might have gone on walking, still vaguely expecting to come upon the stalls which line the Heerengracht and the domed water-gate commanding the Plein, but my legs had grown rebellious. Again a house which stood against the pavement gave me a step to sit on, and once more I found it luxury to remove the weight from my aching feet.

Here the strengthened sun was in my eyes; a young woman who, presently, came over from the other side of the road had reached the kerb before I realised she was someone I knew. Even then my brain refused to throw up her name. She stood before me, earnest, bashful, like a small girl entrusted with some responsibility too large for her years; I was absurdly slow to notice that she had in her hand a piece of paper which she wanted me to read.

It was a telegram, signed 'Dekker'. It said, *'Tilka triomfantelijk strief gisteren nacht.'*

I thought, 'So at last Tilka is dead!' There was nothing remarkable in that. I could not see, to begin with, why Nicolaas had troubled to send a telegram; nor why he should have used the word 'triomfantelijk'—'Tilka died *triumphantly* last night.'

And yet this message greatly affected me. I ceased for a time to be conscious of the bearer, or of any traffic which may have passed along the street. As if I had returned to it bodily I saw the room I had once shared with Tilka, I even seemed to breathe the fetid air which had filled it at my last visit there. The wandering beam of memory will linger to illuminate some fragments of the past with particular distinctness, but it has not often restored a faded scene as vividly as it showed me the thin, grey, crumpled mask which at that final meeting had been all that was left of Tilka's face: the vision brought her so close to me that I could hear as if from a mechanical recording the distant, muted voice, still unmistakably hers, decking with its Polish gracefulness the exacting German words as she talked of my own concerns, and again as she related with the calm of simple credence how a man with bleeding feet had come and offered to nurse the airmen prisoners in her stead. Nor was that experience merely a revival of old sensations. Within the picture of a stifling sickroom—of Lore's watchful presence at my shoulder, the monstrous shadows which one muffled light described on walls and shutters, the lifelike broken flesh and indefinably commanding eyes of the figure on a crucifix—I caught fresh sight of the genius which imbued the friendship of those two women. It was not their courage only which distinguished them from others of their kind; it was (I thought) a special gift for being at once involved in the drudgeries of living and detached from their smallness, for watching even their own distress with eyes which contained a larger scenery. As when, standing in an emptied and silent concert hall, you may seem to hear again the closing bars of a Bach chorale which has lately been played there, so I recovered for an instant the sense they had aroused in me of mysterious splendour, of luminescent joy. As if it had been a talisman I found the voice of my brain repeating the word, *Triomfantelijk.* 'Triumphantly!'—I began to say it aloud, over and over again.

To passers-by I must have offered a spectacle of little dignity—a once-respectable woman in a state of extreme dishevelment, weary-eyed, leaning against a wall and talking to herself, on a winter morning in an increasingly busy street. It was fortunate that the patience of the girl who had brought the telegram at last gave out—that she began to murmur, *'Bitte! ... Bitte!'* gently pulling my sleeve. Responding to her will until my own should get to work again, I followed her across the street, and through the passage under a wing of the ugly house we wandered into the courtyard beyond.

Standing there I searched her face, she mine, as old schoolfriends do in groping recognition when they meet after many years. At length a name came to the surface of my mind, and I said it aloud: 'Agnes.'

It seemed to leave her dissatisfied. We continued in a shy and foolish way to explore each other's eyes; she in turn had to work patiently—as it appeared—to dredge from her brain the name she wanted, but it came at last.

'Ruth,' she said.

I echoed, 'Ruth,' and again, 'Ruth.' But my body was slow to share in this meeting: it was she who, with a grave simplicity, stretched out to touch my hand.

Side by side—our hands still touching—we went into the house, to be greeted by the fumes from a pan of milk which someone had let boil over and by the pervasive bickering of children. Enveloped in that orchestra of inveterate sounds and smells, I realised I was back on the painful course I could never finally escape from—itself my one escape from the despotism of the past; the only course which could lead towards an ultimate tranquillity; the harsh, acceptable, exalting road.

Blechingley
1964—68